Regency

COLLECTION

VOLUME
—11—

THE
Regency
COLLECTION

VOLUME
—11—

Not Quite a Gentleman
by
Paula Marshall

A Lady of
Independent Means
by
Sarah Westleigh

*First published in Great Britain 1999 by
Harlequin Mills & Boon Limited,
Eton House, 18–24 Paradise Road,
Richmond, Surrey, TW9 1SR.*

The Regency Collection © by Harlequin Enterprises II B.V. 1999

The publisher acknowledges the copyright holders of the
individual work as follows:

Not Quite a Gentleman © Paula Marshall 1995
A Lady of Independent Means © Sarah Westleigh 1995

ISBN 0 263 82424 1
106-0003

*Printed and bound in Spain
by Litografia Rosés S.A., Barcelona*

NOT QUITE
A GENTLEMAN

by

Paula Marshall

Paula Marshall, married, with three children, has had a varied and interesting life. She began her career in a large library and ended it as a senior academic in charge of history teaching in a polytechnic. She has travelled widely, has been a swimming coach, embroiders, paints pictures and has appeared on *University Challenge* and *Mastermind*. She has always wanted to write, and likes her novels to be full of adventure and humour.

Other titles by the same author:

* linked
** Schuyler Family saga

+ linked
++ linked

CHAPTER ONE

'Lord, what fools these mortals be!' Shakespeare.

MISS FIELDING, the Rector of Broomhall's eldest child, known to all her friends and relatives as Nan, stood on a tall stool in the Rectory pantry and cursed life. She was busy arranging the first jams of the summer of 1819 on a high dark shelf, away from the light. The oaths she was using were mild, but firm, discreetly intoned beneath her breath.

She privately counted the sum of her annoyances. Her hair was coming down, her old brown dress, despite the presence of an apron made from sacking tied round her waist, was streaked with fruit and syrup. She was perspiring, for the summer day was hot and not really suitable for jam-making at all. Worse, the top shelf was almost out of reach and the only ladder which might have helped her had been taken away by the carpenter who was busy repairing one of the Rectory's bow windows.

Worse still, and by far the most galling, the rest of her family was entertaining itself after the fashion which pleased it most. Her father, Caleb Fielding, was upstairs in his study teaching eleven-year-old Chaz, his youngest child and only son, Latin verbs. Her one remaining unmarried sister, Jane, was out visiting her friend Caroline at her home at nearby Letcombe's Landing, and was doubtless seated idly in the shade, under a cedar tree, a glass of newly made lemonade to hand, flirting with any pretty young fellow who happened to be sitting near by. Her mother, Lavinia Fielding, who had proclaimed herself a helpless invalid after the birth of her last child, was lying on her bed being fanned by one of the undermaids. She was also

9

being read to by Kelsey, once the Fielding children's governess and now by way of being a general factotum in the Rectory.

Only Nan Fielding was working, and suddenly, quite suddenly, Nan Fielding was tired of work, tired of being the dogsbody around whom the life of the Rectory and, yes, the life of the parish revolved. Tired of being nearly twenty-eight years old, past her last prayers, sensible plainish Nan Fielding with only a pair of fine eyes to recommend her to anyone. Although once there had been a young man to gaze into those eyes, and tell her that she was beautiful Anne, his own darling girl...but that young man had been dead and gone many years ago...

How long had this fit been coming on? she wondered, setting the last jam pot neatly at the end of the line. Was it the result of being the family's mainstay ever since her mother had realised how practical dear Nan was after Chaz's birth? Or was it that this morning she had found one of Randal's letters, its paper yellow and its ink brown, tucked away in a drawer and long forgotten?

Or was it the fact of her sister Jane's sheer inconsiderate selfishness, her belief that Nan existed only as some kind of automaton, such as eastern sultans in fairy-stories were reputed to possess, which once wound up was able, tirelessly, to look after their master's interests and fulfil their slightest wants? Her other two sisters whom she had chaperoned, cared for, and seen that they had made good marriages, had been grateful to her for what she had done, and sometimes continued still to do. Only Jane took everything for granted—complained, even, that Nan did not consider her enough...

Above all Jane was intent on making a grand match, much better than any of her sisters, and thought that Nan was too practical, too dowdy to push her interests hard enough against those of girls who had a grander name than Fielding. Never mind that their father was the cousin and heir of Sir Charlton Fielding Bart, the whole world knew that Sir Charlton was only of middling fortune, and being younger than Caleb Fielding was like to die after him. . .

Oh, damn, damn, double damn. To Gehenna with everything, cursed Nan as she touched ground once more. For there on the lowest shelf were two errant pots which she had quite forgotten. And now she would have to climb back on to the chair again, and range them alongside the others. Which only went to show that self-pity was a deluding and disgusting thing—and time-wasting into the bargain.

So, to save wasting any further time, Nan climbed back on to the chair, a pot in each sticky hand. But, alas, in the doing her hair had quite come down—but what of that, for who was there to see it? Which was another observation best not made, for as, invoking Satan and all the devils from hell, Nan leaned sideways on one leg to save having to climb down and move the stool along *again* she overbalanced, and fell, letting out a little scream as she did so.

But good fortune, for once, was with her for she descended headlong, not to the hard stone floor, but into the obliging waiting arms of someone who proved to be a rather large gentleman!

'Well, well, well,' he drawled, having arrived in the pantry in time to catch a nymph, falling, if not from the skies, from a high stool, 'what have we here? A divine armful sent down to me by Jove, no less. A happy portent to greet my arrival in South Nottinghamshire!' And he rewarded the nymph with a vigorous kiss on her shapely mouth. . .

Nan, usually so hardened to the proprieties, so used to acting the part of the Rector's prim eldest daughter—for her bad language was indulged in only in private—surprisingly found that her first thoughts were not those of gratitude for being caught, nor even of anger at being so summarily kissed. Instead, as her saviour continued to hold her tightly to him, stroking her right breast gently as he did so, causing the most alarming tingles to radiate all over her body, long starved of such affection, she could only think, Who in the world is he? And what the devil is he doing here in the pantry? What she should have said, of course, was something in the order of, How dare you, sir? Unhand me at once!

But before she lost her good sense completely and asked him that in those rude terms Nan looked him firmly in the face which was so near to her own. It was most disconcerting, to say the least, to discover that he was not only large, but extremely handsome. His eyes were so grey that they were silvery. His nose was long and dominant, his mouth long and shapely. His hair was fashionably cut and darkly glossy with a frosting of silver in it—borrowed from his eyes, perhaps. And what had brought that trope on? Admiring gentlemen's looks was not the habit of Miss Fielding. Most surprisingly of all, she who knew everyone in the village and the surrounding countryside had never seen him before.

'Pray who, sir, are you? And what are you doing in the pantry?' she finally croaked at him, something odd having happened to her voice as well as to the rest of her body.

The stranger still made no effort to put her down. Which proved that he was not only large, but strong, for Nan, although by no means plump, was a tall woman and well-built. The manly chest against which she was reposing was both broad and warm, and, to an elderly spinster who had not had a man's arms about her for some twelve years, oddly comforting... And she really must stop thinking in the prose of a Minerva Press novel, and start trying to make this unknown rake behave himself! But what with trying to wriggle out of his arms, and stop the jam pots she was still holding from falling on to the floor, she found herself unable to think clearly.

He answered her with a rumbling laugh, and the words, 'What am I doing in the pantry? Saving servant girls from breaking their necks, of course. You don't seem very grateful.'

Servant girls! Her hair, her clothes, her apron, and possibly her language as she fell, must have deceived him as to her true rank. To this humiliation had she come! No wonder Jane looked at her with distaste and the suggestion that even for a chaperon she was rather more of a plain dowd than she needed to be.

She opened her mouth to pour righteous indignation over him for holding her in such a familiar fashion, to inform him that she was Miss Fielding, the Rector's eldest daughter, but before a word could so much as pass her lips he bent his handsome head and kissed her again—full upon her half-open mouth!

It was a polite kiss, if one snatched from a servant girl could ever be deemed polite, and when it was over he took no further liberties with her. She opened her mouth again to inform him that she was not accustomed to being so treated, but the only result of that was that he misunderstood her, and murmured, 'Another kiss for further payment for rescuing you?' This time the kiss was full and lusty, his tongue gently probing her mouth, and touching hers before it retreated.

Hampered by a pot of jam in each hand, Nan could do nothing to defend herself. He was obviously one of those predatory gentlemen who took their pleasure with the women servants of any house where they happened to find themselves. But that was not the worst thing of all. To her disgust Nan found herself enjoying the kiss, and the spicy aroma from either his hair or his linen which surrounded him, and wouldn't have minded if it had lasted longer. Most of the men whom she met smelled only of horses, and wouldn't have dreamed of kissing her; nor would she willingly have kissed them back. But that was no reason to welcome this stranger's advances.

The kiss over, he gently lowered her to the ground, where Nan carefully put the jam pots on the lower shelf and then turned to face him, to discover that he was not only tall but also well-built and beautifully turned out, from the top of his admirably dressed head to the tips of his shining boots. Wealth and power shone from him like rays from the sun.

So what was he doing in the Rectory pantry? She was soon to find out.

'My good girl,' he murmured negligently, 'you may perhaps be able to inform me where the Misses Fielding are this afternoon. Miss Jane Fielding distinctly told me when we met at Sampford Lacy two days ago that she would be at home to me here today and invited me to call. I rang the bell but no one answered. Seeing that the front door was open, and fearing that something was amiss, I took the liberty of entering. Only to find that no one was about. Growing a little alarmed, I took the further liberty of exploring the house—to find not Miss Jane but Beauty herself, working diligently in the pantry, and I just in time to save her from a dreadful fall!'

Speaking thus, he drew a fine cambric handkerchief from his pocket and, murmuring, 'Allow me,' gently wiped the mixture of jam and perspiration from Nan's right cheek.

Nan was suddenly and deeply aware that so far she had not, apart from the question she had put to him after she had fallen into his arms, uttered a word. Shock and surprise—as well as sensual delight—had kept her mute. It would, she felt, be too humiliating to confess that she was the elder Miss Fielding whose cold propriety was known throughout South Notts and North Leicestershire.

And 'Beauty herself, working diligently in the pantry'! How dared he come out with anything so preposterous? He was jeering at her; he must be. She had no idea at all how unlike the lively picture which she presented to her unknown visitor was from the prim one which she saw in the mirror and which as Miss Fielding, the Rector's spinster daughter, she usually showed to the world.

Her hair, whose collapse she had lamented, had
fallen in long waves and ringlets about her face, soften-
ing it. Tawny in hue, scraped back into a tight knot, it
usually looked a dull mouse-brown; loose, it shone with
red and gold lights. Her face, normally pale, was rosy
with the heat and exertion. Her lips, usually primly
straight, were swollen, soft and tender as a consequence
of both his kisses and his caresses—which, shamefully,
she had made no attempt to resist. Her eyes, a deep
turquoise, shone with indignation at being so carelessly
handled, but the intruder was not to know that.

As for her clothing—well, it was how a fine gentleman exepcted to see a servant dressed, so he made
nothing of it. He merely admired the clean lines of the
long-limbed body revealed by the drab dress clinging
damply to it. Those gentlemen who met Miss Fielding
in her normal habitat had never had the opportunity to
discover that she possessed a body at all, never mind a
shapely one.

What Nan would have liked to do was to ring a great
peal over him, to put him in his place, once and for all,
but from what he had just said he was obviously one of
Jane's beaux. And what would he think of the Misses
Fielding if, dressed and dishevelled as she was, she
confessed that she was the Rector's eldest and most
proper daughter? With any luck he would not recognise
her when they next met. She usually took good care to
live in Jane's shadow when she was chaperoning her,
and would make sure that she looked her worst for the
next few weeks.

So, remembering charades taken part in long ago
where she had played the part of a serving maid, Nan
bobbed him a submissive curtsy, offering in a thick
Nottinghamshire accent, 'Lor', sir, the young ladies be
gone over to Letcombe's Landing for the day, and the
rest of the fambly be engaged or out. Be there owt I
can tell 'em? As to 'oo y'are, that is?'

She was a little afraid she might be overdoing things.
The mischievous part of her which no one knew existed,

and which had helped her to survive the years since her mother's withdrawal from the world after Chaz's birth, almost had her pulling her forelock. The large gentleman smiled his lazy and charming smile at her, displaying a splendid set of white teeth.

'Nymph, garlanded with jam and jam pots, if not with flowers, you may tell Miss Jane Fielding that Brandon Tolliver came to pay his respects to her. He is at present residing at Gillyflower Hall and will be pleased to entertain any of the Rector of Broomhall's family. He will also present his compliments to the Rector himself at a suitable date in the near future. You can remember all that?'

'Ooh, I'll try, sir.' And Nan bobbed an even lower curtsy, trying to hide her face as she did so.

'Good girl!' He rewarded her with another smile, and without the hint of patronising condescension which the gentry usually offered to servants. He hesitated a moment, and gave a soundless laugh before pulling a guinea from his pocket. 'That's for promising to remember my message, and my thanks for three splendid kisses—with my apologies to the lad you may be walking out with for stealing them from you.'

He closed Nan's disbelieving fingers over the guinea, made her an elaborate bow and took his bright self away. Nan had just enough presence of mind to give him time to leave the Rectory before she ran into the front drawing-room to watch him striding down the path which led to the gate where a spanking new curricle picked out in sky-blue and gold was waiting for him. His tiger, also picked out in blue and gold, stood beside it. Nan's recent visitor jumped up, took up the reins and bowled away, the tiger now clinging on for dear life at the back.

So that was Mr Brandon Tolliver, who said that he was the new squire of Gillyflower Hall, but who knew so little about his inheritance that he was not yet aware that it was known to one and all as Gilliver Hall. The locals invariably shortened it as they shortened the word gillyflower, or wallflower. But more to the point, who was he and where had he come from?

The whole world knew, or thought it knew, that when curmudgeonly old Bartholomew Tolliver had gone to his last rest his second, much younger cousin, Desmond Tolliver of Broomhall House, would inherit. So where had Mr Brandon Tolliver, silver-tongued seducer of plain servant girls, come from? And was that why Desmond had been called to London shortly after old Bart's death, and had not yet returned? Well, doubtless she would soon find out.

Another surprise was that Jane had said nothing about meeting the impudent Mr Brandon Tolliver, and would doubtless be furious that she had missed him— even if it was her own fault.

Jane was. 'He must have misheard,' she wailed that night after the Letcombes' gig had dropped her off at the Rectory, and she had arrived in time to partake of the tea which Kelsey had carried through for them, dinner at the Rectory having been over for some time.

'I told him that I would be at home tomorrow, not today. Oh, dear, and we had such a famous time together at Sampford Lacy, and he's most enormously rich, and he only talked to me; he wasn't at all interested in Charlotte Alden, Louisa Thurman or Caroline Letcombe, I could tell. Oh, what appalling luck.'

'No need to take on so,' murmured Nan gently. She had quite recovered her balance and her usual sang-froid and was trying to put out of her mind the memory of the shameless way in which she had allowed Brandon Tolliver to kiss and caress her. Brandon Tolliver, indeed, would not have recognised his 'Beauty', who was now wearing a shapeless dark dress, had scraped back her tawny hair beneath a disfiguring cap, and was speaking in her usual self-effacing manner. 'No need at all. He will doubtless be staying here for some time, now that he has inherited. He said that he would be calling again soon.'

'You met him, then?' queried Jane. 'Not that *you* could have had much to say to interest him,' she added a trifle scornfully. 'He's the most amazing quiz. Full of life and fun.'

'So Annie said,' Nan murmured. She was tatting vigorously, an occupation useful for unconsidered spinsters—particularly one who was busy lying by omission to her rather ill-natured sister. At least Jane wouldn't question Annie about their visitor, so no risk that she would discover Nan's fib—that Annie hadn't met him at all! Not that this was the only, or the most important, fib to which Nan treated the family who took her so much for granted.

Jane refused to drop the subject of Mr Brandon Tolliver; she said, with self-satisfaction in her voice, 'I'm sure that his inheriting Gillyflower Hall will have put Desmond's nose thoroughly out of joint. He was always so certain that it would come to him.'

Nan felt a small pang of grief for Desmond, and also felt constrained to reprimand Jane a little for flightiness. 'A most unChristian comment for a parson's daughter to make, my dear, and not one which you ought to utter outside our family circle.' She ignored the face which Jane pulled, and received some small support from Kelsey, who, surprisingly, had never greatly cared for Desmond.

Kelsey murmured drily, however, 'I am sure that Mr Desmond will doubtless be feeling most disappointed, if not to say cheated. After all, the late Mr Tolliver virtually promised him Gillyflower Hall.'

Well, that was the correct thing to say, even if rather lukewarm, but for some reason Kelsey had taken against Desmond, even if he did visit the Rectory frequently, to play chess with the Rector and to talk books with Nan and the rest of the pretty sisters. It was not often that Kelsey took against people, but when she did there was no moving her. Nor could she say why she did. 'I feel it in my bones,' she had once told Nan, 'and very often my bones tell true.'

Which was a bit hard on Desmond, who had always been unfailingly kind in his stiff way to the Fielding family, and to Nan in particular.

Nan briefly wondered what Kelsey's bones would make of handsome, airy Mr Brandon Tolliver who made so free with servant girls. Would she succumb to the charm which he had so carelessly ladled over the Rectory's supposed parlourmaid? And why should she be allowing Mr Brandon Tolliver to monopolise her thoughts?

So Nan shook herself mentally and said, in the most composed manner she could muster, 'I agree; it cannot but be distressing for poor Desmond to be passed over. And pray how did his cousin Brandon, if cousin he be, come to be at Sampford Lacy when you were there, Jane?'

Jane replied petulantly, for she always disliked being questioned closely about anything, 'I'm sure I don't know, Nan. All I know is that he's excellent company, not a bit like Desmond who is so grave and dull. He made us all laugh time and again.'

Now why was it that that comment should cause Nan to have a brief memory of a pair of flashing silver eyes and a curling mouth. . .? Oh, pooh to that! Those eyes would never flash for plain Miss Fielding. . .

In an effort to banish the unwanted memory Nan murmured repressively, 'I am sure that he need not be so remarkably witty as to be able to reduce you and all your friends to hysterics.'

Even Kelsey looked a little surprised as Nan came out with this barbed comment. Jane's response was to pout in Nan's direction before remarking cuttingly, 'One might expect you to talk like an elderly gorgon, Nan. I think that you have forgotten what it was like to be young. Who can be surprised that you refuse to read anything by the author of *Sophia*? Papa's books of sermons are more in your line!'

For some reason these darts from Jane, which Nan was usually able to ignore, hurt her more than a little.

To steady herself she spoke even more quietly than usual. 'It would be as well to remember, Jane, that Mr Brandon Tolliver is almost double your age, that you know very little about him other than that he is a great flirt, and as a very young girl it might be as well for you to go slow with him.'

Kelsey and Jane both stared at her. Jane said, her pretty voice more cutting than ever, 'Now, Nan, how do you know all that about him? I was not aware that you had ever met him. You surely did not gossip about him with Annie?'

Now here was a facer, as young Chaz was often given to saying. For once, Nan's tongue, usually on a tight rein, had run away with her. She chose not to make any comment, merely shook her head and tatted away more vigorously than ever. Least said, soonest mended. After a brief pause during which they all drank tea, Nan finally said, to no one in particular, 'After all, we must always remember that real life is not at all like the life in the novels by the author of *Sophia*.'

'And what a pity that is,' sighed Jane, tossing her curly blonde head and flashing her bright blue eyes as she took from the little basket which she had carried with her from Letcombe's Landing the first volume of a three-volume novel, bound in pretty blue cloth, with an elegant label on the spine which read '*Amelia's Secret*, by the author of *Sophia*'.

'Only think, I have come away from Letcombe with Sophia's latest. Charlotte has lent it to me. She says it is even more exciting and more horrid than the last. One cannot guess what Amelia's secret is, she says, and I suppose I shall have to wait until the last volume to find out! You may have it when I have finished with it. I have quite fallen in love with the hero, Mr Lancelot Beaumains.'

'Oh, I really haven't time to be reading novels.' Nan's voice was subdued. 'And you know how dear Papa disapproves of them.'

'Well, Sir Avery doesn't,' announced Jane. 'He reads

each one of Sophia's as it comes out. He has read all of the Waverley novels as well, and so has Papa, for all that he says that he dislikes novels!'

'I shouldn't make too much of that,' retorted Kelsey, gathering up the tea things. 'What Papas do and what daughters do are two quite different things. But I must confess that I do enjoy Sophia's novels; there is a bottom of common sense in them, and they are so witty. You ought to read them, Nan. You would enjoy them.'

'No time,' Nan returned briskly.

'Lancelot Beaumains is very like Brandon Tolliver,' continued Jane, flicking over the pages of *Amelia's Secret*. 'Very handsome and great fun. He teases the heroine all the time.' She glanced sideways at Nan before taking the opportunity to stake her claim to the infinitely desirable Mr Brandon Tolliver. 'Charlotte Alden says that the *on dit* in London is that he is most immensely rich. He told her that he intends to settle at Gillyflower Hall and improve it. He has sent for an architect and a landscape gardener to begin work at once. He said that he will be attending the Assembly Rooms ball in Highborough next week. I am sure that you would wish me to attend also, seeing that he was *most* particular in his attentions to me—and he will surely expect me to be present.'

One might assume, thought Nan nastily, that from what I saw of him today Mr Brandon Tolliver is '*most* particular' in his attentions to anything female on two legs. Aloud she said, 'Well, that being so, I agree we ought to attend, so long as you promise to conduct yourself properly. I will prevail upon Papa to escort us so that we may all have the pleasure of being introduced to such a charmer.'

Jane chose to ignore the touch of vitriol in this last speech, and exclaimed with delight at the prospect of yet another meeting with the new owner of Gillyflower Hall. It was left to Kelsey to say to Nan, as she extinguished the candles in the drawing-room after Jane had gone to bed, 'Are you feeling a little under the weather today, my dear? I know that Jane was being her usual tiresome self, but it is not like you to bite back at her quite so sharply.'

What to say to that? That I have the most distinct impression of life passing me by and that whereas I was able and willing to shepherd Jane's older sisters about the county and in London because they were so sweet-natured and grateful I am coming to find Jane's little unpleasantnesses to me unbearable? That was the unsayable truth.

But it was not the whole truth. For had it not been Mr Brandon Tolliver's careless kisses which had reminded Nan Fielding that she had once been young, desirable, and desired?

CHAPTER TWO

'So, YOU mean to settle at last, Brandon?'

Brandon Tolliver bent his handsome head and said affectionately to his widowed sister, Mrs Lydia Bligh, who was keeping him company during these early days at Gillyflower Hall, 'Oh, yes, indeed, my dear. I think that I may have found exactly what I was looking for—a pretty, biddable young girl of good, if not great family who will make an excellent mother for my children.'

Lydia Bligh, who was engaged in stitching a fire-screen portraying a pair of rosy cherubs with their arms around each other and their tiny wings extended, gave a great sigh at this, and said shrewdly, 'And who is this paragon—who, I may remind you, will also be your wife, as well as the mother of your children? I take it that you will no longer be keeping the excellent Mrs Emma Milborne—or will you be holding her in reserve when you become bored with your pretty and biddable bride?'

Now this was naughty of Lydia, was it not? Particularly when he was contemplating doing what she had long asked him to do—giving up Emma in order to found a family.

'Oh, you misjudge me,' he told Lydia reproachfully, walking away from her to gaze out of the window across the neglected park, so that she might not see his face. Who knew what she might read there, seeing that she was as shrewd as he was? 'I have pensioned Emma off, and she is to marry her penniless suitor whom she has long adored, but could not afford. We parted on happy terms, I hasten to add.'

'No doubt.' Lydia's tone was satiric. 'Now you may tell me who your child bride is, and I will exclaim in suitable terms at your choice.'

'Unkind,' Brandon murmured, without turning round. 'You met her at the Ameses'. Miss Jane Fielding. She is, in case you don't know, the youngest daughter of the Rector of Broomhall, the living in my gift. He is by way of being the distant cousin and heir of Sir Charlton Fielding of Ryall in Northumbria.'

Lydia laid down her needle, frowned. 'I remember her. Remarkably pretty. Seemed very taken by you. No dowry, I suppose. Has the Rector any income beside his stipend, which I happen to know is a poor one?'

Brandon turned round, a somewhat mocking expression on his face. 'My dear girl, you know that I have not the slightest need to marry money. I am rich, and growing richer. The late wars made my fortune secure, and the India trade grows and is growing. One advantage of being a merchant first and a landed gentleman second is that I may add to my fortune, rather than throw it away.'

'True.' And Lydia smiled for the first time. 'For all your romantic looks, Brandon, you are the hardest-headed creature it has been my fortune—or misfortune—to know. Are you not being a trifle too hard-headed in contemplating this marriage? She will be your wife, Brandon. She struck me as a little shallow and somewhat selfish. Now you are very deep and confounded selfish—not a good mixture, I would have thought.'

'Oh, I think that you wrong her. She is young and will grow deeper as she moves into the world, I am sure.' Brandon frowned a little. 'My information is that the Rector is comfortably placed financially, and that there will be a small dowry. The story is that he wrote a theological book of great profundity some years ago and made a tidy income from it. I must admit that I found that a little surprising, but it is true that from being the usual struggling poor relation of a cleric he became very much richer some five or six years ago—so I suppose that theology may pay more than I would have thought!'

'Your information!' Lydia gave a short laugh. 'No

doubt you put some agent to the trouble of investigating the family into which you think to marry. How exactly like you. I suppose that you know everything that there is to know about them. You really are the outside of enough.'

Brandon threw himself down into a large armchair opposite his sister. 'Knowledge is power, my dear. I know that Miss Jane is a trifle selfish as well as you do, but she is also shrewd, and determined to make a good marriage, I am sure. I also know that she has a dowd for an older sister, who acts as gorgon and chaperon, besides a much younger brother, Charles, familiarly known to all as Chaz. Her mother has retired from the world as a semi-invalid, and the elderly dowd runs the household, including Miss Jane, with a rod of iron, even managing the finances for the Reverend Caleb—he being, I'm informed, as befits a theological philosopher, totally unworldly.'

'Your agent earned his pay. I wonder that he has not listed the contents of the pantry and the colour of the Rectory curtains for you,' returned Lydia. 'From what you tell me, marriage with the dowd might be an excellent business proposition, if it is she who is keeping the Rectory afloat.'

'I like the thought of a pretty face sitting opposite me at breakfast, as well as a pretty face setting the table,' announced Brandon with a wry smile. 'There's a damned fine specimen of the female sex running round the Rectory kitchens, to my certain knowledge. For some reason my agent never mentioned her. As to business acumen, I hire clerks to help me with that. I need a wife for different reasons altogether.'

'No doubt.' Lydia took up her canvas work again, stabbing one of the cherubs in the eye. 'I hope that Miss Jane's sister will be at the ball next week. I like to meet ladies out of the common run, dowds though they may be.'

He was not to be put down, it seemed. 'Now, Lydia, you are not to be contrary. You seemed very happy in

Miss Jane's company at the Ameses'. Try to be happy with her now that you know that I am seriously considering her as my wife.'

'And that's the rub,' said Lydia sharply, attacking the cherub's eye again. 'A pleasant companion at a house party is one thing, but viewing her as your prospective wife is quite another! Especially when you tell me that your roving eye alighted on some underservant when you made your visit to the Rectory to revive your friendship with Miss Jane.'

Brandon looked a little self-conscious as this barb struck home. 'Now, Lydia,' he expostulated midly, 'you know full well that, although I may have many faults, seducing servant girls is not one of them. . .'

'I never thought that it was. But it isn't kind to dally with them, Brandon. Oh, I know that when you see a handsome creature of any station you always wish to pay her your respects, but it is wrong of you to raise any kind of expectation in servants. You are a handsome and powerful man and you scarcely understand the kind of effect you have on such poor young things. It would be the height of unkindness to make them dissatisfied with their own simple-minded village swains. And if you are pursuing Miss Jane Fielding, make sure that you do so after a fashion which will not cause her distress if you change your mind.'

It was Brandon's colour which changed at this. He sprang to his feet, exclaiming a trifle bitterly, 'I had no idea that you entertained such a low opinion of me, Lydia! I see that I have been living in a fool's paradise so far as you are concerned.'

Lydia knew at once that she had hurt him and, little though she had wished to do so, she thought that perhaps it was all in a good cause.

'No, Brandon,' she said, as coolly and equably as she could. 'It is not a fool's paradise in which you have come to live, but a small country district where gossip reigns as queen and where everything which you say and do will be chewed over ad infinitum, where there are few, if any, secrets. You have no notion of how different you will find it from living in a cosmopolitan society, where, with respect to you, a certain licence reigned instead. I am only saying that it will be best for you to go carefully, particularly at the start of your stay here.'

She avoided looking at him while she threaded her needle with some pink wool in order to pick out Cupid's lips, and waited for him to reply. It would not do for them to be at odds, if she was to live with him and be his hostess until he married. Although he had always been kind to her, she knew that in the world in which he had lived for the last twenty years he had always been known as a hard man. She did not want him to be a hard man with her.

Brandon, taking stock of what his sister had said, acknowledged a certain truth in it. He had heard of the narrow-minded nature of country society, and it would not do for him to gain the reputation of being a careless rake before he had so much as settled in it.

He told himself firmly that he would behave himself. After all, he was determined to settle down, was he not? Why else had he pensioned off Emma and decided to make his home in the house he had inherited from his second cousin? A wealthy man in his middle thirties owed it to himself to go carefully, to steady himself, marry a good little wife, and start a family. The time of flirtations, grand passions, confidential little suppers with opera dancers, the squiring of barques of frailty and the cultivation of little bits of muslin must be considered to be over.

It hurt him somewhat to discover that Lydia might suspect him of corrupting the innocent, when he had always been careful not to do so. If he saw the nymph from the Rectory again he must be sure to avert his eyes, ignore her, and think of the ladylike charms of Miss Jane Fielding. He knew that he would be seeing her at the Assembly Rooms ball at Highborough, where he hoped to be introduced to the Gorgon, as Jane naughtily nicknamed her older sister Nan, and also her elderly parent.

Another thought struck him. 'Do you think Cousin Desmond will be present at the Assembly Room ball next week? And, more to the point, ought I to call on him beforehand? He was very short with me when we met at the lawyers in London, which is not to be wondered at. The poor fellow always thought he was to inherit, and I gather that, while not exactly starving, he is not particularly blessed with this world's riches either.'

'I think that you ought to visit him,' said Lydia slowly, relieved that Brandon, good fellow that he was at heart, if a trifle selfish like all men, had not taken what she said too ill, 'if only that if you do he won't be able to say that you met him only to drop him. But from what I gather from Broomhall gossip he is hardly likely to attend the ball; he doesn't often go into society. He has something of a mild *tendre* for Miss Fielding, I understand.'

'Ah, Jane's Gorgon,' smiled Brandon, good humour recovered. ''Pon my honour, Lydia, I am quite agog at the prospect of being introduced to provincial society. It's a pity the Fieldings are merely comfortable—if Miss Fielding had possessed a large dowry, one might have encouraged Desmond to cultivate his *tendre* and to go so far as to offer for her. It would ease my conscience over depriving him of Gillyflower Hall, and set him up for life into the bargain. If I do marry Miss Jane, I shall have to see what I can do for him—tactfully, of course, and without making it look as though I am offering him charity.'

Lydia put down her canvas work, stood up, and impulsively walked over to Brandon to kiss him on the cheek.

'I must never forget,' she told him, seeing that he looked surprised at receiving such sudden and unprovoked affection, 'what a thoroughly good fellow you are at bottom. Such a sentiment does you great credit.

Now if you would only stop calling poor Miss Fielding the Gorgon I should feel so much happier. I know that you have caught the habit from Jane, but it does neither of you credit.'

She paused. 'It is one of the reasons why I am not completely certain that you ought to think of making her Mrs Brandon Tolliver—but she is young, and doubtless her manners will improve with age and experience.'

'Doubtless,' echoed Brandon optimistically. 'Well, the next few weeks should reveal all, I trust.' He smiled his charming smile at her. 'One thing, my dear; I am determined to enjoy country peace after enduring town bustle.'

Afterwards he was to laugh at himself for this piece of presumption. Country peace, indeed! He had lived so long in cities, among the bustle of a corrupt commercial world, that he had come to see the country as an Arcadian place where the only passions present were those of happy shepherds and shepherdesses dancing in the smiling fields. But poverty existed there, as well as in the back alleys of London—aye, and jealousy, hate and revenge too. As he was soon to learn.

Nan, dressed soberly, was seated in the Rectory drawing-room on the same afternoon, writing at a desk which stood in the window and looked out over the front lawn. Kelsey was chaperoning Jane on a visit to Gillyflower Hall, where they arrived shortly after Lydia and Brandon had concluded their conversation.

She was happy to be alone. There were times when she wished herself free of being the Rectory's indispensable guardian and today was one of them. Chaz had peered round the door a moment ago, pleading with her to join him in flying his new kite. He had looked so happy and eager that for a moment she had almost thought to indulge him. And then she had thought of how tired she was, that she had, for various good reasons, not retired to her bed until well after one in the morning, and that this would be the only time of day that she might sit down for a few moments.

'Come on, Nan,' Chaz had urged her. 'You know you like flying my kite, and this is a new one, a stunner—there's no one else to go with me. Please...'

'Take Roger,' Nan had said. Roger was their boy—or rather youth—of all work. Refusing Chaz anything always made her unhappy. From his birth he had been a handsome, biddable child—clever too. In face and body he didn't resemble any of the Fielding men, who were all tawny-haired and big-bodied; even her sedentary father had the build of a bruiser. Instead Chaz was dark, slender and intense, with a pair of flashing hazel eyes shot with green.

'Roger doesn't make up exciting stories about what the kite is doing and where it's flying to like you do,' he told his sister. 'It's forever since you came out with me.'

'I've been so busy lately,' Nan excused herself.

Chaz was possessed of a brand of practical logic foreign to his father and most of the Fieldings apart from Nan. He said, almost angrily, 'Then why can't Jane do some of your work and help you? Instead she's always out jaunting. She's jaunting again this afternoon. At Gillyflower Hall. Why couldn't you have gone over there with Kelsey and left Jane to do whatever it is you're doing?'

'Copying Papa's new book,' Nan told him. 'Jane couldn't do that.'

Chaz's logical mind supplied him with no answer to that incontrovertible statement. He gave something between a grunt and a groan and shot out of the door, crying ungraciously, 'Very well, if you won't come I suppose that Roger will have to do. And if it's Papa's new book you're copying, you'll do that forever. He changes it every day, as well you know!'

Nan resumed writing, although her wrist ached and her eyes were tired. A noise outside disturbed her. She looked up to see that Desmond Tolliver had arrived on horseback and that Jackson, who trebled as coachman, butler and groom, was leading the chestnut which he had been riding round to the mews at the back of the Rectory. Desmond himself was striding smartly to the Rectory front door. He didn't, Nan noticed with a sinking heart, look very pleased with life.

So she wasn't surprised, when Annie ushered him in, that he didn't appear to be his normally equable self. As usual he was tidily, if not exactly fashionably, turned out. Also as usual his manner was severe and slightly aloof. He didn't in any way resemble his wicked cousin Brandon, as Nan had come to think of him since the episode in the pantry.

True, Desmond was tall, but his hair wasn't dark or curly, being an indeterminate lank brown, *not* cut à la mode. His face was tanned and lean, but possessed nothing of the mobile charm which had distinguished Brandon's. He had no naughty look or charming smile for Nan Fielding—and no wonder, thought Nan disconsolately. Here I am in dull dark grey again, a turn-out years old, and my hair is dressed to be out of the way, not to be fashionably dangling around my ears and neck. On top of that, truly on top, I am wearing my duenna-cum-spinster's cap, which quite extinguishes me and makes me look forty.

A thought struck her. Did Desmond also accost housemaids, kiss them vigorously, and stroke them until they were helpless jelly in his strong arms? Did all men, when they were not in drawing-rooms being polite and exceedingly proper, either to pretty young ladies like Jane, or plain old ones like Nan, have that certain look in their eye when they dealt with those who were plainly not ladies? What would it be like to be a 'not lady'?

And why am I thinking such dreadful thoughts, and have been doing so since I met *him*? Nan banished Mr Brandon Tolliver to the dungeons of her mind and concentrated on listening to Mr Desmond Tolliver, who was, as usual, being as proper as proper in everything

which he said to her. Would he have been improper in
the Rectory pantry if he had thought her a housemaid?

'I am so happy to find you in,' he was telling her
earnestly after she had made him sit down and rung for
Annie to fetch them tea. 'I feel most desperately in
need of your cool common sense.'

My cool common sense, thought Nan wildly, while
nodding gravely in his direction. And what has happened to that, seeing as I am constantly thinking of the
dissolute roué who invaded the pantry and very nearly
invaded me?

'I am sure,' Desmond was continuing, still earnest,
'that I need not tell you of the thunderclap which struck
me down after my cousin's death.' He paused, then
continued in melancholy vein, 'It was not that I looked
forward to cousin Bart's death, but I own that the
thought that after it my own monetary cares would be
over did feature in my thinking. I am, after all, only
human.'

This came out after the fashion of a man who needed
what he had just said to be contradicted, but Nan was
only equal to nodding again. It seemed, in the circumstances, the most tactful thing to do.

'So. . .' and Desmond dropped his voice mournfully
'. . .you may imagine what a blow it was for me to find
myself passed over for a cousin whom I was not even
aware existed, but whom the damned— I beg your
pardon, my dear Anne, but I am most overset, as you
see.'

More nodding from Nan seemed to steady him. Yes,
perhaps nods *were* better than words in certain circumstances. If she had nodded at Mr Brandon Tolliver
would he have stopped kissing her? She must truly be
going mad, and now she had lost one of Desmond's
long-winded and lachrymose sentences. She really must
stop wool-gathering.

'Cousin Bart had told his lawyers, it seems, to find his
true next heir, and the property was to go there. They
had to trace back three generations—*three generations*—

to find this man whose grandfather took precedence over mine, and the result was that this upstart, who is no gentleman, has inherited.'

'Upstart,' echoed Nan. 'And no gentleman. Forgive me, but if he is truly a Tolliver, how does that come about?'

'His father had no money and it seems that Brandon was articled as a clerk straight from a country grammar school! A clerk! He rose in the merchant's house where he was employed, saved money, invested it during the late wars, or so I am told, was taken up by the Rothschilds or some such, and made himself a fortune large enough for him to cut loose and start his own house. The war continuing made him richer still, and on the two occasions when the market fell, and others were broken by it, he gambled in the right direction, won, and is now as rich as Croesus. The devil of it is. . . oh, do forgive me. . .he has no need of Gillyflower Hall or Bart's estate, whereas I. . .'

Desmond fell silent. Yes, it really was, thought Nan, full of pity for him, a truly terrible story. On the other hand. . .yes, on the other hand, how strong a character must Brandon Tolliver have been to have made himself a fortune after such a poor beginning. It all went to show that there was much more to him than she might have thought if all she had known of him was the encounter in the pantry.

But she really must say something sympathetic to poor Desmond whom Bart had treated quite abominally, allowing him to think, from when he was quite a small boy, that he was the Tolliver heir. All Desmond now possessed was an impoverished estate, a small country house, Brandon Hall, named after Brandon and Desmond's great-grandmother's family, and the home farm, which had come to him through his mother, the only daughter of a poorish country gentleman. Desmond's father had been one of those who had lost money in the late wars, not gained it, which Nan knew must make his cousin Brandon's successes seem the more galling.

'Not quite a gentleman,' repeated Desmond sadly, when Nan had commiserated with him, made him drink a cup of tea and eat some of the Bosworth Jumbles which were the speciality of Grace, the cook from Leicestershire.

'There is something I really ought to say to you,' he continued slowly. 'When Bart died my first thought was that now I might realise one of my dreams. That is, to marry. And when I thought of who I would like to make my wife my thoughts immediately turned to you.' He was standing now, one hand behind his back, tea and Jumbles alike forgotten.

'After all, Anne, we are both old enough to know that we are beyond passion and its traps. We are both creatures of great common sense. I cannot but admire your housewifery and the businesslike way in which you run the Rectory. The whole world is aware that you are the mainstay of the house and the parish. I felt that we would really deal well together, and that I would gain a wife of whom I, and my mother, would be proud. But, alas, situated as we are, prudence dictates that this marriage cannot be. But I thought that you ought to be aware of the high esteem in which I hold you.'

What sort of kisses would high esteem provoke? was Nan's unruly thought. She supposed that she ought to be flattered by what Desmond had just said. But 'beyond passion', and the confession that he was marrying her to acquire a housekeeper...! Dreadfully, tears pricked at the back of her eyes.

If Mary Tudor had said that when she died the word Calais would be inscribed on her heart, then when Nan Fielding died the words common sense ought surely to be found there.

Desmond was waiting for her to say something, the kind of half-smile on his face which told her that she ought to be profoundly pleased by what he had said

when all that she really felt was the deepest depression.
For if he had truly loved her, then he would not have
allowed such considerations as he had listed to come
between them. He might be poor as the wealthy
counted poor, but many poorer than he had married,
and fathered children. And even if she did not love him
he had been a good friend, and she might have been
tempted to end the barren years, to let others, as Chaz
had suggested, do their share of the Rectory's duties,
and marry him for that alone.

But this passionless recital left her gasping. Nevertheless she rose, and said, her voice shaking with a kind of
grief, and not, as Desmond easily assumed, gratitude,
'You do me too great an honour, sir. I shall always
remember and treasure what you have just told me.'

He took her lax hand and kissed it. 'Oh, I knew that
you would understand, Anne. You will also understand,
I am sure, when I tell you that I shall not be going out
into society for the next few weeks. I feel that I cannot
face the world...the curious and greedy eyes of those
who must know what a blow this has been. I mean to
take my misfortune like a man, but I must retire for a
little. I intend to keep up my connections with you and
the Rector, whom I hope to see before I leave, but I
shall not be at the Assembly Rooms ball to dance with
you.'

'Oh, Papa is at the church this afternoon,' Nan told
him. 'He is meeting the verger and the churchwardens
to inspect the tower, which he fears is in need of repair.
If you care to look in, I am sure that he would be happy
to see you.'

For some reason which she did not quite understand
Nan wanted him to be gone. She wanted to say, I am
Nan, not Anne, and have been since I was a child—
only Randal was ever allowed to call me Anne—so why
do *you* always call me Anne? More, it would have been
better for you not to tell me that you intended to
propose if you were not actually going to do so. And I

dislike the fact that you took it for granted that I would have agreed to marry you if you *had* proposed!

None of which could conceivably be said aloud. Instead she was left to comfort him gently, which by his manner he plainly expected her to do. So, as usual, Nan, not only exercised her common sense, but did her duty.

It was only when he had left that, to her utter astonishment, Nan began to cry. For who was there to comfort her, the plain spinster sister who had not received a proposal, only the information that she might have done so if the potential proposer had inherited the property—which in all honesty he had done nothing to deserve, but which he had counted on since he was a small boy?

Worst of all, it was not only for herself that she was crying, but also for the knowledge that a man whom she had respected and esteemed had revealed himself as a hollow straw, who at the first set-back had collapsed into maudlin self-pity.

And all this because charming, heedless but apparently deep Mr Brandon Tolliver had walked into their lives. What else could they expect to happen? The serpent had arrived in Eden.

CHAPTER THREE

HIGHBOROUGH was a pretty little market town on the banks of the River Soar in North Leicestershire, near to the boundary which divided it from South Nottinghamshire. It was the centre of social life in the region, boasted a large set of Assembly Rooms and had once contemplated turning itself into a spa, but the landowner who had dreamed up the notion had died before he could launch it. Alas, his son was more interested in spending his money on himself in London rather than on the natives of the town from whence a large portion of his rents were derived.

Nevertheless it remained both lively and attractive and on nights when the moon was full there were not only balls at the rooms, but also musical recitals and meetings of the Highborough Literary and Philosophical Society. One of the most ardent contributors of papers to this group of gentleman amateurs was Nan's father, who took an interest in matters archaeological and topographical as well as theological. Occasionally a group of strolling players graced the small stage, and Nan had seen Romeo and Juliet portrayed by ranting thespians over twice their age, but had been so entranced by the music of Shakespeare's words that they had filled her mind for weeks afterwards.

Fortunately today had been fine, the sky was clear and the moon would be high when the time came to drive home from the ball, so that all but one of the inhabitants of the Rectory's ancient coach were in high spirits when they left for Highborough in the late afternoon.

The exception was Nan. She had put on the oldest gown which she had dared to wear, so old and dowdy

37

that Jane had screamed at her when she had walked into the entrance hall ready to leave.

'Pray, Nan, what could possess you to wear that? That is the most monstrous turn-out it has been my misfortune to see you in. You look exactly like the housekeeper on her way to have tea with the lady's maid!'

Nan could almost forgive Jane for her cruel words. Dreadfully, for some odd reason the sight of herself in the long glass in her room had made her want to laugh; she looked such a fright that she was almost a parody of a dowd. She could only murmur, 'Well, Jane, if you wish to shine tonight, you will surely do so even more, seeing that you are getting no competition from me. . .'

Jane had rewarded this piece of nonsense with a disdainful toss of the head. It hadn't so much as occurred to her that plain Nan could ever present her with any competition, but for once had she held her tongue.

What Nan had chosen to wear in an attempt to prevent Mr Brandon Tolliver from recognising her was a dun-coloured brown day dress with some ageing and coarse saffron-coloured lace about its high neck and around her wrists. No one, seeing her in it, could guess that she even possessed a body, let alone a shapely one. She had even found a cap of the same depressing material to wear on her plainly dressed and scraped-back hair. Its saffron lace frill fell forward over her eyes, hiding their beauty. The whole ensemble extinguished her quite.

Yes, there seemed small chance that Mr Brandon Tolliver would identify her as the nymph in the pantry. She supposed that sooner or later he would have to discover his mistake, but the later the better. In a few weeks he might have forgotten the encounter. Doubtless it had been a commonplace one for him!

Nan wronged him in that. Not that he had thought much more about it, and certainly it was the last thing on his mind when he entered the ballroom, Lydia on his arm, looking modish in apricot, to discover that the Fieldings were seated not far from the group of musicians arranged on the small dais.

Jane, who had been waiting for his arrival, fretting and worrying that perhaps the whole occasion was such small beer to him that he might not even turn up, threw him a dazzling smile. The Letcombes were seated next to the Rectory party, and she and Caroline had pulled their chairs together and were quizzing the company over their raised fans when Brandon's entrance drove everything unconnected with him from their heads.

Nan was seated at the back of the room, between the Ladies Alden and Letcombe, both of whom were more than twice her age, but she privately thought that she looked older than either of them.

'And how is your dear mama?' asked Lady Letcombe, more from the need to say something to poor Nan rather than from any real desire to know. 'Still unable to go out? Do you think it possible that we shall ever see her in society again? Caroline!' she commanded in a severe tone, not doing Nan the honour of waiting for an answer. 'Do stop staring quite so hard at Mr Tolliver. Patience is required from you until the Master of Ceremonies brings him over. Is not that so, Miss Fielding?'

Nan, who privately thought that the greatest patience on such occasions as these was shown by unfortunates like herself, who were condemned to spend most of the evening watching others enjoy themselves, gave a cool assent. She would not even have the dubious pleasure of Desmond asking her for at least one dance, as he was keeping to his intention not to attend the ball.

Most of the men in the room were not seated, but were leaning against the walls or the pillars of the hall. Another room, where tables containing cold food and drink were set out, opened out of the ballroom and was reached through a large classic arch. Statues of half-clad nymphs, gods and goddesses stood in niches around the walls of the room.

Jane and Caroline's excitement grew apace. The MC was talking to Brandon and his sister. 'I vow I shall die if he does not come over soon,' Jane announced dramatically. Her card for the evening would have been full by now if she had not insisted on leaving several spaces open for Mr Tolliver. What if he never came over at all? Surely he would, for had he not been *most* particular? He must have meant *something* by that. Jane thought that she would burst, and all that tiresome Nan could do was to tell her to sit still, and not to wriggle or laugh too loudly.

And then the dance was over, the musicians were quiet, mopping their brows, and the MC was bringing Brandon and his sister over towards them. The Letcombes and the Fieldings all stood up together, even though the MC was gallantly waving the ladies down again. Even the Rector, who was heartily bored by the whole business, and who considered dancing barbaric, but was compelled to attend the ball to do his duty by his youngest daughter, found himself pleased to meet again the new owner of Gillyflower Hall.

Brandon Tolliver found the whole business of a provincial assembly ball so quaintly charming that everything enchanted him. His sharp and curious eyes took in Jane and Caroline's pleasure at seeing him again. He also registered the rector's other-worldly but friendly greeting of the man with whom he had talked knowledgeably of the necessity to repair Broomhall's church to speak to him after entertaining the Rectory's housemaid. He recognised Sir Avery and Lady Letcombe, to whom he bowed, and also Kelsey whom he had met a few afternoons ago.

The fright in the hideous brown dress with the ugly cap hiding most of her doubtlessly plain face must be Jane's Gorgon, and so the introduction to her, made across two rows of chairs, proved. It was not surprising that poor Jane complained so much about her. The wonder was that such a pretty little charmer could have such a plain creature for an older sister.

Nan nodded. 'And the other business?' she asked him cryptically.

'Accomplished,' he said with a rare smile. 'I received a letter today which assured me that your latest. . . offering. . .is more than acceptable, and that what they are prepared to. . .give. . .for it is beyond anything which they have suggested before.' He had been choosing his words with care, lest they were overheard. He paused, then asked, 'And your father, my dear? He still suspects nothing?'

'Nothing.' Nan's smile was a little twisted. 'Which we agreed was the best thing. He, being so unworldly, believes that it is his great work on the nature of the Trinity which is responsible for our recent affluence.'

'And when you have finally succeeded in settling Jane, what then?' And Sam Stone gave a meaningful look at Jane, who was now talking animatedly to Brandon on the other side of the room, laughing up into his handsome face, and tapping at him with her fan when he laughed back at her.

For some reason the sight of this gave Nan the strangest pang. She lost kind Sam Stone for a moment, before remembering that he had asked her a question.

'And then nothing,' she answered him almost shortly. 'I have my duty to my parents, you know.'

He shook his greying head at her. He had been a handsome young man and was now a handsome middle-aged one, widowed since his beloved wife had died in childbirth some fifteen years earlier.

'No, I don't know.' He was almost abrupt. 'You have a life of your own, and ought to be able to live it. Only I and God know how hard you have worked these last years, and all unacknowledged by anyone. None of your family is grateful for what they know that you do, let alone what they *don't* know that you do.

'I had not thought to say this here, in such circumstances, but I feel that I must. I honour you above all the women I have ever met. You are unselfish and kind, you hide your light so as not to extinguish Jane's. No, do not deny that,' he told her, raising a hand as she tried to deny what he was saying to her. 'Looking at you tonight I know that to be true, and because I have come to care for you, as well as to admire you, I am asking you to marry me as soon as you are free—when Jane marries, that is. I will see that the Rector and your mother do not suffer as a consequence of your marriage.'

Nan was so shocked by this unexpected proposal and the expression of earnest love on his face that all that she could do was open her mouth and shut it again. For a moment, at the end of his proposal, the world had seemed to stop. Now it was turning again, the dance had ended and her party and that of the Letcombes, together with the two Tollivers, were making for where she and Sam sat.

Sam, seeing this, said rapidly, 'No, do not try to answer me now, my dear. Think over what I have said to you. I love you as well as honour you, and would like to free you from the trap which life has created for you. You may give me an answer when you please, but for both our sakes do not be overlong in your consideration.'

He rose and bowed. 'You will forgive me for moving on. I am supposed to be talking business tonight with Lord Alden, and although the surroundings are not suitable I cannot oppose him, he is such an old friend. You will present my compliments to your father, as I shall leave after speaking to m'lord.'

He had gone. Jane was sitting by her and was talking excitedly about Brandon, and how he had made her laugh, and how much he liked reading the novels of the author of *Sophia*. All this, for once, flew over Nan's head. She was quite overwhelmed by what had happened to her. In one week she had received two unexpected proposals—albeit that the first, from Desmond Tolliver, had not really been one at all!

But this second one from Mr Stone—perhaps she ought to think of him as Sam, was her dazed inward comment, seeing that he was considering her as a possible wife—was indeed a facer. 'Facer' was another of Chaz's favourite pieces of slang which seemed particularly suitable applied to Sam Stone's proposal, which was a genuine one—even if he was also proposing delay to satisfy her sense of duty, she supposed. It was, unlike Desmond's, also very flattering. She had no reason to believe that it was not sincerely meant. And if Sam had spoken only of admiration and care, rather than love, he had not chosen to demean either of them by insisting, as Desmond had done, that they were beyond passion.

Who would have thought it? In effect, elderly spinster past her last prayers though she was, she had already accumulated three more proposals, counting Randal's, made so long ago, than Jane had yet managed. The thought made her laugh to herself. The rest of the evening passed in a haze. Mr Brandon Tolliver continued to be '*most* particular' to Jane, dancing with her again, and taking her into supper.

Nan went into supper with the Letcombes. Lydia Bligh, seeing how isolated she was, took it upon herself, in her kind way, to talk to her, but Nan found herself barely able either to eat or to speak. Her throat seemed to have closed. As she finished her meagre meal she saw Brandon and Jane coming towards her, but the thought of trying to speak to him without giving away her—and his—secret was too much.

She dodged away from them behind one of the pillars and went through a side-door into a long corridor where she sat alone on a stone bench trying to make sense of what was happening to her.

The only thing was that every time she tried to do so the picture of Mr Brandon Tolliver laughing at Jane came into her mind and would not go away. And pooh to that, was her desolate thought. What I really ought to be contemplating is becoming middle-aged Sam Stone's second wife. At least he would be kind to me ...if I were free to marry him, that is...

* * *

Sitting in the carriage on the way home, being talked to by Lydia about the events of the evening, and in particular about Miss Jane Fielding, whom Lydia was coming to agree might make him a suitable, if rather young and flighty wife, Brandon said abruptly, 'You were right to reproach me the other day, Liddy.'

It was a long time since he had used her childhood pet name when speaking to her. 'About what, my dear?' Lydia replied gently, looking out of the chaise window at the peerless moon sailing above the clouds.

'About not being unkind and careless. I was unpleasant to that poor drab creature, Jane Fielding's older sister, and it has been on my mind ever since. I cannot even apologise to her, for to do so would be to demean her further. I was being as frivolous and thoughtless as Jane herself, and there is no excuse for me at my age.'

Well, here was a turn-up, was Lydia's startled inward response. 'You conversed with her, then?' she thought fit to ask.

'No, indeed, I said but a couple of sentences to her, and the second intolerable. Should I marry Jane she will be my sister-in-law and I shall owe some kind of duty to her. Bad for me to begin such a relationship by distressing her as I am sure I did.'

'Oh, she allowed you to understand that?'

'Not at all—or not in words. I could tell by her stance, what I saw of her mouth—which was all that I could see of her face beneath that dreadful cap.' He wriggled restlessly. 'Lord, Liddy, I am turning Methodee, as they say, to trouble myself about such a thing. Never mind; I will try to make it up to her later when. . .well. . .when. . .you know.'

'No, Brandon, I don't,' replied his sister forthrightly, 'and I don't think that you do. Consider. This might reflect badly on Jane as well as on yourself.'

'She's but a child, Liddy, and will learn, I'm sure. . .' He was restless again. He laughed a little, and said, with an attempt to recover his spirits, 'Do you think that it is associating with the Rectory party which is bringing on these thoughts, or is it living in the country? I never seemed to have them in the old days.'

Lydia made no reply; the chaise was turning on to the front sweep at Gillyflower Hall and footmen and lackeys were running towards them. It was no time to be dissecting one's conscience, she thought; the matter would have to wait until tomorrow—or never, perhaps.

CHAPTER FOUR

'NAN, why has not the hem of my blue evening gown been mended? I most particularly asked that it should be seen to immediately.'

'Miss Fielding, the butcher has forgot to send the meat which I ordered; pray will you have words with him? This is not the first occasion on which this has happened.'

'Nan, my dearest girl. You are quite the best reader of novels in the Rectory, but somehow these days you never seem to wish to entertain your poor old mother by treating her to a chapter or two. I beg that you will find a little time this evening to read me some more of the author of *Sophia*'s novel.'

'Daughter, I know that you have been a trifle busy lately, but I did ask you, most particularly, to copy out the latest chapter of The Nature of Grace. At this rate it will never be ready for the printers...'

'Nan, dear, I know that you have very little time to yourself these days, but I would like you to assist me to decorate the church, ready for this Sunday. Mrs Aske, who promised to do so, has taken a fit of the ague and cannot leave the house. You have such a neat hand with flowers. This afternoon would be a most suitable time.'

'Dear Nan, I know that you are busy but I have lost my new kite; the wind whipped it out of my hands, and I last saw it flying in the direction of Gillyflower Hall. I should be most obliged if you would come and help me to look for it this afternoon...'

Nan put her hand to her head and wailed at poor Chaz, 'No, no and no! I have spent the whole morning being badgered by everyone in this house, and it is beyond me to satisfy everyone. You should have taken more care of your kite.'

'Oh, have a heart, Nan. Why, once you were only too happy to fly kites with me.'

'Chaz, take Roger and go and look for it yourself.'

'But I have Nan, I have.' Chaz's face was a picture of misery. 'Oh, why are you such a crosspatch these days, Nan? You used not to be.'

'I used not to be many things,' Nan replied fiercely. 'But time changes us all, Chaz, as you will find out when you grow up.'

'Grow up! Well, if growing up means becoming like you then I don't want to.' And Chaz ran out of the drawing-room where Nan had been busy copying out the Rector's latest treatise.

She put her head down on the desk before her and cursed God and what her life had dwindled down to — the Rectory dogsbody for whom no one really cared, but whom everyone expected to see that life ran easily and sweetly for them.

She sat up again and humbly begged God's forgiveness, and thought instead that Sam Stone was offering her a way out. But did she want that way, and would her parents allow her to take it? She looked out of the window; the sun was shining, a little breeze was blowing. It really was the most delightful summer's day. And she would be unable to enjoy any of it; she was bound to a wheel of tasks.

'No,' she said aloud, to no one at all. She threw down her quill pen, ignoring the string of blots it made on the white paper. Why should she not enjoy the sun? She stood up, pulled on her shawl which she had draped over the back of her chair and walked out of the drawing-room and then the Rectory front door without a backward glance.

Why should she not spend the afternoon in the scents of the woodland around Gillyflower Hall and look for Chaz's kite while she was doing so? Someone was calling her name as she crossed the front lawn. For a moment she hesitated, and turned to see who it was. Kelsey was standing at the front door waving a basket of flowers at her.

Duty almost overcame her, but then rebellion took over. No, Kelsey could manage on her own quite well. She merely wanted Nan's company in order to gossip to her about village affairs, and by the end of the afternoon the only result of it would be that Nan would have acquired a few more chores.

Well, a fig for everything and everybody! She took herself through the wicket gate at the side of the Rectory's paddock where an old grey donkey grazed, and walked along a rutted path through the scrub and woodland.

And I have not even put my bonnet or cap on, she realised. For her cap had irked her by its reminder of what she had come to, and she had flung it off in the middle of copying out the last page before Chaz had interrupted her and sparked off this minor revolt. If only someone would thank her, or show her some affection, then she might feel a little better.

Nan shook herself. It was too bad of her to wallow in such self-pity. She really ought to be looking for Chaz's kite. To find it would give this walk some justification, if justification were needed. She meandered happily along, thinking of nothing, looking up into the trees although she was sure that she was on a wild-goose chase—though a better name for it might have been a wild-kite chase!

She had walked quite a long way towards the Hall when she saw Chaz's lost treasure. It was high in the branches of a somewhat rickety tree, its tail dangling forlornly down. Now the common-sense thing to do would have been to go straight back to the Rectory, tell Chaz or Roger where it was to be found, and they could then have come along and recovered it.

But the spark which had ignited Nan's rebellion had also ignited something else in her. Looking up into the tree, she remembered happy childhood days when she

and Randal had shouted and played in a similar woodland and had, between them, climbed every tree in
sight. Why should she not climb this tree and take
Chaz's kite home as a trophy?

Her skirts would be a nuisance, but what of that?
There was no one about to see her and she could hitch
them up with the help of her shawl. To climb to the
forking branch where the kite was caught and release it
would be the work of a moment. No sooner said than
done. Almost twenty-eight she might be, but her body
had lost none of its agility, and she shinned up the tree
as though Randal was still with her, cheering her on,
and not lying dead in foreign soil, leaving behind only
memories. . .

She reached the forking branch where the kite had
become entangled, and carefully began to disentangle
it. Easy, something sang inside her, but, as always, pride
went before a fall. The tree was old and inwardly
rotten, and even as her fingers began to loosen the kite
Nan heard, to her horror, an ominous creaking in the
branch on which she was perched.

'Oh, hell and all its devils!' Nan's oaths were always
theological, as befitted a parson's daughter, and this
flew out as the creaking grew louder, the branch broke,
and Nan found herself falling without any hope of
salvation and without even having liberated Chaz's kite.
And this time she was falling not from a high stool, but
from a high branch, with the hard ground below. She
had no time to be frightened, only to recognise that she
was lost and falling. The wages of sin were truly
deathly, as well as certain!

Mr Brandon Tolliver had decided that the fine day
demanded more homage from him than merely sitting
in the house and admiring it through a large window.
He had asked his sister to accompany him, but she had
pleaded tiredness.

'You really are the most energetic creature,' she had
told him forcefully. 'Always on the go. Go and be

energetic on your own. I confess that simply to see you there radiating determination makes me feel quite weak. I can only imagine what you think "a little walk" entails!'

He had laughed at her, picked up a stick and set out on a tour of exploration of a part of his property which he had not yet visited. He could see Broomhall and its church in the distance, and perhaps he might even decide to visit the Rectory, talk to Miss Jane, and find some way of being pleasant to the Gorgon. . .

Yes, it was quite delightful to quarter the countryside knowing that it was yours, and that everything that you saw was new and consequently interesting. The track he was following led him to a clearing, where he paused for a moment to look around him. . .to discover that the countryside held more surprises than one.

For a lively young female had climbed one of the taller trees and was sitting astride a branch, showing a fine pair of legs. Her hair had come down and her splendid arms were upraised for she was freeing what appeared to be a kite from the tree's upper branches.

By Jove, it was the servant from the Rectory again! And what a superb specimen of womanhood she was! He had seldom seen a finer pair of female legs, and he had seen a few of them in his time! Brandon stood back the better to enjoy the sight of such a charming nymph. All his good resolutions to his sister and to himself about not pursuing servant girls were flying away at the sight of this one. What a hoyden she must be! By the looks of her she had no doubt given the village lads some pleasure in her time. They hardly deserved such a splendid pair of calves and ankles!

His happy contemplation of the female form divine in action was interrupted by the creaking which had distressed Nan, and was the harbinger of her fall. He started forward to assist her, for such an enterprising nymph deserved more than a broken neck. . .and for the second time in three weeks Mr Brandon Tolliver caught the falling Miss Fielding in his strong arms.

Only this time she came down with such force that although he was able to break her fall she took him to the ground with her, knocking the wind out of the pair of them as she did so...

For a moment Nan had no idea of where she was, or what had happened. She was still held in Brandon's arms, and he was beneath her this time, lying flat among the woodland flowers and herbs, surrounded by their scent. It took a little time for them to recover. Brandon was to discover later that he was bruised. Nan was merely shocked, Brandon's body having protected her from the worst consequences of her fall. His hand still resting on her arm, he sat up as she rolled a little off him, to sit up in her turn, so that they were now side by side, staring at one another. Turquoise eyes met amused silver ones.

'*Again*!' exclaimed Brandon, once his breath was back. 'Do you make a habit of falling from on high, my fair nymph? If so, you must beware. I shall not always be present to save you.'

Yes, it was he, her nemesis, Mr Brandon Tolliver, always about when she was doing something unladylike! And whatever would he think of her? Her skirts were up to her knees, her hair was down, her bodice was torn by her descent through the tree so that Brandon could see the shape of one creamy breast tipped with rose.

It was only too plain what he thought of her! Of its own volition his arm went around her and he heard himself saying, his voice hoarse, 'And does not your rescuer deserve a reward?' And Nan Fielding found herself flat on her back being thoroughly kissed—*again*!—by the desirable Mr Brandon Tolliver who was being '*most* particular' to Miss Jane Fielding.

He was also being '*most* particular' to her elder sister, believing her to be quite other than she was. The devil of it was that Nan Fielding liked behind held and kissed by the strong man whose warm body was so close to hers, who was plainly roused by her and the sight that she presented—so roused that he was doubtless about to try to have his way with her among the greenery of the woodland, the birds calling about them, and Chaz's kite high overhead. . .

It was the thought of Chaz which restored Nan to sanity—that and the knowledge that she would not be able to keep her true identity secret for very much longer—and what would be the result of that? The mind boggled. Even the author of *Sophia* might find it difficult to suggest a way out of this predicament.

But oh, it was hard to say the words which would stop him as their kisses, caresses and sighs grew ever more urgent. And I don't really know him, and he doesn't know me at all, and what sort of man carries on like this with a servant girl, chance met? she thought wildly. And if he really wants to marry Jane, I shouldn't be allowing him to take all these dreadful liberties. . .

And why am I able to ponder moral problems with my brain while my body is busy letting Brandon Tolliver undo it? There being no answer to this, Nan cried, 'No, certainly not,' and pushed Brandon away as strongly as she could, her whole body aching with the desire to clutch him to her rather.

For a moment he resisted her, and then, his head clearing, he rolled away from her, aching himself. What in God's name had come over him? He had never done such a thing before. His love-affairs had always been with willing females well-known to him. He had never been, as he had truthfully told his sister, one for passing dalliance with servants and underlings.

Even as they fell apart they heard footsteps crashing through the undergrowth. Both of them sprang to their feet, rearranging their clothing. Nan undid her shawl and threw it around her shoulders to hide her ruined dress. She could do nothing about her hair. Brandon was in better case, although she noticed, with wry amusement, that a certain amount of buttoning up of his breeches flap was going on. She had, it seemed, stopped him in the very nick of time.

They were thus almost respectable when a small boy, one of the village children, galloped into the clearing to stare incuriously at them. They were the great ones of his world, and what they got up to was always mysterious.

He immediately said the fatal words which Nan had dreaded. 'A fine arternoon to you, Miss Fielding. I've come a-looking for Master Charles's kite.'

Nan heard Brandon's breathing change at this revelation. She tried not to look at him, and said to the child as coolly as she could, 'It's up in that tree, Jem, the one with the broken branch. Run and tell Master Charles where it is, and ask him to bring Roger with him to free it.'

He pulled his forelock at her and ran off, after saying respectfully, 'Yes, Miss Fielding.'

Nan pulled her shawl tightly around her shoulders. Despite the warmth of the day she had begun to shiver. She said formally to Brandon without looking at him, 'Good afternoon to you, Mr Tolliver,' and began to walk away in the same direction as the boy.

Only to be stopped by a strong hand on her arm dragging her around to face a grim-faced man who was staring at her with an expression of profound astonishment on his face.

'Oh, no,' he told her ruthlessly. 'You don't escape from me as easily as this, madam. What game were you playing with me?'

Nan could not resist answering him in kind. 'Why, the same game that you were playing with me, Mr Tolliver, and it reflects little credit on either of us.'

'And that statement, at least, is the truth,' he rasped, his mouth now as straight as it had been smilingly curly until he had discovered who she was. He continued to hold her in such a grip that Nan thought that she would be bruised by it. He was taking in every detail of her present disgraceful appearance, which was so unlike that of the prim Gorgon he was used to seeing, sitting at the back of every room which he had entered in the last three weeks.

Then, as though he were uttering an oath, he came out with a single explosive word, 'Why?' And then again, 'Why?'

'Why what?' demanded Nan, trying to pull away. 'Pray do release me, sir. I have many duties awaiting me at the Rectory.'

His smile was almost ugly as she came out with this. 'Oh, indeed, madam, so I understand. As you must understand the import of my question. Why the double masquerade? You caught me nicely with them both, did you not? The upright spinster lady and the serving maid with a glad eye for the main chance where gentlemen are concerned. With how many men have you played the latter part?'

'Oh, for shame!' exclaimed Nan, still trying to pull away. 'It was you who set upon me in the Rectory pantry, and I was only saving you embarrassment by not informing you that you were like to ravish one of the Rector's daughters while courting the other!'

'Ravish, madam, ravish? You joined in the game so lustily, I thought that you had pleasured half the village.'

Brandon knew that he was being disgraceful, but shame at his own bad behaviour was somehow being transferred from him to her. Even as Nan slapped his face with her free hand he was full of remorse.

He held and clasped that hand too, mastered himself, and began to remember who and what they both were, who a moment ago had been nymph and satyr celebrating their passion in the time-honoured way.

'No,' he said. 'No. I should not have spoken to you as I just did, and you will forgive me. But consider your appearance, then and now. Consider the condition in which I found you—up a tree! Am I to believe that you occasionally grow tired of propriety and abandon it so that you may adventure, unknown and secure in your mode of servant?'

Shame was gripping Nan as well as Brandon. Her walk in the woods, which had begun in what now looked like wicked defiance, had ended even more badly than she could conceivably have expected.

'Believe what you please,' she told him. He was still holding both her hands, but in the lightest clasp so that she could have broken away without a struggle—but somehow she did not want to release herself from him.

More than that, they were both beginning to understand that if they were to meet again in the small society in which they lived they must somehow manage to come to terms with what they had both done after a fashion that would enable them to do so without embarrassment.

Brandon began to allow his intellect to dominate his reasoning, and not his passions. And about time too, he thought dismally. Twice, not once, but twice, I have set upon a woman I have never met before and treated her like a whore. Reason might say that she had responded like one, but what chance had he given her to do otherwise? And who would, or could, have guessed that she was Parson Fielding's prim and proper daughter?

'My sister says. . .' and this time his voice was low and calm, not high and angry '. . .that you are much put upon. Is it possible that occasionally you need some sort of release from the call of duty?'

This was so exactly what Nan had felt earlier that afternoon that she began to tremble. Brandon felt it and drew her slowly towards him, so that they were face to face and breast to breast again, but strangely passionless—as though, Brandon thought afterwards, they had actually achieved consummation and were quivering in the aftermath of it. Strangely, for a fleeting moment each felt that they had known the other forever.

'I have frightened you,' he said, his voice as gentle as he could make it. 'I apologise to you for that. It was neither gentlemanly nor kind of me to speak and behave to you as I did. My sister Lydia frequently tells me that I am no gentleman and I fear that she may be right.'

He took in Nan's white face, her quivering lips. She felt as though everything that she had suffered and endured since the news of Randal's death had all fallen on her together. The attraction which Brandon had for her, and which she surely could not have for him, seemed not only a reproach to her, but a weight she must carry.

And she was being so unfair to both him and Jane. For if he was honest in his pursuit of Jane for a wife, what was she, Nan, doing, to come between them in any way, however unintended?

'If you will allow me to leave,' she told him, her face slightly averted lest it reveal to him more than she wished him to know, 'I will try to find my way back to the Rectory without being seen. It was foolish of me to climb the tree to release Chaz's kite, but I so seldom allow myself to do foolish things that perhaps we can both forgive me for doing this one.'

Her whole mien had become so humble and defeated that Brandon felt himself to be the most utter cur. He let go of her hands and stood back.

'You will permit me to escort you to the Rectory paddock?'

'If you must,' Nan told him simply, 'but I would rather you did not.'

'Oh, I think that I must. I have disgraced myself sufficiently for one day. You must allow me to do some small penance, although,' he could not prevent himself from saying, 'escorting the nymph who lives behind Miss Fielding's mask of propriety is no penance.'

For a moment the passion which had flared up and burned so brightly between them was revived. Nan gave him a half-smile of such sweetness that Brandon almost blinked at it. How could anyone have called her plain? How could he have thought her plain, even when she was the Gorgon?

But then, he had not seen the Gorgon up a tree, her

shapely legs in full sight and her superb body outlined by the dress which was strained tautly around her. And what was he doing to allow his thoughts to stray in such a wanton manner when he had just told himself that he owed it to her to forget all that had passed between them and remember only that she was Jane's elder sister and the Rectory's overworked factotum?

As for the Gorgon herself, she was a mass of seething embarrassment. Walking alongside Mr Brandon Tolliver, allowing him to take her grubby hand, scratched as a consequence of trying to free Chaz's kite, she was only capable of the deepest shame as he kissed the back of it gently. The beautiful eyes which looked up at him were full of tears.

'Come, my dear Miss Fielding,' he said, his voice as kind as he could make it. 'You must not repine too much over what is now past and gone. Try to think of it as an amusing episode from one of the works of the author of *Sophia* and all will be well.'

He was hardly prepared for the result of this well-meaning attempt to lighten what had passed between them. Nan dragged her hand from his violently, put it to her mouth, and exclaimed, 'Oh, no!' Then she turned to half run across the paddock towards the Rectory as though the devil himself were behind her.

'The devil!' exclaimed Mr Brandon Tolliver aloud. 'I shall never understand women, never!'

CHAPTER FIVE

'AN INVITATION,' exclaimed Jane, waving a splendid sheet of cream writing paper at Nan, 'for us all to attend Mrs Bligh's open day of fruit and flowers at Gillyflower Hall! Papa has just given it to me to pass on to you. The whole family, save for Mama, of course, is invited, including Chaz, and we are to stay over for three nights. Is not that monstrous kind of them? For sure Mr Brandon Tolliver is behind this invitation.'

'To stay over,' repeated Nan distractedly. She had just come downstairs after changing out of her ruined dress and tidying up her equally ruined hair. 'We only live a bare mile away. Why should we stay over? We could walk the distance between here and Gillyflower Hall in no time. And what will Mama do while we are away?'

'Oh!' Jane was determined to show her impatience at Nan's backwardness and her equal determination to be a guest at Gillyflower Hall. 'There is to be a ball on the middle night, and a musical recital on the last one. Dear Mrs Bligh has arranged for some musicians to come over from Leicester to play for us, and half the county will be there. We cannot be forever rushing backwards and forwards between the Rectory and Gillyflower Hall every five minutes, as even you must acknowledge! And Kelsey will look after Mama for us. She has already agreed to do so.'

She tossed her pretty head. 'Besides, Papa is quite determined that we shall go. Mr Tolliver is proving *such* a benefactor to the parish, he says, what with providing extra funds to repair the church tower and to replace the pews which have woodworm, as well as giving an endowment to the old women's almshouses.

It will be only right and proper, he says, to support him and his sister in their enterprises.'

The last thing which Nan wanted was to be brought into intimate contact with Brandon Tolliver again, but she could hardly allow her own whimwhams to interfere with Mrs Bligh's kindness, whether Brandon was responsible for them or not. She took the letter of invitation from Jane and read it through, while Jane rushed on excitedly about the benefits which Mr Tolliver and his sister had conferred on the district by coming to live in it.

'I have known that this celebration was proposed for some time,' she announced. 'When Mrs Bligh was at the Letcombes' the other week she raised the prospect of some such enterprise with Lady Letcombe and asked her advice on whom to invite and whom to employ to make a small stage for the musicians to play for the ball, and for the recital the next evening. Only think, Desmond is quite reconciled with them, and has agreed to attend! I would have thought that you, of all people, would find that monstrous agreeable.'

Why me 'of all people'? wondered Nan, putting down the letter. I suppose Jane thinks that Desmond may have a *tendre* for me—the sort that elderly persons have for one another, I imagine! For some odd reason this thought was so amusing that it drove the dismals away a little.

Further excitement ensued. The door was flung open as Chaz rushed in crying, 'Oh, what a brick you are, Nan, to go looking for my kite! It was too good of you after I spoke to you so scurvily. Jem came and told me that you had found it, and his papa helped us to fetch it down from the tree. Was it you or Mr Tolliver who found it? Jem said that he was with you when he met you in Gillyflower Woods.'

Was it Nan's imagination or did a strange silence suddenly fall as Chaz ingenuously threw this grenade into the Rectory drawing-room? Jane stared at her

sister, as did Kelsey, who was busy darning Chaz's
everyday woollen socks.

'You did not,' said Jane, in the voice of a prosecuting
counsel, 'tell us that you went walking in the woods
with Brandon! Pray how did that come about? I distinctly understood you to say that you were too busy to
mend the hem of my dress, or to read to Mama! And
why should you say nothing of it when you came
home?'

Harassed, Nan came out with, 'I suppose, Jane, that
it is allowed for me to have some private life of my
own? I was in the middle of copying out Papa's latest
book when the beauty of the day decided me on a walk
into the woods to look for Chaz's kite. I found it by
chance, just as Mr Tolliver came upon me on *his*
afternoon walk. We exchanged politenesses and he
escorted me to the paddock gate. I understand that he
could not stay to visit as he was expecting a visitor of
his own.'

Now this last was pure fiction, particularly the bit
about exchanging politenesses, but something had to be
said.

'Oh!' Jane was mollified, but not completely so. Chaz
looked at both his sisters. He was beginning to question
a little many of the foundations of Rectory life, one of
them being that Jane had all the fun and Nan did all
the work.

'Why should not Nan walk with Mr Tolliver if she
wanted to?' he asked Jane belligerently. 'He is not your
property yet, nor Caroline Letcombe's either. And
Nan's conversation is always a deal sight more interesting than either yours or Caroline's, I can tell you. Nan
knows about kites and fishing, and the battles of the
late war, whereas all you and Caroline talk about is
your clothes and balls and how to do your hair.' He
roared relentlessly on. 'If I were Mr Brandon Tolliver I
know who I should want to marry——'

'Charles Fielding!' exclaimed Kelsey, as though she

were still his nanny-cum-governess. 'Hold your tongue. You are not to speak to your sister after that fashion.'

He would not be silenced, and roared back at her, face scarlet, 'Why ever not? *She* never chooses her tone when she talks to Nan.'

It was Nan who stopped him this time. 'No, Chaz,' she told him. 'You help neither me nor yourself by speaking so. Apologise to Jane.' She added this hastily, because she could see that Jane was about to throw a fit of the hysterics, and she knew that if Jane did she would be compelled to slap her, and she was fearful that if once she began to do so she wouldn't know how to stop.

'That I won't,' began Chaz furiously, only to have Kelsey rise to her feet, take him by the arms, and say,

'Go to your room, Charles, and only come down when you have recovered your temper. You must learn that it is not always wise to say exactly what we think.'

He pulled away and ran towards the door, to turn at it and shout into the room, 'That may be so, but you are all jolly unfair to Nan, and I am not much better.'

He left behind a silent room until Jane began to speak. 'Papa ought to give him a beating for his insolence to me. Why should I not ask Nan about her meeting with——?'

'If anyone says Mr Brandon Tolliver's name again I shall scream,' announced Nan in ringing tones. 'I am going to my room to enjoy a little peace and quiet. You may fetch me down for supper,' she told Kelsey, 'and perhaps by then we shall all have recovered our tempers.'

But she was still trembling when she opened the door to her bedroom which doubled as her sitting-room and which was her only refuge from the cares of the household. It was a large room at the back of the house, on the second floor, and looked out across the paddock towards Gillyflower Hall and its park, and the winding path on the left which led to it through the wood.

The room contained a big four-poster bed, two

elderly armchairs and a small table which had come from her mother's home years ago, and which had been passed on to Nan when she was a girl. In one corner stood a large wardrobe, in another a small and elegant walnut bureau which her parents had given to her long ago when she had still been young enough to be petted, before her more conventionally pretty sisters had begun to occupy their hearts and minds.

The bureau had a little top which could be let down so that one could write upon it, and also had the advantage of small but strong brass locks on the top and the drawers below it. Nan always wore the key to it on a ribbon around her neck below her dress.

She walked over to the bureau, pulled out the key, unlocked it and let down the top to reveal an ink-well, quill pens, a penknife and a small box of fine sand. Next she opened one of the drawers, lifting from it a pile of paper, some of it written on, some not, which she placed on the top.

She sat down, picked up the quill pen, and sharpened it with the penknife before dipping it into the ink-well. But instead of writing with it she put the pen down, rested her head upon her hands and willed herself to forget everything which had happened that afternoon.

When her heart had stopped bumping and her breathing had returned to normal she picked up the pen again, pulled a blank sheet of paper towards her, and for the next hour wrote steadily and surely, until she heard the bell for supper sounding in the Rectory hall.

She did not want to stop working, but knew that she must. Not to partake of the evening meal would be sure to be remarked upon, and she didn't think that she could stand either Jane's reproaches or Kelsey's solicitude. Far better to break off, go downstairs and, even if she found eating difficult, try to join in the conversation, if only to help poor gallant Chaz.

Besides, Sam Stone had said that he would look in after supper to speak to her father about signing documents relating to the business of the church. She and Sam had already gone over them, and all her father would have to do was append his signature, secure in the knowledge that his lawyer and his daughter would not let him down.

Nan re-locked the bureau and examined herself in the small mirror which hung above the wash-stand. Yes, she looked pale, but not unduly so. Her cap was a little awry, but that was soon straightened. She sighed, smoothed down her skirts and prepared to go downstairs, the very model of propriety who would never, ever climb a tree or lie willingly in Mr Brandon Tolliver's strong arms being made love to!

Nor, she discovered regretfully as she talked with Sam over the tea board, which had been brought in on his arrival shortly after supper was over and Chaz had been sent to bed, did she wish to marry Mr Samuel Stone. She had thought of him as a kind and helpful uncle for so long that the idea of being his wife was odd and strange, and she knew now that she could not accept him even if it was possible for her to free herself from the prison of servitude which her life had become. To do so would be fair neither to him nor to her. For he would want of her what she could not give him. She was not so innocent as not to know that he would require of her more than friendship, and friendship was all she had to offer. She did not look forward to telling him so.

Over the teacups, before he retired to do business in the Rector's study, Sam mentioned that he too was invited to the house-warming at Gillyflower Hall. 'I have been doing some business for Mr Tolliver,' he announced, holding his cup out to Nan for another offering. 'I expect that you will all be there?'

'Indeed, indeed,' replied the Rector before Jane had time to assure him eagerly that yes, of course they would. 'I am not over-partial to such jauntings as these, but it would not be fair to Jane and Chaz to deprive them of such a pleasant outing.'

'And Nan,' remarked Sam drily, looking at her over the rim of his cup.

'Oh, yes,' said Nan's papa vaguely. 'She will be going too—to look after Jane and Chaz and see that they behave themselves,' he remarked, smiling at her. 'I am sure that she will enjoy the recital on the last evening. The rest of the programme is designed more for the youthful members of the party, I believe.' And his benign smiled encompassed them all.

Sam put down his teacup and saucer with a disapproving rattle while inside Nan something shrieked, Oh, Papa, do not consign me to the almshouses yet. For that, she knew, was where poor parsons' unmarried daughters went, if none of their brothers or sisters wished to offer them a home. Would she go to Gillyflower Hall as the elderly maiden aunt if Jane married Brandon? The very idea made her shudder.

Her trembling start was noticed by no one except Sam, who, looking a little alarmed, asked gently, 'Are you feeling quite well, Nan? You are very pale tonight.'

'Nothing,' lied Nan. 'It was nothing. Someone walked over my grave, perhaps.'

'Oh, what a horrid saying that is,' Jane said, and later, when Sam and the Rector had retired to his study to do business, she remarked a little acidly, 'From the way that Mr Stone looked after you and his "Are you feeling quite well, Nan?" one might think that you had an elderly beau there.' And she gave a scornful little laugh at the mere idea.

A great blush swept over Nan; she could not help herself. Jane laughed harder than ever at the sight of it. 'Oh, never say so! What, Nan, are you eager for the privilege of being the second Mrs Stone?'

Even for Jane this was rather more spiteful than usual. Nan stood up. 'Better perhaps than being the only unmarried Miss Fielding, Jane, and now, if you will excuse me, I shall retire for the night. I had a long and arduous day.'

She heard Kelsey begin to reproach Jane for her

rudeness to her sister as she left the room, and missed
Jane's answer: 'Lord, Kelsey, what a fuss about nothing.
She must know as well as the rest of the parish that she
said her last prayers long ago. I sometimes wonder if
Nan was ever young.'

'So happy that you were able to come—and that the
day is so uncommon fine!'

Lydia Bligh had said this or some variant of it so
many times on the first day of her small fête, as she
chose to call it, that she began to wonder how sincere
she sounded.

She had invited what looked like the whole of the
district, and the whole of the district had chosen to
attend. They were processing by her as they arrived in
the large drawing-room at Gillyflower Hall, whose tall
glass doors had been opened on to the terrace which
overlooked the park where her earlier guests were
already taking a turn. A cold collation was to be served
on the upper lawn, and the servants were already laying
it out.

Brandon, who stood beside her, looked particularly
fine in a charcoal-coloured jacket, cream pantaloons,
black silk socks—just showing—and light black shoes
decorated with silver rosettes. His cravat was a miracle
of his valet's art, it having taken the man, Brandon had
declared, half the morning to achieve such perfection.
His hair was fashionably wind-blown—another magic
trick of his valet's. He was being charm itself and no
one would have guessed that he had spent the morning
looking out for the Rectory party and one member of
it—Miss Fielding—in particular. He was, he knew, supposed to be looking out for Miss Jane Fielding—or that
was what the world and his sister Lydia thought.

Just as he had begun to wonder whether they were
going to cry off—perhaps Miss Fielding was ill, or the
parson—he saw them ushered through the double
doors by the butler, and heard their names cried aloud,

so that Lydia swung round to greet them, before passing them on, one by one, to him.

Who was he looking for? Again, most supposed Miss
Jane, who appeared absolutely enchanting in a cream
silk gown decorated with rosebuds. Little silk rosebuds
ran along the neckline of her dress, and one was tucked
into the pale blue sash around her waist, another nestling among her golden curls. She had never looked so
lovely, so ethereal, and she knew it. Beside her, Chaz
had been wrestled into a youthful imitation of the
clothes which Brandon was wearing, and it was plain
that he was a handsome boy who was going to be a
handsome man. Behind them, as always, Parson
Fielding was his usual vaguely charming, flyaway self,
and beside him. . .

Yes, beside him was Miss Anne Fielding, wearing a
deep purple gown with a high neck which looked,
Brandon thought, as though it might have done duty
for the mother who was never seen. This judgement
merely confirmed his percipience, for it *was* an old
gown of Mrs Fielding's, cut and trimmed to Nan's size.
Even Nan's cap, whose frill drooped on either side of
her face, had been her mother's. Thrift was a necessity,
as well as a virtue, at the Rectory. Any spare money
went to buy Jane's clothes, and ultimately, it was hoped,
a husband.

If anything, Nan was more extinguished than ever.
No strand of her glossy tawny hair could be seen, and
her eyes were hidden in the shadow of the dreadful
cap. Worse still, the ugly dress hid the beautiful body.
So how was it that Mr Brandon Tolliver, surveying the
Rectory party, felt a dreadful spasm of desire, not for
the elegant fairy on the front row, but for the elderly
dowd at the back? A dowd who was trying to avoid
looking at him.

And he must not look at her. He bowed over Jane's
hand, held it a little too long, told her how pleased he
was to see her again and how charming she looked.
Jane was always at her best when being admired. She

sparkled prettily at both him and Lydia, saying everything that she should on such an occasion.

Chaz was greeted with the words, 'And how are you,
old fellow? Did you manage to recover your kite? Does
it still fly?' Brandon showed such genuine interest in
Chaz's doings, complimenting him on being a member
of the village cricket team at such a young age, that
Chaz thought what a splendid fellow he was, who surely
deserved better as a wife than an empty-head like Jane
or Caroline.

Talking to the Rector, Brandon changed tack again,
referring knowledgeably to his book *The Nature of the
Trinity*, of which he had taken the precaution of reading
the first few chapters and skimming the rest. Nan's
father was duly left with the impression of what a well-
informed man Mr Brandon Tolliver was, for all that he
was a mere merchant who, the Rector understood, had
not been brought up as a gentleman. Nevertheless he
possessed a splendid presence and was obviously learning to conduct himself as a gentleman should. Parson
Fielding was very conscious of his own claims to
gentility.

Lydia was busy doing the pretty at his side to yet
another guest when Miss Fielding was finally presented
to Mr Brandon Tolliver. She could not help but note
that he looked more superb than ever. More handsome, too. He strongly resembled the portrait of his
great-grandfather, Adolphus Tolliver, who had been a
good-looking as well as clever man. In that, Nan
thought, Brandon was the first of his descendants to
resemble him. She could only wish that she had similar
claims to be remarked upon.

He bowed. She bowed. He took her unwilling hand,
bent over it and kissed it, saying, 'A pleasure to meet
you at last, Miss Fielding,' as though he had not seen
her several times in various drawing-rooms as the
Gorgon, and twice as a nymph whom a wanton shepherd might pursue.

Nan tried to remove her hand quickly, but he hung

on to it, and turned it over gently, to reveal the marks of the many different tasks which she did upon it. There was a little callus on her second finger which her quill pen had placed there as a result of constant use. Brandon frowned a little at the sight, and reluctantly surrendered the damaged paw. Both parties were only too well aware of the frisson of pleasure which went through them whenever they touched. Nothing like that ever happened when he had held Miss Jane Fielding's hand, was Brandon's thought, while Nan's was, I haven't felt *that* since Randal left me to go to the war.

'I am pleased that you saw fit to accept our invitation, Miss Fielding. Jane thought that you might refuse it.'

Nan could not resist saying, 'Jane is not always correct in her suppositions, Mr Tolliver.'

Equally, Brandon could not help replying, 'Indeed, Miss Fielding, nor am I always correct in mine, as you well know.'

Nan flushed scarlet, and said in a low voice, 'I thought that we had agreed to forget the past, Mr Tolliver, and start anew.'

His eyes on her were frank. 'I have to inform you that I have a problem, Miss Fielding. It is difficult for me to do so.'

'Then perhaps I should not have come.'

Brandon was suddenly remorseful. 'No, indeed; I should have held my tongue. You have little enough of amusement in your life, I understand. Try to enjoy the next few days, I beg of you. You deserve a taste of pleasure.'

The silver eyes were so kind and serious as he said this that Nan had difficulty in repressing a sudden gush of tears at such unwonted consideration. Goodness, what can be happening to me? she thought. I am turning into a regular watering-pot. I must remember that he cannot be sincere, that he probably still sees me as. . .prey. After all, I behaved so loosely with him that he may conclude that that is my true nature. . .and that he may yet profit from it. . .

'I ought to move on,' she told him, for Lydia was passing the next guest on to him, and reluctantly Brandon allowed her to go.

She walked across the terrace, down the steps and into the garden, to be greeted by Jane with the words, 'Why, Nan, whatever was Brandon finding to talk about that he should engage you at such length?'

To which Nan's only answer was a repressive and totally untruthful one. 'Oh, I suppose that he means to make all his guests feel wanted, Jane, and as, so far, we have exchanged so few words, he doubtless thought to make sure that I felt as welcome as those whom he had already favoured with many.'

Which left Jane thinking yet again how elderly and pompous Nan was beginning to sound, but which also reassured her that for Mr Brandon Tolliver the younger Fielding sister must be the one in whom to take an interest. A belief which was reinforced when presently Brandon made his way into the garden to inform her that he was to be one of her partners at the luncheon table, Lord Alden's son, George, being on her other side. The servants had finished their work and the food was waiting for their masters to eat.

Lydia, Brandon thought, had excelled herself. Besides cold ham and beef, good bread, Stilton and Red Leicester cheese, and great slabs of newly churned butter from the dairy which was part of the appurtenances of Gillyflower Hall, there were huge bowls of strawberries, as well as peaches, and dishes of whipped cream. The peaches had been brought from the hothouses of Lydia's new friend, Lord Alden, who lived at nearby Alden Hall, Gillyflower Hall being without a proper hothouse, although Brandon had great plans for one.

To eat with the fruit and cream there was a variety of cakes and biscuits, including a large Madeira cake, Threadneedle biscuits, a speciality of the Tollivers' cook, and Jumbles, a Leicestershire delicacy often called Bosworth Jumbles—presumably because of the battle fought there! The recipe for it had been acquired from the Rectory's cook. Lemonade for the ladies and Cambridge milk punch for the gentlemen were carried from the house by the footmen at the last moment so that they arrived cool and fresh.

The guests stood around exclaiming at the feast. Nan found herself alone for a moment; Jane was on Brandon's arm, and Chaz had found a new friend, Tim Alden, while her father was in earnest conversation with the Rector of the neighbouring parish about the necessity of putting down the hedge priests who were attracting the local villagers to their impromptu open-air services.

'This is all very fine, is it not? And, I dare say, required a great deal of Cousin Brandon's money to fund it,' hissed a gloomy voice in Nan's ear as she took in the splendour of the tables. It came from Desmond, who then remarked, 'Remiss of me, Nan. I should have greeted you formally, I suppose, but as such old friends. . .' And he let the sentence die. He was dressed in dark, slightly outmoded clothing, and his cravat was a drooping modest thing. Was it Nan's imagination or did he look more faded than ever as a result of his cousin's being so completely à la mode?

He smiled wryly, and added, 'I should not speak so. It was good of him to invite me, offer me an olive-branch, but I had much rather I had not needed one.'

Unspoken were the words, Had I inherited then I would have been giving this house-warming party and not him. Instead he went on briskly, 'I am to take you in for luncheon, Nan, or so my cousin Lydia informs me.'

Desperate to say something, anything, to lighten the occasion for them both, for the sight of Jane hanging on Brandon's arm and laughing up into his handsome face was doing strange things to Nan's temper, she remarked coolly, 'How does one take a person *into* luncheon when it is held *outside* in the garden,

Desmond? And how will our hostess to be able inform us that it is served?'

Before Desmond had time to reply, the answer itself appeared. A round-faced youngster whom Nan recognised as the elder brother of Jem, who had come across Brandon and herself on the day on which she had found the kite, came out of the Hall. He was wearing a brilliant page's uniform in scarlet and gold, rather like a miniature guardsman, and he was carrying a large brass gong which he banged several times with a huge drumstick before piping shrilly, 'Luncheon is served, m'lords, ladies and gentlemen.'

Lydia offered her arm to Lord Alden, Brandon took in Lady Alden and one by one the guests processed in rough order of rank around the luncheon table. Rough, because Brandon took the view that appropriateness in one's partners at meals, so far as enjoyment was concerned, took precedence over everything else—so Lydia had placed him between Jane and Lady Alden, while Nan had been given Desmond and sat opposite them.

She thus had the agonising experience of watching Brandon being '*most* particular' to Jane. It did not ease her sore heart to consider that if she had judged Mr Brandon Tolliver correctly those merry eyes of his would be looking at pretty women like Jane, not plain ones like herself. She did not consider the compliments which he had paid her on the two occasions in which she had lain in his arms to be anything more than lures designed to trap a poor girl into letting him have his way with her.

For some reason the mere idea of Brandon having his way with anyone had Nan going hot all over. Desmond, who was busy haranguing her about the folly of local manufacturers in bringing in the new weaving machines, which resulted in so many men being laid off, provoking radical dissent and violence, looked keenly at her and remarked, 'Are you well, Nan? Your colour seems very high today.'

The other day it had been her pallor which had caused remark, Nan remembered acidly. Presumably these days she never possessed the correct complexion. She replied, her voice trembling slightly, 'I fear that I am feeling the heat today, Desmond. It is not usual for me to sit in the open in order to eat.'

He might have appeared to be carrying on a conversation with Jane which occupied his whole attention, but for all that, to his secret annoyance, Brandon had also been sharply aware of Miss Fielding and her conversation with his gloomy cousin Desmond.

He could not prevent himself. He leaned forward, remarked solicitously, 'If being outdoors is too much for you, Miss Fielding, then I am sure that Lady Alden and your sister will release me so that I may escort you into the shade of the Hall, and send for some cooling drinks.'

Lady Alden might have agreed to his suggestion, but Jane didn't want to; that was plain. Nan stammered, 'Oh—oh, no, I am not so troubled that I need you to disturb yourself, Mr Tolliver.'

'No disturbance,' Brandon told her, at the same time that Desmond, looking annoyed, came out with, 'No need to put yourself out, Cousin; I will escort Nan into the Hall.'

'But I neither require nor need anyone to escort me indoors,' almost wailed Nan at the improbable sight of the two cousins glaring at one another over a dispute about which of them should have the honour of looking after the dowdiest creature at the party.

Lydia Bligh was staring at all three of them in disbelief, particularly at Desmond's angry scarlet face. Sits the wind in that quarter? Well, who would have thought it? was her inward comment. And as for Brandon, well, who would have thought any such unlikely thing as that he would be taking note of plain, upright Miss Fielding—who was not quite so plain when one took a good look at her?

Had Brandon been taking a good look at her, and if so, when?

Matters were not improved by Jane saying angrily, 'I am sure that there is nothing wrong with Nan. She is never ill, you know. Why, even when the whole Rectory was laid up last winter with the shivering ague she was still on her feet looking after us all. She is as strong as a horse.'

This unflattering last sentence had Brandon looking in astonishment at the little fairy whom he had thought, like all pretty girls, to be 'sugar and spice and all things nice', as the nursery rhyme had it. And even if she was not quite like the little boys in the same rhyme in being made of 'slugs and snails and puppy dogs' tails' there was still more than a touch of bile, he was beginning to grasp, in most of Jane's remarks to her sister.

For her part, Nan felt like shouting aloud, Why, you selfish ninny, I was as ill as the rest of you, but *someone* had to stay on their feet and see that the house was warm, the sheets and nightwear changed, medicines doled out, and that drinks of water and hot lemonade were in constant supply. How dare you compare me to a horse?

'Please,' she said in agony, aware that the whole table was staring interestedly at her—her at whom no one ever looked, but always took for granted. 'I am not in the least discommoded. Pray allow me to continue my meal at table.'

'If you are absolutely sure,' both men began together, Desmond now glaring at Brandon, who was looking daggers at him.

'Yes,' she told them, while Lydia, aware that as hostess she should have nipped this in the bud, but had been too shaken by the reaction of both Desmond and Brandon to think straight, announced in a firm voice, 'I am sure that we must all allow that Miss Fielding is the best judge of her condition. May I suggest, Miss Fielding, that instead of lemonade you take a glass of

Cambridge milk punch? I am sure that will set you up wonderfully.'

She signalled to the nearest footman, who ran to do her bidding, placing before poor Nan a huge glass cup, foaming to the brim with a concoction of which one of the major components was brandy!

And there was nothing she could do but drink it! She dared not demur, for Lydia's intervention had brought her end of the table to its senses, and they all began to eat the delicious food before them as though nothing out of the ordinary had occurred.

'What the devil is that fellow to you?' whispered Desmond in Nan's ear once the meal was over and they were walking along the terrace, ostensibly admiring the view towards Leicestershire. 'Why should he be so particular towards you?'

Nan was feeling the effects of two glasses of punch for Lydia had insisted on her drinking another. She said, with a light laugh, finding her words a trifle difficult to articulate, 'Why, Desmond, don't take on so. He's particular to all women, as I'm sure that you must have noticed.'

'Only to pretty ones,' returned Desmond unfortunately.

The devil got into Nan, or the Cambridge milk punch was talking out of turn.

'Then he must think me pretty,' she announced defiantly.

Desmond, who had just realised the insult he had put upon her, replied a trifle uncomfortably, 'Then you are admitting that his behaviour towards you has been——'

'Has been nothing.' Nan's voice was as hard as she could make it. 'Forgive me, Desmond, but I don't propose to put up with your inquisition any longer.' Before he could open his mouth again, she was striding away from him, past the swing which Brandon had caused to be erected and on which all the pretty young things were taking turns to be pushed by Brandon and the unmarried men.

She was seeing the beautiful garden through a blur of tears. Shame and embarrassment had prevented her from enjoying the excellent food which the Tollivers had provided. She did not see Brandon look after her as she walked blindly on, towards the tiny lake with its small pavilion where the Tolliver women had, for two centuries, sat to admire the view and sketch or do their canvas work.

Oh, to be away from everyone forever and ever. But even an hour would do. No one would miss her. She was out of everyone's sight, and she could half recline on the marble bench in the shade and close her eyes, maybe doze a little. She had written far into the night because she was going to be unable to carry out her self-appointed task while she was at Gillyflower Hall, and not for the first time she wished that she had been left at home on her own. That would have been perfect bliss.

Doze she did—to be wakened by the sound of someone walking along the gravelled path which led to the pavilion. She shrank back, determined not to be discovered. A man stood in the doorway which was merely an open arch, and the man was Brandon Tolliver, the very last person whom she wished to see.

CHAPTER SIX

BRANDON almost didn't see her, but he must have heard the rustle of her dress, for he moved forward so that his dark silhouette was sharp against the bright blue late afternoon sky behind him.

'Miss Fielding?' His voice was tentative, questioning, then sure, as his eyes adjusted to the gloom and he saw her, huddled into a corner of the marble bench. 'Ah, there you are. Are you ill? May I assist you in any way?'

As earlier his solicitude distressed rather than reassured Nan. She sat up straight, and her voice betrayed nothing of the inward agitation which shook her every time she met him.

'No, indeed, Mr Tolliver, although it is kind of you to ask. I came here to enjoy the water and the sun, and in the half-dark I fear that I dozed off.' And then, anxiously, 'Have I been missed?'

Brandon walked further in, and waved Nan down as she began to stand up, sitting down himself on another bench set into the wall opposite Nan, after asking her for her permission to do so.

'Alas, no. You have not been missed, although you have sat here for some time. I say alas because it pains me to see that none of your party appears to show you any real consideration, although Chaz did ask me a little time ago whether I knew where you were. But he barely stayed for an answer. I saw you walk to the pavilion and realised that I had not seen you return. The rest of my guests have gone to their rooms to prepare for the evening.'

He paused, wondering at his own solicitude for the upright woman opposite to him who was allowing no shadow of emotion to cross her face. He was not usually wont to worry about such unconsidered creatures as Nan Fielding seemed to be.

So why was it that he was feeling anger that no one *did* consider her? He did not pause to answer his own question, but merely went smoothly on—Nan had already noted that his voice was a beautiful one, deep but not too deep.

'I took the liberty of sending one of the footmen to your room with a fresh bowl of flowers and a message. He came back to inform me that you were not there. I met your father on his way to the library—he told me what a splendid collection of books I possess, but appeared to have no idea of where one of his own possessions was!' He stopped, allowing Nan to enjoy this small joke—which she did with a slight nod of her head.

'Growing worried, because you seemed both ill and tired today, I decided to search for you myself—so here I am.' He looked around the pavilion, then asked, 'And do you like this building as well as the view?'

'I have always,' replied Nan truthfully, 'liked everything about Gillyflower Hall, but I had never seen very much of it until today. Your cousin Bart was quite the recluse, as I suppose you know.'

'So my lawyers told me. I am pleased that it pleases you, though.' He hesitated. 'I suppose we are breaking all the canons of etiquette by remaining together alone, in such a confined space.'

'I should not let it trouble you.' Nan's tone was earnest. 'I am so remarkably elderly and respectable that no one would think that anything was untoward if we were found together.'

Brandon made a short vexed exclamation and jumped up. Nan had already learned what a very vigorous person he was, and that she had annoyed him by what she had just said was betrayed by his bodily movements as well as his speech.

'No!' he exclaimed violently. 'Just because the whole world chooses to demean you—including my cousin

Desmond, for all his supposed admiration of you—it does not mean that you must demean yourself. It is time someone took a little care of you, instead of you spending your whole time caring for others. Are you never let out of prison? Was that why I have twice found you climbing on to stools and trees—to free yourself?'

'How very melodramatic of you, sir.' Nan tried to keep her tone as light as possible, but he could see that she was shaking, and he could not guess the cause.

He was the cause. He and none other. The shuddering became worse when Brandon walked forward to take her by the arm, exclaiming, 'Earlier today you were overheated, and now you are cold! No wonder that you are shivering. Come, let us walk you back to the house, and you must allow your maid to put you in a warm bath to restore you.'

It was not the cold which made Nan shiver, but his nearness. That and the weariness which had overcome her ever since she had reached Gillyflower Hall. Paradoxically, it had not been while she was pursuing her labours around the Rectory that she had felt tired, but at the moment when they had ended, and she was supposed to be enjoying herself, with servants around to satisfy her every whim.

Unresisting, Nan allowed Brandon to take her arm and walk her back towards the house. 'Suppose someone sees us?' she ventured, only for him to reply robustly,

'Nonsense, my dear Miss Fielding; you have just informed me that your sober presence must disarm all criticism—I will not have you change your mind ere five minutes have passed. That would be to make you too like most of the other women in society!'

This sally made Nan laugh, and, encouraged, Brandon began to talk idly and lightly to settle and soothe her. 'As you may imagine,' he began, 'when the tea board came around, shortly after luncheon we all began to discuss the author of *Sophia*'s latest offering.

Discuss, of course, is the wrong word, because we were all in agreement. The very young ladies, Jane in particular, could not sing her praises loudly enough.' He stopped, laughed a little under his breath.

'And you, Mr Tolliver?' Nan could not prevent herself from asking. 'Were you in agreement, or do you find novels such as Sophia's frivolous and rather tiresome?'

'Oh, no, not all.' He shook his handsome head. 'Far from it. My trouble was that the rest of the company was busy praising her for the delicacy of the romance, saying, and I am quoting others, how sweetly pretty her writing is, how charming; whereas I, on the contrary, admire her for her astringency, the delicate irony which suffuses all that she writes, the insights which she displays into the darker sides of our nature. I must tell you that I hope that she does not come to live near me! I should not like that cool, probing eye turned on me and my doings. I say she, but, of course, she may be he—although I do not think so. What is your opinion, Miss Fielding? I should value it.'

Nan was silent for a moment while she debated on how to give this difficult question an honest answer. She finally came out with an equivocation. 'Jane will tell you that I do not read novels, so I fear that I cannot enlighten you.'

He looked at her sharply, and found that to do so had the oddest effect on him. He wanted to tear off the disfiguring bonnet, dress her in something more suitable, and hope to see again the nymph who had sat astride the tree branch. All this havering about the author of Sophia was a blind to try to disguise from himself the strong and strange impression which the rector's eldest daughter had on him. It was Jane he was supposed to be fixed on, not Nan!

He found himself murmuring, 'Then you should read those by the author of Sophia; you would enjoy them. And despite what I have just said I should very much like to meet her, but one conjectures that she might be ninety. . .'

He rolled a comic eye at Nan and had the pleasure of hearing her laugh before she added gravely, carrying on the game he had begun, 'And carries a huge green umbrella and has a poodle called Pericles, which never behaves itself in company.' They were laughing together at the picture this presented when they reached the gravel path which led to the hall.

Brandon stopped, and released Nan's elbow which he had been lightly grasping, a touch which was helping to render her delirious and was doing no less for him if he were to be honest with himself, and said gravely, 'Whatever I may have hinted earlier, Miss Fielding, I am only too mindful of the need to preserve your reputation. I suggest that we part here, and that you go into the Hall alone. If any should be so bold as to question you, you may tell them the truth: that you were tired and fell asleep in the pavilion, awoke, and found your way home. No need to start any gossip by adding that you were with me.'

He bowed, before he left her with the words, 'I look forward to seeing you at supper. We are informal again this evening. That is Lydia's way and one which I too prefer.'

To tell the truth, even if it was only a part of the whole truth, appeared to be a habit of Mr Brandon Tolliver's as well as hers, was Nan's thought as she walked into the pleasant room which was to be hers during her stay at Gillyflower Hall. She had hardly sat down before there was a knock on her door. A little maid stood there, saying, 'Excuse me, ma'am, I'm Mary. I've been sent by the master to look after you while you are at the Hall. He said that you would be needing a bath. The footmen will be following shortly with the warm water, and meantime you must allow me to prepare you for it.'

Mesmerised both by Mr Brandon Tolliver and his splendours, Nan made no demur, but sat quietly on a large sofa ranged at the bottom of her four-poster bed as a procession of servants made the big, free-standing bath in the adjoining room ready for her.

Downstairs, Mr Brandon Tolliver, who was beginning to wonder if he was running slightly mad, because he had never felt like this about a woman since he was a green boy first discovering the opposite sex, was speculating on what kind of nymph Miss Nan Fielding most resembled when little Mary helped her into the warm water he had so thoughtfully provided for her!

However, tempting she might be supposed to look with her clothes gone, her dress for supper was no better than that which she had worn for lunch. While Jane was wearing amber gauze floating over amber silk, Nan was sensibly dressed like the chaperon she was in puce—another of her mother's cut-down dresses. Her cap was the saffron horror which she had worn at the Assembly Rooms. Lydia had mixed up her guests for supper, and Nan was now seated at the far end of the table. Fortunately her partner was Sam Stone, who had arrived a little earlier. He had told Brandon that business might prevent him from arriving before luncheon.

What a dismal turn-out! had been Sam's internal comment when he had greeted Nan in the drawing-room before supper. If she accepted him he would make sure that Mrs Samuel Stone had some new clothes. They might not be able to rival Lydia Bligh's luxurious and fashionable amethyst silk gown, enhanced by the diamonds which her late husband, an India merchant, had bought for her, but she would not be ashamed before the world as she was at the moment. The money going into the Rectory was being spent on everyone but Nan, apparently. Well, that would have to stop, preferably once Jane married this personable youngish man Tolliver, who was not, Sam decided, quite a gentleman, but none the worse for that.

The port which was circulated after the women had left was first rate, though. The Tollivers knew how to set a good table, was the universal comment. The cigars were first rate too, and the talk wasn't bad either. They were discussing shooting, about which Brandon was knowledgeable, when he threw into the conversation something which had happened to him in the previous week.

'Have some careless shots around here, do you?' he asked, swirling his port around in his glass, holding it against the light and admiring its ruby-red. The county had already discovered that he was a discriminating rather than a heavy drinker.

Lord Alden, one of the heavies, drawled, 'Not so you'd notice, Tolliver. Why?'

Brandon, making little of it, replied, 'I was walking in the woods near to your land, Alden, when some damned fool nearly took my head off. Took my new hat instead. Frightened himself as much as me, I suppose. I heard him running off, but couldn't catch a glimpse of him.'

'Might be some Luddite, of course, loosing off a shot at one of us,' offered Sir Avery Letcombe. 'Not that there's been much of that round here lately—not since Cullen was hanged at Highborough eighteen months ago.'

'That was the man who shot and killed Mason, the manufacturer, was it not?' offered Brandon, trying to make light of what had happened to him. 'I thought that after his death his gang of Luddites had all been rounded up and their weapons confiscated.'

'True,' said Alden, 'but one never rounds up *everyone* on these occasions. Besides, your cousin made quite a few enemies on the Bench. He was a harsh sentencer, and they might be taking it out on you.'

Brandon thought this improbable, preferring to believe that it had been an accident, although not quite the kind of accident he liked. His main worry, which he didn't confide in the others, was that he couldn't imagine what the shot had been meant for, if it hadn't been meant for him. None of his fellows seemed to take the matter very seriously. Even Parson Fielding remarked in his gently hazy manner, 'That sort of thing has probably happened to most of us at one time or another.' He blinked at the company and they all nodded polite agreement.

In the world in which Brandon had made his fortune one took nothing on trust. One minded one's back, and he had come to believe that few incidents of this kind ought to be lightly passed over. But he was a new man in this part of Nottinghamshire, and was well aware that he was not yet considered to be quite a gentleman for all his old name and his ownership of Gillyflower Hall. They knew that he had started life as a clerk. That he had been more than that in his time, had worked before the mast while on the way to his fortune, they might guess, but couldn't know. He had no mind to antagonise them by making heedless accusations.

But his values weren't theirs, and however much of a veneer he had acquired, and was still acquiring, they never would be completely. His cousin Desmond, who had seen Brandon shoot, remarked in a friendlier tone than he had yet used to him, 'They're not all as careful with their weaponry as you are, Brandon, nor are they such good shots. Whoever it was was probably ashamed of what he had done, and made off before you could reproach or reprimand him.'

More nods followed, and the matter was forgotten by everyone except Brandon—and Sam Stone, whose wise old face was thoughtful.

The arrival of the gentlemen after their post-supper drinking was eagerly awaited by all the ladies, none, surprisingly, more eager than quiet Miss Fielding, seated in a straight-backed chair in the corner among the other older women, watching the young girls playing spillikins to while away the time until the interesting part of the evening began. Chaz had left with the ladies and had gone to his room some little time before. Nan's eagerness related to the appearance of Mr Brandon Tolliver.

The conversation around her was abuzz with excited speculation about which of the Royal Dukes would marry next in order to give the throne an heir, now that the Prince Regent's only child, Princess Charlotte, had died giving birth to a stillborn baby. All the Dukes had large families by their various mistresses, but none of these was, of course, eligible to succeed to the throne.

The next source of mild uproar was the latest fashion in dress, and the new hairstyles, which were somewhat longer, Lady Alden said knowledgeably, than those which had been popular for the last twenty years.

Nan could not take part in any of this. She knew little or nothing of the doings of the Royal Family, and was hardly likely to be able to afford new toilettes or a new coiffure. On the other hand, the foibles of those around her always engaged her interest, so she was, if silent, never bored. 'So restful, Nan Fielding,' was the common cry. It was fortunate that they had no notion of what she was thinking!

In came the gentlemen in various stages of sobriety. Either, Nan noted, Brandon Tolliver held his drink well, or he had not been drinking heavily. He walked over to the table where the young misses were engaged in spillikins and naughtily reduced them to hysterics by his antics. Young George Alden, Lord Alden's heir, again made a dead set at Jane, and various other young men engaged themselves with various other eligible young females. Only Jane had two ardent courtiers.

And only Nan was left to sit alone and composed, her hands clasped together on her unbecoming puce knees. Sam Stone, who had been caught by Sir Avery Letcombe for advice on some legal pother he was engaged in, cut short Sir Avery's maunderings as quickly and politely as he could in order to make his way over to her.

'You are enjoying a break from your labours, my dear?' he asked her, solicitude in his voice.

Mischief glinted in Nan's eyes. Whatever happened to her, she thought, cheerfulness would always break in. 'What would you say, sir, if I answered that I am most uncommonly bored?'

'That it is the kind of answer I can imagine the author of *Sophia* giving one of her characters to say, but not yourself.'

Nan's eyesbrows—beautiful ones, Sam always thought—rose slightly. 'You are able to make a distinction, then?'

He laughed at that, causing a few heads to turn. What *could* severe Miss Fielding be finding to say to amuse that old stick Sam Stone so?

'It is of that which I must speak to you, and immediately. There is a rather fine picture gallery opening out of this room. We could take a turn along it, and I could speak to you in some privacy without causing comment. You will allow?'

Nan nodded, and rose. She put her hand on Sam's arm, and he led her from the room, through the double doors, and into a corridor which ran the width of the house. Assorted Tollivers looked down their haughty noses at them, among the views of Italy and the paintings by Salvator Rosa which a mid-eighteenth-century Tolliver had brought back with him from the Grand Tour.

Sam stood in front of a view of Vesuvius in eruption, and said softly, 'It is your publisher, Mr Murray, my dear. He is no longer happy, or I may say willing, to keep the identity of the author of *Sophia* secret. He thinks that the mystery has gone on long enough. He is hinting that to reveal who the author is would enormously increase sales which are already large.'

'He would not think so if he *were* aware of who the author of *Sophia* is,' remarked Nan irrepressibly. For the truth was that some six years ago, using Sam as an intermediary, she had sent the manuscript of *Sophia* to Mr John Murray, the publisher who had helped to make Lord Byron both rich and famous. It was the earnings from *Sophia* and the novels which had followed it which

were saving the Rectory from penury, not Parson
Fielding's dim piece of outdated theology.

And all of them had been written at her little bureau,
either at dead of night when the Rectory had gone to
bed, or early in the morning when only the servants
were up. The first, *Sophia*, had dealt with the adven-
tures of a parson's daughter in the great world, after
Nan had spent her first season in London, chaperoning
her younger sister Madeline, and observing the passing
show with a cynical eye.

She and Sam had insisted on the secret being kept,
and at first Mr Murray had been willing to oblige them,
but now he had apparently changed his mind.

'He is talking of sending one of his employees to
Broomhall to meet me, and to try to winkle the truth
out of me. Mr Murray is apparently certain that his
author is a son or a daughter of a clergyman, and I
suppose his man will spy out the land, after trying to
wheedle me into revealing all.'

Nan suddenly became agitated. 'No,' she said, her
hands rising to cup her scarlet cheeks at the mere idea
of being unmasked. 'No. On no account must you give
me away. It is of all things necessary that I remain
anonymous. Think of the scandal, the distress Papa
would feel if he knew what paid for his bread and
butter.'

'It is high time that he did know,' riposted Sam, his
kind face alight with anger. 'To work as you do on top
of everything else, and to receive nothing in return, but
to be neglected and passed over for those who are not
worth tuppence beside you.'

Passion suddenly rode on his usually impassive features. He put out an impulsive hand to grasp one of
hers. 'Give me the answer I wish for now. Marry me,
Nan. Let me free you from the wheel of servitude to
which you are bound. I would allow you to continue to
write, if you so wished, but not as you do now, before
and after a hard day's work.'

Nan disengaged herself gently. 'Oh, Sam, I have

thought long and hard of your kind proposal, and my decision is that it would be unfair to you for me to say yes. I should be marrying you out of gratitude, friendship and, yes, a desire to escape the trap which my life has become. But you deserve better than that. I value you, that's true. But not in the way in which a wife should value a husband.'

She knew that there was another reason why she ought not to marry him, or any other man, but she could not tell him of it.

He turned a little away from her, to mutter, 'You are an honest woman, Nan, and I knew what your answer would be. Why cannot you be like the rest of your sex, looking only to the main chance? Then you would accept me. If I thought that you would ever find a man who wished to marry you, and would value you as I do, then I might feel a little happier at your refusal, but as it is. . .' He pulled out a large handkerchief and blew his nose vigorously. 'As it is, I fear that you may live and die exploited and unconsidered.'

Nan closed her eyes against his pain. She did not want to lose a dear friend, and said, 'We may remain friends, I trust?'

In a gesture such as she had never seen him make before he took her hand in his again to kiss it, and to say, 'Always, my dear. We have been friends since we first met, have we not? I could not relinquish my chaperonage of the author of *Sophia*. That would be to make my life even duller than it is.'

His faded eyes were twinkling at her as he spoke. There were many, Nan knew, who thought him a prosy man, a stick, but she knew better, and was only sorry that she could not give him what he most wanted: herself.

'And,' he continued, relinquishing her hand, 'if you wish me to help you retain your anonymity, I will do so—although I warn you, you will not be able to keep it forever—secrets can never remain secrets permanently.'

'I know that,' Nan told him. 'Nevertheless I wish to keep this one as long as possible.'

'What Sir Walter Scott could not do will be beyond you, I think,' he said—for Scott had wished to be known only as the author of *Waverley*, but in the end had been, in Sam's words, 'smoked out'.

'I will leave you now, my dear,' he said. 'I will ask you to consider Murray's wishes again, but the other business is dead and buried. Friends we are, and friends we will remain, I hope.'

Nan watched him go. To compose herself she turned towards the landscape again. Yes, Vesuvius was still bursting into flames.

She was seeing it through a blur of emotion. Not tears, but something else was moving her. A voice from the rear of the gallery said, a touch of mockery in it, 'I see that your elderly admirer has left you. For a young woman who makes little effort to attract, I judge that you are being uncommonly unsuccessful. I gather from something that my cousin Desmond has said that he has some vague aspirations towards your hand as well.'

'You are ungentlemanly, sir—particularly if you have been eavesdropping on our conversation.' For Nan was a little worried that the secret of the author of *Sophia* might no longer be a secret to her host.

'I do not need to overhear anything, my nymph in disguise,' Brandon drawled, his eyes hard on her. 'The looks your middle-aged swain casts in your direction tell all.'

Nan's face told him that she thought that others might have seen what he had done. He laughed softly. 'Oh, no, my dear. Your friends and family are blind when you are concerned. They take you so much for granted that if you danced a hornpipe on the front lawn they would assume that it was someone else they were seeing!'

Nan could scarce repress a laugh at this unlikely picture. She managed to return earnestly, 'Your absence will be remarked on, sir. You are the host, and you should not dally here talking with the least considered of your guests.'

'All my guests are considered,' he told her, as irrepressible outwardly as Nan was inwardly, 'and no one will miss me, for I have supposedly left to arrange some matters for my guests' convenience tomorrow.'

'Jane will miss you,' Nan could not stop herself from saying. His presence had the most dreadful effect on her. Her heart had begun to beat rapidly; a strange quivering swept over her body. Moths had invaded her head. She knew what all this meant, and oh, she ought to stop herself from feeling it, but could not.

He said something under his breath which sounded uncommonly like, 'Oh, damn Jane,' but he couldn't have said that. She must have misheard.

'Some of your guests might wish to visit the portrait gallery,' she informed him.

'What, and desert the pleasures of the drawing-room?' he retorted. 'They are all on fire over some child's games with counters, the men inspired by drink and the ladies by excitement.'

He was now so near to her that the silver eyes seemed to be filling all her world. Nan had nowhere to retreat to. And she needed to retreat, for he put up a hand to tip her cap up, causing it to fall backwards to the floor, revealing her tawny locks, her waves and curls which were trying to escape from their tight confinement.

'Sir, you are no gentleman to do such a thing.' Nan was vigorous, not complaining.

'I know.' His voice was as lazy as he was. 'I have never claimed to be one, and I don't like most of those whom I meet.' And he put both hands on the wall to hold her there without touching her, while he leaned forward to kiss her oh, so gently on the lips.

Oh, what bliss! She had forgotten what lovemaking was like. How sweet it was, how dear. Nan closed her eyes and he saw straight away, for his own were open, that she was not resisting him but welcoming him.

Oddly, at the sight of this surrender, the conscience which his sister claimed that he did not possess began to reproach him. He must remember that he was dealing with no flirt, no lady who was, behind a mask of virtue, as much of a lightskirt as the whores and courtesans she affected to despise. Instead he was in the despicable position of assailing a virtuous and untried woman who was unversed in the art of coping with double-dealing men.

He released her, which was difficult, for he had discovered to his surprise that to be with Nan was temptation itself. She looked at him with great eyes, and half whispered, 'I repeat, sir, your behaviour is most ungentlemanly. You are supposed to be "*most* particular" towards my sister Jane, and here you are being "*most* particular" to me. That is a scoundrel's part.'

'Oh, I am a scoundrel,' he assured her, and despite all his good resolutions he kissed her again—determined to prove that what he had just said was true, he thought afterwards, a little bitterly.

Nan was trying not to kiss him back, an almost impossible task. Somehow she managed it, somehow she pushed him away, just at the moment when his conscience pricked him again.

She found that she was panting, but composed herself sufficiently to move away from him and pick up her despised cap, as he pulled away from the wall, leaving her free to go. During the whole short episode he had touched Nan only with his mouth; his hands had remained on the wall and his body away from her. For some reason this had aroused him more than if he had been free with her. But that small contact had been enough to do its work on him.

When he looked up again Nan was gone. She was back in the drawing-room, with only one thing on her mind. And that one thing was that not only had she fallen in love with Mr Brandon Tolliver, who was most decidedly not meant for her, but that she desired him with a desire beyond anything which she had made her heroines feel for the heroes whom they desired!

What Brandon Tolliver had on his mind was that yes, he truly was running mad. But after a somewhat sane fashion, he recognised ruefully, because he had already started to cool his manner a little towards Jane Fielding. But nothing could mitigate the distressing fact that he was being '*most* particular' to two sisters at once — something which no gentleman should ever be.

Nan had hardly sat down again before Desmond, who had been stationed in a corner, watching the goings-on around the big table set aside for games, with a supercilious expression on his face, came over to be supercilious to her.

Nan knew that expression. It had seldom been directed towards her, more usually towards her flightly sisters, and anyone of whom Desmond disapproved — and he disapproved of many. Its presence this evening meant that she was his target.

He began without preamble. 'Where have you been, Nan? I have been unable to find you. Your father thought that you might have retired to your room. Did you?'

This abrupt and rude questioning angered Nan almost more than she would have credited if she had thought about it beforehand. 'You are neither my husband, my father nor my chaperon, Desmond. You have no right to submit me to such an inquisition. What I care to do is my concern not yours.'

'It is my concern when I have seen the fashion in which my cousin looks at you. I understand that he is a dangerous man where women are concerned. You would do well to avoid him. He cannot be after you other than to deceive you. I am informed that his marriage plans are fixed on Jane. You are supposed to be advancing her claims to him, not competing with her and putting both your reputations at risk.'

Nan rose to her feet. 'I am going to my room now. If all you can do these days, Desmond, is rebuke me for

my conduct, then I would rather that you did not
address me at all. It is also unkind of you to speak of
your cousin as you do, when you are a guest in his
home.'

'Which should be mine, if we all had our rights, as
you well know.'

'No, I don't know, Desmond. Pray release me.' For
as he had bitten out the last sentence at her, his face
furious, he had also taken her by the arm to detain her.

'No,' he said, 'you will hear me, Nan. . .' His voice
tailed off, for Brandon had returned from what Nan
suspected was his purely imaginary errand, invented to
track her down in the picture gallery and make love to
her when Sam had gone. The cousins were a good pair,
she thought disgustedly, both bent on embarrassing her
in their different ways.

'Everyone happy?' queried Brandon cheerfully, as
though he were slightly foxed—a ploy which didn't fool
Nan, seeing that he had been stone-cold sober only a
few moments ago. 'Shouldn't like to think that you had
only come here to be miserable.' And his silver eyes,
now shrewd and hard, were on Desmond's hand, which
was still incontinently clutching Nan's arm.

Desmond let go of it, and Nan, to preserve the
proprieties, for she didn't want the cousins warring over
her twice in one day, bowed to them as formally as she
could.

'You will both forgive me, I am sure,' she announced,
'but if I am to be happy I must retire to my room. Jane
does not need me to chaperon her with so many others
present, and I am not used to experiencing such excitement as I have encountered today.'

Both men followed the progress of her straight back
across the room as she left it. Desmond met Brandon's
eyes again, and knew without being told that his
cousin's intervention had been quite deliberate. He
said, his voice as harsh as Brandon's had been genial,
'You understand, I suppose, that Nan needs protecting.
Her experience of life is that——'

'Of a parson's daughter,' Brandon finished for him. 'Yes, I do know, Desmond, but I thank you for reminding me of it. Now, I understand that you are quite a whist player, and my sister, being aware that the senior members of the party have had their fill of childish games, is making up some tables to please them. Your presence there would be valued.'

There was nothing for Desmond to do but go and play whist, and watch Brandon have the most disgusting good luck, while his own remained poor, as usual. Brandon was watching Desmond, and his face was inscrutable as he did so. What had surprised him was the overwhelming desire to knock the fellow down on the spot which had come over him when he had seen Desmond bullying Nan. His own share at bullying her after a different fashion had stopped him from doing anything rash, as much as his wish to maintain the proprieties of polite life. Yes, he really was fit for Bedlam, and all since he had arrived at Gillyflower Hall!

CHAPTER SEVEN

'A BOATING party! How excessively delightful. And what ought I to wear, my dear Mrs Bligh? For one would not want to be other than exactly *comme il faut*!'

Well, thought Nan acidly, the next morning after breakfast, even if Jane was not a member of the *haut ton* she was certainly making a good fist of giving Lydia Bligh the impression that she was! Her one short season in society in Nan's company, with their father's cousin, Lady Fielding, had undoubtedly given her confidence, if not genuine polish.

'Something simple, my dear, will be all that is required from you and your sister.'

'Oh, Nan? Will you want to come too, Nan?' was Jane's reply to that, in a voice which suggested that Nan certainly wouldn't.

A slight frown crossed Lydia Bligh's face, and Nan, who had been busy deciding that a boating party on the Soar was the last event which she wished to attend, found herself saying, in as cool a voice as she could manage, 'Of course I shall wish to go, Jane. I have never been on a boating party before. "Excessively delightful" seem to me to be quite the correct words to use.'

This earned her a sharp look from Lydia Bligh. Cool though Nan had been, the touch of mockery which she had not been able to prevent herself from betraying when she had echoed Jane's fulsome tone had not escaped her hostess. I must be more careful, she thought. Splendid nullity is my line, not comments *à la* author of *Sophia*. I must save those for the book I am writing.

Jane's self-satisfaction was so great that she, at least, heard nothing amiss, although she did frown a little

when Brandon strolled towards them, because it was to
Nan that he spoke after bowing politely to her sister
first.

'And will you enjoy a morning on the river and an
alfresco picnic afterwards, Miss Fielding?'

Nan answered him as calmly as she could, aware that,
as usual, the mere sight of him had set her heart beating
wildly—something which she must never betray to him
or to anyone else.

'I am not quite sure, Mr Tolliver. I was thinking that
perhaps, after all, a quiet morning seated in one of the
arbours in the garden, with the author of *Sophia* for
company, might be a happy alternative.'

'Oh, no, it wouldn't,' he assured her rapidly, with as
much vigour as politeness would allow him when con-
tradicting a lady. 'I won't have you shutting yourself
away. You are not yet ninety, don't own a poodle and
the weather is such that a green umbrella is not
obligatory. . .and——' He paused, his eyes on her merry.

'And. . .?' prompted Nan, astonished to hear that he
had taken such note of what she had said to him
yesterday evening—and beginning to flirt with him in
consequence, much to his pleasure.

'And. . . Cinderella shall go to the ball with the other
young ladies; I insist. Isn't that so, Lydia?' he called to
his sister, raising his voice a little. 'Miss Fielding must
not play truant this morning, must she?'

Lydia looked up sharply, as did Jane and several
others present, Lydia because she had never heard that
tone of voice from Brandon before, Jane and the rest
astonished that an unconsidered and elderly chaperon
should be engaging so much of their host's attention.

'Only if Miss Fielding felt unwell could I possibly
recommend her to miss this morning's fun,' was Lydia's
obliging answer. She knew that that was what Brandon
wanted to hear, and wondered again what his game was
with poor, downtrodden Miss Fielding. He could surely
not be acting out of simple kindness—could he? Not
that Brandon could not be kind, but it was rare for him

to attach himself to other than the more obvious beauties in any company he was in.

'So, there it is,' Brandon announced triumphantly. 'Both your host and hostess demand your company, Miss Fielding; you cannot possibly refuse it.'

For the first time Nan became fully aware of the glares which the young women of the party were turning on her. Jealousy, the green-eyed goddess, was having a field day at Gillyflower Hall. She muttered something indistinct, which the brother and sister took as agreement, and Lydia, whose powers of management seemed to be as great as her brother's, announced that Nan would be in the leading carriage with herself, the one which Jack Coachman would be driving. Desmond would also be a passenger. Chaz would go in the gig with young Tim Alden and equally young Jack Letcombe, with Tim's tutor, Mr Figge, to keep them in order.

Jane, who already knew that she would not be travelling with Brandon because he had arranged to go on horseback, was to be George Alden's passenger in his curricle. They had been friends since childhood, and familiarity in this case had certainly bred a little contempt: Jane took his adoration of her for granted.

This decision of Lydia's to seat her with the other most eligible male catch had the effect of raising Jane's spirits at the expense of depressing those of every other young woman in the party. After all, thought Jane triumphantly, if she could not be driven by Brandon, then to partner George was certainly the next best thing! It would be very much more fun than to have to sit with Lydia Bligh and make polite conversation, so Nan had not really gained very much after all by travelling in the first carriage.

And she would be sure to call Brandon over to her when the party set off, thus ensuring that both her beaux would be dancing attendance on her at once.

Consequently, when all was decided, she retired to her room to dress herself with care, putting on her most

attractive straw bonnet with the daises, and demanding
to borrow Nan's only good shawl. 'For I take cold so
easily, you don't, and Mrs Bligh says there might be
quite a breeze on the water, so do let me have it,' she
said, thus making sure that she looked as fetching as
possible—at her sister's expense.

Nan handed over the lacy thing, one of her few pretty
possessions, with an inward sigh, but if she wished to
secure a husband for Jane as soon as possible, then
some sacrifice must be made. So now she had to make
do with her second-best, worn beige wool wrap about
her shoulders. Her dress was second-best too, another
cut down from one of her mother's, but it was rather
better than her usual turn-out, being high-waisted, in
cream muslin, trimmed with some rather pretty lace on
the neck and sleeves. Her cap was not quite so disfiguring either; it was lighter and finer than usual, in a
cream lace which matched the muslin.

Altogether she did not feel too unhappy as the party
set off, with a great deal of laughter and chatter from
the young people, and a great deal of decorum from
their elders, including Nan. The Tollivers' big old-
fashioned coach in the rear carried the servants and the
food which the party would require after an arduous
morning spent amusing themselves on the water.

Once or twice on the ride to Highborough Brandon
pulled level with their carriage to converse with them,
and Desmond unbent enough to point out the land-
marks of the country round about, which was now
Brandon's adopted land, or so he said.

The boatyard where small pleasure- or rowing-boats
could be hired was on the edge of Highborough, just
where a rash of white-fronted villas had recently sprung
up, built by the newly rich manufacturers who were
spending their profits from the mechanical looms. A
group of sturdy men stood about hoping that the gentry
might choose to hire them, rather than take on the
burden of rowing themselves. They had been alerted
beforehand, by a messenger from Gillyflower Hall, that

the Tollivers' party would be arriving that morning, and Brandon decided on seeing them that everyone's pleasure would be enhanced if the local oarsmen were used.

He was also keenly aware, having been poor himself, that, given the poverty of the area, his money would be highly welcome to men whose own source of livelihood had disappeared.

One of the men approached him and offered his barge as a source of transport for 'my lord', as he insisted on calling Brandon, and some of his party.

It and his horse were ready, he said, and perhaps, if 'my lord' didn't want to hire him for his own use, then his servants could be taken on board, along with the party's food and drink. The carriages and horses were to be left behind at some stables near by.

Nan was delighted by the whole business. The freshness of the sunny day, the breeze arising from the river, the smiling faces of the boatmen who were only too pleased to oblige 'my lord', and the cheerfully competent fashion with which Lydia and Brandon organised their pleasure, entranced her beyond words.

One sturdy youth handed her into a rowing-boat in which Desmond and Lydia already sat; another took up the oars. Brandon, who had decided that he must stop being '*most* particular' to Nan—in public, that was, in private being another matter—had put himself in a boat with Jane and George Alden. Consequently Jane was on her highest ropes of pleasure, with George looking daggers at 'that old man', as he privately called thirty-five-year-old Brandon.

Brandon, for his part, was alternately amused and appalled by his own duplicity, for he found himself looking ahead for a glimpse of Nan even while he was engaged in flattering Jane and annoying George.

Sleepy cows stared at the noisy throng as they were rowed downstream towards the Trent into Leicestershire. Rails, ducks, geese and swans sailed around them, the swans stately and the ducks busy.

Nan trailed her hand in the water, wishing that she had a parasol with her—one like Lydia's, a confection of pink and white lace—to shield her complexion. I shall be a milkmaid's brown on top of everything else about me that is unfashionable, she thought ruefully, but oh, what a dream of a day!

The terrain through which the river meandered had grown increasingly wild and woody, and was a place where it seemed that no man had set foot, since it was uncultivated, with natural stands of trees and tall hedges everywhere. Unimproved by Capability Brown and his followers it might be, but it had the beauty of the natural, and so Nan told Lydia and Desmond. 'One might imagine fairies and elves treading among the undergrowth, and Oberon and Titania waiting to greet us when we reach journey's end.'

Desmond stared at her. How unlike practical Nan to be so romantic and poetic, his expression said, but Lydia Bligh, who was beginning to find the eldest Fielding daughter both intelligent and witty behind her façade of dull modesty, murmured appreciatively, 'What a charming thought. And Bottom, will he be there, Miss Fielding, or shall we find the Duke and his bride?'

This further reference to *A Midsummer Night's Dream* passed over Desmond's head, he being more used to reading books on political economy than poetry, but Nan smiled at it, and continued the game she had started.

'Or shall we,' she went on gaily, 'if we stay here until night falls, come across the lovers and help them to untangle themselves before Puck can confuse them by his tricks?'

She was aware that she was giving herself away a little to all her hearers, and when Lydia laughed appreciatively at what she had said she coloured a little, and decided to be silent in future. She had an important secret to keep, and to betray her own flights of fancy too often might be to reap a harvest she did not want!

It was of all things necessary that the author of *Sophia* remain anonymous.

Anonymity, therefore, must be her own refuge. She fell silent, and remained so until the party reached its destination, whereupon she forsook the boats and the barge to watch the swans from the safety of the bank. Desmond, again by his expression, obviously preferred the dull, silent Nan to the witty, talkative one, which almost had her talking again, but wisdom kept her dumb.

Jane was not dumb. Her charming voice could be heard as she tried to hold both her admirers' attention at once. Eating the splendid cold collation, which was set out on damask tablecloths spread out on the grass, with bottles of white wine and lemonade tied with cords to nearby bushes, swinging gently in the river water to keep them cool until the party was ready to drink from them, she managed by some art to have half the men, both young and old, hanging on every light word she uttered.

And very light they were, thought Nan grimly. She sat between Sam Stone and Desmond, both of whom, in their different ways, tried to entertain her. But, alas, nothing could keep her thoughts away from Brandon.

He was as splendid as ever in his fashionable turn-out, which was absolutely all that it should be for a boating party in summer. He was wearing light nankeen breeches, light boots, a tan-coloured jacket of the finest wool with brass buttons, a cream-coloured shirt, to match the breeches, presumably, and a cravat which was just short of extravagant, as befitted a day in the country. He was, Nan decided savagely, much prettier than she was.

He certainly made all the other men, even the younger ones, look dull by comparison. His conversation sparkled too. He was telling Jane, Caroline and Charlotte of a visit he had paid to Macao, years ago, when he had been only a lad and had worked before the mast. Listening to it, punctuated by the girls' ready laughter, Nan suddenly became aware that he was cheating. He was embroidering a story from a book of Eastern fairy-tales which she had read long ago, and pretending that the adventure had happened to him.

'And the Sultan,' squealed Jane, entranced. 'Did he really promise you any bride you wanted because you had brought him the golden cup which he had coveted? Whatever did you say to that?'

'Oh——' Brandon was equal to anything '—that I had a bride at home, and that my religion did not allow me more than one. To which his answer was that that seemed to him to be a poor sort of religion, and that I ought to convert at once to his and have as many as I pleased, as soon as possible. He would personally arrange it for me...' He paused tantalisingly.

'And what did you say then?' asked Caroline Letcombe, her eyes as large as saucers.

'Only that it was as impossible for me to break my vow to be faithful to my one wife as it was for him to break his vow not to be faithful to any of his many wives.'

Nan, who had been trying hard not to listen, and to keep her face impassive, broke down as this ingenious and lying tale reached its witty and untruthful ending, and began to laugh helplessly. Desmond hissed angrily in her left ear, 'I am disappointed at you, Nan, that you are amused by such a flibbertigibbet as my cousin is proving to be. One wonders how he ever made a fortune. He seems formed only to keep silly young girls entertained.'

Having no answer to make to that which would please Desmond, Nan said nothing. Sam whispered in her right ear, 'For my part I find Mr Tolliver's efforts to keep his younger guests entertained quite charming. He appears to have an imagination to match your own.'

There was no answer that she could make to that either. Brandon, his tales over, rose from where he had been sitting and made his way to his sister's group, just as the footmen arrived with glasses of white wine and lemonade. Offered a choice, Nan for once accepted the wine, only to meet Desmond's disapproving eye again.

It must have attracted Brandon's notice, for he sat down on a tree stump near by to stretch his long legs and remark, 'So happy to see that you are enjoying yourself, Miss Fielding. You are, I hope, pleased that you obeyed my orders and joined our little jaunt?'

'We are all enjoying ourselves,' remarked Lydia a trifle severely. She was again put out by Brandon's making such a dead set at Nan. He had spent the morning behaving himself, but perhaps it had been too much to expect that he would go on doing so once the afternoon had arrived.

'I was about to propose,' she went on, 'that after we have recovered from our meal we should take a short walk into the country. The young man who rowed our boat here——' she waved a hand at him where he sat enjoying his luncheon with the servants who had begun to eat theirs '—tells me that there is a very pretty little green lane behind us, which in spring is edged with bluebells. It is shady, so we may be out of the heat of the afternoon sun.'

'Whatever you wish, my love,' smiled Brandon lazily. 'Were the ground a little more open, I would have suggested that we might bring along a cricket bat and ball, and enjoy ourselves with them, but I was informed that there was very little flat land round here. On the other hand, what could be better than to enjoy a country walk after a country meal and a country row downstream?'

And so it was arranged. The party lay back, dozed and prosed—even Jane and her friends eventually fell silent—until Brandon decided that they had all been sedate for long enough, and mustered everyone for the walk except Lord and Lady Alden and Sir Avery and his wife, who cried off for their various reasons. The two women preferred to sketch; they had brought their books and crayons along with them. The two men preferred to stay behind to drink Brandon's good wine, although that was not the reason they gave for doing so.

The lane and the views from it were pronounced as charming as the young boatman had said. Chaz and the other boys ran on ahead, Mr Figge panting after them— *they* were not interested in views, pretty or otherwise. Nan, walking along between Sam and Desmond, who seemed to be having a silent struggle as to which of them was her cavalier, found their combined presence oppressive, until Lydia Bligh removed Sam, asking him very prettily to be her escort. 'For,' she told him, 'I need a strong arm to help me over the stiles, and Miss Fielding does not need two!'

The real reason was that encouraging Desmond to pursue Nan might result in his winning her for his wife, which would neatly remove her from Brandon's orbit. Much though Lydia liked Nan, Brandon had begun by favouring Jane, was still doing so, and Jane must therefore properly be considered to be the young woman he ought ultimately to propose to. If he would not behave himself, then she must arrange matters so that he did.

Jane, unaware that Nan was any sort of threat, was unwisely provoking Brandon by encouraging George. That, she hoped, might bring him to a firm decision to make Jane Fielding his wife. Caroline and Charlotte, her two best friends, had not given up hope of securing Brandon for themselves. Like Jane, neither of them saw Nan as any sort of threat. George Alden was pursuing Jane in the hope that she would come to her senses and realise that Brandon was far too old and passé for her.

Nan was trying to hide from herself the fact that she was strongly attracted to Brandon to the degree that she could not stop thinking about him. Brandon was equally drawn to Nan, and to his horror was finding more and more that merely seeing her roused him, whereas Jane, while superficially even more desirable, created no such urgency in him.

Desmond and Sam were at last aware that they were

rivals. In his head, Desmond was composing reproaches to Nan along the lines of, You surely are not serious about accepting that jumped-up attorney's attentions, Nan? He is old enough to be your grandfather!

Sam for his part, was thinking, It is devoutly to be hoped that Nan does not favour this sour puritan of a man who would make her life a misery if she were ever to marry him. He would never forgive her for being the author of *Sophia*, let alone consent to allow her to go on writing her novels if she were his wife.

All this seething emotion was, of course, neatly hidden under the good manners of the party. Only Chaz, Tim and Jack were free to express their high spirits, along with their desire to find a suitable place to fly Chaz's kite which he had thoughtfully brought along with him.

Mr Figge was not sharing in their joy. He had not thought, when he had been an undergraduate at Oxford, that life would condemn him to shepherding small boys, trying to teach them Latin grammar and escorting them around the countryside. Earlier he had enjoyed an all too brief conversation with Chaz's elder sister, the commonsensical Miss Nan Fielding, so he too was sharing in the general gloom, but was hiding it as successfully as everyone else.

What made matters worse was that it was as though they really were walking through Arcadia, that happy rural country where everything grew in abundance without anyone having to do any work. The only member of the party besides Brandon who knew that this was an illusion was Nan—but she, like him, was not sharing her knowledge with anyone.

Unaware that the sunny afternoon might hold unexpected perils for them, the little party walked on. It gradually straggled over some distance, with Lydia, Desmond, Sam and Nan at the front, and the others strung out behind them. Lydia was about to call a halt, judging that they had gone far enough, when her little group reached a small clearing where Mr Figge and the boys were waiting for them.

At the far end of the clearing was a kind of tent made from a grey blanket draped over several poles of wood. In front of it were the remains of a fire. Above it a rusted iron cauldron hung from a tripod made from tree branches. Before the tent stood a woman, at the sight of whom the bright afternoon and their idle pleasure was dimmed.

The woman was filthy. She was a caricature of a woman, her face hollow, her body gaunt. She cradled a dirty baby in her arms, and the sour smell of poverty hung about them both. She held the baby towards Lydia and said one word, which at first was not understandable, but which Nan suddenly interpreted as 'Mercy'.

Shocked, no one moved or spoke. The woman cried out again, this time moving towards Lydia, who said faintly, 'Poor creature, what are you doing here?'

Desmond, pushing Nan, Chaz and the boys behind him, exclaimed harshly, 'Away with you, woman! Begging is an offence, as well you know, and squatting too,' for he had correctly interpreted what the presence of the makeshift dwelling meant. To squat on land for more than a certain length of time gave you certain rights over it, much to the annoyance of more orthodox landowners.

The woman cowered away from him. Lydia, more sympathetic to her misery than Desmond, repeated gently, but almost reproachfully, 'What are you doing here, so far away from any village? You should have applied to the parish for help.'

It was not that Lydia meant to be unkind but the comfortable life which she had lived for so long had sheltered her from such sights. She received no answer, the woman merely letting loose another harsh cry, so that Nan, who had originally been shocked into silence and immobility, gave way to her own deepest feelings at the sight of the woman and her neglected child.

More, of all of them, she alone could see that the woman was near to collapse, so that she was not surprised when her eyes rolled upwards and she fell slowly to the ground.

It was now Nan's turn to exclaim, to push by Desmond, to run forward and bend down to rescue the baby, who had rolled away from its mother to lie among the rough grasses and weeds by the side of the lane.

Nan picked it up. It appeared to be under six months old, was unhurt, and had set up a feeble wailing. She clutched it to her bosom to comfort it. Desmond, with a look of disgust on his face, joined Lydia in bending down to examine its mother cursorily.

He straightened up, to say, 'She has only fainted; she appears to be still alive,' almost as though he regretted the fact. Lydia gave a little exclamation at the harshness of Desmond's words and, sitting down on the ground, cradled the woman's filthy head on her knee.

Nan, while cuddling the baby, had grown aware of how cold it was; its pinched features were blue despite the warmth of the day. She thrust it at Sam, saying, 'Here, hold it for me a moment, please.' The baby's crying grew louder still as Sam took it clumsily from her, which allowed her to strip the shawl from her shoulders, before reclaiming the child in order to wrap the shawl closely about its shrivelled little body.

'Oh, really, Nan!' exclaimed Desmond, unmoved by the tender way in which she was hugging the baby to her, and the entranced expression on her face, which was holding Sam in thrall. 'Whatever do you think that you are doing? For all you know it is suffering from some foul disease. Put it down.'

'If hunger is a foul disease,' retorted Nan, 'then that is what is wrong with it, and I shall certainly not put it down until its mother has recovered and we have found some means of feeding it.' For the baby had seized the forefinger with which she had been stroking its cheek and had begun to suck it vigorously, until a wailing cry announced that it had found no sustenance there.

No one thought fit to answer her. Lydia had managed to get the woman, who had regained consciousness, to sit up, and just as Desmond began to expostulate with Nan again Brandon and the rest of his party, who had been dawdling and picking wild flowers on the way, arrived in the clearing. He took in the situation at a glance and said in his pleasant voice, 'Squatters?' And then, 'Deserted by the husband?'

But talk was not all he did. He joined his sister in examining and questioning the woman. They spoke in low tones together for a moment, then both stood up, Brandon announcing, 'It seems that her husband, who was a weaver, turned away because of the new machines, has either deserted her or is lost, or injured, for he has been gone for several days, and she has no food left, and she fears that the child is dying.'

'But that,' Desmond remarked stiffly, 'does not mean that Nan needs to risk contagion by nursing it, as I hope that you will tell her, cousin.'

Before Brandon could reply, Chaz forestalled Sam Stone, who was about to protest at Desmond's discourtesy to the woman he loved and respected, by crying firmly, with a baleful glare at Desmond, 'Hoorah for Nan, I say. The Bible tells us, or so my papa says, that the Good Samaritan should not pass by on the other side, and Nan is the best Good Samaritan I know. Why, she even found my kite when no one else would trouble themselves to look for it. If she's not allowed to hold the baby, then I will. Although I don't like babies much,' he finished glumly.

This brave declaration lightened the mood of the party wonderfully, the only member of it who remained unhappy besides Desmond being Jane, who muttered audibly to Caroline, 'I must say I wonder at Nan for wanting to hold anything quite so dirty.'

Giving her a sharp look, Brandon strode across the clearing to Nan, saying, 'My dear Miss Fielding, you will allow me to take the baby from you for a moment.' When she began to protest at losing it, he added, with his most dazzling smile, 'You may have it back, I promise you.'

He held the baby as carefully as she had been doing before fulfilling his promise and handing it back to Nan.

'Nothing seems to be wrong with it but hunger, I dare say,' he offered in his usual cheerful manner. 'No need for us to wrangle. I suggest, Mr Figge, that you return to the river with the boys and ask two of the footmen to make an impromptu stretcher, and bring it here so that Mrs Blagg and her baby may be carried back to the barge and thence to Gillyflower Hall. She tells me that she is a sempstress, and I am sure we can always find room for another at the Hall.'

Desmond's answer to this was, 'Your kind heart does your credit, cousin,' said after a fashion which suggested that it didn't. Then he added, 'But such indiscriminate charity will mean that you will find yourself at the mercy of every bold beggar in the district.'

'No, indeed.' Brandon's tone was equable. 'I have no intention of housing or caring for every beggar in the district, only this one poor woman and her child whom we have come across today.'

Chaz, who had been about to leave with Mr Figge, said approvingly, 'Nan is not the only Good Samaritan, then, Mr Tolliver. Neither of you passes by on the other side.'

Brandon answered him a little wryly. 'I think you flatter me, Chaz. But yes, on this occasion I cannot let my sister and yours be the only ones to offer succour to the needy.' He cast a glance at Nan as he spoke. Something in her transfigured face as she held the poor starving baby to her touched him so deeply that he was compelled to turn away from her. In doing so he found Sam Stone's eye on him, and knew that he had in some sort betrayed what he was beginning to feel for Nan Fielding.

But what *do* I feel for her? he asked himself as they all walked soberly back to the river. Such a strange mixture of compassion, friendship, admiration and lust.

Whatever can it be? He dared not admit to himself that it might be love, for had he not decided that that emotion did not figure in his calculations as to his marriage and his future life? He was not even sure that he thought that it existed outside the haverings of poets and inside the covers of Minerva Press novels.

CHAPTER EIGHT

SECURE in the knowledge that poor starving Mrs Blagg had been fed, put to bed in the servants' quarters at Gillyflower Hall, and that a temporary wet nurse had been found for the baby by Lydia in the shape of the butler's wife, whose own baby was in the process of being weaned, Nan felt able to attend the ball that night.

Not only the guests at Gillyflower Hall were to be present, but also many from Highborough, and a few of the villages round about. The night was serene, the moon was high, the musicians from Leicester, who had arrived while they were on the river, were gifted, and the ballroom had been decorated to perfection with flowers from the gardens under Lydia and the head gardener's supervision.

Nan made her way downstairs some time after Jane had burst into her room and demanded to accompany Caroline and Charlotte, who were both being chaperoned by Caroline's elderly aunt. 'You surely do not need to stand guard over me all the time,' had been her ungracious comment. Nan had not argued with her. She was feeling a strange sort of satisfaction after having persuaded Brandon and Lydia to allow her to carry the baby all the way back to Gillyflower Hall—much to Desmond and Jane's disgust.

There had been one untoward incident on the way home which had frightened Nan more than it should—for what was Mr Brandon Tolliver to her, other than someone who was occasionally briefly kind? After their first passionate interchanges, that was. Brandon's horse, Nero, had been brought round to him when they were all assembled in the carriages again. Mrs Blagg had been put in the servants' coach, a little to their disgust, she being so very dirty.

Brandon mounted with his usual athletic ease. He was one of the few men Nan knew who did not possess the beginnings of a paunch through over-eating and indulgence in strong drink. Even Desmond, she had noticed, had begun to put on weight. The sight of Brandon on horseback was almost enough to make her forget her joy in having a real live baby to herself for a few moments, or rather the joy changed and centred on Brandon and his attractive presence. . .but her pleasure in his athleticism was not to last long.

A dog belonging to one of the boatmen ran out and frightened Nero. He gave a snorting plunge and for a moment Brandon fought to control him. He had just done so when one of the girths snapped—and Brandon was then fighting desperately to stay on board Nero and not to be thrown. A battle he was doomed to lose. He was thrown headlong, to land face down on the ground, and, for one heart-stopping moment, to lie quite still.

Heart-stopping for Nan, that was. One moment she was secretly drinking in the sight of him mastering Nero with such power and grace, and the next moment he was—what and where was he? Only the baby in her arms, she realised afterwards, had stopped her from disgracing herself by leaping from the carriage and going to his assistance. All the other women began to wail and exclaim while George Alden, who had been about to take his seat in his curricle, ran over to where Brandon lay and was the first to reach him and examine him to find out what damage had been done.

Fortunately not much. For Brandon was already stirring by the time that George bent over him, and George helped him to sit up.

'How goes it, old fellow? No bones broken, I hope,' he enquired anxiously.

'I don't think so,' muttered Brandon. He was both shaken and winded, aware that he had been fortunate in not pitching on his head. 'I shall be A1 at Lloyd's in a minute, I hope.' And he put his head down as a wave of faintness swept over him.

Meantime one of the attendant grooms had caught Nero and was inspecting his saddle, which had slipped sideways.

'His girth snapped, sir,' he announced, running over to where George and now Desmond were helping Brandon to his feet.

'Best not ride back,' George told him. 'There's room in one of the carriages, I'm sure.'

Brandon wanted to say no, but common sense prevailed. He allowed himself to be walked over to the Letcombe's carriage and take his place with them. There was a great bruise starting up on one side of his face, his fine coat was covered in grass and his breathing was still disturbed.

From where she sat Nan gazed at him, agonised, unaware of what her eyes were telling poor Sam, who, having had Brandon's inner feelings revealed to him, was now witnessing Nan's. He knew at once that she had not accepted him because her heart was given to the charming rogue which he suspected Brandon to be. No one who had made such a great fortune at such a relatively early age could, Sam was sure, be other than hard and devious beneath all the surface attraction.

But Brandon was a strong man, and Nan was a strong woman. Sam was old and wise enough to know that like called to like. Whether like would get like was quite another matter. The odds were that Brandon would marry for reasons of prudence, or of prestige, and neither would lead him to lay his heart or his name at Nan's feet. What was important was that Nan should not be hurt.

His admiration for her grew as she kept her composure while Brandon lay back against the cushions of the Letcombes' carriage and slowly regained his senses. After a few moments he had recovered enough to assure his travelling companions that he had suffered no permanent damage.

'Which was just as well,' he told Lydia cheerfully, when they were safely back at the Hall. 'Just think of the brouhaha it would have caused if you had been compelled to cancel everything tonight if I *had* broken my neck and was laid out in state in the big drawing-room ready for the undertakers!'

Lydia shuddered. 'Never say so, my dear. Even to think of it. . .' And she shuddered again. 'You are sure that you will be able to attend the ball tonight?'

'Quite sure,' he told her. He had, she was pleased to note, regained his normal cheerful manner. 'Oh, I'm bruised, but nothing fatal, thank God.'

'You should reprimand the grooms.' Lydia was energetic. 'Quite wrong of them to allow you to start out with a frayed girth.'

'Oh, yes.' He seemed a trifle abstracted, she thought, which was perhaps not surprising in the circumstances. He did not tell her that he had gone round to the stables shortly after his return to the Hall and had asked to examine the broken girth.

Ned, the head groom, had looked steadily at him and said gravely, 'I thought that you might ask that, maister,' and had taken Brandon over to where the saddle lay on some staging at the back of the stables.

He had said nothing more, but stood back while Brandon examined the girth. His expression had remained impassive until Brandon had stared him straight in the eye and said, 'Now, Ned, do you see what I think I see?'

Ned had pursed his lips. 'I did think as how I might be mistaken, but I see that I am not. . . I think. . .' He had paused, not wishing to say the unsayable.

'That the girth was three-parts cut through, quite neatly, so that it was only a matter of time before it parted and I was thrown,' Brandon had finished for him.

'Aye. But who would do such a thing and why? You

might have been killed. I do know that there was nothing wrong with the saddle when I put it out. I always check the girths, and have taught all the lads to do the same. Sim swears that it was whole when he saddled Nero, and I do not think that he was lying.'

Brandon had thought a moment. He didn't think that either Ned or Sim was lying, and said so. 'Which leaves us with this. That the girth was cut deliberately while it was at the stables by the Soar, during the time we went upriver.'

'Aye, maister—but who would do such a thing?'

'Who indeed? Malcontents, Luddites, Jacobins angry at all gentlefolk and landowners—happy to see one pitch on his head and not get up again.'

He had not added that he was not quite satisfied with this as an explanation, even though Ned was nodding his head in agreement. After all, this was the second time since he had arrived at Gillyflower Hall that an odd accident had happened to him. He was thinking of the shot which had so narrowly missed him. More prudent, perhaps, not to dwell too much on them. Coincidence might be at work, but for some reason Brandon's intuition, which had helped to make him a fortune, told him that there was more to his run of misfortunes than that. Meantime he must watch his back.

He was not watching his back when he stood among his guests at the ball. He didn't think that here, among his own people, coincidence would strike again. Above his head, on the painted ceiling, Jove rode in the clouds, a thunderbolt clutched in his right fist, to remind mortals that one might plan one's life, but one could not command life to follow the plan.

Apparently Mr Brandon Tolliver could not even command that Miss Nan Fielding would be present at a ball in his own mansion. He took a rapid look around the big room to see that Jane was the centre of a circle of playful young men and women, and that most of the house party were present as well as those guests who had come from Highborough and round about to take part in the ball.

But no Miss Fielding. He turned to Lydia and said, as apparently aimlessly as he could, 'I don't see Miss Fielding among the chaperons, Lydia. Is she unwell, do you think? She seemed cheerful enough on the way home when she was holding Mrs Blagg's baby.'

How like Brandon to remember Mrs Blagg's name, and how unlike him to trouble over Nan Fielding.

'She seemed well enough when we returned home, Brandon. Perhaps she is feeling a little tired and is resting in her room. Why do you ask?'

'Oh,' he offered, as vaguely as he could, 'the poor woman seems to have a dull time of it. She is not so very much older than Jane and the rest, but seems doomed to sit on the back row of life among women who are old enough to be her mother or her grandmother.'

'But she does have to act as Jane's mother, as you will allow, seeing that her true mother is a permanent invalid.' Lydia paused, then, against her better judgement, pursued the matter.

'Why are you troubling yourself about her, Brandon? She is hardly the sort of person in whom you normally take an interest. You have already caused a little comment by publicly arguing with your cousin Desmond over her. I have also had occasion to remind you not to make servant girls unhappy by your attentions. How much more distressing it would be if you gave the poor woman incorrent notions about your intentions towards her.'

'I have no intentions towards her!' he exclaimed, a trifle stiffly. 'But she is a guest here, and I would like her to be happy. Perhaps you could send a footman to ask if she is quite well, if she needs anything.'

Lydia's expression of astonishment grew. 'Well, really, Brandon...' And then, 'No need to trouble yourself. I see that she has just entered the room and is talking to Lady Letcombe. There! I hope that sets your mind at rest.'

'Only trying to be a good host, Lydia. If I ask her for a dance, you will not think that I am about to seduce her, I trust.'

'No,' Lydia shot back. 'Only that I find you unfathomable. You will be losing Jane to young George Alden. He might not have your fortune, but he will inherit his father's title one day, and he is nearer to her in age than you are.'

Brandon muttered something under his breath which fortunately Lydia did not hear, and bowed to Lady Letcombe who, with Nan in her wake, was crossing the room. Nan, he noticed, as did his sister and Sam Stone, to say nothing of Desmond, was looking more *comme il faut* than she had previously done at Gillyflower Hall. Her duenna's cap was not quite so extinguishing as usual, and her dress of cream silk, although more suited to a dowager, enhanced her complexion rather than diminished it as most of her other clothes did.

They all bowed to one another. Formality was more treasured in the country than the town, Brandon was discovering. Lady Letcombe monopolised Lydia, to leave Nan and Brandon together, much to Lydia's annoyance.

Nan tried not to let Brandon dazzle her overmuch with his splendour. Evening black became him so well. The touch of silver in his black hair, his broad shoulders, narrow waist and long legs were all enhanced by the fashionable clothing which fitted him so snugly. As usual his cravat was a valet's dream of heaven, and tonight he wore round his neck a quizzing-glass which depended from a black cord. He lifted it to examine her, remarking coolly, Lydia's reprimand still sounding in his ears, 'You look well tonight, Miss Fielding. That colour becomes you.'

Well, he could hardly praise anything else about my turn-out, was Nan's irreverent thought, but nevertheless her cheeks glowed with pleasure at the small compliment, and when he finished by saying, 'And you will take a turn on the floor with me, I hope. I promise to behave myself tonight,' she felt almost dizzy with delight.

The smile she gave him transformed her face. So much so that Brandon decided at once that he ought to provoke it more often.

'Lydia told me that the next dance is a waltz. Will you waltz with me, Miss Fielding?'

And he put out his strong and shapely hand, so that for good manners' sake Nan was compelled to take it, saying breathlessly, 'But I have never waltzed in public before.'

He held on to her hand to lead her on to the floor almost against her will. 'And if not in public when did you waltz, Miss Fielding? You intrigue me.'

'Oh,' she told him, aware that many eyes were on them, including Jane's furious ones. 'When I taught my sisters in the Rectory parlour before they had their season in town. But I always took the man's part—so I fear that if you insist on dancing with me you may find that I will lead rather than follow.'

To her secret delight Brandon gave her his dazzling smile, the smile which made the silver eyes crinkle, which affected his whole face and was no mere slight movement of his lips. 'Oh, now you intrigue me even further—to have a lady who leads! But,' he could not resist adding, 'I think that you have led twice in our encounters already.'

Nan's blush was all-enveloping. For some reason being reminded in such a public place as a ballroom floor of what had passed between them in the pantry and in the woods seemed tremendously exciting, almost wicked. Before she could make any reply—and what reply could she make?—the music had started, she was in Brandon's arms and was being whirled around the floor.

And she was certainly not leading. Brandon was most definitely doing that, and she could think of nothing

more delightful. She knew now why Lord Byron, of all
people, had condemned the waltz for being immoral,
for surely it must be immoral for her to be feeling such
extraordinary pleasure in Brandon's arms. She was tall
enough for him to need to bend his head only a little to
look into her eyes, and when he did so the strange
dissolving feeling which being with him in the pantry
and the woods had caused was upon her again.

It lightened her footsteps, as well as her heart, so
that Brandon felt that never before had he waltzed with
a partner who seemed almost to be his other self, so
exquisitely did she follow him and the music. Lead,
indeed! No, far from that, she was following him perfectly, and the delicate scent of lavender, mixed with
warm and living Nan, which rose from her was strong
in his nostrils, and was seduction itself. Lydia was quite
wrong. He was not seducing Nan. She was seducing
him, merely by being her own sweetly modest self.

And this is heaven, and I am in it, and I wish the
music would go on forever, was Nan's thought. It will
come to an end all too soon, but I shall have this
memory to take away from Gillyflower Hall, to hold to
me in the endless dark winter nights. Not since the
long-ago days when Randal and I roamed the woods
together in Hampshire have I felt such pleasure.

She was unaware of the many jealous and critical
eyes on her; among them, Desmond's and Jane's were
hard and angry, Lydia's and Sam's rueful. I might as
well have saved my breath, was Lydia's reaction. What
can he be thinking of? For I know him too well; he
can't be serious. Her eyes met Sam's and they
exchanged a wordless message. How do we save her
from misery and disillusionment?

It was over. The dancers and the spectators were all
clapping. Brandon was bowing to Nan, and she was
bowing back. He took her hand to lead her off the
floor, saying into her ear, 'You need no lessons on
following, Miss Fielding. You could give lessons your-

self, so sweetly do you obey your partner's lightest touch.'

'You are pleased to say so, Mr Tolliver.'

'No.' They had reached the edge of the floor. Brandon turned towards her, having released her hand. 'No, Brandon, I beg of you. We are friends at last, I hope. And in return I may call you Nan. Or would you prefer Anne?'

Anne was the name which Randal had known her by, and it was sacred to him. It told of a past time when she had been young, happy and hopeful.

'So long as you promise to continue to behave yourself, then you shall be Brandon, and in return I must be Nan. That is my name in Broomhall.'

If Brandon thought this answer a trifle odd he did not say so. He lifted her hand and kissed it. 'Now enjoy yourself, Nan. I think that Mr Stone is waiting for you, and I must play the part of mine host until the tower clock tells me that the dance is over.'

Yes, but her pleasure had ended with the music. He was leading her to a chair, not at the back, but next to Sam, who was looking at her with his kind eyes. Nan felt that she was floating on air. Sam thought that Nan looked transfigured—which was perhaps only a different way of saying the same thing.

'You are enjoying yourself?' he asked her.

Her reply, she thought later, was fit for Jane. 'Oh, famously!' she began enthusiastically, before catching herself and slowing down into normal staid Miss Fielding again. 'And I thought I would not, this afternoon. But Brandon—Mr Tolliver—sent word to me by a footman that the poor woman we rescued is sleeping and the baby has been fed and is sleeping too.'

Sam made appropriate noises, even though his heart was heavy. Like Lydia, he thought that Mr Brandon Tolliver was being a mere heartless seducer, who, even if he did not intend to ruin Nan, would at least make her very unhappy by causing her to entertain false hopes.

A quadrille followed, and Sam duly led her on to the floor, just cutting out Desmond who had been slow to cross the room to them. Desmond, however, made quite sure that he was all present and correct, as the saying had it, when her dance with Sam was over, in order to ask Nan to partner him in the country dance which followed.

While they were waiting for the music to begin he asked her if she would take a turn with him in the adjoining drawing-room, 'Where,' he announced, 'it is cooler and not so oppressive.'

By his expression he was about to read the Riot Act to her again, and so it proved when they finally found themselves in the big empty room with no one to interrupt them. Nan made a straight line for a wall of coloured prints by Gillray and Rowlandson satirising the follies and foibles of society. But Desmond was not to be diverted by such simple means.

'I wonder at you, Anne,' he began again, so that Nan irreverently pondered on whether or not to suggest to him that some slight variant on this mode of address to her might be no bad thing if he wished her to take him seriously.

'What have I done this time?' she asked him patiently as he paused to make the seriousness of what he was saying apparent to her.

'You must know, being so *au fait* with what should and should not be done by unmarried laides, that you ought not to have waltzed with such a philanderer as I have already informed you that my cousin is reputed to be. What kind of example, one wonders, do you think that you are setting poor young Jane? It is not surprising that the freedom with which she speaks and acts is already being commented on. I feel that my duty to you and to your family demands that I make you a formal offer of marriage so that I may be able to protect you both from those who would exploit and deceive you.'

For a moment Nan hardly knew what to think, let alone what to say.

'Am I,' she asked him, quite dazed, 'to infer from what you have just said that you are proposing marriage to me, Desmond? And after such a strange fashion, too.'

His expression was so wounded when this came out that it was almost comical.

'My dear Anne, I thought that I had made myself sufficiently plain. I fail to see how anything which I have just said could conceivably be construed as "strange" in any way.' And the inverted commas around 'strange' were heavy in his voice.

'Oh!' exclaimed Nan, almost ready to stamp her foot at him. 'Do you never listen to what you say to me, Desmond? You cast doubts on my judgement, on my chastity, on Jane's behaviour, which differs not at all from that of any other high-spirited young girl, and then you offer to marry me—not because you love or care for me, but because you wish to act as a kind of moral arbiter to me and my family. The only person you left out of the equation was Chaz. Do you propose to be his guide, philosopher and friend as well?'

'I thought, after all the years which we have known one another, my dear Anne, that you could take the love and the care for granted. And of course I should be willing to assist *Charles*——' and he trod heavily on the formal name '—to learn to moderate his present rash behaviour, although that task ought properly to be left to his father. I do grasp, however, that your father is so spiritually inclined that the assistance of someone who is a trifle more knowledgeable about worldly affairs——'

As this pompous sermon showed no signs of drawing to a close, Nan could not contain herself. 'Pray stop,' she exploded. 'Just because Chaz does not greatly care for you is no reason for you to go on so, and as for poor Papa. . .'

At this point she ran down, partly because she realised that were she to continue she would say something unforgivable, and partly because she suddenly understood that Desmond was so armoured in right-eousness that nothing she could say would make any impression on the carapace of certitude in his own judgement which he carried around with him.

'I thought,' she resumed lamely, before he could begin on another lecture to her, 'that you had decided that you were not rich enough to afford a wife and so were unable to propose to me.'

This statement, Nan immediately realised, was an unfortunate one. It merely served to start him off once more on another self-serving diatribe.

'I conceive it to be my duty——' he began grandly, so that Nan interrupted him again, first putting her hands over her ears.

'No, Desmond, please stop. If I hear the word duty again I think I shall scream. It is only fair to tell you that despite the great honour you have done me in asking me, with all my imperfections on my head, to marry you, I must refuse your kind offer. Do not ask me again, I beg of you, for my answer will always remain the same.'

She saw the thunderstruck expression on his face. 'My dear girl,' he said heavily, 'I do not understand you. Are you sure that that is the answer which you wish to give me? I had always assumed that were I to offer marriage to you you would be only too happy to accept me. After all, you are getting on in years, are not likely to marry unless you do accept me, and this is your last chance to achieve an establishment of your own. Common sense alone would dictate. . .'

'No!' Nan almost screamed at him. 'Pray do not speak to me of common sense at all. I am sick of exercising common sense. Please leave me. You have your answer. I wish to remain your friend, Desmond. . . I want to be alone. Please!'

Whether it was the frantic way in which she spoke, or whether he finally understood that she meant her refusal, Nan was never to know. He dithered for a moment, opening and shutting his mouth like an agitated goldfish trapped in a bowl, before he finally grumbled at her, 'Oh, very well, but I warn you, I shall not ask you again. So if this is mere girlish megrims. . .'

The face that Nan rewarded him with after this unkind remark had him muttering again, 'Oh, very well. . .' before he turned and left the room.

Nan had scarcely drawn a thankful breath at his going when he opened the door again to fire his final arrow at her. 'And if you think that my unprincipled cousin will propose to you, Anne, you are very much mistaken. He will want someone young and pretty with a good dowry. I doubt that even Jane will satisfy him.'

He closed the door. Nan flung a cushion from the sofa at him as he opened it again—to fire another broadside at her, presumably.

But instead the cushion hit Brandon amidships as he came in.

'Now what have I done?' he asked her, pulling a comical face as he neatly fielded it, and tossed it on to a nearby armchair.

Nan burst into tears.

Brandon was across the room at once, to sit by her and take her in his arms. 'No, you are not to cry. I won't have it. He isn't worth it. What on earth did that pompous ass, my cousin, have to say to you which could distress you so?'

'He proposed to me,' Nan sobbed at him, wetting his beautiful cravat.

'And that is a cause for tears? Most women would be pleased.'

'Not by the manner in which he proposed to me.' The tears which she had held back for so long, had suppressed since the terrible day on which she had learned of Randal's death, flowed even more rapidly.

Brandon said nothing for a few moments, and then, in a confidential tone, came out with, 'I shouldn't repeat gossip, I know, but it might cheer you a little to learn that Desmond has proposed to three young heiresses during the past year, and they have all turned him down!'

Nan offered him a watery smile. 'I suppose that was why he decided that he might as well settle down with me!' She could not prevent a loud sob from punctuating the end of the sentence.

'Come, come.' Brandon's voice was mock-severe. 'I am not a flowerbed to be watered, and it is not like you to be less than brave.'

'Brave!' Nan raised her head and stared at him fiercely through her tears. 'What do you, or any man for that matter, know about being brave? Oh, I don't mean brute courage as on the battlefield or in a duel. No, I mean the enduring of the unending littleness of daily life which is most women's lot.'

There was no answer Brandon could make to that. His own life had been wide-ranging and adventurous. He had no notion, he knew, of what life might be like for a spinster in her late twenties in a quiet country village. What he did know was that he was becoming aware that he should not be holding Nan to him so lovingly. If it was temptation merely to see her, then what was having her in his arms likely to do to him?

As though she had caught his thoughts, Nan murmured into his chest, 'You have left your guests again in order to speak to me, Brandon. You will be missed as I will be. This is most unwise; we shall occasion even more gossip.'

'No one will miss either of us yet,' he assured her, unwilling to leave her before necessity compelled him to do so. 'The whole party, even Lydia, who is being squired by your papa, is on the floor performing a country dance. Desmond, who might be permitted some suspicion of what we are up to, was, by the direction he took, on his way to his room. We are safe for a few more minutes yet.'

Safe for what? was Nan's sleepy thought. Tears over, she was caught in the languor of strong emotion's aftermath, and this, plus being held against a man's rapidly beating heart, was so comforting that she would willingly have remained there until he chose to move. . . Yes, all that she wanted was to be held. . .by him. . . She closed her eyes and relaxed against the strength of him, his heartbeat lulling her to sleep. . .

Brandon Tolliver did not consider himself to be the most sensitive of men, but he was sensitive enough to be aware that the last thing which Nan needed in her present state of mind was to be made love to. What she really wanted was to be cherished. What he wanted was quite another thing, but that could wait.

The very thought of making real passionate love to Nan, seeing that he was holding her so closely to him, was rousing him. Which had him moving a little away from her, unwilling to distress an innocent maiden lady. Besides, he really ought not to be pursuing her, putting temptation in her way unless he was quite sure in his own mind why he was doing so.

For, after all, had he not decided that what he really wanted for a wife was a pretty, reasonable biddable young girl, who would be an ornament on his arm when he went into the great world, who would grace his home, give him children, and make few demands on him—a trophy, in fact, to confirm his success in life? Someone to whom he need make no real commitment. Someone with whom he would have the kind of relationship which would enable him to take a lover when he pleased. Someone, in short, like Jane Fielding. He would make exactly the sort of marriage, indeed, which most of his contemporaries engaged in.

He had never once contemplated marrying a clever and strong-minded woman of mature years who would demand commitment from him, for that was Nan's nature; she would want him to surrender something of himself to her. He had always been, as Lydia had once told him, 'the cat that walked by itself', arranging his life to suit himself and no one else. He had no intention of changing that, either by marriage or by any other sort of tie.

The kindest thing which he could do for Nan Fielding was to walk away from her—as his sister had suggested—speaking to her only when politeness demanded, and not be putting her in the way of developing a hopeless *tendre* for him. That would be of all things the most unkind, would it not?

Wryly, he was also aware that these sane and honourable notions seemed feasible only when he was not with her. And now madam was going to sleep against him. By its cadences, the music floating in from the ballroom was drawing to its close, and they must not be found here together—and alone. He must leave her, having behaved nearly as badly as his sister had feared. Perhaps, after all, he ought to have encouraged Nan to think again...to reconsider...to accept his cousin's proposal.

More than his dislike of seeing her promised to another strangled that thought at its birth. Anyone but Desmond, perhaps even that old attorney who so visibly mooned after her, would be better... No, not him either.

'Nan,' he murmured gently in her ear, dropping the lightest of butterfly kisses on to her tawny hair. Her duenna's cap had slipped away, and her usually restrained curls were springing loose.

'I must go,' he whispered. 'For both our sakes. It would not do for us to be discovered here alone.'

'Oh!' Nan sat up, suddenly wide awake. 'Whatever am I doing? You have let me go to sleep,' she informed him accusingly.

She saw his long mouth twitch, the silver eyes flash. 'So I have,' he agreed gravely. 'You seemed to be in need of it. Let me prescribe for you.' He put on a solemn owlish face, looked at her over imaginary half-frame spectacles. 'For many years, I suspect, you have devoted yourself to working and caring for your family without respite. I give you, therefore, permission to retire to your room and rest—if that is what you wish. You may make your excuses prettily to my sister, while

I reappear in the ballroom through the far door—like a genie in a pantomime—ready to look after all my other guests.'

He had a silver tongue, Nan thought—and so informed him.

His reply, she thought, was a little bitter. 'So I have often been told.'

He had disengaged himself, and was rising from the sofa. Her magical moment with him was in the past. He was sorry for the poor old maid, she thought, and now he would be off to be kind to someone else. . . She had no doubt, though, that if he wished he could be cruel or stern. . .anything he pleased.

Well, he had chosen to be kind to her for a short time, and that must be enough. She must not, dared not, hope for more. So after a little while, when her tears had dried and the scarlet they had provoked in her face had died down, she did as Brandon had suggested—made her adieus to Lydia and prepared to mount the stairs to her bedroom.

But the evening was not yet over for her.

CHAPTER NINE

NAN had a foot on the stairs when Jane shot out of the door to the ballroom.

'Wait, Nan.' Her voice was harsh and peremptory, so much so that the look Nan turned on her was an astonished one. Jane's face was scarlet and angry. She advanced on Nan as though she were going into battle.

'Why are you doing this to me, Nan?'

Nan's reply was not entirely truthful. She said, as innocently as she could, 'I don't understand you, Jane. Doing what?'

'Oh, don't pretend. You know perfectly well what I mean! You knew how taken I was with Brandon and he with me, but you have done nothing but make eyes at him since you first met, and now you have danced the waltz with him. That is almost a declaration of something or other, is it not? He should have asked me to waltz, not you. What did you say to him to persuade him to do so?'

Now she could be truthful. 'Nothing, Jane, nothing, I assure you. And you must know, as well as I do, that it would be quite improper for you, as a young girl, only just out, to waltz with a man of Brandon's age. Your reputation would suffer if you did so, whereas I...'

'Whereas you, being elderly, and past her last prayers, I suppose, could hardly be considered to have a reputation worth keeping or losing,' Jane flashed spitefully at her.

This was really too much, even from a sister who rarely considered her feelings. Nan clenched her fists and said as coolly as she could, 'I do not make the rules by which we live, Jane, but like you I have to abide by them.'

'Then leave Brandon alone, and cease making

sheep's eyes at him. I saw him first, before you did.'
This came out as childishly as though they were arguing
over the possession of a doll. 'Why don't you make us
all happy and agree to marry Desmond?'

'I don't intend to marry anyone, and for your benefit
I have just refused to marry Desmond. Now I wish to
go to bed. I am very tired.'

She saw Jane's lower lip protrude as it often did
when she was being particularly selfish, whether the
selfishness was concerned with a man or the ownership
of a box of bon-bons. Nan's words flew out of her, of
their own accord, almost as though she had not willed
them, as words had done when she had been a lively
young girl, younger even than Jane was now.

'One thing, my dear. If you wish to keep a man, or
inspire him to marry you, let me give you a piece of
advice. Do not pout and groan at him overmuch. Men
like pretty, biddable young things, not scowling, ill-
tempered ones.'

'Oh!' Jane almost shrieked. 'I'll have you know I
have no intention of taking any notice of what an
elderly prude, long past her last prayers, who has never
managed to marry a man, says to me. I don't believe
that Desmond ever offered for you. If he had I'm sure
that you would have jumped all over him, and the
wedding would be arranged for next week — or sooner.'
She tossed her pretty head in the air, and shot back
through the door by which she had come, determined
not to miss any more of the evening's fun.

Any desire to sleep which Nan had possessed flew
away after Jane had left her. Was it true? Had she been
making sheep's eyes at Brandon? Had anyone seen, or
was it that Jane had noticed something which no one
else had? The eye of jealousy was as keen as the eye of
love.

Nan did not think that Jane loved Brandon. She was
at an age, and of a disposition, not to love anyone other
than herself. She had seen and attracted Brandon
before anyone else in the neighbourhood had met him,

and he had constantly behaved towards her in a '*most* particular' way, as she had said, to give her the impression that he was interested in her. Jane did not persevere with men, young or old, who seemed to be immune to her charms.

And, if so, it must be especially galling for her to see Brandon taking a sudden interest in the despised elder sister for whose way of life she had always shown such contempt, not knowing that it was Nan, as the author of *Sophia*, who had made her own, and the Rectory's, comfortable life possible. It was absolutely necessary, then, for Jane's sake, that she should discourage Brandon, and cause him to stop his strange pursuit of her. Once again Nan asked herself in the small hours as she tossed and turned, sleep coming and going, What does he really want with me?

Brandon didn't know what he wanted with Nan Fielding. He had never been in such a pother over a woman before. Nothing in his sensible arrangement with Emma Milborne, or the other accommodations he had come to with various other young and willing women, had prepared him to deal with Nan Fielding. What on earth had led him to start the whole business off by wandering into the Rectory's pantry? It was enough to teach him not to go adventuring—that was to be left for his business, not his social life.

And, more, why had he not passed by on the other side when he had found her again, up a tree? And what on earth had the commonsensical and proper Miss Fielding been doing up a tree, freeing her brother's kite? Why couldn't she have walked back to the Rectory and found an underservant to do it for her, and have thus spared him temptation? Jove, what legs she had... He dragged his fevered mind away from mental contemplation of them—and of the rest of her.

And why could he not sleep for thinking of her, when it was Jane who should have been occupying his thoughts? And what was the business she had with the

ageing attorney which should so preoccupy her? For
Brandon's intuition told him that there was more to
their association than Sam Stone's desire to make her
his wife. There was something odd going on at the
Rectory, and the oddity centred on the mysterious Miss
Fielding—who would not let him sleep, damn her!

Like Nan he tossed and turned, before exhaustion
claimed him in the small hours, his last thought being, I
must be going mad to let a woman trouble me so, for,
like most men, he agreed with the poet Byron. 'Man's
love is of man's life a thing apart, 'Tis woman's whole
existence.' So what was he doing to allow the business
of Nan Fielding to take such a large part of his life?

He and Nan were not the only ones to be thus
troubled. Jane, too, and George Alden, to say nothing
of Desmond Tolliver and Sam Stone, were beset by
love's cross-currents, and perhaps only Parson Fielding
and young Chaz, dreaming of kites and plum tarts, were
free from the attention of the little god of love. Plenty
of time for Chaz in the future, though, however serene
his present!

Nan expected the last day of the house party at
Gillyflower Hall to be as fraught as the first two, but no
such thing. The guests all straggled down to breakfast
one by one, the last arriving just as a cold collation was
served in the big dining-room. A wind had risen during
the night, strong enough to make eating luncheon out
of doors troublesome.

Even Desmond seemed to have recovered his spirits
and went out of his way to be pleasant to her. Brandon,
on the other hand, seemed to be going out of his way
to avoid her. She told herself that this was an eventuality much to be desired—a piece of pomposity which
gave her no comfort at all, even if Jane was happy to
have her admirer back again.

Her pretty laughter rang out more than once. She
was much admired by the older gentlemen of the party,
although Desmond's one scowl that day was directed

towards her enthusiastic enjoyment of his cousin's attention.

Sam Stone left towards noon. A messenger had come from his office to say that he was required there urgently—an important communication had come from London. He feared by what was said that Mr Murray was badgering him again about the identity of the author of *Sophia*. He had been much alarmed at breakfast-time, and happy that Nan had not yet come down for it, when Lady Letcombe, reading letters which had been forwarded to her from Letcombe's Landing, had given vent to a loud cry.

'Only think!' she exclaimed, putting down a much crossed piece of writing paper from a correspondent whose handwriting seemed to be distinguished mostly by its large and excitable scrawl. 'It is the *on dit* all around town that Mr Murray has said that he may soon be able to announce the true identity of the author of *Sophia*! Even more exciting, he says that she—he is sure that it is a she—lives somewhere in South Nottinghamshire, near to the borders of Leicestershire. Only fancy if that be true! Why, Sophia might even be one of us! What a thing!'

An excited buzz from the ladies drowned all male conversation. Nan, who had arrived just as Lady Letcombe had finished speaking, showed Sam a white, scared face. He shook his head imperceptibly, to reassure her that he had not given her away.

Brandon, seated next to Jane, drawled in his most teasing fashion, 'I suppose that Murray is setting this rumour on its way to increase the sales of the author's next novel. I have seen the advertisements for it in the public prints. He is making sure that when it arrives in the bookshops there will be queues down the street in case something in it will betray her identity.'

Sam nodded, and even Nan acknowledged the truth of what Brandon was saying. But she was also forced hard up against the fact that what Sam had told her recently was true: she would not be able to keep her secret much longer.

She sat quiet. Lady Alden, next door to her, anxious that Nan should not be left out of the conversation, remarked to her, 'Whoever she is, she knows country society as well as town. She has a pretty wit on her, and in my opinion must be well on in years to be able to see all our foibles and portray them so accurately. I have been trying to think who I know who might be the author, but I confess that I am at a loss. My guess is that she may be a he after all. What do you think, Miss Fielding?'

She was always kinder to Nan than Lady Letcombe, whose private judgement of her, made to the other women the night before, after Nan had retired, was, 'She is such a bore, my dears, so strait-laced, so proper. The only thing which seems to occupy her mind is the ordering of affairs at the Rectory and in the parish!'

Lady Alden's reply to that had been incontrovertible. 'Well, dear Lady Letcombe, knowing how matters stand at the Rectory, with a mother who has retired from the world and a father who was never in it, if she does not order affairs, who will?'

Lady Letcombe's answer had been a dismissive snort, and after it Lady Alden had determined to be kind to the poor thing, seeing that no one else would be.

Nan said slowly, 'I have really no opinion on the matter. I would have thought a lady more likely, but a sensitive gentleman might perhaps be able to talk so knowledgeably on matters usually discussed by the female sex.'

'Ah, Miss Fielding,' Brandon put in as he walked back from the sideboard with a large plateful of cold sliced ham. 'You think it possible for gentlemen to be sensitive, then?'

'Some men. . .' Nan was reflective '. . .seeing that men are more usually than women the poets and philosophers who make informed pronouncements on matters of the heart, although I believe that that may be because women are supposed to be quiet on such topics, whereas men are encouraged to speak their thoughts aloud.'

'Bravely spoken,' said Brandon as he prepared to demolish his breakfast. 'So, you are suggesting, Miss Fielding, that we must look suspiciously at everyone if we wish to determine who the author of *Sophia* is, not just the fair sex?'

Sam could almost feel Nan's agony as the discussion continued. She had already raised several eyebrows by her remark on the difference of what was expected from men and women. To bring matters to a close, he stood up and announced briskly, 'Well, seeing that Murray has chosen to break his silence, it is possible that we may all soon know the truth. Uninformed speculation is invariably useless.'

'True,' remarked Brandon, who was beginning to draw some astute conclusions about the possible relationship between Sam Stone and an author who was supposed to live in the district, although the real truth as to Nan's involvement was still far from his mind. 'And all we have at present is the knowledge that whoever it is knows more about our souls and the well-springs of our behaviour than is comfortable.'

He gave a mock-shiver, said something half under his breath to Jane, who laughed appreciatively at it, and the subject of the author of *Sophia* was temporarily abandoned.

Later, before he left for Broomhall, Sam spoke to Nan, who was sitting on the lawn in the shade of a stand of cedars, enjoying the unusual sensation of being completely idle, with no task awaiting her, and no shrill reminders from the rest of her family about what she ought to be doing for them.

'My letter is from Murray,' he began without pre-amble. 'He is trying to put pressure on me to give the author of *Sophia* away. I do not know how long I can hold him off. He requires an instant answer, a reassur-ance that I have done my best to persuade Sophia to reveal herself. He threatens to send his man here to talk to me, to put further pressure on me—and play Paul Pry around the neighbourhood, no doubt.'

Nan sat up, her beautiful peace disturbed. 'You will not give me away?'

'Indeed not. Although I fear that your secret may soon be no secret. You ought to consider what your course of conduct will be then.'

Nan sat bolt upright, all colour draining from her face. Brandon, engaged in a game of cat's cradle with Jane, was also surreptitiously watching Nan, and wondering what Sam Stone could be saying to her to affect her so.

She shook her head, recollected that she was doubtless being observed, and tried to smile before saying, stiff-lipped, 'I never thought that I should be so successful, although God knows I am glad of it, seeing how much money it has brought in.'

'And will bring more in,' Sam told her quietly, also trying to look as though their conversation was innocuous, 'after you are unmasked. Think of the uproar when Scott was discovered.'

Nan closed her eyes. 'Oh, but I do not want that, you know I don't. . .but what will be will be, I suppose. Papa would say that we are all in the hand of God, although I sometimes wonder how much God really cares about any of us.'

This was a strange remark from a parson's daughter, but Sam made no gloss on it. His own religious belief was shaky these days, and he frequently wished that he had Caleb Fielding's childlike belief in a benevolent deity. Looking round the world as it had been wagging for the last thirty years or so, with the emphasis on war, revolution, poverty and distress, Sam had strong doubts about that. But he never voiced them, and sat each Sunday in his family pew at Broomhall, enjoyed singing the familiar hymns—and wished that he still had the unquestioning faith of his youth.

'We have to follow the path laid out for us without complaint,' he told Nan gently, 'and you know that I would marry you as soon as I could acquire a special licence if only you would accept my proposal.'

Nan might have been tempted by this renewed offer if she had not met Brandon Tolliver. All that she could murmur was, 'You flatter me, but it would not do.' She did not say, Find someone nearer to your own age who will make you happy, not a woman young and flighty enough to hanker after the impossible dream of finding her true love who will sweep her off her feet and carry her into realms unknown to kind, prosaic Sam.

'I am not worthy of you,' she told him earnestly, and meant it.

In the end, because her talk with Sam had ended with his renewed pledges of help to her and her expressions of gratitude to him, the happiness of her day was not diminished. Even though Brandon never came near her, turning his attention on Jane again, Nan was aware that he was always conscious of her presence, as she was of his. It was as though some unseen chain stretched from him to her and back again, finer than gossamer, stronger than any spider's web, so that each knew without looking that the other was there, and both were communicating without speaking.

Nan knew without being told, in the same way that she knew the innermost thoughts of her characters about matters which she had never experienced, that Brandon desired her—and that she desired him. But only in the world of fancy, she told herself firmly, can we ever consummate our love. We are kept apart by barriers as fine and firm as the thin cord which unites us, and which, sooner or later, for my own peace of mind, I am bound to sever. He cannot be for me. I lost the right to have him for a husband long ago.

Because she had found Brandon, even if only to lose him, seated that evening in the big drawing-room, listening to Mozart, Haydn and Handel, beautifully played by the musicians from Leicester, Nan also discovered something in the music which she had never found before: an affirmation of the heights and depths to which the human spirit could rise and fall. That night she slept peacefully and dreamlessly as she had not slept since the day on which she had met Brandon in the pantry.

Renunciation might bring its pains, but it also brought its pleasures too, even if these were bittersweet and known to few.

'Damn,' said Brandon violently. 'Damn everything!'

He, who usually knew why he did and said everything, did not know why he was cursing. He only knew by her manner, by the expression on her face, by the very tone of her leave-taking, that he had lost Nan.

There was a new serenity about her, and he knew what it was. He almost knew the moment when she had withdrawn herself from him—when he had felt suddenly and shockingly alone, even though he had been fooling with Jane and the others at the time.

He had known by then that he could never marry Jane, and bitterly regretted that he had ever put her in the way of thinking that he might offer for her. What he had said and done with her before he met Nan had bound him, had kept him from being able to be honest with Nan—that, and the nature of their first encounters.

How could he have ever thought that he could spend the rest of his life tied to such a pretty little empty-headed charmer with no thought beyond her appearance and her immediate pleasure? He must have been mad. Yet he had arrived at Gillyflower Hall fully determined to offer for her as soon as possible.

Now he no longer wished to marry her, and the woman he did wish to marry had decided on renunciation. The calmness of Nan's gaze, the coolness of her voice as she had thanked him for her three happy days, the way in which she had spoken to Lydia, all told him that she was about to sacrifice herself again for the family which hung around her neck like a millstone.

Only when all his guests had gone on the following morning could he give vent to his feelings, raging and prowling around his study, cursing the misfortune that had made him meet the one sister before the other.

Finally he tried to acknowledge Byron's dictum and resume the public life whose demands made plain the differences between the lives of men and women. He rang for Carteret, his secretary, a middle-aged man with a weary, cynical face, and told him to send for Thorpe, the ex-Bow Street Runner who carried out his investigations for him, and whose discoveries had helped to keep him on his way to creating a large fortune which was founded on a secure base. Not for him the doubts which his rivals faced when they contemplated courses of action. Thorpe —and others like him—was there to discover and reveal to him the secrets which he was not supposed to know.

Thorpe arrived a week later. He entered Brandon's study with his usual strong air of being engaged in a conspiracy with someone or something. He refused the seat which Brandon offered him.

'I allus prefer to stand. Think better that way. Well, what is it this time?'

Such surly independence, a refusal to see him in any way as his master, usually amused Brandon. Today he was beyond being amused.

'More than one thing,' he said curtly. 'Several things. All of equal importance.'

Thorpe's heavy brows rose. 'Difficult, that,' he muttered. 'I likes some sort of order.'

'Well, I'm sorry.' Brandon's tone was untypically nasty. 'I usually like obliging those whom I pay heavily to carry out my orders, but today I can't.'

Or won't, thought Thorpe, who knew his man, and that behind Brandon Tolliver's airy charm lurked a quite different sort of man—stern and hard. But something was rattling him today. His usual control was missing. Thorpe's feral eyes gleamed. Nice to see m'lord not at ease for once. He wondered who and what was responsible.

Brandon saw the gleam, and damned himself internally at the same time that he changed his manner to his normal one.

'I think that someone is trying to kill me,' he began, bluntly for him, 'and I want you to find out who and why.' He briefly outlined the two attempts, the failed shot and the cut girth, Thorpe nodding as he spoke.

'Now, no one knows of the cut girth except the two grooms who discovered it. I mentioned the failed shot to a party of local gentry and they all dismissed it as some disgruntled Luddite trying to kill, maim or frighten a local landowner. . .'

'But you don't think so,' finished Thorpe. 'Especially after the second attempt. Anyone else want to do for you? Benefit by doing for you?'

'No, I don't think either try was accidental. As for those who might benefit. . .' He hesitated. 'I've a cousin who thought he was inheriting the whole of his and my cousin's estate until the day the will was read, when he found that I had inherited it. But. . .he's a poor thing. . . I can't quite see him. . .'

He hesitated again. 'On the other hand, look what he lost and I gained, and he knows that I was already richer by far than the value of the estate he lost. . . And then there's the possibility—a slim one, I admit—that it might be a failed business rival getting back at me. . .'

'So's you want me to look into it—and him—and Luddites—disgruntled grooms. . .and anythin' else.'

Brandon nodded. 'That's it. Now, I've another task for you—or tasks. I want you to find out everything you can about the affairs of Caleb Fielding and his family. He's the Rector of Broomhall, and when I say family I mean family. I paid the lawyer Stone to tell me all about the Fieldings and the rest of the local gentry before I settled here, but I'm not satisfied that he was completely frank with me, which is why I sent for you. And, connected with that, I want you to ferret out all you can about Stone himself.'

He paused. 'There's something odd going on involving the Fieldings and Stone, and I've a mind to know what it is.'

Some expression on Thorpe's face disturbed him.

'What is it, man? What have I said that has you looking at me as though I'm a shilling lacking a penny?'

Thorpe's mouth twitched. 'Only that one reason why I didn't mind taking on this job for you in this God-forsaken part of the world is because as how I've been hired to do another here, and I thought I could combine the two. What I didn't know was that the two jobs might be related.'

Brandon knew that Thorpe thought that all places outside London were God-forsaken, but the news that someone else was interested in Broomhall's affairs was something of a surprise.

'Could you be more specific?'

His tone was acid, deadly—the tone of a man who had made a fortune before he was thirty.

'Confidentiality is what I allus promise. . .but what you know might help me with the first job—kill two birds with one stone—and what I know might help you with yours. So. . .'

'So. . .?' echoed Brandon as Thorpe paused tantalisingly.

'So, my other man wants Stone investigated because Stone is involved with some man or woman who writes novels under an anonymous name, and my man wants to know who the writer is. Stone knows and won't tell. My man needs to know for financial reasons, he says. What do you know, Mr Brandon Tolliver, sir? About Stone. Or is it all gin and moonbeams with you?'

Brandon took no offence. Thorpe was doing him a favour by telling him of his other assignment. 'I suspect that Stone is involved with the writer. I also suspect that there *is* some kind of a mystery involving Stone and the Fieldings, but I've only my bones to tell me so. That's why I'm hiring you—to find out if my bones have begun to let me down. They have never done so before. I don't think that the attempts on my life have anything to do with Stone or the Fieldings—they are a separate issue. That's all.'

'And damned small that "all" is. It'll cost you, is all I can say.'

'Anything, so long as you are discreet.'

'I'll use Miller as well; proper yokel-seeming Miller can be—you remember him, I'm sure. Cost a bit to keep him drinking in the local, but you won't mind that. Get him some work in the parson's household, perhaps—or, better still, have him ferret around Stone. I'll put a word in for him as a groom, or a gardener. Gentry often need gardeners. At the worst, take him on yourself. He can complain about your high-handed goings-on and tempt other people to tell him what they wouldn't if they thought that he was loyal. . .'

'Anything,' Brandon said. 'Anything, but keep away from here unless I send for you. Arrange a pick-up for your reports with Carteret. Remember, I want answers to my questions as soon as possible. I have another strong feeling that a further attempt will be made on me, and I don't want it to succeed.'

'That you don't,' agreed Thorpe. 'You shouldn't be so bloody rich, sir. Annoys people. Not me,' he added.

'Carteret will see that you leave here without being seen—as you arrived here. Here's some guineas as a retainer.' And he passed over a small purse.

Later, when Lydia came into the study, he sat with his booted feet up on a small occasional table, a ledger thrown to one side. He was stifling a yawn, and looked the picture of indolent boredom, not at all like a man who had just paid a discredited Bow Street Runner to spy on all his neighbours and relations because someone was trying to kill him, and the others were hugging secrets which he felt that he ought to know.

He particularly wanted to know Miss Fielding's secrets. Being a man who had a few himself, he was always aware when others had them.

But for the life of him he couldn't imagine what they were, and for the first time when he had sent one of his agents on his way he wondered whether he was doing a wise thing. . .

CHAPTER TEN

'IT MIGHT be conjectured that if a handsome man of good birth and great fortune were to offer for a moderately good-looking young woman with a paltry dower she would accept his offer on the instant. No such thing: Nan's response to Brandon's proposal was to reject it outright. . .'

Oh, Satan, Belial, Beelzebub and Mephistopheles, she had done it again! She had written her own name and Brandon's instead of that of Louisa Gascoigne, her heroine, and Henry D'Eyncourt, her hero! Now she would have to rewrite the whole page, and this was the third time she had done such a thing since she had started work on her novel once the whole Rectory was safely in its bed and sleeping.

And Henry was not in the least like Brandon, being stern, upright, full of honour, and he would never, under any circumstances, kiss a servant girl in the pantry. Nor was Louisa like herself; she was a kinder, cleverer version of Jane. She must be going mad, and she had no time to go mad. Her fourth novel was about to be published, and she had promised, through Sam, that the next would not be long in following it.

So it was imperative that *Dearly Beloved*, as she had already named it, should be taking shape, not wandering about because her mind was on her own affairs and not those of her imaginary beings.

Come to think of it, would she refuse Brandon if he offered for her? She would be compelled to, would she not? There were, after all, very good reasons why she could never marry anyone, even if there had been occasions when she had thought that she might take Sam Stone's offer seriously.

The spoiled sheet of paper carefully torn up and

consigned to the waste-paper basket, Nan began again, making sure this time that it was Henry and Louisa whom she was fetching from the back of her mind, not Nan and Brandon. She must concentrate on the task before her, but for once the activities of her hero and heroine were less riveting than those of the men and women among whom she lived.

She and Jane and their father had been home for some days before her mother had referred to what Jane had told her of their visit to Gillyflower Hall. They had been in her mother's little drawing-room which opened off her bedchamber, and from which she could look down the village street and watch the passing show.

Nan had been reading to her from *Amelia's Secret*, which Jane had recommended to her mother, and which Nan, who knew it off by heart and was heartily sick of both Amelia and her secret, was doomed to go on reading until all three volumes had been disposed of. It had been late afternoon, almost time for dinner to be served, when Mrs Fielding had sighed, closed her eyes, lain back in her armchair, and announced, 'That will do, my dear. A most interesting tale, and you read it well. I think that I could manage a roll and a little soup now.'

Nan had put down her book and stood up. She had barely done so when her mother had opened her eyes again and said, 'Before you go downstairs, I think that there is something I ought to say to you. Pray sit down, my dear. I dislike it when you tower over me so.'

Nothing, thought Nan, that I ever do pleases my mother. I wonder what it is that I have done wrong this time?

She was soon to find out.

Mrs Fielding made herself comfortable again. She was still a handsome woman, and despite claiming constant ill health had a rosy complexion and glossy blonde hair. Jane greatly resembled her as she had been in youth, if the little miniature of her by Cosway was any guide. She had not left her upstairs rooms these eleven years or more. She rose daily from her bed to walk into her drawing-room, to gaze out of the window, and to admire the view, before saying, 'I don't think that I will venture downstairs today,' to whoever happened to be with her at the time.

She was quite happy to allow Nan to run the household and carry out all the parish duties of a parson's wife, including regular visits to the sick and poor, but she always made it quite plain that she would manage everything so much better than Nan did—if only her wretched health would allow her to do so.

'Jane has been telling me of your visit to Gillyflower Hall,' she began, 'and I was a trifle disturbed by what she told me. It seems that although you knew that she had formed a *tendre* for Mr Brandon Tolliver and he for her you constantly put yourself forward when with him, to a degree which occasioned gossip on more than one occasion. Wait. . .' she commanded as Nan, her fine control broken for once, opened her mouth to deny what her mother was saying.

'Pray allow me to finish, Anne. She also told me that it was common gossip that Desmond Tolliver had offered for you, and that Sam Stone was showing a distinct interest in your company—again to the point of unkind comment.

'Now, that is most unlike you, and I have no hesitation in asking you to resume your more usual modest conduct. You know that it is important that Jane should marry, and marry well. Mr Brandon Tolliver would make her a most suitable husband. You also know, without me telling you, that it is not possible for you to marry anyone. We agreed on that long ago. I hope I do not have to remind you again that it is your duty to undertake those duties from which I am debarred and never to put yourself forward in any way.'

She closed her eyes, then opened them again, to say, in the most patient and long-suffering voice which she could achieve, 'I do hope that I shall not have to remind you again, Anne, what your place in the world must be.' Without changing her tone, she added, 'Pray tell Cook to be sparing of the pepper when she prepares my soup for me; she rather overdid the seasoning on the last occasion on which she served it. You really must learn to control the servants a little more, otherwise they will always take advantage of you.'

This time, before she closed her eyes again, she waved Nan away, as though she too were one of the servants about whom she was complaining.

Remembering this conversation brought the tears to Nan's eyes again. To be reprimanded so harshly, yet so casually, between two peremptory orders about her mother's dinner, had almost been enough to overset her. She brushed the tears away with an impatient hand, picked up her quill pen again, and began to write about Henry and Louisa's love-affair as rapidly as she could, in order to try to forget her own stunted life. Her mother was...what she was, and nothing now would change her.

At Gillyflower Hall, Lydia Bligh, who had suffered from insomnia since her late husband's death, had walked to the windows of her bedroom from which she could see the back of the Rectory. She glanced at her little fob watch to check the time. Two-thirty on a fine night, with the stars out, and, yes, there was a light in the back bedroom of the Rectory again.

This small mystery had occupied her since the first time that she had noticed it—not long after she had arrived at Gillyflower Hall. Someone at the Rectory was frequently awake far into the night. For her own part she rarely lit a candle, preferring to lie in the dark after drinking a little water, and reciting to herself some passages from Pope, an author whom, though now out of fashion, she greatly admired.

So intrigued was Lydia by what she had seen that the next morning she idly asked her maid, Nellie Forde, whether she knew who it was who worked far into the night at the Rectory. The servants, she shrewdly thought, would be sure to know the answer. For some reason she did not think that it could be the Rector — his unworldliness did not lie in working beyond the midnight watches.

Sure enough, Nellie told her, as she was arranging her hair, 'They say in the Rectory kitchens that Miss Fielding works late at night, ma'am. They know because of the number of candles she uses. They think that she is making a fair copy of her father's book.'

Greatly daring, she added, 'Jackson, their butler and man of all work, thinks that she probably writes much of it for him. They know that he gives her the notes for his sermons and she finishes them off for him!'

Does she, indeed? was Lydia's inward thought. Poor thing, to work both day and night as she does to keep the Fieldings afloat. I wonder that her mother allows it. And then she thought of the impression which both the Fielding parents had made on her when she had visited the Rectory: that the Rector's unworldliness lay in letting his eldest daughter do much of his parish work for him, and his wife's pleasant and charming selfishness, her easy life, was also accomplished by exploiting that same daughter.

All the more reason, then, for Brandon not to exploit her, and so she told him that afternoon at dinner.

He was looking particularly well. He had spent the day in the open air with his agent, and had worked up, he said, a healthy appetite. He, at least, unlike Mrs Fielding, was not eager to complain about his victuals. 'Commend the cook about the roasting of the rib of beef,' he informed Lydia as he poured himself another glass of good red wine, 'and tell me whatever it is that you are bursting to impart.'

Lydia thought, not for the first time, how shrewd her brother was behind his charming mask. 'I was about to inform you of some news concerning Nan Fielding which ought to make you think twice before you exploit her in any way, seeing how much she is exploited already.' And she told him about the light in the bedroom and what Nellie Forde had discovered about Nan's midnight work.

'Writing into the small hours, copying out that damned pedantic rubbish for her father! When does unworldliness become rank selfishness, tell me that? And the mother. You have met her as I may not, she being permanently upstairs in her suite of rooms. What do you make of her?'

Lydia was a little guarded. 'Not very much. She looks well enough. The doctor goes twice a week, I understand, and is perfectly happy to allow her to live a sedentary life. If you asked me my honest opinion. . .'

'Oh——' Brandon was sardonic '—by all means tell me your honest opinion. I rarely have the good fortune to hear many of those from anyone!'

Lydia made no comment on this piece of cynicism. 'Well, then, Brandon, I think that nothing much can be amiss with her. She has been living after this strange fashion for eleven years, since her son was born, and so far as I can tell has not deteriorated in health since.'

Brandon threw his napkin down quite violently. 'And all on the back of one poor daughter, as I see it. Jane never appears to have any duties and I gather the two other sisters were chaperoned by Nan and made good marriages. They appear to have lived like ladies also, never raising a finger, or so one infers from what Jane says. It is quite intolerable.'

'But it is not our business, Brandon—except that you must not do anything to make her hard life harder.'

'No, indeed; nor may I do anything to make it easier.'

'The thing I wonder at,' pursued Lydia, 'is that she does not accept either of the offers which your cousin Desmond and Sam Stone have made to her. To marry either of them would relieve her from servitude, and both offers are from most suitable men.'

For some reason Brandon did not like to hear that Nan Fielding had received offers from most suitable men. Still less, he knew, did he wish to hear that she had accepted either of them. Oh, yes, he was being a real dog in the manger, was he not? He was making no offer to her himself, but was wishing that others might not!

He became aware that Lydia was waiting for an answer, and said, as casually as he could, 'You could do something to ease Nan's lot by inviting her over to Gillyflower Hall—to take tea, or to talk of those matters which women value but which men do not.'

Lydia nodded and said no more. Best to keep silent from now on about the Rectory affairs, since anything which she might wish to say to Brandon *vis-à-vis* Nan Fielding was sure to be taken ill, and she was not used to quarrelling with him. Their relationship had always been harmonious—a pity to spoil it by allowing the Rector's daughter to come between them.

For the next few weeks Lydia kept to this good resolution. She did not invite Nan over to the Hall, although Jane was in and out with Caroline and Charlotte, but she did send her a short letter telling her that Mrs Blagg and the baby were doing well, that Mrs Blagg was proving to be a good sempstress and had been taken on to the permanent staff at the Hall. She stifled her bad conscience over leaving Nan to her fate by telling herself that she was doing her a favour in not encouraging her relationship with Brandon.

As Brandon said nothing more of Nan, she began to hope that he had forgotten her, but she could not have made a graver mistake. He could not remove her from his memories, the principal one being the sight of her holding Mrs Blagg's baby with an expression of such tender joy on her face. His own serious pursuit of Jane had been halted by her relative indifference to the fate of both mother and child by contrast with Nan's compassion.

He was seated at breakfast one morning when Cartaret brought in the first letter from Thorpe. It was short and to the point. He had discovered nothing yet about 'the main business', as they had agreed to call the attacks on Brandon.

As for Mr Sam Stone, he deals only with local people. His main client, who sees him more often than any, is Miss Fielding from the Rectory—which I thought that you might like to know, being interested in their doings. By the by, the Rev earns very little from his writing, a cully of mine from London informs me, so the Fieldings' income does not come from that.

Thorpe added a PS.

As Mr S never sees anyone out of the way, if he is running the author of *Sophia*, then he, or she, must be someone local. He goes to Highborough once a week, but only to Paget's Bank, or to his Gentleman's Club, next to the Assembly Rooms.

Brandon tossed the letter to one side. It told him nothing that he did not already know...but something niggled even as he dismissed it...

He had already suspected that Parson Fielding's theological tomes sold poorly...but...if his only income was the miserly stipend from Broomhall Parish, and nothing came from his rich relatives, then how was it that the Fieldings lived so well, had a houseful of servants and were able to afford a London season to launch Jane on the world?

Something Lady Letcombe had said quite idly in his presence recently, when watching Jane and Caroline romp together, had, without his knowing it, stuck in his mind. 'I remember when the Fieldings first came to Broomhall they had hardly two halfpennies to rub together. It was quite distressing—so much more pleasing to us all to see them so comfortable these days.'

So what had made them comfortable?

Brandon picked up the letter and read it again.

'His main client, who sees him more often than any, is Miss Fielding from the Rectory...'

He began to attack the problem of the Fieldings with the remorseless cold-blooded logic, intermingled with intuition, which had made him a rich man even before he had inherited his cousin's property.

Item: the Fieldings are comfortable, who were poor.

Item: this is not through Caleb Fielding's writings, nor his stipend, nor through any income from his rich relatives.

Item: Sam Stone is almost certainly acting for the author of *Sophia*, who is a local personage.

Item: his most constant client is Nan Fielding. All Broomhall believes that this is so because she manages her father's business, mostly his profits from his theological writings—but as he has none this belief must be mistaken.

Item: Miss Nan Fielding is an uncommonly clever, well-read and observant young woman.

Item: Miss Nan Fielding works far into the night—as Lydia has discovered and as I have recently confirmed for myself—by spying on the Rectory through the kitchen window at Gillyflower Hall at three a.m.

Item: Miss Nan Fielding, therefore, must be the author of *Sophia*, is earning considerable sums of money, and is deceiving everyone, including the sophistical parson whose unworldliness is a cloak for his blind selfishness.

Item: Nan Fielding, therefore, is the prop and mainstay of the parsonage in every way—including the financial one.

Brandon stood up, cursing steadily. Could he conceivably be correct in his suppositions? Was he imagining things? Put it to the test, he informed himself coldly. Would you gamble good money on this supposition? And if the answer is yes, then it is likely that you are correct.

He had read and been entertained by *Sophia* and the author's other novels, but he had not examined them to look for clues as to their true author. Before he finally made up his mind he would read her latest to see if he could find echoes of Nan's voice in it.

Noise and conversation outside told him that Lydia was finally up. He strode over to the double doors, flung them open, and hurled at her as though she were one of his clerks, 'Lydia! Pray listen to me. You have a copy of that woman's latest novel, have you not?'

His sister stared at him. 'Do you mean the author of *Sophia*, Brandon? Of course; why do you ask?'

'Because I want to read the damned thing, that's why! And as soon as possible, too.'

All his usual careful charm was missing. What bee could possibly be buzzing in his bonnet that he wanted to read a novel at nine in the morning on a fine summer's day?

The sight of his sister's outraged and puzzled expression restored Brandon to his senses as she said coolly, 'You will find *Amelia's Secret* on the desk in the library. It is quite her best.'

Good humour suddenly restored, Brandon kissed her on the way to collect it. 'Blessings on you, my dear. You are always so charmingly helpful.'

What was even more surprising than his sudden desire to read a novel at such an hour was that he went through *Amelia's Secret* with the same speed and intensity which he usually brought to his financial papers. His brow furrowed, and giving the occasional snort of laughter, he did what he had never done before: read every word instead of dipping in and lightly browsing. He had spoken to Nan as though he had previously given to the author of *Sophia*'s novels the kind of attention which he was at present devoting to *Amelia's Secret*, but he had only been uttering a half-truth.

At the end of the morning he put the book down. He had already recognised several of the characters in it. Parson Fielding was there, gently mocked, and Jane, her sister. Oh, it was an idealised portrait of her, it was true, but Jane was the undoubted inspirer of the heroine, Amelia. And the older woman, her friend and adviser, the epitome of common sense, was Nan herself.

But Lancelot Beaumains, her hero, who the devil was

he? That handsome, upright, brave creature, once a soldier and now a landowner of liberal tendencies, caring for his tenants? No one like that frequented the fields, woods and drawing-rooms around Broomhall and Highborough, that was for sure.

But the country in the book was that which lay around them, and Bridgeford, the little town by the River Rill, was Highborough, near to the Soar, no doubt of that either.

He ate his luncheon savagely, hardly knowing what he put into his mouth. How was it that no one had seen what he had seen? But then, they had not been looking for it, as he had been. And Sophia's voice was Nan's, with an added acerbity which must be hers in secret, for the face which she showed the world was, if he was correct in his suppositions, not quite the true face of Nan Fielding. As, he acknowledged to himself, the face which he showed the world was not his true face—so who was he to criticise Nan?

No, he didn't wish to criticise her, he wished to admire her all the more for her gallantry, as well as her ability to write clearly and wittily.

He picked up his stick from the little cloakroom off the hall and set off to walk through the woods and ponder on the enigma which he thought that he had uncovered.

Unaware that Brandon had pierced to the heart of one of her mysteries, Nan was in the drawing-room patiently copying the Rector's latest chapter out in her finest hand, hoping that this time he would not suddenly determine to revise it again—for the fifth time—so that all her careful labour would go for naught.

Upstairs, in his study, her father was teaching Chaz. Jane was over at the Letcombes' and Kelsey was in the kitchens, superintending more jam-making, so the house was quiet for once.

Until a door banged and there was the noise of feet as Chaz thundered downstairs, his father, voice raised for once, shouting after him, 'Boy! Come back immediately.'

The drawing-room door was flung open and Chaz stood there, shaking, his face scarlet, his eyes full of tears.

'Oh, Nan, Nan, what am I to do? He never listens to me, never. I don't want to be a parson, but it is all that he can say to me—that I must be one. And today, because I construed everything correctly, and my Greek exercise was completed without a fault, he ranted on and on about what a great scholar I should make when I went up to Cambridge as he had done.'

Nan stood up, just as Chaz flung himself into her arms, saying, 'But why has that occasioned such a storm?' for she could hear her father walking agitatedly about overhead. He would not demean himself, she knew, by coming after Chaz, but would expect her to send him back upstairs again to be punished.

'Oh, Nan, you're the only one who ever listens to me,' Chaz wept into her chest. 'I told him that I had no intention of going to Cambridge, of being a parson, but that I wanted to be a soldier. I know that I find all book learning easy, but I would die if I stayed indoors all the time, and could not be in the open with the horses and the dogs. I would rather sign on as a humble trooper than be a curate—yes, I would. And he told me that he would thrash me daily if I ever said that I wanted to be a soldier again.'

Nan stood transfixed, hearing another boy saying similar things to her—that he too wanted to be a soldier, not to sit tamely at home waiting to inherit his father's estate, or waste his time going to university.

Were all boys the same? Did they all wish to wear a brave scarlet coat, regardless of the fact that war meant death and destruction more than it meant fine clothes and marching bands? Randal had died so soon after he had entered the Army, after his father had been persuaded to grant him his wish and buy him a commission.

'Papa could not afford to buy you into the Army,'

she told the sobbing boy, 'so it is foolish of you to provoke him for nothing.'

This prosaic piece of advice was unlikely to afford Chaz any comfort, or any hope that his future might change—but she was unable to offer him anything better. Time was making it painfully obvious that he was temperamentally unfitted to follow in Caleb Fielding's footsteps—yet what else could a poor young man with a good brain do but enter the Church and hope for preferment? Even if she earned enough money to buy Chaz a commission, her father would never allow it, and that was that.

He gradually stopped sobbing as she stroked his dark head. Finally he broke away from her, dashed his hand across his tear-stained face, and said slowly, 'I suppose you're right, Nan—you always are. I had better go upstairs to apologise to him.'

'Better so,' Nan told him gently, resisting the urge to kiss his soft cheek. He must learn, and learn soon, that men must put a brave face on things, that tears were for women, and that what couldn't be cured must be endured.

Which was exactly her own case, after all. To make matters even more difficult, Desmond chose to call and be admitted into the hall just as Chaz shot upstairs again, the marks of his distress plain on his face, his greeting to Desmond perfunctory, to say the least.

His comment to Nan on Chaz was typically critical. 'The sooner that boy is sent away to school, the better for him. He needs strong discipline, and your father is too kindly to see that he gets it, I fear.'

'Whereas you would,' Nan retorted, Chaz's hopeless misery still with her.

Desmond never heard criticism of himself. 'Indeed,' he said complacently, 'and one of the benefits of your marrying me would be that I could see that Chaz was set on the right course.'

This unfortunate remark did not improve his chances

with Nan at all. She wondered why he had come—to lecture them all, presumably.

But she did him a little injustice there. He had brought with him from his gardens a couple of baskets of early plums and several great bunches of flowers—surplus to his own requirements, he told her—somewhat ungraciously, she thought. He had the unhappy knack of making even his kind actions sound grudging.

Such generosity made Nan feel compelled to ask him to stay a little; in any case, he showed no sign of wanting to leave. She accordingly rang for the tea board—they had eaten a late luncheon, as had Desmond—and invited him to take supper with them later.

With the best will in the world Nan had no real wish to entertain him; she had far too much to do. Her father would expect the chapter to be rewritten before the morrow, which would mean that she would have to neglect Henry and Louisa, and she would much rather have been attending to them than to her father's clotted prose.

Chaz clattered by the window, proudly carrying his kite, on his way to the open country beyond the woods; small Jem, squat George and tall Roger were in attendance. Well, at least *he* was happy again, having placated his father.

Jane arrived with the tea board, Caroline Letcombe in tow, and they began to drink tea, eat Bosworth Jumbles, and drive Desmond slowly mad. He had been hoping for a few sober words with Nan, and hung on in the hope that Jane and Caroline might retire to Jane's room to giggle and laugh together about life, hairstyles and clothes.

Her afternoon's work was definitely lost. Nan resigned herself to that, and consented to listen to Desmond prose on about the coming trial of the Luddites who had wrecked Harvey's Mill at Highborough; he showed no pity for the poor wretches who had lost their livelihood to the new machines.

Not that Nan condoned machine-breaking, but she had only to think of the men's poor wives and little children to realise that, hard though her own life might be, it was as nothing to the sufferings of the very poor.

After that Desmond complained gently about the changes Brandon was making to Gillyflower Hall, changes which Nan privately thought long overdue, and had the advantage that extra work was being brought to the district, for all the changes meant that more hands would be needed, both temporarily and permanently. He droned on remorselessly until Nan was hard put to it to stifle a yawn. Constant working far into the night was beginning to take its toll.

Desmond had just begun what she hoped was his final peroration when Chaz, his face on fire, shot by the window, hallooing. She saw Jackson come from the kitchens, and one of the grooms from the mews. By their expressions something was up.

'Goodness,' yawned Jane. 'Whatever is the matter with Chaz *now*?'

But her indifference was soon to disappear when Chaz flung open the door for the second time that afternoon, exclaiming breathlessly, as Jackson and the others made for the woods, 'Only think, Nan! When we were on our way home we came upon Mr Tolliver in the woods. He was being attacked by some rough men who took to their heels when we arrived. We don't think that he is badly hurt, but Roger and George stayed with him while we came for help. . .'

Jane's response was to throw up her hands like a heroine in a play, and exclaim, 'Oh, how very dreadful!' in a die-away voice.

Nan's response was to do something totally unexpected and untoward, quite out of character. She turned as white as any sheet, as Chaz said later, and fell forward in a faint. Exasperation with life and Desmond, extreme exhaustion and the news that Brandon had been hurt all combined to overset her quite.

CHAPTER ELEVEN

'WHAT a pother about nothing,' Brandon said, but the voice in which he said it was faint, his colour was poor, and he sat half propped up on the big sofa in the Rectory's downstairs drawing-room.

Mr Hampton, the local doctor-cum-surgeon, had been sent for—he had assumed, when Chaz had come panting to his door with the news that he was wanted at the Rectory, that Mrs Fielding had had another of her mysterious turns which no care of his, or any nostrum he might prescribe, seemed to be able to cure, they came and went so erratically.

'Mr Brandon Tolliver attacked and hurt!' he had exclaimed when Chaz had finally gasped out the true nature of his errand. 'Luddites, no doubt! Whatever is the world coming to?' A question to which he required no answer since to his mind the world had been going to the dogs since the French Revolution of 1789, when he had first arrived in Broomhall.

'You are wrong, sir, quite wrong,' he told Brandon now, pushing him back against the cushions as he tried to rise. 'You have suffered a heavy beating, your left wrist is damaged, and it is a wonder that nothing has been broken. You will be one vast bruise tomorrow, I fear. Today you must remain here and rest, no going home until the morning, and then only if I give you permission. You were fortunate that your attackers were interrupted, or Mother Linley would have been laying you out in your coffin!'

'But she isn't,' grumbled Brandon, even though he was happy to lie down again, for his head showed a disturbing tendency to swim whenever he tried to do anything vigorous. A bruise was purpling his cheek and one of the blows had damaged the top of his left

shoulder, but his attackers had been disturbed before
they could do him any mortal harm.

He had consented to having his wrist bandaged and
to his arm being placed in a sling made from one of
Parson Fielding's black silk scarves. Desmond and the
Rector himself, who had deigned to come down from
his study, stood about looking concerned, and making
suitably sympathetic remarks. Kelsey, holding a bowl
of warm water, assisted the doctor in his ministrations,
and it was to her that the doctor gave orders as to how
the patient was to be treated. Nan, who would normally
have been taking charge of affairs, had been banished
from the room when she had recovered from her faint,
as had Jane, who, having seen Nan drop like a stone,
had decided to do the same herself.

'Much liquid, a low diet, and rest,' the doctor finally
ordered. 'Some port—but not too much, mind—will be
beneficial.'

'You cannot really mean that I am to remain here
until tomorrow,' Brandon protested, his voice strength-
ening as he began to recover a little from the shock of
the sudden attack on him, so near to the Rectory. 'I
cannot allow Mr Fielding's household to be so
burdened.'

'No burden at all, my dear fellow,' Caleb reassured
him. 'It is my Christian duty to play the Good
Samaritan. You may stay here as long as the doctor
deems necessary. Miss Fielding will prepare a room for
you.'

So what Brandon had privately feared would come
true was already doing so: any playing of the Good
Samaritan in practical terms would fall on the already
overburdened Nan—and where was she this afternoon?

He was enlightened a few moments later when
Parson Fielding asked the doctor to be good enough to
examine his daughters, who had retired to their rooms.

'They both fainted on hearing the dreadful news of
the attack upon Mr Tolliver, I am told.' He hesitated a
little, looking puzzled. 'I can understand Jane's fainting,

she is such a sensitive creature, but Nan, now, that is a surprise. She is usually of a much tougher fibre. It was, I gather, her collapse which precipitated Jane's.'

He frowned. 'I trust it is only a passing malaise. My wife has come to depend so much on Nan's good sense about the house—and she is busy copying out my latest work as well. I should be sorry if anything happened to render her unable to carry out her duties.'

Shaky though he felt, Brandon might have come out with something unforgivable as this piece of crass insensitivity was poured over his aching head, had not the door opened and the subject of her father's selfish fears entered.

Nan's pallor was pronounced, but when she spoke she was as composed as ever. 'So stupid of me to be so childish as to forget myself, and make myself unable to be of use,' she announced. 'I trust, Mr Tolliver, that you are not greatly hurt?'

She could hardly look at Brandon, she was so worried for him. She had sat in her room, in a stew of misery, twisting her hands together, and the moment her legs had become steady enough to take her downstairs she had made her way to the drawing-room.

'It was most fortunate,' Brandon told her, 'that your brother and his companions arrived just as the ruffians were about to finish me off. It is kind of you to ask, but should you be downstairs? You look as though you need the rest which the doctor has prescribed for me more than I do.'

It was as much as he dared to say before her father and his cousin Desmond. Desmond indeed, frowned heavily, and added as soon as Brandon had finished, 'Just what I was about to remark myself, cousin. Nan must not overtire herself. She has a heavy load to bear.'

Another selfish swine willing to see her exploited, and not to say or do anything to assist her, was Brandon's internal reaction to that. He could not help continuing, as though Desmond had not spoken, 'One reason why I should like to be conveyed home is that I do not want to add to Miss Fielding's burdens.'

'Oh, no burden, no burden at all,' Nan cried hastily. Nothing, no, nothing should deprive her of the most delightful burden of all—looking after Brandon Tolliver. The mere idea was so exciting that colour returned to her cheeks, her whole body vibrated, and she felt as though she could do anything, anything at all, if that anything had to do with *him*. Brandon saw the change in her, and registered again that Miss Nan Fielding, when roused beyond her usual state of passive endurance, looked twice as handsome as she normally did.

'You are sure?' he asked her gently.

'Oh, quite sure. Think nothing of it. It is my Christian duty to look after those in need of succour,' she explained, consciously echoing what her father had often said, in case anyone should think that there was more to her eagerness than was proper.

Brandon didn't think nothing of it—he knew the extra sacrifices she would be called upon to make—but said no more. He could almost feel Desmond's irritation at his speaking to Nan after so personal a fashion. He was not surprised when his cousin said, as though the idea had just occurred to him, 'If the burden is intolerable, and it worries you, cousin, then I will take the liberty of driving you home. I shall be most careful not to jolt or distress you in any way by driving too fast.'

But the doctor, who had just returned from examining Jane, who was lying in her bed looking interesting, and who had announced that she too might rise and, like Brandon, partake of a low diet only, was having none of this.

'By no means,' he said bluntly, 'and I would ask that Mr Tolliver be put to bed as soon as one is prepared for him. I shall call early tomorrow,' he added severely, 'and I want no loose talk of him being driven around the country before he is well enough to be moved again.'

Desmond gave way with an ill grace, while Brandon, anxious to be rid of him, placed a hand across his eyes and murmured in a low voice which immediately had Nan looking worried, 'If you are intent on being of assistance, cousin, you could perhaps go over to Gillyflower Hall and inform Jenkins, my valet, that I need nightwear and a change of clothes. I wish you may also inform my sister of what has happened to me, and that I am safe, if a trifle damaged. She will be growing worried by now, seeing that I should have returned from my walk some time ago.'

'And I will see that the constable is informed of the attack on you,' said Caleb Fielding, showing a little practical sense for once. 'Although I think that the miscreants may be long gone. Luddites and Jacobins, one suspects.'

Privately Brandon doubted any such thing. He had done nothing to either Luddites or Jacobins to provoke three attacks on his person, and he was beginning to harbour quite different suspicions. They could wait until he saw Thorpe again. He must ask Carteret to set up a meeting through the system of private post which he and Thorpe had arranged.

In the meantime he wanted to enjoy the delightful ministrations of Miss Nan Fielding, who was hovering about him, her fine eyes anxious, her father's book and her own novel alike forgotten. To be of use to the man whom she now knew that she had come to love—what could be better?

Only his knowledge of the extra duties which he was creating for her by his presence at the Rectory spoiled Brandon's pleasure in being the subject of Nan's care and attention. A room was prepared for him, and Jackson was called on to help him up to bed where he was promptly served his supper.

His cousin had grudgingly visited Gillyflower Hall

and had returned with Brandon's valet, who was found temporary quarters in one of the rooms above the mews—not exactly the kind of accommodation he was used to, but needs must, he told himself.

Nan watched with sad amusement as Jane invaded the drawing-room where Brandon lay on the sofa while his room was being made ready for him and offered to read to him. 'Something light, or something improving?' she prettily begged him.

He cried off, announced that his head would not allow him to concentrate on anything more serious than his next meal, and a comfortable long sleep after it, so Jane was unable to play her role as a ministering angel to the injured. Nan busied herself with organising the kitchen for two extra guests at supper—Desmond and his cousin—and spent some little time explaining to her mother what all the commotion downstairs had been about.

'How splendidly convenient!' Mrs Fielding announced, as though poor Brandon's attack had been kindly arranged by God to be of service to her family. 'Now that he will be here for a few days he will have time to get to know dear Jane better. Being with her daily, and seeing her in the bosom of her family, will surely convince him that he need look no further for a bride.

'I do trust, Nan, that you will make yourself scarce when they are together—let Kelsey act as chaperon. There can be no question that he might turn his attentions to *her*! In any case you will have quite enough to do in the way of extra duties without dancing attendance on him. Jane can perform any little errands about the house which he may require.'

Nan said nothing, being too busy wondering what these duties might be which Jane could perform, she being singularly unable to do anything other than beautify or entertain herself—neither of which talents could be seen as being of any real benefit to Brandon—other than that of pleasing his eye, that was.

All in all, by the time that she climbed the two flights of stairs to her room she was feeling that poor Henry and Louisa had grown very far-away and distant. The effort of reviving them both, and ending the scene which they had begun at such outs with each other that she could hardly imagine how she could ever make them be at ins again, seemed beyond her. All that she really wished to do was sleep.

Nevertheless, after she had undressed, not troubling to ring for the maid whom she shared with Jane, washed herself at the big wash-stand, had slipped into her sensible flannel nightgown with its large collar trimmed with a little cheap lace, undone her long tawny hair and brushed it until it shone and glowed, she felt refreshed enough to sit at her desk and begin to work again.

Unaware that in the distance at Gillyflower Hall an insomniac Lydia Bligh had registered that Miss Fielding must be at her work again, Nan wrote steadily along for some three quarters of an hour. She paused once, to laugh briefly as she thought up an amusing ploy which would have her hero and heroine incensed with one another just as it seemed that they were on the verge of reconciliation.

She also noted, a little drily, that in her mind's eye, on the stage on which he performed, Henry was growing to resemble Brandon Tolliver more and more. She was just reminding herself that she had given him blue eyes, not silver ones, when she heard a noise outside on the landing. She shook her head; she must be imagining things. The only other bedroom on the top floor besides her own was barely furnished and unoccupied: the servants slept either in the mews or in the atticks above Jane's bedroom.

There it was again—a sound as though someone had stumbled. Perhaps someone had entered the house for nefarious purposes, although why they should then mount to the top floor Nan could not imagine. She rose, picked up the candle by which she was working, crossed the room and carefully opened the door on to the corridor which led to the small landing at the turn of the stairs. . .

Brandon Tolliver slept almost immediately after he had eaten the light meal which Kelsey had taken up to him. After that his valet helped him out of his clothes and into his fine lawn nightshirt. He was more shaken than he cared to admit, although he also thought that the doctor's insistence that he should stay at the Rectory was rather nonsensical. He was not so overset that he would not have been able to manage the drive back to Gillyflower Hall.

On the other hand it was perhaps no bad thing for him to be made even more aware that Jane was not for him, and that Nan was even more exploited than he had imagined. Perhaps while he was here he could make up his mind what he ought to do about her, and his almost certain knowledge that she was the author of *Sophia*.

He fell into an uneasy sleep while thinking of her, and when he awoke in the small hours she was the first thing which came to his mind. The devil! What was wrong with him that he was mooning after a young woman past her first prayers—or for that matter any young woman at all? He would not have mooned after Jane if he had decided to marry her, that was for sure.

Now wide awake, and not likely to sleep, he lit his candle and looked about him for a book. Alas, all that was to be found in the way of reading matter was a copy of Parson Fielding's turgid masterpiece, and some aged numbers of *The Gentleman's Magazine*, hardly the most exciting reading even at the best of times, and this was most definitely not that. Not when all that occupied his errant fancy was the thought that Nan Fielding was sleeping directly overhead, with her hair down and all her clothes gone except for a nightgown. . .

Damnation! Simply to think about her was enough to rouse him—in God's name, he had not been as excitable as this about a woman since he had been a green boy! Perhaps it was simply the unorthodox manner in which he had met her—but no, there was more to it than that.

He tossed and turned. His shoulder and his wrist ached, his cheek throbbed. . .and somewhere else ached too, and was even more unassuagable than the rest of him.

The watch on his night-stand told him that it was two o'clock. Was she awake, writing, or had she finally blown out her candle?

Brandon sat up. Her room was above his. His room was opposite to the stairs which led to the upper floor. It would be the work of a moment for a man used to moving about without drawing attention to himself to mount the stairs and to check whether there was a light under her door. Why should he not do so? Risky, no doubt, but he had taken such risks before and got away with them—and he had nothing better to do with himself.

Between his varying aches and pains, further sleep was unlikely for the moment. Besides, the rest of the family slept in the far wing, the rooms on the floor he was occupying being dedicated to the Rector's study and a now unused nursery.

He crept cautiously out of his bed, picked up the candle, opened the bedroom door and began to mount the stairs. He reached the landing in time to see that, yes, there was a light under what must surely be Nan's door. A light, but no sound. It told him very little— other than to confirm that the light he had seen from Gillyflower Hall *did* come from her room as his sister had said.

Time to return—for how could he explain his wandering in the dark on the upper floor of the Rectory if anyone should discover him? Brandon turned towards the stairs. But his injuries had made him clumsy; he stumbled, recovered, and stumbled again, falling against the wall of Nan's room.

He swore to himself and stood still for a moment.

There was no sound of movement from her room and perhaps she had heard nothing, or, if she had, had discounted it. But he was wrong, for even as he was reassuring himself the door to Nan's room opened, and she stood there, her beautiful turquoise eyes huge, her tawny hair unbound, candle held high, staring at his guilty self as though he were Mephistopheles in person, come to tempt her. . .

For a long moment neither of them said anything. Brandon wondered for one glorious and impudent instant whether he ought to claim that he was delirious, and in his raging fever had wandered—he knew not where. He could stagger a little, fling his hand across his brow and moan at her, but no, he would not cheat her thus—and, what was more to the point, he didn't want her to react in such a way as to bring the servants along on the run. He shuddered at the inferences which might be drawn if they were discovered alone, in their nightwear. . .

'I could not sleep. I thought I heard something, feared a burglar, and came to inspect. I do apologise for disturbing you.'

Nan roused herself from the paralysis brought on by seeing a large and handsome gentleman clad only in his nightshirt. She was aware that his silver eyes were hard on her, mostly because of the charming spectacle she presented with her glowing hair hanging down to her delightfully rounded bottom. What would it be like, he mused, while she gathered her wits to answer him, if he stripped off her ugly gown, removed his own, and pulled her glorious tresses around them both. . .?

'As you see,' Nan finally managed, astonished by her own coolness, 'there is no one here but myself.' She paused, and said, a little naughtily, 'You were perhaps fevered, imagined what was not there. I think that you ought to return to your bed as soon as possible. You might take a chill, and that would never do.'

Her eyes were steady on him. Yes, he would pretend to be feeling weak, stagger a little, dammit. He wanted to enjoy the sight of her so informally clad for more than the few minutes she was offering him.

So Brandon did clutch his brow after all, muttering hoarsely, 'Yes, a fever. . .' adding something indistinct in the way of mumbling explanation, since invention told him that to be too specific about what might ail him would be unwise. He leaned forward against the wall, his candle wavering dangerously about as he did so.

'Oh. . .' Nan, prepared to dismiss Brandon briskly, found herself holding him up instead. Through the nightshirt she could feel his hard, warm body as, leaning against her, he could feel her soft curves. The excuse of not dropping his candle had him staggering backwards into her room to sink into an armchair, at the same time that he gave a surreptitious look about him. . .

Nan was too preoccupied to notice Brandon's deceitful goings-on. She took the candlestick from his unsteady hand and placed it beside hers on her desk, before going to the jug on the wash-stand to pour him a glass of water.

His drinking it with avidity was not all deceit, for Brandon found to his astonishment that he really did feel decidedly shaky. Small wonder, what with a battered torso, a damaged wrist and shoulder, wandering about a strange house in the small hours, and avidly desiring an accessible female with whom he was now alone.

Mixed with Nan's feelings that she really ought not to be tête-à-tête in her own bedroom with Mr Brandon Tolliver in the small hours was the very real temptation to her common sense that he presented. Half of her wanted him gone as soon as possible, but the other half, the half which no one but Nan knew that she possessed, wanted him to remain with her come what may. . . Like Brandon—and some of her characters—she was beginning to think in exclamation marks and little dots. The sane part of her, which was rapidly sinking beneath the waves of passion, told her that she was doing so in order not to think of what they stood in place of—the vision of herself in Brandon's arms.

'You are feeling a little better?' she ventured as she saw colour begin to return to his ashen cheeks.

He was not lying when he told her that he was. His recovery was enabling him to look over to her desk where he could see two small piles of paper, an inkstand and a quill pen. Nan, who was being as deceitful in her way as Brandon was in his, felt compelled to explain why she was still up and about in the middle of the night.

'I was copying Papa's book,' she told him earnestly. 'I had no time to work on it today, and time, you understand, is of the essence.'

Which was, she thought, about the biggest thundering lie she had ever come out with, seeing that the book and a half which her father had written had taken most of his fifty-five years to accomplish; indeed, the first one had only been finished at all because of Nan's devoted secretaryship. But the explanation would have to do.

Brandon did not believe a word of what she was saying. He was more than ever sure that it was the warm hand of the author of *Sophia* which was holding his slightly fevered brow. To her horror Nan found herself stroking him gently and to touch him was temptation indeed. In another effort to excuse her forward behaviour she said gently, taking the naughty hand away, 'You really ought to return to your room as soon as possible. You should not be out of bed.'

'Nor should I be in your room.' Brandon stirred himself at last. The temptation which Nan was presenting to him had become so great that what he wanted more than anything in the world was to hurl himself into a tub of cold water to stifle desire. If he remained much longer in her company he was in danger of falling on her and throwing her on to the bed. How could she be so damnably cool? That alone was enough to excite any normal red-blooded man.

Nan was not cool at all. She wanted him gone. The

devil was whispering in her ear, and Nan knew all about the devil and his works and did not want to encounter him, or them, again.

She watched Brandon rise reluctantly and make his way to the door. Before he left he turned to take one last look at her. The candle behind her on her little desk created an aureole of golden fire around her tawny head and body, adding to the enchantment of the night. For Nan the light it cast on him enhanced the strength of his face and the power of his body, barely concealed by his thin nightshirt. Her shiver was the result of passion, not of cold.

They stood staring at one another, until Brandon gave a muffled groan and, before she could stop him, strode towards her and caught her to him. He tipped her head back so that her hair fell like a shining waterfall down her back, his two hands cradling her skull. His mouth came down on hers with such magnetic force that Nan's shudder of desire in response to it consumed her whole body. She felt his hard arousal through his thin nightshirt—and felt her own knees weaken in an instant response to his urgency. She was on the verge of offering herself to him without reserve.

No, something shrieked inside her, no. He must have come here to seduce me, as he would have seduced the servant he took me for when we first met. I will not be his whore—for what would be the end of that but shame and misery in exchange for a few moments of passionate fulfilment?

With as much strength as she could muster she wrenched herself away from him, whispering fiercely, 'No, Brandon, no,' and lifted her swimming head to stare him full in the face.

His eyes, she saw, were blind. Desire had him in its thrall. So she repeated her refusal as loudly as she dared, fearful that she might wake the house, and if she did, what then? What then?

Still he resisted her, reaching for her mouth again, his hands beginning to roam her body, arousing sensation of such sweet delight in her that it took all Nan's moral as well as physical strength to place her hands on his chest and thrust him away from her.

Brandon blinked.

His eyes changed; he saw her again. Sanity returned. He said hoarsely, stepping away from her, his face full of passion shot with remorse, 'I'm sorry, Nan. Oh, I'm sorry; I shouldn't have done that, but the good God alone knows how much I was tempted. . .how much merely to see you undoes all my good resolutions.'

Nan shook her head at him, and said as coldly and severely as she could, for he was not for her, 'No, Brandon, you shouldn't. And as for temptation, you brought that on yourself when you came to my room uninvited. Recollect it is Jane to whom you have been paying your attentions.'

But he took no note of what she was saying. Jane meant nothing to him, and Nan meant—what?

Someone whom he should not violate. Someone whom he must respect. Someone with whom he must not be found in the dead of night.

Brandon took her hand, kissed it, and started down the stairs. On reaching his room he fell shuddering on the bed. He was not a man who had needed to practise much self-denial in life or in love. He had always taken what he wanted, when he wanted it. He had never forced a woman, or been wanton or cruel, only, as he was now coming to recognise, he had always been selfish in his attitude towards them. For the first time he was having to take heed of the needs of another in a wholly selfless fashion, and the experience was not only new, it was disturbing. He was sailing in an uncharted sea, without a chart or a pilot, and his destination was unknown to him.

CHAPTER TWELVE

'Now, Jane, leave the poor man alone, do,' commanded Kelsey briskly. 'He needs to rest and you are moithering him.'

Jane rattled the backgammon dice angrily, and pouted across at Brandon who was reclining on the sofa and had been playing a losing game against her, partly because his conscience, that new-born baby creature, had been troubling him over Nan, and would not let him concentrate.

'I am keeping him amused, not troubling him,' she riposted angrily, waiting for Brandon to support her, but he had only been playing the game to keep her happy, and to stop himself from thinking about her sister. He didn't know which hurt him the more, his head or his heart.

'He doesn't look particularly amused,' remarked Kelsey acidly. 'Have you no duties to follow? Nan might welcome a little help today. I know that she is troubled because she is falling behind in her copying of your papa's book.'

'Nan has gone out this morning. She said that she needed to visit Mr Stone's office, so she cannot be too exercised about falling behind!'

Kelsey's answer to this was to lift the backgammon cup from the table and remove it, so that the game came to an abrupt stop. Jane's intention to protest again was stifled when, after a knock on the door, the little maid came in to say, 'Mrs Bligh has called, Miss Jane, and has asked if she may be allowed to speak to her brother—if he feels sufficiently recovered, that is.'

Jane's petulance was immediately dispelled by Lydia's arrival. Mrs Bligh was reassured to discover that Brandon had not been as badly injured as she might have feared. She thanked Jane, Kelsey and the absent Nan for their care of him, and handed over fruit and flowers from the newly restored Gillyflower Hall hothouses.

Jane, who was finding that having Brandon at the Rectory was proving less satisfactory than she might have imagined, preened herself a little, and sent Kelsey into the kitchen with the flowers and fruit so that she might have Brandon and Lydia to herself.

For some reason of which she was not entirely sure, Brandon was slipping away from her. When he had first arrived at Broomhall she had been certain that a proposal from him was only a matter of time. But his extreme attentiveness had slowly leached away, had turned into polite indifference, and she was sure that, of all unlikely things, it was Nan who was interesting him rather than herself!

Now how could that be possible? She had boasted to Caroline and Charlotte that she would be Mrs Brandon Tolliver before the summer was out, and it was the loss of face which Brandon's defection would cause her which troubled her more than the loss of his love, or of hers for him. What was worse was that she had discouraged George Alden, who had more than once been on the point of proposing to her, because he seemed so much less exciting as a possible husband than Brandon did with his charm, his maturity, and the slight air of mystery which had caused George to remark disapprovingly to her that his father thought him 'not quite the gentleman' for all his old name.

Kelsey brought in the tea board during the mid-afternoon—a country habit, since it more commonly followed dinner in fashionable circles. Chaz had come in, and between large helpings of sandwiches and pound cake was quizzing Brandon about his life in London. The whole party had become uncommonly merry when the door opened and Nan arrived, looking rosy.

Jane was just handing Brandon his cup of tea when

he saw Nan come in. He looked up over it, and for a
moment he forgot everything except that she was back
with him. It hit him with the blinding force of a revelation that, whatever else, he loved her, would always
love her, and had never known before what true love
was. His whole expression changed before he recollected where he was—and that he was a man who never
gave his true feelings away if he could possibly help it.

Jane saw.

Nan saw.

Oh, not Jane's stricken face, but Brandon's, with its
momentary expression of revelation before it resumed
its usual cheerful impassivity. For a brief moment her
own face reflected his.

Jane saw Nan's face too.

In that moment Jane grew up. Jealousy roared
through her. She knew at once that she had lost
Brandon, that he would never now propose to her. She
did not even want him to. She would die rather than
have a man who preferred her plain elder sister to her
own beautiful self. But if she was not to have him she
would make sure that Nan never would. How she did
not know. But she would. . .she would. . .do anything
. . .anything. . .to thwart the treacherous lovers.

A few moments before she would have pouted, been
petulant, shown her anger with the pair of them, even
if they were not aware of why she was showing it. But
her new maturity told her to bide her time, to pretend
that nothing had happened while she waited for her
revenge.

She was, indeed, very lively, very much the girl who
would do anything—yes, anything—to ease Brandon's
malaise and to help Nan. She even offered to go to the
kitchen to order extra tea when Lady Alden and George
arrived. Lord Alden was over at the Assizes and sent his
compliments and best wishes to Mr Tolliver, and the
hope that he would soon recover. As Jane bounced
busily out of the room on her unaccustomed errand Nan

wondered whatever could be the matter with her usually idle sister!

But she had no time to worry about that or anything else; the necessary work of the house engaged her. Later the Aldens were offered supper, which they declined—much to Brandon's relief; he was beginning to feel tired. She left Jane to play the gracious hostess, and once the arrangements for supper were in train, and she had discovered that her mother was willing to let Kelsey read to her for once, she retreated to her room to think over not Brandon and her love for him— that would have to wait—but what Sam had told her when she had seen him earlier.

'Murray is determined to have you unmasked,' he had said, bluntly for him. 'He sees more profit in that than in carrying on the excitement about your anonymity. That is beginning to die down, he says.'

'My unmasking would die down too,' Nan offered robustly. 'Particularly when it became plain to him and everyone else that a dull clergyman's daughter is the author of *Sophia*.'

'I suspect he is willing to take that risk. Besides, you may be sure that he will think up some other ploy to keep your public entertained.

'But it is not only that of which I wish to speak. You must take care, my dear. This attack upon Mr Tolliver may signal that none of us is safe. I have become aware that not one man but two is roaming the neighbourhood of Broomhall, enquiring not only who the author of *Sophia* might be, but also wanting details about your own family and Mr Tolliver's cousin, Desmond. I cannot think what else they can conceivably hope to discover.

'Anyway, one man has been discreet, the other clumsy. The clumsy one offered my clerk, Knowles, money. He knows nothing, and therefore was able to tell the man nothing, and handed him his guinea back. Even had he known he would have said nothing, he tells me.'

'Asking around the neighbourhood about our family as well,' echoed Nan thoughtfully. She seized on this point because it was the one which troubled her even more than any questions about her novel-writing. Please God, the past would remain safely dead! She shuddered.

Sam saw the shudder and misread it. He thought it was her authorship which troubled her, and said tentatively, 'Would it be so very terrible for you if the truth were known, my dear? It would free you from the burden of work you carry and would surely not distress your father overmuch.'

'Oh, you do not know him,' sighed Nan wearily. 'He has such a sense of honour. . .' She could not use the true phrase to describe her father's character, because had she done so she would have said 'sense of self-importance', and that would never have done. She could not confess to Sam that she had long ago judged her father and mother with the clear eye which she wished that she did not possess, but which made her such a powerful writer. So she concluded, 'It would trouble him greatly.'

Sam shrugged at that and said, 'You know best, my dear,' in a doubtful voice and did not pursue the matter further. . .

She heard the visitors leave, heard Jane come upstairs and go to her mother's room, and wondered a little that Jane had not chosen to remain with Brandon. On her way downstairs she met Kelsey in the hall carrying a silver salver with a glass of port on it.

'Your papa left word before he rode to the Letcombes' to dine with them this afternoon that I was to see that Mr Tolliver was kept supplied with this.' And she indicated the port. 'Would you help me by seeing that he gets it? Cook is in a fantod about supper. Jane has said that she cannot endure the thought of salmon this evening, and salmon is all she has! I need to smooth her down.'

The last thing which Nan wanted after her stressful

afternoon was to have anything to do with the equally stress-inducing Mr Brandon Tolliver, but since Kelsey often tried to make Nan's hard life a little easy she felt she must try to help Kelsey whenever she could.

She found Brandon not reclining on the sofa but seated in the big armchair which faced the window and the back garden with its lawns and shrubbery. He seemed withdrawn and a little pale, but rose at her entrance. She carried the salver over to a small occasional table standing by his chair, and made to withdraw without speaking. Since the sure and certain knowledge that she both loved and desired him had struck her down last night, she wished to have as little as possible to do with him. Safer so.

It was not to be. He put out his hand and caught her by the wrist.

'Why are you avoiding me?'

His voice was as hard and blunt as though he were speaking to a recalcitrant clerk. He was showing her the face of the man of power which he truly was and which, so far, Highborough and its neighbourhood had never seen. He could hardly have looked or sounded less lover-like but, like Nan, in order to try to fight off desire he needed to control himself, and the effort of doing so was having its effect on him as well as on her.

Nan stood quite still. She looked away from him, for to look at him, feeling as she did for him, was more than she could bear.

'You know perfectly well why I am avoiding you. And now please release my hand. I have work to do.'

He gave a violent exclamation and tightened his grip. 'Damn your work, Nan. Look at me! No, do not turn away; I won't have it; look at me. Look me in the eye and say that again; I dare you.'

Nan looked him in the eye as he commanded, then dropped her own, and repeated in as colourless a voice as she could summon up, 'You know perfectly well why I am avoiding you.'

His face hardened still further; his grip grew almost cruel.

'No, I do not.' He was doing his damnedest, he knew, to make her confess her true feelings for him. He knew also that he was being cruel, but he could not help himself.

It was Nan's turn to look stern, to say, 'You must know, Brandon, that when you met my sister Jane you were so particular in your addresses to her that everyone assumed that at some stage in the near future an offer for her hand would shortly follow; you cannot pretend otherwise.

'Not only did she tell me so, but your sister, as well as all Jane's friends and acquaintances around Highborough, thought the same. Until she met you it seemed inevitable that she would marry her childhood playmate George Alden—a most suitable match.'

Brandon slackened his grip on her hand and said, his voice stifled, 'I had not met you then. I was not to know that——'

Nan interrupted him. 'To know what, Brandon? That you were so flighty in your attitude towards the female sex that you could be off with the one and on with the other, when you had allowed the whole of the county to assume that you were dead set on marrying Jane? For you were, were you not?'

'I can be accused of many things, but flighty is not one of them,' was his stiff response to that. 'And I made Jane no offer, no offer at all. . .'

'And that is no matter either. If you were not flighty, then you must admit that you behaved unscrupulously towards a young girl with little experience of life, and your withdrawal after being so particular will be as badly seen as though you had jilted her. You know as well as I do what that will involve for her future prospects. You see, I don't think you understand how different country morals and standards are from those of the town, of London. You were so conspicuous in your attentions to her that you might just as well have proposed.'

He was still holding her hand.

'Every word you say is a dart which pierces me to the core. Would you really have me propose to a female I do not love, when the one whom I prefer to her is standing before me?'

She must be brave. He must understand that even if he did not propose to Jane she could not allow herself to have anything further to do with the man who had been so treacherous towards her sister. If only they could have met before he had so much as seen Jane. . . But no, even that would not have done. She could not marry him; she could not marry anyone.

'I think that you did not love Jane when you made yourself so particular to her, nor when you thought of proposing to her, as I am sure you once did. But in any case it is for you to decide what you intend to do. . .'

So far, Nan thought, he has said no direct word of marriage to me, although he has said much of admiration, of preference—and of desire. Is it simply lust he feels for me, and I for him? If so I *must* refuse to have anything more to do with him, for it will not last.

Brandon lifted the hand which he held and kissed it tenderly. 'Nan. . .' he began.

The door burst open and there was Jane, staring at them, at Brandon holding Nan's hand, which he gently released at the sight of her sister, his sentence left unfinished.

'Oh, there you are, Nan. Kelsey was asking if Brandon had finished his port. I see that he has not.'

The prosaic words, flung into the storm of passion which, despite the coolness of their speech, had been consuming Nan and Brandon, had the effect of quenching it. Brandon sighed, snatched up his glass of port and drank it in one giant swallow before replacing the glass on the salver. Nan picked up the salver and moved away to leave Brandon alone with Jane, the last person on earth with whom he wished to be tête-à-tête.

No need to worry, though. Jane was almost as cool towards him as her sister had been. Looking at her, at her charming unspoilt beauty, her little air of command, he could understand why he had been so attracted to her when they had first met, but oh, how he wished that it had been Nan whom he had met at Sampford Lacy and then he would not be caught up in this damned confounded tangle.

He tried to be pleasant to her, ate his supper at table—the first meal at the Rectory which he had not taken as an invalid—and announced firmly that come what may he would return to Gillyflower Hall in the morning, for among the letters and papers which had been brought over to him earlier were some which demanded his instant attendance in London.

He did not also tell his kind hosts that among them was a report from his spy, Thorpe, concerning the Fielding family which had made him begin to think most furiously. Thorpe had written:

> I have to inform you that Parson Fielding and his family left their previous living in Hampshire rather abruptly around the time of his son's birth. As I understand them, the circumstances were vague, and I would prefer not to confide the details of the matter to paper. I will report to you on your return to Gillyflower Hall.

Now, what the devil could that be all about? Brandon wondered. Was Thorpe manufacturing mysteries to justify his pay, or had he uncovered another secret? Useless to speculate; he would know more on the morrow, or the day after. Meantime he must go carefully. It had been his intention to challenge Nan over the question of her authorship, but living at the Rectory and seeing how vulnerable she was had changed his mind over that.

Whatever else, he must not hurt her more than he had already done—or Jane either. Who in the world would ever have guessed that, having seen and been

mildly attracted by the younger sister's youthful and
heedless charm, he would then fall headlong for her
elder sister's character and gallantry? And, yes, for
Nan's mature beauty, which was not of the common
kind, enchanting when first seen, but was more like a
difficult strain of music, which after a time, once mastered, was more attractive than the melody easily
understood at the first hearing.

He shook his head again, astonished at his thoughts.
He had never been an introspective man, but knowing
Nan was beginning to change him, for she challenged
all that he knew, or thought that he knew, about
women. And he was beginning to understand that she
was hedged about by secrets. One of them, he was sure,
concerned her mother, the woman who was so seldom
seen, the woman who lived in her suite of rooms
upstairs, and whom few had ever seen or spoken to.

Lydia had been graciously allowed to visit her once,
and had told him that she was well-informed, spoke
trenchantly about the affairs of the day, and of the books
she had read. He wondered whether Nan resembled her
at all, and what had led to her life of retreat—which
depended on Nan's utter selflessness. . . All thoughts led
to Nan these days—and that was another new thing for
him.

Both he and Nan went to bed that night not to sleep,
but to think about the other. 'Star-crossed lovers',
Shakespeare had called Romeo and Juliet, and each
thought ruefully that his description applied to them
both.

'Well, one of the Rectory's secrets is on the verge of
being revealed,' Thorpe told his employer two days
later as they sat in Brandon's study at Gillyflower Hall.

'You are about to inform me,' Brandon could not
resist saying, 'that you have discovered that Miss
Fielding, the Rector's eldest daughter, is the author of
Sophia.'

Thorpe, who had accepted the chair which Brandon

had offered him, and a large helping of good sherry, raised his glass to him in mock-salute and offered Brandon his congratulations. 'No need to have employed me. You have teased it out for yourself—while you were over at the Rectory, I dare say.'

'Before that.' Brandon was brief. 'Being more with the lady simply confirmed my suspicions.'

'And those of others.' Thorpe was equable. 'There was another spy in the neighbourhood—Murray's, the publisher's man, no doubt. He has been making his enquiries, and I don't think that Miss Fielding's secret will remain one much longer. I bribed the clerk at Paget's Bank in Highborough, who told me that Sam Stone personally pays into Parson Fielding's account the bank drafts which come from Murray. I don't doubt but that he took a guinea or two from Murray's man as well.'

'No secret can be kept forever,' was Brandon's comment to that, 'however careful one is. Which leads me to your other enquiries—I am not so forward in discovering the answer to those, I do confess.'

He was amused by the wryly cynical expression on Thorpe's face. 'Oh, no,' his man said simply. 'I am sure that you know the answer to one of them. Your cousin, Mr Desmond Tolliver, is certainly, as I believe that you suspected, behind the rather clumsy attempts on you, including the last one.'

Thorpe looked at Brandon's bandaged left wrist. 'I understand that Master Charles Fielding and his friends came upon his latest nasty effort. I have found the villain whom he hired, wormed Master Desmond's involvement out of him when he was getting drunk upon his hirer's payment, and frightened him away from undertaking any further villainy by pretending that I am still the Bow Street Runner which I once was. He gave me the name of another rogue who was his accomplice. What do you want me to do? Put the frighteners on Master Desmond? Or do you want to do that yourself?'

'God knows what I want! I want this not to have happened. Think of the scandal if it were revealed! And it would rebound on me, as you well know. I am the stranger, the interloper—"Not quite the gentleman",' he added, mimicking Lord Alden's measured and stately tones. 'If I had not existed,' he went on, 'then Desmond would have inherited and all would have been well. As it is. . .' He shrugged.

Raised eyebrows told him that Thorpe was waiting for him to finish. He went on, 'As it is I want you to watch him, act as *agent provocateur* even. I believe that you did that when you were with the Runners. Keep me informed of all that passes. He might prefer to hire a more subtle villain like yourself, rather than the incompetent simpletons he has been lumbered with so far.'

A nod told him of Thorpe's agreement. 'And then you deal with him—as you have dealt with others.'

Brandon nodded. 'Draw his teeth, quietly, when I have the evidence of his villainy. I want no man hanged on my account, and, damn him, he is my cousin.'

'True. Now, as to the other matter to do with the Fieldings. They came here from Hampshire, from Frensham Major, a small town with a richer living than this one—which you will allow was a strange move for a poor man. . .

'The parson's patron there was one Sir Frankfort Scott. Scott's eldest son, Randal, and your Miss Fielding were childhood playmates. When she reached sixteen Sir F gave orders that the friendship was to end: they had turned into sweethearts. He intended his son to marry wealth, a rich heiress, not a penniless parson's daughter. The son, Randal, was desperate to be a soldier, and as a reward for giving up the girl his father bought him a commission in the Army. He was sent to the West Indies, and died there, of the yellow fever.

'At the same time Mrs Fielding was with child with Master Charles, and Miss Fielding suffered a long illness after Randal Scott left to be a soldier. The doctor ordered the two women into the country, for their health, it was said. Miss Kelsey looked after the parson, and the other three girls, while he threw up his living and came north to this one, found for him by his cousin Sir Charlton, as soon as his missis had given birth to Master Charles and was fit to travel.

'Mrs Fielding became an invalid permanently when she reached Broomhall, saying that bearing Master Charles had ruined her health. Miss Fielding, by now recovered, and being the oldest of the children, took over the burden of looking after the family with Miss Kelsey's help.

'So you see, first Miss Fielding lost her sweetheart, and then became the family drudge, by all accounts.' He stopped.

'And that's it?'

'All that I could discover, yes. The only odd thing is, as I said earlier, that of Parson Fielding giving up his good living for a poor one, but I gather Sir F went a trifle mad when he realised that his son and the parson's daughter were serious, like. Social living between the big house and the parsonage a bit difficult after that, one supposes.'

'Hmm.' Brandon rested his chin on his hands and thought of poor Nan, sweetheart lost, her mother withdrawn, devoting herself to a life of sacrifice—and all from the age of seventeen. Somehow something seemed to be missing from the story.

But it did account for her attitude to him, and to men in general, if for nothing else. He remembered the middle-aged autocrat Carrington Beaumains, Lancelot Beaumains' father, in her novel *Amelia's Secret*, who had tried to ruin poor Amelia's life for her. No doubt who *he* was modelled on, if Thorpe's story was true. Which, of course, it was.

He pulled open a drawer in his desk, took out a purse full of guineas, and tossed it over to Thorpe, who took it without counting it.

'More of that,' Brandon told him, 'when we have

settled my cousin Desmond's hash for him without the whole neighbourhood being thrown into an unseemly pother. The less pother, the more guineas for you, you understand?'

'Understood.' Thorpe rose. 'You don't want me to pursue the Fielding business any further?'

'Nothing further to discover.' No need to tell Thorpe that he was off to London for a time, would visit Frensham while he was at it, and try to find out anything he could. He had a merchant friend who knew the Scotts: Sir Frankfort had been a successful plunger in the stock market, and he was sure he could think up some useful excuse for visiting him.

He was not sure why he was going to such lengths, but in his business dealings it had been his usual habit to quarter his ground like a general before battle, and it had always paid off. Social life was no different, and the vultures hovered above its unsuccessful participants as well as the gods bearing wreaths for those who succeeded.

Brandon had every intention of succeeding, in love as well as in business life. It was for that reason that the next day, while his valet finished the packing of his bags, and while his post-chaise was being readied for him, he sat at his desk composing a letter which he had never thought he would write. He had, indeed, delayed writing it until the morning, for in a way he was surrendering the independent life which he had lived since he was sixteen. But he had slept badly and the reason, he knew, was that he wished that he had written the letter earlier, or had made the effort to offer for Nan in person.

It was, of course, to Miss Nan Fielding, and it contained not only a proposal of marriage, but a declaration of love from a man who had always laughed at the notion that love existed. He had expected to find the writing of it difficult, but as he began he discovered that the words flowed from him in a steady stream of passionate expectancy. It was as though he had found harbour at last, and having done so he was freed from all the constraints which he had bound around himself from the day he had been sent out into the world to make his way in it. He wrote:

> My dearest Nan,
> You will forgive me, I know, for writing to you when you have not given me permission to do so, but I must inform you that I have found in you the woman whom I never hoped to meet, the woman to whom I could give not only my love, but my unbounded respect and admiration. My respect is for the selfless manner in which you look after your family, and my admiration is for the cheerfulness with which you have performed, and continue to perform, your unending duties.
> This being so, I humbly ask you to consent to marry me, as soon as the ceremony may be arranged after I have approached your father and asked him for your hand in proper form. Do not fear that our marriage will leave your family financially unprotected. It will be my duty, as well as my pleasure, to care for them and ensure that they are not financially harmed.
> Whatever your decision is, I shall respect it, as I love and respect you, but I can only hope that it will go in my favour. I have loved you from the moment that you fell into my arms in the Rectory's pantry, and I hope that you will allow me to finish in marriage what we began then.

So far Brandon had written in the careful script which he used in his business letters, but now he finished in an impassioned scrawl.

> Oh, my darling, my dearest love, do say yes, and make both of us as happy as I know we can be. Your loving and humble servant, Brandon Tolliver.

He sanded the paper, folded it, sealed it with the seal which he had inherited from his cousin Bart, and carefully wrote Nan's name on the front. He rang for Leeson, his most trusted servant, and told him to deliver it to Miss Fielding at the Rectory. 'I ask you most particularly,' he said, 'to make sure that if you are unable to deliver it into her hands, then you will give it either to Miss Kelsey, the housekeeper, or to Jackson, the Fielding's man of all work.'

Leeson assured him that he would, and set off on his errand. All Brandon's servants were particularly eager to see that his orders were promptly and punctually carried out, for they found him a hard but fair master, who rewarded well those who served him well.

Brandon, on his way to his chaise, watched him go. Surely Nan could not refuse such an offer, made from the heart as it was? He would live in hope until he returned from London. It was annoying that his presence was required there at this juncture, but he had learned to live with expectation, and he thought that Nan would find it difficult to refuse someone with whom she was so obviously passionately taken.

Leeson walked briskly to the Rectory, to discover that Miss Fielding was not in. She was making parish calls to the poor, Jackson said, in company with Miss Kelsey, for whom Leeson asked when told that Miss Fielding was not available. But Mr Tolliver had told him to give the letter to Jackson, failing anyone else, and so he did.

The letter was duly placed on the silver salver which reposed on a small side-table in the Rectory's entrance hall for Miss Fielding to pick up when she returned from her errand of mercy. It rested there for the best part of an hour until Jane reached home after a ride with Caroline Letcombe. She recognised Brandon's hand and stared at the name of the addressee. Jealousy rode on her shoulders. Jackson saw her pick it up and remarked, 'Mr Tolliver's man Leeson left that for Miss Fielding.'

'Oh, indeed.' Jane waved the letter in the air. Whatever could Brandon be writing to Nan about? She made for the stairs, throwing at Jackson over her shoulder, 'I will put it in my sister's room for her to read when she returns.'

Jackson thought nothing of that, if he thought at all. The Fieldings were given to such small and helpful acts, particularly Miss Fielding. It was perhaps a blessing that Miss Jane was being a little more thoughtful than she had been of late.

Jane's thoughtfulness actually took her into Nan's room. She was about to place the letter on Nan's desk when jealousy and curiosity both overcame her.

Why ever should Brandon be writing to Nan? What could he have to say to her that was so urgent that he should send a letter to her on the day that he left for London? The small hesitancy which had the letter hovering in Jane's hand over Nan's desk stretched on and on. . .

And, almost as though her hands belonged to someone else, Jane found them opening Nan's letter, carefully preserving the seal so that she might refasten it—to read it feverishly, listening for any sound from downstairs which might herald her sister's return.

He was proposing to Nan! She was his darling! His dearest love! Oh, the devil, how dared he? It was she, Jane, to whom he had been '*most* particular'! And then the villain had transferred his attentions to Nan! And what had he been doing in the Rectory pantry with Nan—and when? At the very thought of Nan in Brandon's arms, Jane's hands—without her consciously willing them to—crumpled the letter, breaking the seal into pieces, so that she would be unable to reseal it.

She stared down in horror at the crumpled paper— and the full enormity of what she had done struck home, so that she stood trembling. She would not now be able to give Nan the letter without letting her know that she had opened it and read it. . .

Even as she thought this the devil prompted Jane. Why should she not keep the letter? Why give it to Nan at all? Brandon did not deserve her; he didn't deserve anyone—and nor did Nan if she had been pursuing an intrigue with him behind everyone's back. If Brandon received no answer he would assume that Nan had turned his offer down. Besides, wasn't it likely that Nan would turn the offer down? He obviously half thought that she would—and what could he mean by all the work that Nan was doing to keep the family going? The maunderings of someone besotted, no doubt.

All the time that she was thinking these distressing and unpleasant thoughts Jane had been walking out of Nan's room, along the landing, down the stairs—the letter pushed into her hanging pocket—and up the other stairs to her own room, where she took the letter out of her pocket and pushed it out of sight to the back of the drawer in her little dressing-table, beneath a small pile of pocket handkerchiefs. She could neither bring herself to destroy the letter nor to hand it back to Nan with an apology for having opened it.

Putting it into the drawer made it almost as though it had never been delivered. She would pretend that it had not, and, doing this, she tried to persuade herself that she had not meant to injure Nan when she had intercepted and opened it. She heartily wished that she had never seen it.

But the damage had been done.

CHAPTER THIRTEEN

UNAWARE that Brandon had sent her a love letter proposing marriage, Nan returned from her afternoon of charity, to learn from her mother, who had watched Brandon's small procession make its way through Broomhall, that he had left for London—'or so Jane says'.

Left for London! Unexpectedly Nan found that to think of Brandon not being near by at Gillyflower Hall carried more than a hint of desolation. Which was stupid, she reproached herself. She had lived for nearly twenty-eight years without Brandon, and must most probably resign herself to living many more without him.

The long littlenesses of Rectory life surrounded her. Jane, for some reason, was being uncommonly irritable. She snapped at Nan when Nan asked after George Alden who had visited Letcombe's Landing while Jane was there. Jane's irritability grew worse as the evening wore on, for the sense of guilt which she felt over Nan's letter grew stronger, rather than weaker, with time. Always before, when Jane had done something naughty, she had been able to shrug it off, but this time the enormity of her sin began to overwhelm her as the days passed by.

She could hardly bear to speak to Nan, repeatedly snapped at her, and was even cross with her devoted admirer George Alden, who sadly put it down to the absence of that cad Brandon Tolliver. Jane herself could hardly bear to think about Brandon—she was beginning to wonder why she had thought him attractive at all if he had been able to make her do anything so wicked as steal his letter to Nan.

Of the three most involved, Nan was, for the

moment, the only happy one. Jane was living in a hell of her own making, and Brandon was wild to return to Broomhall to discover what answer Nan had sent to his letter. He was as conscientious as ever in his dealings with the Rothschild brothers whose letters to him had drawn him back to London. He and they were satisfied with one another, and his business with them was completed much sooner than he had expected, so that he made his way to the Fieldings' old home in Hampshire two days earlier than he had hoped.

Frensham Major was a small and pretty town, visibly rich, which made Parson Fielding's translation to the poorer living at Broomhall even more mysterious. Sir Frankfort had expressed his willingness to entertain Mr Tolliver at his home, and had even asked him to stay for several nights if he so wished.

He was, Brandon discovered with some amusement, a pompous man, exactly like Carrington Beaumains in Nan's novel. He had obviously been handsome in youth, and had worn quite well, although he was now heavy; his wife was another matter altogether. She was a duke's daughter, and proud of it, and Brandon had no doubt, after taking dinner with them on a late and sunny afternoon, that she was the one who had resisted Nan as a possible bride for her oldest son.

He met the heir, Hervey Scott, who resembled his mother in being large and blond, unlike his father who was large and dark. He was sluggish, too, and Brandon found it difficult to believe that he resembled poor dead Randal, his elder brother and Nan's lost love. Nan could never have loved such a stolid lump as Hervey Scott was.

'Broomhall?' drawled Lady Scott at dinner, over a delicious rack of lamb—she kept a good table, which accounted for the family's size. 'Isn't that where the Fieldings went, Frankfort, my love?'

She knew perfectly well that it was, was Brandon's sardonic reaction, but he allowed Sir Frankfort to confirm his wife's belief before Brandon remarked that the Fieldings were still at Broomhall.

'And the eldest daughter, Nan? Is she still unmarried?' Lady Scott asked. 'She and my poor dead Randal had a tiresome romance, a rather ridiculous *tendre*, you understand. The girl was a perfect hoyden. Not at all suitable to be a wife for a Scott, as I think Randal realised before he went to the wars. We should never have let him have his way and become a soldier.'

She raised a handkerchief to tearless eyes, rather because she was expected to than because she was genuinely moved. Hervey stolidly ate his dinner. He could hardly be expected to mourn his brother's death, seeing that he had inherited as a result of it. Brandon deplored the cynicism which the Scotts were inducing in him, and he could only be grateful that Nan had been spared marriage into such a tasteless *galère*.

But a hoyden when she was young? Yes, he could believe that of the woman who had fallen into his arms in the pantry and whom he had found up a tree, rescuing her brother's kite. Lively young Nan Fielding still existed beneath the armour of propriety which she wore as the Reverend Caleb Fielding's eldest and responsible daughter.

It was difficult to know how to answer her. He decided to be bland. 'Oh, no, Miss Fielding has not married, although two of her younger sisters have already made good matches, and the youngest, Jane, is expected to do so.'

'Too clever for most men, one supposes,' offered Sir Frankfort, in a remark which was slightly vicious, or rather shrewd, whichever way you wanted to take it. Both, probably, was Brandon's somewhat uncharitable thought, seeing that Sir Frankfort's keen eye for a bargain or a deal was causing him to double the considerable fortune which his father had left him.

Later Brandon drank tea in a magnificent drawing-room filled with Chippendale chairs, a sideboard by Hepplewhite, and some superb china set out on shelves around walls hung with a marbled paper of great beauty and equally great expense. His eye was caught by a small portrait of a tall dark young man wearing hunting clothes and carrying a sporting gun. Behind him was a groom flying a kite.

Lady Scott saw the direction in which he was looking. 'My poor son Randal. One of Thomas Phillips' better efforts. Worth a second look, I always think.'

Indeed it was, was Brandon's reaction, but perhaps not for the reason which Lady Scott assumed.

'You will allow?' he asked, and walked over to inspect the portrait more closely.

Lady Scott chattered on behind him, but Brandon ignored her, parts of the puzzle which the Fieldings presented falling slowly into place as he carefully examined Randal Scott's boyishly handsome face.

'I hear that Mrs Fielding is now an invalid,' Lady Scott volunteered to his back. 'I understand that she has been so since before the birth of her last child and only son. Charles, is he not? She had to go deep into the country away from the bustle of the town when she became enceinte with Charles.'

'Yes.' Brandon sat down at last. There was a rather strange look on his face, and his dislike of the self-satisfied company he was in grew with each moment. The poor Fieldings, to have found themselves involved with such a graceless and selfish crew! Sir Frankfort was particularly appalling, because Brandon's own clear-sighted self-assessment informed him that were he to continue living a life in which he only cared for himself, his pleasures and making money he would probably end up like him.

Politeness kept him anchored in Frensham for two nights. Before he left he promised to pay Sir Frankfort and Lady Scott's respects to the Fieldings—'they were, after all, of good family, if a trifle eccentric', was Lady Scott's epitaph on them. He thought grimly that if Lady Scott knew the whole truth about the Fieldings, which he now thought that he did, she might feel constrained to reach a different verdict.

All in all he was happy to be on his way back to Gillyflower Hall, and Nan, again. Visiting Frensham had had the effect of making him love her more than ever—and had also filled him with a fierce desire not only to get into bed with her, but to shelter her from the world's despite.

Nan was too busy trying to cope with her family to spare Brandon much thought. Only at night when she was alone did she permit herself the luxury of remembering her times alone with him.

It was bad enough that her father had revised the last two chapters of his book again, that her mother was having a fit of the restless megrims which made her send for Nan every hour or so, usually on some imaginary pretext connected with her health, but as a kind of rancid icing on a singularly dry cake Jane was driving everyone mad by her temper, her tantrums, and her frequent unexplained fits of sobbing.

Questioned by Nan and by Kelsey as to what was wrong with her and should the doctor be sent for, she threw them off, exclaiming pettishly, 'I have a fit of the megrims these days; my head hurts and my nose is sore!'

'That is because of all the crying you have been doing,' remarked Kelsey bluntly. 'Really, child, you have been making the most unseemly fuss over Chaz's not being as respectful to you as you think he ought to be.'

This was because her latest crying fit had been caused by a quarrel with Chaz which had ended with him informing her what a poor thing she was compared with Nan. 'Now, *she* knows how to talk to a fellow, and you don't. You've never once helped me to fly my kite.'

For some reason—oh, but she *did* know what the reason was—these days the mere mention of Nan's name was enough to send Jane into a fit. It reminded her too much of Brandon's letter, which, although it lay physically upstairs in her dressing-table drawer, also lay heavily on her conscience, and she could find no way of ridding herself of her unwanted burden. She felt like the unfortunate man in the fairy-tale who was doomed to carry a heavy load with him everywhere he went, and who saw no prospect of ever being rid of it.

Nan said, exasperated, 'I thought that you had arranged to visit the Letcombes today, Jane. For goodness' sake, go upstairs, ready yourself, and tell Jackson to bring the carriage round for you. You will feel better after a good gossip with Caroline.'

Such kindness from the sister whom she had betrayed was almost the last straw. Jane's eyes filled with tears. For a moment she almost gave way, told Nan what she had done, gave her the letter and begged forgiveness.

And then she thought of Kelsey's reproaches, of what Nan would think of her—and Brandon...and she allowed herself to be persuaded to visit the Letcombes, to try for a little time to forget the pains and penalties which followed sin and plagued the sinner. Nan watched her carriage go down the drive, her face puzzled—for her sister's behaviour was most uncharacteristic. Then she shook her head, and forgot Jane's megrims while she performed the endless and busy tasks of her day.

Late in the afternoon Kelsey came in and told her that Brandon had returned from London. He would be present, or so his man had said, at Sam Stone's soirée the following evening, when half of Broomhall and district—or rather the gentry portion of it—would turn up for the ladies to take tea and coffee and eat cake, and the men to drink his good port in his splendid gardens. The news had Nan singing under her breath as she helped Kelsey to make jam of the first of the summer's plums.

I shall see him tomorrow, she thought, and talk to him, and that alone will be bliss—like playing gold harps in heaven and singing with the archangels! A flight of fancy which had her laughing at herself.

Brandon was not so happy.

There was no letter from Nan waiting for him. He had made straight for his study and the small pile of correspondence put on one side for his return, sure that her letter would be there. But no. She had not answered him.

Oh, but she had! By her silence, she meant refusal. He swore nervously to himself, his brow black. By God, he would neither repine nor surrender! He would carry the attack to her. She should not so lightly escape him. He knew that she loved him. It was written on her face and on every line of her body when they met, so what nonsense, what piece of piff-paff, what quirk of imaginary morality, could be keeping her from him?

He would convert her! No missionary to a savage island would be as sincere as he would be in his campaign to make Anne Fielding his wife. He would not have her devoting her life to her selfish family. No, indeed, she must devote it to selfish Brandon Tolliver instead!

Like Nan he laughed at himself a little. He would not descend on her immediately—that would be boorish—but he would be seeing her at Sam Stone's. He would find a secluded part of Sam's splendid gardens, and he would begin his campaign there. And if he could not make Sam Stone's soirée Nan Fielding's Waterloo, then he would find a better site where he would bring her to surrender at last.

Just as though he were one of the Scots Greys going to that last great battle, Brandon dressed himself as splendidly as he could. The day was hot, so he wore a light short jacket, a cravat which was not too confining, but whose understated and well-bred elegance was yet another tribute to his valet. His hair was brushed into a modified Brutus cut, and he would have been blind not to be aware that he was a man who would always attract a second glance. Not only his clothes but his height, his shapely body, honed to muscular perfection by the hard work of his early youth, were always sure to draw admiration. The Tollivers had been famous for their looks, and he was no exception.

Nor was his cousin Desmond, even if his clothing was of a more sombre cast. He was the first man Brandon greeted when he made his way through the glass doors of Sam's drawing-room into the gardens, a glass of port in his hand. He was looking for Nan, but seeing Desmond was always a bonus. By Thorpe's latest report, read that morning, his agent had almost drawn Desmond into the snare where Brandon could confront him with his villainy and—if he was lucky—draw his teeth.

But today he was joviality itself to his cousin, even if his eyes quartered Sam's garden for a sight of Nan.

And there she was!

Oh, damn the clothes she was wearing! He would see, when they were married, that she was dressed to show off the perfect body, the creamy complexion, the great turquoise eyes and the splendid tawny hair. Mrs Tolliver would be the envy of all, and no mistake!

Today she was the envy of no one, but Brandon did not love or desire her the less. She was the pearl of great price, hidden away from the multitude, if not in the gutter, then in the drab drawing-room of a thankless father. He would pick up the pearl, polish it, and put it in a perfect setting, so that all should envy him. . .

Why, he thought in wonder, I am like to run mad, I want her so, and I want the world to see what a treasure they have passed over.

Who would have thought it? Lydia, watching him, suppressed a sigh, for she read him truly, and hoped that the brother whom she loved would find haven with a woman whom he loved and who loved him.

'Miss Fielding,' he said, and bowed to her punctiliously. Jane was by her side, but he did not see her. He saw only Nan in her drab dark grey gown with its

Quaker-like white linen collar and its three-quarter-length sleeves. He wanted to tear it off, not only to make joyful love to her, but to replace it with something more suitable.

Before the others they made small talk. Not only Lydia, however, was aware of how much of a blind that was. Poor suffering Jane, and Sam Stone, also watched and endured. Lydia saw Sam's eyes on the lovers, and, moved by the anguish she saw there, felt constrained to say something to him to relieve it.

'They are meant for each other,' she told him gently, and though she uttered neither name he knew of whom she spoke. 'She will soften him, and he will make sure that she does not constantly sacrifice herself for others—if he persuades her to marry him, that is.'

Sam said, through stiff lips, 'I want her to be happy, whomsoever she chooses. And your brother is nearer to her in age than I am.'

Lydia nodded, put her gloved hand on his arm, and murmured, 'Come, let us leave them together. It is easy, I know, to say what can't be cured must be endured, but it is a motto of whose truth I have painfully come to be aware.'

They moved away. Sam gave up his dream of a life with Nan, but, almost without knowing it, another life was opening up before him as he escorted Lydia Bligh to a table where a light summer punch stood. Serving Lydia with a cup of it, he began, for the first time, to forget Nan a little.

Brandon could not forget Nan, nor Nan Brandon. With a light touch on her arm he led her away from the rest of the company, down a long alleyway to a corner of the garden where a stone Cupid stood behind a bed of roses. For a moment Jane made to follow them, but, seeing George with a group of friends, gave up the notion and instead joined them, and tried not to worry over whether Nan and Brandon would discover, either at once, or later, that Brandon's letter had gone astray.

Without knowing it, luck was with her. Near to his

love, Brandon could see that there was almost a transparent look about her. For the first time she betrayed a fragility which troubled him, and which was owing, he knew, to the double life she was living. Working both during the day and the night was taking its toll of her. Whatever he said, he must not distress her.

Nan felt that she must say something, and that something must be innocuous. 'You are back earlier than you expected, I believe?' There! Surely that was banal enough for anything?

Apparently so. His silver eyes glinted. He said, gravely, 'Indeed. For once the Rothschilds moved quickly—I am usually a little too impatient for them, but this time their impatience matched mine. We agreed, and the business was done.'

'That is a whole world of which I know nothing,' Nan told him.

'As I know little or nothing about being a member of a parson's family,' was his riposte to that.

'That is little enough to know,' Nan sighed back at him.

Just to be with him was enough. He had taken her hand in his, and was swinging it gently as Randal had done when they were children. But she was not a child now, and nor was Brandon. He was very much a man. Even at the end, before he had left for the last time, Randal had still been a youth, with his man's strength yet to come.

'You have made your choice, then,' Brandon said, his eyes hard on her now, 'and it is to stay with your family. You will not regret what you have done, or reconsider?'

Nan found this a little ambiguous. She concluded that he meant the choice she had made when she had agreed to act as the family's mother and guardian, once her mother had retired from life. So she answered him with a little sigh. 'A hard choice, I know. But what is left to me? One's duty has to be done, and a parson's daughter is the person most likely not only to know that truth but to obey it.'

Brandon would have preferred there to be a little regret in her voice, some acknowledgement of what they must both be suffering as a result of her decision to refuse his offer. Not answering him had apparently been her way of refusing him. Was it a kinder way? He thought not.

Having her so near, and being alone with her, was causing him to forget all the good resolutions he had made to go slowly with her, not to disturb her, or attack her with his love.

'Nan!' he exclaimed hoarsely, taking her by the shoulders and swinging her around to face him. 'I beg you to reconsider, Nan, I love you, worship you. You can have little doubt of that now.'

Holding her was compounding his distress. He bent down, kissed her on her tender mouth, murmuring, 'To see you is enough to make me want to break each of the ten commandments. Slowly, one by one. Surely, as a parson's daughter, you will relieve me of that temptation? You already know that I am willing to offer you everything which is mine. My name, my fortune—and, dare I say it to you, my body. Think carefully, my darling, before you refuse me.'

His kisses grew stronger, his hands more urgent. Nan replied in kind, her senses swooning to the degree that she saw nothing odd in what Brandon was saying to her—for when had he made her such promises before? Only—and she did not know this—in the letter which she had not received.

For a second they were 'The world forgetting, by the world forgot,' but even as their passion mounted the consciousness that they might be disturbed at any moment moved them both. Both stood back together, the warning bell of prudence having sounded for them both at the same moment. In this, as in everything else, they lived and thought as one.

'No!' The word exploded from both of them.

Nan said, almost shyly, hanging her head, as she stepped back from his embrace, 'You told me that I must know how deeply you feel for me, Brandon. Now how should I know that, seeing that so far we have said much of mutual attraction, of desire even, but nothing more than that?'

Even in the throes of thwarted passion, for Brandon's body had responded as strongly to having Nan in his arms as a virile man's might have been expected to, he had enough rationality left in him to understand the true sense of what she was saying.

She was telling him quite plainly that he had given her no indication that his feelings for her were more than those of passing desire, of lust. But he had written to her much more than that, had he not? Oh, but he had; he had bared his inmost soul to her in his letter, had he not? And asked her to marry him. Something which he had never done before. And she had rejected it, and him, had she not?

But had she? The look she gave him was limpid, filled with truth. Nan would not flirt or palter with him. If she had read his letter she could have no doubt of his love, or his intentions.

Like a trapped animal trying to escape from the pit into which it had fallen Brandon's mind twisted and turned as he contemplated this unexpected puzzle.

What if?

What if?

What if she had not received his letter?

Was that possible?

He had given Leeson the letter to deliver and he had said that he had handed it to Jackson—so she must have received it.

But, by every word she had uttered, she had not.

So it had gone astray. She had never received his proposal, the letter which he had written with so much love, and, much though he now longed to propose to her again on the instant, he could not do so until the mystery of the letter had been solved. He wanted nothing to mar his offer when at last he made it, solemnly and in proper form. To rant about lost letters would be desecration. More, he did not wish to propose here in Sam Stone's garden where they might be interrupted at any moment.

Thought was rapid but, even so, Brandon's silence lasted longer than he supposed. Her eyes suddenly filling with tears, Nan assumed that perhaps, after all, he had been toying with her.

'You would wish to return to the others,' she ventured, not wanting to look at the stone Cupid, the little god of love who seemed to have been playing games with her.

'Not quite yet,' he said, his voice hoarse again, with desire, mixed with anger, for he thought that he knew who might have been playing tricks with Nan's letter. 'Not before I have told you how much I love and honour you. So much so that I will not treat with you here. What lies between us must be, and shall be, done in proper form. I shall not assail you again, and here is my word on it.' And he went down on one knee before her, taking her work-worn little hand in his to kiss it reverently.

'Bear with me for a time, my love. Trust me and all shall be well.'

'No, Brandon,' she told him. 'Wait. I cannot be for you.'

'No,' he said, in his turn. 'Make no decisions now, my love. When the time comes you will, I know, accept me. Think only that I love and honour you. Hold that to you in the dark watches of your long nights. For the moment let us return to the others.'

Nan was silent. There was something compelling about him, almost as though he was willing events to go in the way in which Brandon Tolliver wished them to go—had ordered that they go. For once she would be will-less, she decided, and she walked away from the stone Cupid, down the glorious flower-bordered alley. Never in her life had she felt as she did now, Brandon by her side: that every nerve in her body thrilled at his presence, as though he were a master musician, plucking at his violin.

Of all those present there were three who had noticed their absence, and watched them return. They were Jane, Desmond Tolliver and Sam. Although he had surrendered all hope of making Nan his wife, Sam still felt that it was his duty to care for and to protect her since no one else would. He needed to speak to her, and when Brandon had departed to take Desmond to one side and talk lightly with him as though he had no idea that it was his cousin behind the murderous assaults on him Sam made his way to her.

Like Brandon he thought that she looked frail, and like Brandon knew the true reason why. He handed her a glass of lemonade and offered her a plate of his cook's best biscuits before he said, 'You must bear with me for what I have to say, Nan. Murray's spy has discovered your identity. He has written to me and asked me to so inform you. He intends to make the news public any day now, and you must be ready for the excitement it will inevitably cause. There is nothing more that I can do to protect you. And, you know, we were always aware that in the end discovery was inevitable.'

Nan nodded, feeling numb. It was simply one more blow to fall on her hapless head.

She had turned so white on hearing this unwanted news that Sam put his hand out to steady her. 'Come, my dear, sit down, I beg of you.' He led her away from the crowd into a seat by a gap in a small hedge which separated them from the big lawn, where the majority of his guests were gathered.

Once there he began to speak again, to try to reassure her. 'One good thing about your identity being revealed is that you will not need to work at dead of night, and I shall persuade your father that your burden must be lightened. There is no reason why Jane should not spend some of her time copying your father's book.

I am fearful that carrying out all your many other duties on top of your writing will result in your falling into a decline.'

Nan smiled shakily. 'You are kind to say so, Sam. But I am sturdier than that. Allow me to sit and think a little of what I must say and do when everyone learns that I am the author of *Sophia*. I must confess that were it not for the money which has helped to make all our lives easier I would wish that I had never started writing, never sent *Sophia* to Mr Murray.'

Sam hesitated. There was something else which he needed to say to her. Yes, he would say it.

'My dear,' he began, as gently as he could, 'I am of the opinion that we have not deceived everyone.' He paused, and in that pause Nan spoke, her breathing growing a little rapid.

'Why, Sam, why do you think that? And who could have guessed?'

'Perhaps I should not have said anything, my dear, but you are intelligent enough to be aware that in such a profession as mine one picks up hints and clues not only from what people say, or don't say, but from the very manner in which they say it.

'Last week Mr Brandon Tolliver came to see me. He was speaking generally of parish matters...of your father—of whom, by the way, he is not an admirer. Something he said stuck in my mind. He indicated that your father did not deserve your devotion to him and the parish, which was, he hinted, in addition to all the other work which you did and which helped to sustain your family's style of living. He told me that he was worried about your health, and sought my assurance that I would try to influence your father to lighten at least that part of your labours—of which he knew.

'There was something strange, a little guarded in his manner. Looking back, I am sure that somehow he knows that you are the author of *Sophia*. He has said nothing to you on that score?'

Nan felt as though she had taken a hard blow in the

stomach. She faltered, 'O—only of how much he admires her writing. He has repeatedly told me that. . .' And she stopped. 'I fear you may be right. But he has said nothing to me—nothing direct, that is.'

Could it be true? Had Brandon somehow guessed? Had he even used his formidable wealth to hire a spy of his own to check what he thought to be true? And should she be distressed if he had? Was that why he so constantly spoke to her of her many labours? Had he guessed that night when he had come to her room? And had he come to find out whether his supposition was true, as well as to take the opportunity to make love to her? And what did his knowledge, and his silence about it, tell her of him, and of the love which he now said that he had for her?

These were puzzles more important and more serious than any puzzle which she had invented for her novels.

Memory gave her the final clue which told her that, yes, he did know. He had spoken to her so often of all that she did for her family, and almost his last words to her had been to tell her of his love, and he had added, 'Hold that to you in the dark watches of your long nights.' Yes, he knew. And delicacy—yes, she was sure now that it was delicacy—had prevented him from saying anything to her—even if it had not been very delicate of him to pry into her secret life!

Another person to exercise delicacy was Sam. He saw the changing expression on Nan's face, and guessed that she wished to be alone. 'I have not troubled you?' he asked.

'No,' was her reply. 'On the contrary.'

Sam left her shortly after that, leaving her seated well away from the hubbub of the rest of the party—to which she could see Brandon contributing in his usual cheerful manner, and she thought once again how much more complex a man he was than his social behaviour would lead anyone to understand.

But she was not to remain alone for long. Desmond came through the gap in the hedge by which she sat and said a trifle reproachfully, 'Why do you insist on hiding yourself away this evening? First you disappear altogether, and then you tie yourself up with that dry stick old enough to be your grandfather.'

'Oh, come.' Nan's laughter was genuine. 'Even to call Sam my father would be an exaggeration, Desmond. And I wish to be alone; I feel a trifle weary tonight.'

'No wonder, with your family sticking to you like leeches, leaving you so little time for yourself.'

Well, at least he had noticed that, as Brandon had done, even if his language was a trifle coarser than his cousin's. He continued, 'I suppose it is useless for me to renew my offer to you, so I will not make it. But I must continue to warn you about my cousin. . .'

Nan shook her head at him, but he still grumbled on for a few moments before beginning again on his disapproval of Jane, ending with, 'She is flightier than ever tonight. I cannot think what has got into her.'

'Only her youth, I suspect.'

Nan was not being entirely truthful. She thought that there was something almost feverish in Jane's manner, something unnatural in the way in which she had been avoiding and cutting Brandon, who until this week had been the one person on whom her undivided attention had been centred.

'I wish that *he* had never come here, and not just because he inherited everything instead of me. Since he arrived everyone seems to have taken leave of their senses. It is Brandon this and Brandon that, until I am sick of the sound of his name. Nothing seems to be able to be done without him. . .'

'Perhaps because he is so able,' returned Nan equably, punning a little.

'He does not need you to champion him when he has everyone else,' barked Desmond.

'Not quite everyone,' Nan remarked quietly. 'As you know, he has been the subject of some nasty attacks. He was sorely hurt that time when he was on the way to the Rectory.'

She seemed to have said something right at last, for Desmond nodded and said stiffly, 'Ah, well, Nan, envy is present everywhere in these benighted times. I thought that things might reform when the war ended, but no, Jack is determined to believe that he is as good as his master, and often desires to kill his master in order to prove his point. Poor Brandon has undoubtedly been the target of Luddites. I always said that they should have hanged more than Cullen for framebreaking and attempted murder. Cullen's associates were dealt with too lightly.'

Nan said nothing. Visiting the poor—and even prosperous Broomhall had its share of them—she daily saw the misery of those families where the wage-earner had lost his work because of the introduction of the new machines, and consequently she could not so lightly dismiss the sufferings of others.

She also thought that Brandon, who was not a textile manufacturer, unlike Linley whom Cullen had shot, was a strange target for Luddites, and said so.

'You are wrong there, my dear.' Desmond's voice was insufferably patronising. 'They see us all as enemies and my cousin is so rich that he is bound to have roused a great deal of hatred among Radicals and dissidents. He is too easy, as well, and therefore they think that he must be an easy target. He should be more careful of himself.'

Nan shuddered and turned the conversation into other, more cheerful avenues. She could hear Jane's feverish laughter as the group of which she was a part walked towards them. Desmond looked his disapproval of her, but said nothing. Nan seemed in a strange contradictory mood this afternoon and did not want to destroy completely what small rapport still lay between them.

Seeing Nan, Jane winced. She had George Alden in tow, and he was only too happy that she was ignoring Brandon and concentrating her attention on him. She was flirting outrageously with him, and he was enjoying every minute of it. The girls in her set were only too painfully aware that, having lost Brandon to her, they now appeared to be on the brink of losing George as well.

The only consolation they had was that Jane could not marry both George and Brandon—plus the indisputable fact that at the moment it did not appear that Brandon wished to marry any of them.

He had been sufficiently careful in his recent pursuit of Nan to protect her from any criticism that she was pursuing him, or that he was more than ordinarily interested in her. Once he had proposed and been accepted, for he was sure that in the end he would be, then there might be a little gossip behind their backs, but Mr Brandon Tolliver was such an important local personage now that no one would dare to be at open outs with him for long over anything, least of all his choice of a wife.

Unaware of the direction in which Brandon's thoughts were going, for like everyone else in Broomhall and district she could not imagine that he would ever seriously contemplate marrying Nan, Jane still hoped that somehow his interest in her might revive.

The summer lightning which split the clear blue sky above them, and seemed an omen to her of better things to come, had her exclaiming, 'Oh, look! What can it portend?' For everyone knew that such manifestations had a deeper meaning, and Jane could only hope that that meaning might centre round, and favour, her.

She was soon to discover whether or not her wish might come true—and in what fashion!

CHAPTER FOURTEEN

'NAN FIELDING is the author of *Sophia*! Now that I do not believe.' Lady Alden, who had been reading her correspondence while her family ate their breakfast, waved her letter about as though it were a flag which she was using to semaphore with.

'But my sister Belville assures me that it is so, and that the news is all round London that Mr Murray has announced that the author of *Sophia* is a country parson's daughter—that she is Miss Fielding of Broomhall in South Nottinghamshire, and that a new novel by her will be on sale in the bookshops before Christmas! I must say, Lord Alden, Charlotte, George, this beats all! What a sly creature she must be! I am sure that neither her papa nor her mama had the slightest notion that she was doing any such thing as writing novels.'

The entire breakfast-table at Alden Hall was staring at her. George Alden, who had always seen Nan Fielding as the plain and dull elder sister of the pretty girl whom he loved, was particularly disbelieving.

'Oh, surely, Mama, Lady Belville has grown light in the attic. When would Nan Fielding find time to write *Sophia* and the other novels? Her entire day is taken up with running the Rectory and the parish, looking after her mother and Charles, and chaperoning her sisters.'

His mother said with great amusement, 'Oh, pooh to that, George. Such a busy creature as she is would find time to do anything! Now I know why sister Belville said that that unpleasant snobbish creature in *Sophia* was just like Lady Letcombe. . .' Her voice died away as an unhappy thought struck her. 'I hope no one considers that I resemble any of the freaks in her novels.'

Charlotte Alden said wistfully, 'I should like to think that I resemble Sophia. But yes, Mama, what a sly thing she is. Sitting there listening to us, and then writing about us without saying a word—and looking as though butter wouldn't melt in her mouth.'

Lord Alden, who had been busy reading *The Times*, put the paper down before saying, also amusedly, 'And that, of course, explains why the Fieldings have been flush lately, after being as poor as church mice for so many years. I never did believe that Fielding's great theological work could possibly have sold so well as to put them in Threadneedle Street after they had been sailing up the River Tick for so long!'

This conversation was being repeated, with variations, all over Highborough and district, as well as in London. Nan's worst fears had come true. Mr Murray had broken his word, revealed all, and had gained—at the expense of Nan's peace of mind—an enormous number of extra subscribers. The only benefit to her was the increased money which this would bring in— but at what a personal cost. Money was being won and lost in London clubland, for bets as to the sex of the author of *Sophia* had become commonplace. Many had thought that only a man could write anything so trenchantly witty and downright.

Did her father and mother know? was the delicious question which everyone in Highborough and district asked themselves. Was it possible that they could not? But the rector was so unworldly and his wife so withdrawn from society that it was considered that the truth could lie either way.

Lady Alden, together with George and Charlotte, descended on Gillyflower Hall straight away to pass on the news and find out what Brandon and Lydia thought about it. Disappointingly Brandon was out, paying calls in Broomhall, but Lydia was, as usual, pleased to see them and exclaimed in the most satisfying manner at the exciting and scandalous news.

Like everyone else in South Nottinghamshire, her first reaction was one of disbelief, and then she said in her thoughtful, sensible way, 'Of course, one was always aware that she was clever, and I know that Brandon admires her mind, but not as clever as that! You are sure that your information is correct, dear Lady Alden?'

'Oh, my sister Belville is always up to the minute and would never send me such a piece of news without being sure of its truth. She writes that Mr Murray himself made the announcement—so it is straight from the horse's mouth, my dear.'

Delighted by Lydia's response, Lady Alden ordered the carriage to be made ready again that afternoon, and personally passed on the message to three more families, enjoying the sensation that she created. Life in the country usually ambled along as though it were a fat old horse, and such a splendid titbit as this was sure to provide plenty of excitement until the next scandal came along.

Brandon, who already knew Nan's secret, but not that it had now been made public, had missed the Aldens by about five minutes. He was on his way to the Rectory, but not to discuss the author of *Sophia*. His errand was quite a different one. He knew that Nan always spent Thursday morning visiting Broomhall's poor, Kelsey attending, so that when he reached the Rectory and asked Jackson if Miss Fielding was in he was not at all surprised to be told that she was not.

Saying that he would call again when she was, and that Jackson need not see him to the door, he made to turn away, but then appeared to change his mind, and called back Jackson who was on his way to the kitchens.

'Oh, by the by, Jackson, you may remember that my man, Leeson, called about a fortnight ago with a letter from me to Miss Fielding, with express orders that you be sure to see that she received it as soon as possible. I take it that the letter was given to her?'

Jackson thought for a moment before replying, 'Oh, indeed, Mr Tolliver. She was out when Leeson called, so I put it on the salver for her to find when she returned. I distinctly remember Miss Jane picking it up and telling me that she would take it to Miss Fielding's room and place it on her desk so that she would be sure to have it immediately.'

The look which Brandon gave him was an enigmatic one. 'Thank you, Jackson. You have greatly relieved my mind. I had the notion that it might have gone astray.'

Now, what was all that about? was Jackson's reaction when Mr Tolliver had closed the door behind him. I wonder if the letter went astray somehow? I'd better have a word with Miss Fielding when she returns.

The deceitful, thieving bitch! Brandon was cursing Jane inwardly all the way down the path from the Rectory front door to the garden gate. He had no doubt now of what had happened. She had seen his writing on the letter, and had stolen it before Nan had had the chance to see it.

He was so lost in anger that he almost passed Jane without seeing her. She was returning from her walk, and was a trifle horrified at the sight of Brandon leaving the Rectory. There was no way in which she could avoid meeting him. For a moment she thought that either he had not seen her or was cutting her, and that she might be able to escape having to speak to him, but at the very last moment, even as he was passing her, he came out of his trance and saw her.

The mood of blind rage which had seized Brandon when he had realised that his worst fears were true and that Jane had stolen his letter to Nan ebbed a little. He saw how wan and dejected she appeared; her usual bright looks and airy charm were smudged. She had the air of one who was utterly wretched.

Conscience smote him hard—a new experience for

him. For had he not created the situation which had lured Jane to commit her wanton act of jealousy by having sought her out and favoured her beyond all other women, to the degree that his partiality had been gossiped about and speculated on—as his sister had warned him?

And then what had he done but withdrawn from her? And even if he had done it gently that must also have been the subject of unkind gossip, and, unwittingly, without meaning to, he had diminished her in the eyes of her small world.

He checked the angry words which were almost on his lips, bowed, and said in his most gentle voice, 'Good morning, Jane; I trust I see you well?'

So weighed down was she by her sin, and her fear of him which had followed it, that Jane could scarcely look at him, let alone speak. She nodded mutely, tears springing into her eyes.

Shocked by her reaction, and by the fact that she was about to walk on without so much as a word to him, Brandon said urgently, 'Stay, Jane; there is something which I must say to you.'

'No!' Her voice was faint and fear distorted her pretty features. She seemed almost on the verge of fainting.

'Yes, Jane. I must talk to you, for both our sakes. And I must apologise to you, profoundly. Without meaning to I have caused you a great deal of misery.

'When we first met I was so enchanted by your charm——' and that was no less than the truth, he acknowledged '—that I committed an error of manners. I was too partial to you, exposed you to gossip, and that was unforgivable of me. You must put it down to my sad lack of knowledge of how to behave in good society. In the circles I frequented before I came to Broomhall no one would have thought twice that I was showing such pleasure in the company of a charming young lady.

'I know that you will find it difficult to forgive me,

but I also know that, though you and I may be friends, we are not suited to each other in any other way. Like all of us, I find it difficult to confess a fault, but I trust that you will find it in you to forgive a sinner. We must all hope that our sins will be forgiven, as you, a parson's daughter, must surely know.' And he looked keenly at her.

He knew! Somehow he knew, was Jane's wild reaction to this. Astonishingly, however, he was not saying so. It was as though the weight of the letter, which was still hidden in her drawer upstairs, had been magnified a thousandfold and was pressing on her poor bruised heart.

She also knew something else, something important: that what he had said about them not being suited to each other was true.

She had never known him. She had been entranced by his difference from all the other men whom she knew, by the power of him, and by his fine body and good looks. But behind all that was the true Brandon, a clever and ruthless man of whom, little by little, if she had married him, she would have become afraid. He was complex and she was simple. He could, as he was showing her, be compassionate, for she was sure that he was sparing her, but she could never have lived in comfort with a man who knew his fellow human beings and their frailties so well.

Jane could never have articulated any of this. She knew it instinctively—and, once she did, the lure of him slowly disappeared, never to return. He might one day be her friend again, but nothing more.

'There is very little for me to forgive, but confession is said to be good for the soul,' she managed hoarsely at last, for she must say something, and he was waiting so patiently and, yes, so humbly for her to speak. 'Do you find it so, Mr Tolliver?' And she used his full name deliberately to show that she was severing any last emotional tie which might once have bound them together.

Brandon was surprised by her question, yet at the same time he acknowledged that by putting it to him she had touched on the truth. He *did* feel better now that he had confessed the wrong which he had unwittingly done her.

'Yes,' he said, equally simply. 'As much all of us who need to confess our wrongdoing.' So saying, he looked steadily at Jane after a fashion which seemed to penetrate her soul.

'I will remember what you have said,' she whispered, dropping her head as the weight which she secretly carried seemed to increase with each word that passed between them.

Brandon amazed himself by saying, as she bowed again and moved away, 'My good wishes go with you, Jane. I know that you will always do the true and right thing.'

Oh, yes, he had spared her; she knew that. But why had he done so? He was obviously aware that she had stolen his love letter to Nan.

And then, in her new maturity, the answer came. So that I may repair the wrong I did without knowledge of it going further to create scandal and distress. I, and no one else, must tell Nan what I have done, give her back her letter—for he must hope that I have not destroyed it—but even if I had he would want me to tell her the truth and beg her forgiveness.

Jane couldn't wait, for even as she made this decision the burden which she had carried since she had stolen the letter disappeared. She began to run down the path, away from him, to fetch the letter from its hiding place and wait for Nan's return.

'Nan.'

Kelsey was abrupt. They were standing in the hall, taking off their bonnets, and Nan had just announced that a pot of tea might be a good reward for their morning's work among Broomhall's poor, when Kelsey

decided to speak to her of something which had been
on her mind for some little time.

'Is there something wrong with Jane? Has she given
you any indication that she might be feeling ill? Her
manner is quite changed. She has had a fit of the sullens
for the last two weeks or more, and when she is not
sulking she is inclined to fits of unexplained sobbing.
Yesterday, when I asked her if she was feeling unwell,
she fled from the room crying even harder. I can get no
sense out of her these days.'

Nan, too, had been worried about Jane. She was
usually so high-spirited, so full of herself, that to have
her walking about like a grey creepmouse seemed as
unnatural as though the sun had decided to rise in the
west instead of the east.

'She has said nothing to me about anything. In fact,'
Nan continued slowly, for the thought did not please
her, 'she has taken to avoiding me lately.'

The unwelcome notion that Jane's misery over
Brandon's ceasing to be *most* particular' to her might
have something to do with her patent unhappiness had
been worrying Nan ever since her sister's manner had
changed so dramatically. But she could hardly tell
Kelsey so. Especially since she was only too well aware
that Brandon had changed towards Jane after he had
begun to be *most* particular' with her.

But he had now, it seemed, abandoned Nan herself.
Despite the fact that he had spoken to her of love and
marriage at Sam's, his manner to her had been most
odd, and in consequence she was unable to trust him,
leaving her to feel desolate and unhappy. Unlike Jane,
however, she was keeping her misery to herself. It was
one more secret which she could share with no one.

Further conversation with Kelsey brought no answer
to the riddle which Jane, as well as Brandon, had
become. Then another riddle was presented to her by
Jackson. He had been hovering while she and Kelsey
talked, and finally came forward, an odd look on his
face, to ask her, somewhat diffidently, 'The letter which

Mr Tolliver left for you on the day he travelled to London—you found it in your room, I trust?' He did not mention Jane's role in promising to deliver it—as general factotum he had learned never to say too much of what he knew.

'A letter for me, from Mr Tolliver?' Nan's surprise was patent. 'I have not received one. You are sure it was placed in my room?'

'That was my belief,' replied Jackson diplomatically.

'Perhaps it was mislaid on my bureau. It is never very tidy. I will look for it.' Nan sounded cool on the outside, but inside her mind was whirling. Brandon had sent her a letter on the day he had left for London!

Why? And why had she never received it? And was that why her last conversation with him had been so. . . so. . .odd. . .?

All the way up to her room the mystery of the letter and the equal mystery of Jane's behaviour occupied her mind. She could only hope that Jane might soon come to terms with the fact that she could not have everything which she wanted from life. It was a lesson which Nan had been compelled to learn eleven years ago, and it was one which she would never forget.

To her surprise, there on the landing before her room, where once Brandon had stood in the dead of night, was Jane. She had been crying and her face, usually so carefully tended, was smudged with tears. On seeing Nan she hung her head, turning it away from her sister's gaze. The reality of what she was about to do smote her hard. But she must be brave, because only by being so could she purge herself.

'I want to talk to you, Nan. Could we go into your room?'

Nan was surprised by her sister's humility. Usually Jane was impatient with her, was only too happy to suggest that her elder sister was behind the times, scarcely worth wasting words on.

She opened the door, and waved Jane into her one armchair, the one in which Brandon had sat pretending

that he felt ill. The memory of him caused her cheeks
to flush, and for once it was Nan who was rosy and
Jane who was pale.

Jane refused to sit down, and said with surprising
dignity, for she felt that she was going to her execution
and the only way in which she could endure it was to
suffer it bravely, 'No, thank you, Nan; I prefer to stand.'

Perforce Nan was compelled to stand as well. She
wondered what was coming, for Jane suddenly gave a
great sob and, all bravery gone, blurted out, 'Oh, Nan,
I have done a terrible thing. I have committed a great
wrong, and I did it to you. Brandon sent you a letter
before he left for London. I stole it, and read it, and
hid it away—and I have never had a happy moment
since!'

Her sobs turned into a storm of weeping as she came
out with the truth at last. She flung herself into the
chair which she had just refused, buried her face in a
cushion, and, shoulders shaking, cried as though her
heart would break. The true enormity of what she had
done had struck home at last at the sight of Nan's
stricken face as she had come out with her confession.
For the first time in her short and selfish life she was
feeling for another, and it was almost like the pangs of
birth, so strong was the pain.

'Stole my letter?' echoed Nan. 'My letter? From
Brandon?' The letter which Jackson had just asked her
about? Jane's misery, added to her confession, temporarily bewildered her. And then she exclaimed, in a rare
spurt of anger, 'Look at me, Jane! What can you mean?
You stole a letter which was meant for me? I cannot
believe it—even of you.'

These last harsh words from a sister who had
patiently endured her petty bullying and small jeal-
ousies further undid Jane, but she had the courage to
lift her streaming face from the cushion, and stand up—
as cautiously and warily as though she had suddenly
grown old.

'This letter,' she said tremulously, and she took it

from her reticule. 'I found it on the salver the day Brandon left for London, and I told Jackson I would see that you received it, but I stole it and read it—and I know, once you have read it, that you will never forgive me. Never. I would never have forgiven you if you had done such a terrible thing to me.'

She did not tell Nan that Brandon had discovered the truth, and had worked on her to confess, for she knew—how did she know?—that he would not want her to do that. Instead, without more ado, she handed Brandon's battered letter to her sister who took it without a word, an expression on her face which Jane could not read.

Before she could speak Jane made for the door, crying as she reached it, 'I know that you will never forgive me, but I pray that you will try, although I know I don't deserve it.'

All her bright beauty had gone, all her pretty grown-up ways which charmed all those about her. She was once more the small girl who had stolen Nan's old doll and deliberately drowned it in the stream because she thought that Nan had been overly harsh to her.

But the letter was no doll, and, although Nan had forgiven her the drowning, once her sister had read Brandon's letter, Jane thought that there could be no forgiveness.

Nan made no attempt to read her recovered letter. She had devoted her whole life to her family, but she would have been the last to claim that that made her a saint. For a moment she was almost faint with rage and anger against the sister who had betrayed her. But the memory of the child that Jane had once been was strong within her.

She said slowly, 'I want to read my letter when I am alone, Jane. It will be difficult for me to forgive you, but I will try—because of the love we once had for one another. You are my sister, after all.'

There was something so patient and dignified about Nan as she stood there, so brave, that Jane had her second revelation of the afternoon. She suddenly understood how hard her sister's life was, how selflessly she had lived it.

She could not help herself; she flung herself on Nan and, tearless now, hid her face on Nan's breast. 'I will try to be good in future,' she whispered. 'Being bad is so unpleasant. Try to forgive me.'

For a moment the sisters clung together, until Jane pulled away from the comfort of Nan's arms. She smiled a watery smile. 'I will go now and leave you to read what Brandon wrote to you. I hadn't the heart to destroy it, and it was like the burden on the back of the old man of the sea.'

Nan nodded. She knew all about such burdens. 'Go and bathe your face,' she told Jane practically and sensibly, 'and change your dress. You will feel better then.'

It was all that she could offer, and when Jane had gone Nan sat down in the armchair which Jane had cried all over, and read Brandon's letter, and knew why Jane had said that she would never forgive her, for it was a declaration of love such as she could never have hoped for.

And every word must have been a dagger in Jane's heart, as every word was like incense and balm to Nan. He loved her and wanted to marry her, and that was riches indeed, but she put her face in her hands and, like Jane, wept.

For, of course, she could never accept him.

Broomhall and district was in a ferment over the news that Nan Fielding was the author of *Sophia*. The only family which remained in ignorance of the news was that of the Fieldings themselves. No one quite knew how to broach it to them. The etiquette for such a situation did not exist. Sam sent Nan a note telling her that the news was out in Broomhall. She read it shortly after she had read Brandon's letter, and sat mute on her bed, trying to order her thoughts.

It was plain from her recent conversation with Jane that she was still ignorant, for had she known she would have been sure to mention it. So there were some small mercies to be thankful for. What did distress her was what her father and mother would say when they found out what she had done. She knew that she must go downstairs and confess that she was the author of *Sophia* before the news reached them from other lips.

She had just determined to do so when there was a knock on the door and Jane came in again. She had taken Nan's advice and washed herself, re-dressed her hair and changed into a pretty cream muslin dress decorated with rosebuds. There was a new reserve in her manner; she would never be so frank and free in company again.

She was carrying a letter. 'Lady Alden has sent me an invitation to spend some days with Charlotte,' she told Nan, adding hesitantly, 'I may go, may I not? She says that her sister will chaperon us, so that you are not to worry that we shall run wild.'

She paused, and added something which she would never have said before her confession of guilt. 'Do not worry that I will say or do something stupid, and if you think that I ought to stay and help you here I will send a message back to say that it is not convenient. The boy who brought the letter is waiting for my answer in the kitchen.'

She was so humble that Nan hardly knew her. 'Of course you may go,' she said gently. 'It will be a good thing for you to be away from the Rectory for a few days.'

And away from Brandon, thought Jane. I can face Nan, but how can I face *him*? But she said nothing, and both went to her room, Jane calling on Kelsey to help her to pack, for Lady Alden was sending the carriage round for her at two o'clock if it was convenient for her to visit.

'Take Margaret with you for a lady's maid,' advised Nan, who thought that she might feel better if she did

not have to face Jane for a few days, particularly if the
storm over *Sophia* was about to break over her head.

Jane's arrangements made, Nan went downstairs to
find her father and confess her sins, but, alas, he was
not in. He had gone to a parish meeting, Kelsey said,
and would not be back until dinner. 'Which, at the
present rate,' she added meaningfully as she stowed
Jane's clothes for her visit into a large hamper, 'might
be rather late in being served.'

So that was that. The evil moment would have to be
postponed.

Of all the great ones who lived in and near Broomhall,
Lady Alden was by far the most frank in her manner,
and the most free with her opinions, but Lady
Letcombe ran her a close second. She was visiting
Broomhall that afternoon and after a happy coze with
several of her friends about the deceitful way in which
the Fieldings had carried on over Nan's authorship, for
they surely must have been in on the secret, she had
the great good fortune to see Parson Fielding dawdling
home after his parish meeting.

She stopped her carriage, an open one, by the simple
expedient of ramming the coachman in the back with
her parasol and commanding him loudly to stop
immediately.

He duly obliged and she leaned over the side to
beard her friend even as he was turning in at his own
gate.

'My dear man,' she roared imperiously at him as he
swept off his hat and made her a low bow, 'I vow that I
shall never forgive you for keeping your daughter's
secret from such an old friend as I am. You have not
been neighbourly, sir, not neighbourly at all, and so I
said to Letcombe when we heard the news. It would
have been more proper to hear it from your lips than
from someone who is merely an acquaintance of yours!'

A faint expression of alarm passed over the Reverend
Caleb Fielding's placid face as one of his patronesses

came out with such an oblique reprimand. His face
showed its bewilderment. Lady Letcombe recognised
that he was nonplussed, and, being no fool, at once
grasped the reason for it.

'What?' And now her roar was as genial as that of a
dragon which had found another source of treasure to
add to its hoard of gold. 'Never tell me that the naughty
gel has not informed you that *she* is the author of those
witty books which have had all society agog! I wonder,
given all that she accomplishes for you and the parish,
that she has found the time to write them, but talent, I
understand, will always find a way. No doubt, though,
the knowledge that a parson's daughter is Sophia will
sell even more of them, which is doubtless why Mr
Murray has broadcast her identity to the world.'

Poor Caleb Fielding, feeling as though someone had
fired a cannon before his garden gate, and that the ball
had carried his head away, stammered nervously at the
great lady who was so mercilessly quizzing him. 'Oh—
oh, madam, forgive me; I am sure that you have been
misinformed.'

'Fiddlesticks, my good sir! I'll have you know it is in
all the public prints, and is going the rounds of society.
Are you sure that you have not been aiding and abet-
ting your daughter's saucy plot, sir?

'What a party of tricksters the Rectory has been
sheltering! Letcombe and I wonder at you all; he is
quite sure that such a quiet creature as your daughter
could not have carried this off by herself. She must
have had an accomplice, and who better than one who
is already an author of note? You must bring her over
to dinner, and the toast will be the author of *Sophia*.'

So speaking, Lady Letcombe rammed her unfortunate coachman in the middle of his bruised back again
and was swept away in a cloud of self-satisfied
patronage.

The dazed Rector stood stock-still, his head buzzing.
A thousand questions were swirling through a mind
which had originally been a sharp one before indolence

and self-satisfaction had taken it over. His expression
growing ever more baleful, he walked rapidly into the
Rectory to find Nan immediately and ask her whether
Lady Letcombe had been telling him the truth.

There was one important question to which he did
not particularly desire an answer. Was it from Nan's
writings that the money had come from, which had
made the Fieldings' lives so easy in recent years, and
not from his theological masterpiece? Such a notion did
not bear thinking on. His *amour propre* and his intellect
both rejected what must, he instinctively knew, be the
true answer.

Rage and hurt pride battled within him and boded ill
for Nan.

Nan, seated in her mother's room, overlooking the
main road which ran through Broomhall, had seen
Lady Letcombe accost her father, seen her gesticula-
tions, and her father's distressed response to the great
lady's hectoring.

She did not need to be told of what had passed
between them. She knew only too well, by the unaccustomed speed with which her father was walking and by
the expression on his face, that the arrogant busybody
who was driving away so speedily had just informed
him who the author of *Sophia* was. For a moment she
contemplated flight. It was too much to bear on top of
everything else which had fallen on her during this
dreadful afternoon.

The strength of will, the courage, which informed
everything Nan did prevented her from doing any such
thing. She became aware that her mother was speaking
to her. She was reclining on the sofa at the other end
of her private drawing-room and was looking in singularly good health for a woman whose invalidity was a
by-word.

Mrs Fielding's rosy face, her carefully dressed hair,
her well-cut deep blue gown of the latest mode, all
enhanced her appearance of happy and self-satisfied

middle-aged charm. Beside her Nan, overwhelmed by the cares and revelations of the day, felt extinguished, and that in some way she had changed places with the mother who had battened on her for so long.

'What can you be staring at, Nan?' her mother remarked petulantly. 'Do begin to read. You know how much I want to find out what happens to poor Amelia.'

Nan picked up *Amelia's Secret* wishing that she had never written it, nor any of the others. Being poor and eating bad food might be better than comfort purchased at such a cost to her health and her peace of mind. She opened the book just as her mother remarked unkindly, 'Really, Nan, do you need to look so fly-away? Even your hair needs to have a brush and comb run through it. I can scarcely bear to look at you.'

Amelia's Secret was put down again as Nan stood up, trembling a little.

'You will forgive me, Mother,' she remarked as coolly as she could, the worm turning at last, 'if I leave you to read *Amelia's Secret* yourself. If you wish me to appear a little more *comme il faut* than I do, then you must give me time to be so. Between organising the parish, the household and the kitchen, transcribing and rewriting Papa's book, arranging for you to be properly dressed, organising Jane's affairs so that she looks her best in order to catch a wealthy husband, and seeing that Chaz behaves himself, I have scarcely the time to put my clothes on, let alone make the effort to transform myself into a fashion plate.

'But, since you wish it so much, I am sure that you will make the sacrifice of releasing me from my duty as reader in order to arrange myself more to your liking.'

She turned on her heel and walked steadily to the door, her mother calling angrily after her, 'Come back here, my girl, and do as I bid you!'

'No,' replied Nan, without turning her head. She heard her mother's angry indrawn breath, but put her hand on the doorknob all the same, just as the door was forcefully thrust open by her father.

She had seldom seen such an expression of rage and temper on his handsome face. He was usually almost bovinely placid, accepting his easy life as no more than his due, the Rectory revolving around him when it did not revolve around his wife and his youngest daughter.

He caught Nan by the wrist as she moved to pass him, ignoring his wife's imperious call of, 'You come pat, Mr Fielding, indeed you do. Nan needs reminding of what her duties are in this house, and so I trust you to inform her.'

'Anne, I require an explanation from you.' His tone to Nan was peremptory in the extreme, and he was calling her by her long-disused proper name. His wife tried to engage his attention, but he continued to ignore her, betraying the depth of his distress: he was a man who prided himself on his punctiliousness towards everyone around him.

He released Nan's wrist but continued to address her, both his colour and his voice high. 'It is you to whom I must speak, Anne, and I prefer to do so before I speak to your mother. I have a question to put to you to which I demand a truthful answer.'

The day of reckoning was upon her. Nan swung slowly round to face him. Her hands, clasped behind her back, were gripping each other tightly.

'Yes, Father,' she said, her head high, determined to meet her doom with courage. 'What is it that you wish to know?'

'Is it true, as Lady Letcombe has just informed me, that you are the author of this. . .novel. . .' he picked up *Amelia's Secret* from the table on which she had placed it '. . .and of all the others written by the author of *Sophia*?'

A gasp was wrenched from Mrs Fielding as he asked this question in a voice which she had never heard from her husband before, so harsh and bitter was it. Her eyes were trained on Nan again. She saw her daughter's face grow ashy pale, saw her sway a little, before she replied, her voice as steady as she could make it, 'Yes, Papa. That is the truth.'

Her father closed his eyes, then opened them to say in a grating voice, 'And I suppose that you did not inform me of what you were doing because you knew that I would not have allowed you to do such a thing. You, a single young woman, to write this.' And he held poor Amelia up by two fingers as though she were contaminated.

It was no less than the truth, as Nan acknowledged. 'Yes, I wrote it and sent it to Mr Murray, who liked it and published it. Yes, I knew that you would not approve of my either writing it or selling it. But I don't think that you and Mother quite understood me when I told you after we came to Broomhall that your stipend was barely enough to feed us, let alone clothe us. It was certainly not enough to keep Mother in comfortable idleness and give the girls a London season, and Chaz an education when the time came. And so I wrote *Sophia*——'

Before she could say any more in her defence her father put up a hand and interrupted her. For the first time in his life, thought Nan irreverently, he resembled the Old Testament prophets of whom he so often spoke in the pulpit. Only the long white beard was missing.

'Sin and defiance and lying are no less so,' he thundered at her, 'even if they result in the accumulation of earthly wealth and luxury. God must have wanted us to suffer in poverty; it was not for you to deny Him. Besides,' he added a trifle pathetically, 'there was the money from my book to help us.'

Nan closed her eyes. She must tell him the truth, whatever the cost. 'There was, and is, no money from your book, Papa. It did not sell. I found that out when we came to Broomhall and took over your accounts. Mr Stone told me what our true financial circumstances were. It had not mattered previously that your book had not sold; your stipend at Frensham Major was more than enough to keep us in comfort.'

'Ah, yes, Sam Stone.' The Rector's underworked intellect, now working again under great stress, had correctly informed him who must have helped his daughter to carry out her wicked plan. 'It was he, I suppose, who assisted you to deceive me and the world——'

Now it was Nan's turn to interrupt him as the devil took hold of her. 'And feed you all,' she proudly announced. 'Never forget that, Papa. Without Sam and *Sophia* we might have starved.'

'And I am to be mocked because of you and Sam and *Sophia*. Considering all that you have done in your short life, I can scarcely bear to look at you. You have humiliated me before, and this second slight which you have placed upon me is the last I intend to endure from you.'

It was the first time that he had admitted that he had known exactly what had happened twelve years ago. Nan bowed her head, the tears springing to her eyes.

'I did not mean to hurt you, Papa, then or now. This time I meant to help you.'

But her appeal to him was unavailing. His pride had been powerfully injured. His book had been a failure, and Nan's books had been successful. He owed the very bread in his mouth, the clothes on his back to her, and he could not endure the knowledge. Only his belief that such a thing would mark him out as a savage was preventing him from threatening to thrash her for her sins.

Instead he held his face away from her and ground out, 'No matter. You shall not help us again. Whatever the cost you shall not stay here to be my permanent reproach. You will go to your room and remain there until you leave the Rectory for good. Kelsey will take over the running of the household.

'You, Mrs Fielding——' and he swung on his wife '—will resume your duties as mistress of this house, since your refusal to do so has led our daughter into sin and wickedness. You will come down to supper, and carry out all Anne's duties—including the copying of my latest book. As for Anne, she shall be sent to Aunt Smithson's to be her companion, and if we must retrench to make up for losing her earnings, then so be it.'

'No!' Nan cried violently. 'I do not deserve to be treated so harshly! Do not send me away where I may never see my family and Chaz again. I have worked faithfully and long to see that we all lived a happy and fulfilled life. I did not care what sacrifice I made to do so—the only one I was not prepared to make was the one which would have followed your forbidding me to do what I did. I am only sorry that I did not immediately tell you the truth when Sam informed me that Mr Murray was about to reveal the author of *Sophia*'s identity to the world.'

But he had turned his back on her, and all she stood for, to cry at his wife as imperiously as Lady Letcombe had cried at him, 'Get up, woman, and go downstairs. You have been idle too long, and I have been wrong to allow it.'

The last thing Nan heard as she left the room was her mother's sobs. The Rector had reassumed the authority over his life and home which he had long abdicated. Nothing would ever be the same again.

CHAPTER FIFTEEN

REMARKABLY, on that evening, Brandon Tolliver was one of the few people who was not thinking or talking about Nan Fielding. The first reason for this was that he had decided to be patient after his conversation with Jane. He would let events take their course. Or, rather, he would wait for Nan to reply to his letter when Jane at last gave it to her, for he was sure from her manner that Jane had not destroyed it. She was, he had decided, weak, not wicked.

If in the next few days Nan did not reply to his letter, then he would visit her and make one last great push to win her. Since his visit to Frensham Major he was no longer puzzled by her insistence that she could not marry him. He knew why she thought so, and it was up to him to convince her that she was mistaken.

The second reason was that once he was back in his study Carteret handed him a note from Thorpe, asking to see him at their secret rendezvous. 'Matters are drawing to a conclusion,' his agent had written.

Brandon stared and sighed at the hastily scrawled words. He could have done with having to deal with this at another time, when his mind was not centred on Nan, but, on the other hand, he was also relieved that he might be on the point of drawing Desmond's teeth, thus enabling him to enjoy his quiet life at Broomhall.

Before he had arrived in South Nottinghamshire he had told himself that he would be bored, but he was beginning to acknowledge that the charms of a rural existence were stronger than he might have thought. He had spent his life in the bustle of the commercial world, in great cities, mostly living in the *demi-monde*, that world which was a kind of mezzanine floor between the respectable and the completely *déclassé*, and now

he had discovered that he wanted more from life than
excitement. He wanted stability, the respect of his social
equals, a family of his own, and a settled home with the
woman he loved in an area whose natural beauty
appealed to him.

He was still pondering on this when at just about
the time that Nan's father was condemning her to
banishment and exile, he met his agent Thorpe, in
an out-of-the-way little inn on the other side of
Highborough. Like Thorpe he was dressed inconspicu-
ously, nothing of the gentleman about him. He was
young Brandon Tolliver again, rising in the dangerous
world which he was on the point of conquering with the
help of such tools as the man he was meeting.

'Well, what is it?' he demanded, nursing his tankard
of ale.

'All and more than you wanted, sir,' responded
Thorpe. 'Our man has grown tired of delay. He has
hired me and some other villains to do his dirty work
for him. He wishes us to attack and kill you, either by
beating you or shooting you, from ambush. He intends
to be present himself to see that the job is properly
done on this occasion after his previous boss shots.

'He knows that most evenings you stroll away from
the park at Gillyflower Hall into the scrub and waste-
land outside it to take your ease after dinner, not far
from the point where the earlier attack on you failed.
He thinks that since you were attacked there once
before you would conclude that lightning does not
strike twice in the same place, and not be particularly
wary.'

'He knows that,' replied Brandon lightly, 'because I
continued the habit when I realised who was trying to
kill me, and told him I was doing so because I thought
that he would probably attempt that particular gam-
bler's double bluff, and in the doing would trap
himself.'

Thorpe nodded. 'With a little help from me, that was
what he decided on. From tomorrow evening we shall

be waiting for you in the clearing in the wood between Gillyflower Hall and the Rectory where the path turns sharp right. You know it?'

Brandon nodded. Of course he knew it. It was where he had seen Nan up the tree, rescuing Chaz's kite.

'We are supposed to attack you there. We shall begin to do so, and then, at a suitable point, when he is fully involved, my mates and I will take to our heels without warning, shouting that we are on the point of being discovered, leaving you alone with him. At least, that is what I suggest to you that we do. It may be that you have other ideas. You will, of course, be armed and ready for us whatever plan you adopt.'

The beer Brandon was drinking was poor—warm and sour; it matched his mood. He grimaced as he swallowed it and placed the pot down on the grimy table. 'As usual I was right to trust you to come up with a plan which seems feasible,' he said. 'Go ahead, and with luck no one will be injured.'

He had no wish to harm his cousin, only to defeat his murderous plans and frighten him so much that he would abandon them. He had not wanted anyone else to learn of Jane's treachery to Nan, and neither did he want Desmond's villainy made public. Best that it lay between the two of them so that it might be forgotten provided that Desmond would have the common sense to understand that the last thing which Brandon wanted was a scandal.

And so it was arranged. Brandon rode home to Gillyflower Hall hoping that this chapter in his life might soon be closed, without recriminations and without bloodshed. This over, he might be able to think of Nan again, not merely enjoy the memory of her in his dreams.

The Aldens could not help but notice how uncharacteristically quiet and subdued Jane was when she arrived in mid-afternoon. Only Lady Alden noticed the trace of recent tears, and chose to say nothing of them.

She had hoped, before Brandon Tolliver had arrived in the district, that Jane would make a suitable wife for George. She was not rich, she would bring no large dowry with her, but then, she need not, seeing how wealthy the Aldens were. Better for George to marry someone suitable, even if she had little money, than someone who would bring a fortune but who might make him unhappy.

True, the child was a little flighty, but she obviously appealed to George's protective instincts, and her family was good. Lady Alden knew all about Sir Charlton and the well-born Fieldings up north. If Parson Fielding could hold on he might yet be a rich landowner himself!

Well, if Jane chose to moon over Brandon Tolliver that was her privilege, but George would make her a better husband...

Organising dinner, chatting to some of her London cronies who had come to stay, she forgot Jane, who, again unusually, did not sparkle at the dinner-table.

Lady Alden was not the only one to notice Jane's changed manner. George, sitting by her, found that her usual liveliness was missing and regretted it. Once the gentlemen's after-dinner port-drinking was over, he walked through to the drawing-room to find her. Again, strangely, she was not part of the group of younger women enjoying themselves by playing at speculation while they waited for the men to appear.

He looked about him. His mother interpreted his glance correctly. 'Jane is in the little cabinet next to the library, I believe. She said that she had a slight headache, and might look at some of your father's new prints instead of joining in the game with the other girls.'

His mother was right. He found Jane, but she was not looking at prints. She was sitting on a small sofa, staring blindly at the opposite wall. Something, he knew, was wrong.

'I trust you are well, Jane? You seemed a little *distraite* at dinner.' Now this was daring of him—to make such a personal remark to a young girl—but Jane, staring blindly at him, took no note of it.

Her stare became less blind. She suddenly realised that George was, after all, quite a personable man. During her fascination with Brandon she had thought him young and callow, but now that that was over almost miraculously George had changed back into the beau whom she had been proud to acknowledge.

But did he want to acknowledge her? New maturity told her that recently she had been cruelly indifferent to him, and that she might as a consequence have lost his admiration—which had suddenly become precious to her.

She gave a great sob. Alarmed, George sat down beside her as he saw the tears threatening to fall. A large handkerchief of the latest fashion, edged with lace, depended from his pocket. He withdrew it and handed it to her, saying, 'Oh, do not cry, my darling girl. You will break my heart if you do.'

Jane's answer was to take his handkerchief, give another wailing sigh and hold it to her eyes. After she had wiped them she said, 'Oh, you must not be kind to me; I don't deserve it.'

She meant because of the way in which she had recently treated him, but George took no note of that. Her manner to him had changed completely; she had reverted to the Jane whom he had once known and loved, the girl whom he hoped to marry.

'Oh, no,' he replied swiftly. 'I don't believe that. You deserve all and more which the world has to give you, I am sure.'

Jane lowered the handkerchief to look at him over the top of it. All, apparently, was not yet lost.

'Do you really mean that?' she asked him tremulously.

'Of course.' His answer was gallant in the extreme and, fixing her with his earnest brown eyes, he said, almost humbly, 'I suppose I ought to ask your papa for permission first, but I can't wait. I must know my fate.'

And, improbably, unromantic George slipped down on to one knee, took her hands in his—she had dropped his handkerchief in surprise at his sudden action—and kissed them.

'Dear Jane, I am asking you to be my wife—pending your papa's permission, of course. Oh, do say yes. I am sure that when we are married we shall be as happy as we were when we played our childish games together.'

A great surge of the deepest affection for him swept over Jane. He was not as handsome, clever or rich as Brandon. But he was kind George who loved his horse and his dogs and would love his wife with the same unthinking devotion.

Let Nan have Brandon; they could be clever together. And now that at last she had done her duty, as Nan had always urged her to do, and told the truth—purged her sin, as Papa would have said if he had known the terrible thing which she had done—she could accept George.

And, it would not be because he could make her Lady Alden and thus cause the other girls to envy her, or because it would extinguish the hurt of losing Brandon, but because she had discovered that she loved him and the simple life which he was offering her.

Brandon had been right. She and he were not suited, but she and George were. She looked up at George, tears forgotten, and said, as simply as a child, 'Of course, George. I shall be honoured to be your wife. I have always loved you.'

Which, she was about to discover, was no less than the truth. So much so that when, on George's arm, she met Brandon again, she could not understand why she had found him so attractive.

Alone, locked in her room, Nan contemplated the dismal future. Her father had already informed her that when she was sent to Aunt Smithson, that elderly tyrant, to be her companion her aunt was to make sure that she had no access to pen and paper. 'There will be no more novel-writing,' he had ordered.

Until the arrangements for the journey were made she was to remain in her room, and Broomhall was to be informed that she was suffering from one of the low fevers common in summer. Kelsey, and no one else, was to bring her meals.

During her first morning's imprisonment, after a sleepless night, she heard Chaz come running up the stairs, to beat on the door of her room, shouting in a despairing voice, 'You are not to go, Nan; don't let them send you away. I won't let them. You are the only friend I have. No one else is kind to me—not Papa, not Mama and not Jane. I want to go with you.'

His hammering redoubled when she said, trying not to sound defeated, 'Oh, Chaz, you must do your duty and remain here.'

The noise he made when she told him that brought her father up the stairs to drag him away. A moment or so later, he came into Nan's room, saying, 'I will not have you encouraging Charles to mutiny against his parents, Anne.'

Nan looked steadily at him. 'You know perfectly well that I did not encourage him, Papa. I told him to do his duty.'

'As you must learn to do yours,' he told her brusquely, and left her.

The day dragged on interminably. She had run out of paper, so could not write. Sam had promised to bring her some that morning, and when Kelsey brought up her luncheon she asked if he had called.

Kelsey put the tray on Nan's small table which stood in the window. 'He called with a parcel for you. Your father gave orders that he was not to be admitted again, refused to accept the parcel and handed him a letter which told him that he was transferring his business to an attorney in Highborough.'

Nan swallowed. Her throat seemed to have closed and she could not eat the food which sat before her.

Her whole world was falling about her ears, and she could not longer hope that her father might change his mind and relent sufficiently to allow her to remain in Broomhall.

From her window she watched the daily life of the household go on. She saw the undermaid feed the chickens, the gardener gather up vegetables for the evening meal and flowers for the house. Beyond the lane she could see the path which led to the scrub and small wood, and ultimately to Gillyflower Hall. Perhaps Brandon would come along it; perhaps. . . But it was foolish to think so. Her father would not admit him either, if he said that he wished to speak to her.

Shortly after luncheon she saw Brandon walking briskly along the path to the Rectory and through the paddock gate. She had no doubt that he was calling on them, even though from her room she could not hear the front-door knocker. But a few minutes later she saw him walk away down the path, back to his home. He had been turned away.

In mid-afternoon Kelsey brought her a cup of tea, and told her that Mr Tolliver had called and been informed that Jane was at the Letcombes' and that Miss Anne was ill and confined to her bed.

After Kelsey had gone Nan lay on her bed in a half-doze and let her mind roam. She was walking with Brandon in the woods; his hand was in hers. But was it his hand or Randal's? She looked up at her companion and it was Randal. For some time now she had found great difficulty in remembering what he really looked like; time was causing his image to fade ever more rapidly.

But in her dream he looked exactly as he had done on that last afternoon they had spent together. The sun was on his eager face, his eyes shone—and oh, he looked so desperately young, little more than a boy! He would always remain so, she knew, while she was the prisoner of time in another way, for each year took her further away from him. He remained forever young, while she. . .she slowly aged.

They looked at one another as they had done then. She tried to say his name, but the word would not come, and he began to fade, leaving her in her dream as he had left her in reality. As he finally disappeared both sleep and dream ended, and she was back on the bed, knowing that in some strange way she had finally said goodbye to him.

'To live and love again,' Nan said aloud as she awoke, and wondered why she did so. She rose from the bed, and for some reason—why she did not know—she tried her bedroom door. It was open. Either Kelsey had forgotten to lock it or had deliberately left it unlocked.

The orange light of late afternoon filled the room. Inside was prison, outside was freedom. Without thinking, almost in a trance, Nan picked up her light cream shawl and threw it around her shoulders. She had dressed herself, as an act of defiance, she thought afterwards, in her one good dress, which was also cream and fashionably cut.

She pushed the door open cautiously and, still cautious, walked downstairs. No one seemed to be about. Her mother would doubtless be napping—downstairs now, not in her own room—and Kelsey and the servants would be in the kitchen preparing dinner. Her father would be in his study. He had reclaimed the manuscript of his book when he had visited her, and would probably be working on it.

Once in the black and white flagged hall, Nan walked along it to the garden door, trying to make as little noise as possible. She had no idea of what she was going to do. She had no plans, either to leave or to stay. But where could she go? Who would give her refuge? She had thought for a moment of going to Sam and asking him to help her, but she also shrank at the thought of the scandal it would cause if she did. She only knew that she wanted to be out of her prison and in the open.

The garden door led to a path which ran down by the side of the back lawn, through flowerbeds bright with summer blooms. There was no sign of the gardener— he was probably drinking tea in the kitchen at this hour.

Then she walked through the paddock and the gate which led to the path through the wood and the scrub which Brandon had taken earlier. Did she hope to meet him? If so, what would she say? Still in a dream, as though she were lying on her bed, Nan walked on. Shock and distress held her in thrall.

The wood was shady and cool. She followed the path until she reached the small clearing where Brandon had found her up a tree, trying to free Chaz's kite. She supposed that she ought to think of him as Charles now that her father had belatedly taken charge of his family again.

Tiredness overwhelmed Nan. She had slept badly on the previous night, and poorly on many nights before that. She walked slowly to the back of the clearing, out of the sun, to a small hollow with a bank of grass where bluebells grew in the spring. To lie there and sleep. . . to forget—perhaps to dream that she was hand in hand with Brandon, for Randal had gone, her home had gone, and she was alone, and might please herself.

Out of the sight of man and beast, free from reproach, Nan lay down and, released from servitude, slept sweetly among the summer flowers.

Brandon had loaded his pistol and had thrust it into the sash which he wore beneath an old-fashioned half-coat which would cover it. It felt large and clumsy, and his one prayer was that he would not have to use it.

He was now worrying about Nan as well as the coming confrontation with Desmond. When he had called at the Rectory he had asked Jackson if he might speak to her, and Jackson had begun some talk of her being unwell when Caleb Fielding had arrived in the hall to ask testily, 'Yes, Jackson, what is it?'

'Mr Tolliver is asking whether Miss Fielding is at home——'

Caleb Fielding had interrupted him, his voice frosty and indifferent. 'Neither of my daughters is able to entertain you, Mr Tolliver, Miss Jane Fielding because she is visiting the Aldens, Miss Fielding because she is unwell; she has a low fever.'

For some reason Brandon did not believe him. There had been something in Parson Fielding's manner which he did not care for, some hint of something wrong. But what? Only his intuition, finely honed by many years of hard bargaining, told him this; he had no real evidence. Perhaps it was the way in which her father had uttered Nan's name...

He had bowed. What else could he do? 'You will convey my sympathies to her, I trust?' he had said politely. 'And I hope that she will soon be well.'

Remarkably for a man who always insisted on conforming to the most exact protocol of social life, Parson Fielding's only reply had been a mannerless nod before he had turned away and entered his drawing-room again. Nothing to do for Brandon, then, but to go home and brood a little, and eat his dinner, while he waited for the hour to arrive when he might offer himself as a target for his cousin's villainy.

Sighing, he rose, and put his head round the drawing-room door to tell Lydia that he was about to take his after-dinner constitutional. Then he set off down the path through the wood to the clearing where he had encountered Nan Fielding that fateful day—which might be a good omen or a bad one; only time would tell, and that time was upon him.

He was in the clearing before Thorpe and his two accomplices sprang at him. For a moment or two Thorpe managed a determined-looking scuffle on Desmond's behalf, the latter emerging from the trees to watch, half hidden, the villainy being carried out for him. The sham fight was realistic enough for Brandon to collect a few bruises—he told Thorpe afterwards that he ought to deduct a guinea of his pay for each of them! It was ended by the arrival of a fourth man, whom Thorpe had hired as a look-out, who came running from the opposite direction to Gillyflower Hall, shouting, 'Run! We are discovered!'

Brandon had wondered how Thorpe would contrive to entangle Desmond and leave him behind while he and his untrustworthy cohorts fled. He did it by the simple expedient of catching Desmond round the waist as he ran by him and throwing him bodily towards Brandon, shouting, 'There's your man, master!' before disappearing down the path and into the wood, his part in the evening's work over.

Desmond's sudden arrival nearly took Brandon to the ground, but he steadied himself, caught Desmond by the throat, and snarled at him, 'So, cousin, not Luddites, nor Jacobins, but my own kinsman thought to hire bravos to kill me!'

Desmond recoiled. Here was a Brandon whom he had never met, someone quite different from the easy, genial man whom half the county thought that it knew. A man with the face and demeanour of a man of power, a man to be frightened of.

'No, cousin, you are quite mistook,' he gasped, half choking under Brandon's grip. 'I came upon you by accident, was about to help you——'

'Oh, damn that for a tale,' roared Brandon, now shaking Desmond as though he were a terrier. 'Those men you hired were mine, sent out to trap you. Their leader has worked for me for years, and has disposed of more than one piece of filth for me. I ought to have let him dispose of you, but you are my cousin, and I don't want your blood on my hands, even if you didn't mind soiling yours with mine.' He threw Desmond from him, and his cousin, holding his damaged throat, fought for breath.

It was useless, quite useless, thought Desmond bitterly. Brandon knew. *How* only the devil Brandon obviously was could have told him. 'Oh, damn you, damn you,' he choked hoarsely. 'To have everything while I have nothing. To be ousted by someone who has come up from the gutter—yes, I know that to be true; you have only attained respectability recently. . .'

'If you're respectable, then God save me from respectablity,' was Brandon's tart reply. 'I ought to hand you over to the constables for arrest and trial, but, God help me, you *are* my cousin, and I don't want the scandal of a trial, or your hanging on my conscience. If you promise to behave yourself in future, and leave me in peace, then I'm willing to overlook what you have repeatedly tried to do to me. I want your word on it, mind.'

He saw his cousin's face change. Saw the hate on it, and sighed. Common sense told him to hand him over to the law, but even if blood counted for something a quiet life counted for more. He saw Desmond's inward struggle before, still clutching his bruised throat, he managed to mutter ungraciously, 'Very well; you leave me no choice. I will leave you alone in future, but don't expect me to be other than sorry that I failed.'

It would have to do. Brandon sighed, shut his eyes for a moment, and then said, 'That could have been better expressed, but it is better than nothing. Remember that I have Thorpe and his men as evidence of your villainy. That should stop you from further nonsense of this sort.'

He wondered afterwards if it was the last contemptuous sentence which caused what happened next. Desmond had been half turning away from him as he had begun to speak, but as Brandon finished he swung round, dragging a pistol from underneath his coat to point it at Brandon. He too had been secretly armed, and now he was using his weapon to intimidate, perhaps to kill. Brandon's concealed pistol was of no help to him, since it would take too long for him to draw it and try to counter his cousin's last desperate move.

'Damn you,' Desmond snarled, 'I'd rather swing than live to endure the contempt of such as you. Tell me

why I should not kill you here and now, and let the law
take its course. I've nothing left to live for. You've even
taken Nan Fielding from me.'

The black hole at the end of Desmond's gun stared
at Brandon as he contemplated death. What a fool he
had been! He had misjudged the lack of mental balance
of the man before him, and was about to pay the price
for it. He stood quite still, head high as Desmond cried
desperately, 'Beg, damn you, beg; I'd as lief you died
on your knees as on your feet so long as you die.'

But Brandon shook his head, refused to speak, either
to beg or to argue—for he could see that Desmond's
sanity was poised on a knife-edge—and tried to stare
his cousin down.

CHAPTER SIXTEEN

NAN'S brief sleep was ended by noise and shouting voices. She stood up unsteadily, leaned forward to peer through the bushes and branches before her to find out what could be happening.

She saw the end of the attack on Brandon. She saw Thorpe throw Desmond at him, and heard what followed. It all happened so quickly. Time seemed to have speeded up. She was behind Desmond and could only see Brandon plainly. She was not surprised by his power for she had always known that he possessed it. At one point she thought that she might show herself, but the sheer enormity of learning that Desmond had deliberately set out to murder his cousin held her still. Besides, it was something which the cousins must settle between themselves; it was not for her to intervene.

Until Desmond drew his pistol and threatened Brandon. At that point she climbed through the scrub, and on Desmond's last words she called at his back, 'Stop it, Desmond, stop it immediately!' as though she were a teacher in a dame school admonishing an unruly child. Afterwards she shuddered. Suppose the sudden sound of her voice had caused him to fire the pistol? Suppose. . .?

As it was, Desmond, surprised and alarmed, swung around to face her, the pistol hanging lax in his hand. Brandon, with the pistol no longer trained on him, jumped forward in order to catch Desmond by the arm which held it, to wrench it from him, to fire it into the air, at the same moment that Nan appeared in the clearing.

In some strange way Nan's arrival seemed to unman Desmond. All of his desperate desire to destroy his cousin leached out of him. He made no attempt to stop

Brandon from overwhelming him, knocking him to the ground, and placing his booted foot on his breast. Only then, when all was safe, could Brandon look at the white-faced Nan, an expression of mixed joy, pride and gratitude for his salvation on his face.

'Thank God, my darling! Had you not come I was done for. But your father said that you were in bed, ill. . .' His voice trailed off at the sight of her sad face.

Below him Desmond writhed and coughed, until Brandon removed his foot and allowed him to sit up.

Only for him to meet Nan's indignant stare. 'For shame, Desmond! Brandon generously spared you, and the thanks you gave him were that you again tried to kill him! You deserve to hang for that alone!' This forthright declaration had Desmond avoiding her eyes and hanging his head. His shame was doubled because Nan had been a witness of his treachery.

Brandon had drawn Nan to him and, his arm around her, the pair of them confronted Desmond as he rose, slowly and painfully, from the ground, a caricature of the cool and self-righteous man he usually presented to the world.

His head still sagging, his manner distraught, for Nan's arrival had restored him to common sense and normality, he ground out painfully, 'I suppose Nan is right. It was the act of a cur to try to take your life when you had just given me mine back. I think that I've been light in the attic ever since you came to Gillyflower Hall.'

It was as though for the first time he was struck by the enormity of what he had been doing. To sit alone, allowing hate to fester and boil inside him, to hire men of straw to help him to kill his cousin was one thing— but for Nan to discover what he had been doing was quite another.

He stretched his hands out to her, wordlessly pleading for understanding, and when she shook her head at him he muttered painfully, 'I thought that I had lost everything—the lands, the Hall, and you.'

'Your honour, Desmond,' Nan cried passionately. 'You were still left with that, and now you have thrown it away. And you never had me, any more than you had Cousin Bart's lands. You simply thought that you deserved them, as you deserved me, without doing anything for them. I am sorry that you did what you did, sorrier still that you descended into murderous self-pity when you should have been thinking about the future of the lands you *do* own, which you have allowed to fall into a sorry state.'

Brandon was hard put to it to stifle a grin as Nan came out with this typically Nan-like piece of sound and down-to-earth common sense. It was plain that Mrs Brandon Tolliver would never allow her husband's fortune to diminish. She would soon put him back on the right track if he strayed from the straight and narrow. In the same fashion she had practically and robustly found a means to restore the fortunes of her family. Marriage to her might have saved Desmond, but she would never have married a weak man, and Brandon thought that like Jane, despite his cousin's attempt on his life, Desmond was basically weak rather than wicked.

'Go home, cousin,' he told him gently. 'Try to forget what has passed here today. Be sure that Nan and I will say nothing of what happened. It was not my fault that Cousin Bart wrote his will as he did, merely my good fortune—the first I ever gained without working for it, I do own.'

Desmond nodded. He was quite defeated. He knew that he would never again attempt to harm his cousin, but the knowledge that he had tried to—and failed— would always be with him. His head sagged again as he muttered, 'I suppose that Nan is right—that I should thank you for sparing me, and that I will do now, but you would not expect me to be happy because I have given you yet another occasion to demonstrate what a kind and splendid fellow you are! Now I will go back home, if you will so allow.'

What more to do? Desmond would have to live with his conscience and both Brandon and Nan were aware that nothing that they could say or do would comfort him, or restore his lost self-respect. Later Brandon, hard-headed as ever, was to say to Nan, 'He should find a rich widow who will take him in hand, but I doubt that he ever will.'

Meantime they watched him walk slowly away, down the path towards the Rectory where he might regain the main Broomhall road. Nan suddenly shuddered and clutched at Brandon's arm. Too much had happened to her during the past twenty-four hours, and between relief that Brandon was still alive and distress at her own sad condition her head was swimming. She wondered if her flight had been discovered and what she would do now. Perhaps she could try to make her own way back to her room, and hope that her absence had not been noticed.

And after that, what?

But Brandon, having Nan almost in his arms again, was not about to let her go. Now that he could think clearly about something other than his cousin, and his own possible imminent death, he could see how pale and thin she looked. Her father had said that she was ill, was confined to her room, and if that was so how had she come to be wandering in the woods? Here was a puzzle he ought to solve immediately.

So when Nan released her grip on his arm and made to return to the Rectory, he caught her hand in his and turned her into his arms. 'No,' he told her, 'no. You must rest again. I can feel that you are shivering.'

Now that danger was over, Nan had begun to shudder, and the clearing was turning slowly around her. . . She had eaten almost nothing since her father had sent her to her room the day before, and exhaustion was beginning to claim her.

Brandon caught her as she fell, muttered an oath—what in the world had been happening to his beloved?—and lowered her gently to the ground, to strip off his coat, to fold it into a pillow and place it beneath Nan's head so that she might lie in some small comfort on the hard ground.

What to do to help his darling? He remembered Lydia dealing with a parlourmaid who had fainted. He tried to imitate her by kneeling down beside Nan and picking up her hands in order to chafe them gently. She was deathly cold, even her lips were white, so he put her hands down and carefully gathered her to him, to share his warmth, her heart against his, his warm cheek against her cold one. He began to kiss her gently, as though, like the Prince in the fairy-tale, he could bring Sleeping Beauty back to life.

Semi-consciousness had given Nan a new kind of beauty. Loss of colour only served to reveal the pure planes of her face, the elegant bone-structure which would keep her lovely even into old age when those whose looks depended on blonde curls and pink and white prettiness had descended into ordinariness. Oh, that she would consent to be his, his peerless love, neglected by the uncaring and unseeing who had passed over her gold in favour of base metal, leaving her for him to find. He would care for her, make sure that she would never again descend into the depths of suffering which he suspected that she was enduring.

'Oh, my love, my love,' he whispered into her tawny hair. 'Wake up so that I may tell you how much I love and worship you—not only for your looks but for the selfless way in which you care for those around you.'

She stirred a little, and to his delight, as he kissed her near her shapely mouth, Nan turned her head and gently kissed him back on the corner of his, so that his whole unruly body tingled with the joy of it, and began to make demands on him which, in honour, he could not fulfil.

Nan was in heaven. Warmth returning was bringing full consciousness back again. She was in someone's arms, and the someone was loving her as she had not been loved for years—if ever. The someone must be

Brandon, and, if so, how had he come to be in her bedroom?

But once her eyes were open she found herself not in her bedroom but in the dim and shady green of the wood between her home and his, and, memory swiftly returning, she remembered all that had passed. Not even memory, though, could compel her to pull away from him, and the next time that he kissed her she first responded, and then whispered, pulling her mouth away from his, 'We should not be doing this, Brandon.'

To which his answer was, 'Why not? I am enjoying myself, aren't you?'

Somehow that wasn't the point. The point was that if she did not return soon she was sure to be missed, and so she ought to tell him. The mere idea, though, was distressing. She began to shudder again.

Brandon felt her change of mood from quiet acquiescence to unhappiness. He held her closer to him and murmured in her ear, 'What is it, Nan? What is distressing you?'

She tried to pull away from him completely, to avert her face, but he would not let her. In some way he must compel her to confide in him, but he must do it gently, without bullying her. He muttered into her ear again. 'Nan, your father said that you were ill, were confined to your room. But here you are, and you look ill, but not in the way his tone to me implied. You must have been fit enough to walk from the Rectory to the clearing—and, by the by, your collapse has prevented me from thanking you for my life.'

This brought an immediate response. Nan turned her averted head, looked at him earnestly, and said, 'I don't think that Desmond really meant to kill you—though he might have done so accidentally, I do admit, by disturbing the hair trigger of his pistol. He was merely playing at villainy.'

While secretly acknowledging that this might be true, Brandon returned, his mouth twitching slightly, 'Well, if what he was doing was play, then I hope never to see

him in earnest. He would have made fricassee of me by
now!'

Nan, without thinking, put a hand over his mouth.
'Oh, do not say so,' she cried. 'It was bad enough to see
you threatened—but to think of him succeeding...'
And she shuddered again.

'No, we won't think of that,' Brandon agreed. 'Let us
talk of other things. What is wrong at the Rectory, Nan,
that you should be in such a state? Was it because your
father discovered that you were the author of *Sophia*?'
He saw by her expression that he was right.

'Yes, but how did you know? Oh, not that you knew
I wrote *Sophia*—Sam told me that he thought that you
had guessed some time ago. Can you read minds that
you knew that, and know that something is wrong?'

'A little,' he said gravely. 'People give themselves
away, Nan, in many ways. With their eyes, their bodies,
their hands as much as their tone of voice. Tell me what
has happened and I will help you. How you shall know
in a moment, but we need to speak of what is distressing you before we go on to more pleasant things. What
did your father do when he found out?'

Nan averted her face again. She could not tell him
for very shame. To be sent away as though she were a
criminal! But the nearness of Brandon, the scent of
him, so secretly and deliciously male, the kindness in
his voice, his kisses, his... She was growing maudlin.
Yes, she would tell him; she would.

'He went a little mad, I think,' she said slowly. 'I fear
that he saw it as an insult to him. I had no idea he
resented me so. He said that he would rather we all
starved than that we should live well on what I
earned...'

Brandon ground out an oath which made him sound
like a wolf howling. The slightly feral quality in him
which Nan, if no one else, had scented had never been
plainer. She fell silent.

'And?' he asked. 'There must be more to it than that.
What did he do?'

Yes, she must tell him, but only if she held her face away from him. 'He ordered me to my rooms, to remain there locked in, until I was sent, like a parcel, to be a companion to my old aunt Smithson in North Yorkshire. He said that he would instruct her never to allow me to have ink and paper so that I could not disgrace him again by writing another novel.'

It was, after all, easy to confess, once one began. Perhaps that was why Roman Catholics set such store by it. One felt purged.

'Kelsey brought me my food. Either she forgot to lock the door or she left it unlocked deliberately, and so I decided to take a walk before I was shut away forever.'

Brandon uttered another oath, beneath his breath this time. It was a good thing that Parson Fielding was not near by. The wolf would have made short work of him.

Once started Nan could not stop. Besides, there was something else which she must confess to him.

'What made it worse was that Jane had just told me that she had stolen the letter you sent to me.'

The memory of it was suddenly so strong that Nan stopped... Then, 'Your letter,' she murmured brokenly. 'Your dear letter, the only true love letter I was ever sent, and she took it. If she hadn't had a fit of conscience I might never have been able to read it... and then Father came in and said...and said...' And she began to rock herself, her knees drawn up to her chin, her head bent, her glorious hair, once more undone, streaming about her.

Brandon said nothing of the part he had played in Jane's change of heart. Instead he put his arms around Nan's shoulders to lift her against him once more. 'What did the letter say, Nan? Tell me that.'

'It said——' and now the drowned turquoise eyes were looking straight into his loving silver ones, pleading for mercy '—it said that you loved me and wanted to marry me.'

'Yes, Nan, and that is no less than the truth. You will marry me, Nan, won't you? There's no need for you to worry about being sent into exile; you shall be the Queen of my heart, and wherever I am there shall your kingdom be.'

He had had no notion that he would say anything half so romantical, but it had flown out of him, a statement of love quite unlike anything the cynical and hard-headed man he had been until he came to Broomhall would ever have said.

'Oh, what a lovely thing to say to me, but. . .' And now the tears began to fall in earnest, for Nan was finding that the emotions and pains of the last few weeks were turning her into the kind of watering-pot which she most despised. 'But, oh, Brandon, I love you so dearly, and I can't marry you, I can't, I can't.'

She burrowed her head into his chest as she cried out these words, and the sobbing grew worse, for oh, she loved him even more than she had loved Randal, for that had been a child's love, and now she was a woman and loved him with her heart and mind, her body and her soul—but she could never be his.

Brandon stroked her hair, lifted her head away from his chest, tipped his hand under her chin and murmured as gently as he could, 'Why should you not marry me, Nan, when we both love one another so much?'

'Oh. . .' wailed Nan, trying to look away from him and failing. 'I am not fit to marry you, or any man. I am a fallen woman,' she wept at him. 'Chaz is mine, not Father and Mother's.'

'I know,' Brandon told her simply. 'I know that he is yours, and it makes no difference to me, truly. What happened in the past, when you were only sixteen, means nothing to me, except that I would willingly be a father to Chaz—if I could.'

Nan swept on unheeding. 'Oh, that's not all. The worst of it is that I don't regret what I did—which makes me doubly fallen, and consequently unfit to marry anyone.

'I met Randal secretly on the last night before he left for the Army—our parents had forbidden us to have anything to do with each other—and somehow we both knew that it was all that we were ever going to have. It seemed inevitable when we made love, although I never thought at the time of the possible consequence for me, because I loved him so much—but even if I had I wouldn't have behaved any differently,' she added with a defiant sniff. 'At least Randal had that before he died, even if he never knew about Chaz.'

Her sobbing redoubled. 'To save my reputation, as well as the family's, Mother arranged everything. She was quite different in those days. I think that she used what I had done to compel me to be her servant so that she could have the life of the lady which she had always wished to be.

'I was never sure, until yesterday, when he reproached me with it, that Papa knew what we, she and I, had done. She said that it was she who was with child, and went into the country for her health, taking me with her. And Chaz was such a dear little baby. They wouldn't let me hold him or feed him when he was born. They bound my breasts up to stop the milk from coming.

'If he had been a girl, Mother would have given him away, but she and Papa had always wanted a boy so she took him home as hers, and we left Frensham Major for fear that the Scotts might find out the truth. They hated us all because Randal was in love with me and they wanted him to make a grand marriage. Which in the end was just as well, because Chaz has grown up to look exactly like Randal did when we were children together.'

She drew several gasping breaths. 'And Chaz has never been mine, even though I am the only one who really cares for him. He's not a bit like the boy Papa wanted—someone meek and scholarly, like himself. If any man ever showed an interest in me, Mother always reminded me that I was a fallen woman and could never marry a good man.'

During her sad recital she had, without willing it, clung closer and closer to Brandon, who tightened his own grasp on her, kissing the top of her head gently, and when at last she fell silent he murmured, 'There, there, my darling, you shall have as many babies as you wish, and I promise you that you shall feed all of them. And I am not a good man, so you may marry me as soon as I can arrange it.'

Even as he spoke he was remembering how she had clutched Mrs Blagg's baby to her that day on the Soar, and her transfigured face as she had petted it. He knew why her father and mother had behaved as they did — to save her — and themselves — from shame and disgrace — but he also knew that as a result of it they had exploited her and blackmailed her unmercifully, turning her into the family's drudge.

Nan had been so preoccupied in telling her sad story to Brandon that his acknowledgement that he already knew that she was Chaz's mother had almost passed her by. Remembering now, she looked up at him with great drowned eyes and stammered, almost reproachfully, 'Y-you s-said that you knew that Chaz was mine. How could you know?'

'My darling, he is so unlike you all, and you love him so, when it is quite patent that no one else in the family does, and that made me curious, as did several other little things, including the way in which your parents used you so unmercifully. My agent had told me that you came from Frensham Major to Broomhall, and I wondered why your father had left a rich living for a poor one. So I visited Frensham and the Scotts on a pretext which was not quite a pretext, and there I saw Randal's portrait, and, yes, Chaz is the image of him.'

'So now you know, and you know why I can't marry you, and there's an end of it.'

Brandon gave a short laugh and shook her gently. 'My darling love, you have been a martyr to your family for so long that you have forgotten how to be anything else. Didn't you hear what I said to you about babies? I want to marry you, Nan, so that you can give me the babies we both want, free you from drudgery, and allow you to write your novels in the day and not in the middle of the night. You see, I mean to be the husband of the author of *Sophia*.'

'Oh,' cried Nan, her eyes suddenly starry. 'You cannot mean that, knowing what I did, and that I am not ashamed of it.'

Brandon held her away from him for a moment to look deep into her eyes. 'Oh, Nan, I have just told you that I am not a good man, and I know that I am not quite a gentleman and never will be. If we are to judge one another and condemn each other for our past sins, then how can *you* bring yourself to marry *me*? My whole life, or at least the life the county thinks it knows, is a lie. I never went to grammar school, except for one half-year, and I was never articled as a clerk, never made my way diligently up a reputable counting house to make my fortune by hard work and honesty.

'No, indeed! My father, the younger son of a younger son, gambled away what little we had on the Stock Exchange and in the gaming halls around the Haymarket. The bailiffs turned us out of our small house in Chelsea when I was ten years old, and we ended up in a tenement near the Docks, where my father drank himself to death and my mother died of shame and despair.

'Lydia, who is several years older than I am, went for a lady's maid, and I. . . I worked for the biggest fence and thief in London doing any job he cared to give me so that I might not starve—I had no trade, you see. When I had saved enough to start a little business of my own, I tried to make money honestly, or at least reasonably honestly, seeing that I had no desire to hang—which my old master did, soon afterwards.

'I had a talent for being a merchant and broker, and soon had enough capital to set up a decent home of my own, and save Lydia from servitude by sending for her to come and run it for me. By hook or by crook—and crooked some of it was—I made myself a fortune with the help of a wealthy India merchant who saw me as the son he had untimely lost. He married Lydia, and I suppose that he was the piece of luck which we all need if we are to succeed in life with only our wits to help us.

'You see, Nan, I was a user and a manipulator of men—and the succession of women whom I set up as my mistresses, until I grew bored and pensioned them off. I was a liar and a cheat, and when I grew rich enough I awarded myself an invented life to replace the one I had lived, first in the underworld and then in the *demi-monde*—a life of respectability when, in truth, Lydia and her late husband were the only claims I had to it—that and Cousin Bart's unexpected bequest which made me a country gentleman.

'When I met Jane I thought that she was exactly the kind of wife I wished to have. Someone young and charming, a kind of trophy for the poor boy who had risen from the gutter. Someone to whom I need make no real commitment, who would be compelled to let me go my own way, in exchange for being the mistress of a noble establishment.

'And then I met you. It was like a thunderclap. For the first time I met a woman whom I desired beyond reason, but also to whom I could talk as I had never talked to a woman before—as I could never talk to Jane. A woman who gave and never took, who lived her hard life uncomplainingly and with pride. A woman whom I wanted as the mother of my children. I saw how empty my past life had been, and I wanted to fill it. I never thought that I could love anyone as I love you.

'It is *you* who will be honouring *me* if you become my wife. Marry me, Nan, and save me from nothingness.'

He had released her, made no claims on her by

touch, made no effort to make love to her, to persuade her to do as he wished. All the arts he had practised on men and women to gain what he wanted from them were laid aside. If she came to him, here and now, after he had placed the truth of him before her, as she had placed her own truth before him, then he knew that they would be blessed indeed. True love and true lovers needed nothing of compulsion.

They were kneeling now, facing one another, as they might kneel in church before the priest who married them. Nan put up a hand to touch his face. 'You were so brave—to survive your dreadful beginning. Whatever you say of yourself, you are honourable as well as brave—else you would not have told me the truth of your past.'

She stroked his face, and saw a smile begin to dawn on it, but still he said nothing—everything had been said. Or, perhaps, nothing needed to be said. Since the first moment when they had met in the pantry they had been one soul, not two. Only time had been needed to bring the two halves permanently together.

Her hand still on his cheek, Nan leaned forward to kiss him on the lips, a gentle kiss, a chaste kiss, a kiss to which for the first time he did not physically respond, except that as she withdrew his eyes dilated as hope dawned in them.

'Of course I will marry you, Brandon, as soon as you wish.'

He gave an exultant cry before he took her into his arms. 'Oh, my dearly beloved—for that is what you are, Nan—I can scarce wait to say the words "till death us do part!" I remember the parson saying them when Lydia married Henry, and they made no real impression on me then. . .but now. . .'

They were both shaking as the emotion of the moment swept through them. Slowly Brandon lowered her to the ground to hold her in his arms there, still refusing to do more than kiss her gently, though every fibre in his body demanded consummation. But that must wait. He would honour her by waiting; he would not fall on her hugger-mugger to remind her of what love, heedlessly fulfilled, had once done to her.

Nan felt the same. She could not really remember what it had been like to make love on the one and only time when she and Randal had clung together, in desperation rather than passion, before he had gone from her forever.

I am reborn, she thought, I who had never hoped to find love again, and warm in Brandon's arms, her head against his chest, happiness working on her, she slept. Afterwards she thought with wonder that almost from the first she had felt so secure with him that sleep had come easily to her—she who had always found it difficult before.

Once Brandon would have mocked a man who, with his willing love in his arms, held off, and was happy to cradle her as she slept. What a waste, would have been his sardonic comment on such an ass.

But they had all the time in the world, and he would let her rest before he took her to Gillyflower Hall, for he had no intention of allowing her to return to the Rectory, to reproach and exploitation. If Nan's parents had discovered that she had gone, then let them worry a little over what might have befallen her.

Twilight was all about them before Nan woke. Lydia would begin to worry—would already be worrying as to why he had not returned—might even be fearing the worst. But that did not matter. Nan's face, now rosy, because she was loved and treasured, was turned trustingly to him.

'What do we do now?' she asked him, her voice trembling a little.

'We go home,' Brandon said, holding out a hand to help her up.

'To Papa?' Nan shivered, her rosiness fading a little.

'No, I said *home*. To Gillyflower Hall. Lydia will chaperon you. My only worry is that I have exploited her too. She needs a husband and a home of her own.'

Nan could almost see him thinking this over. He shook his head and said abruptly, 'No matter; time to deal with that later. You shall not go back to the Rectory until I have arranged matters for you there. I shall begin by asking for your hand.'

Nan shivered again.

'What is it, my darling? What troubles you?'

'Chaz,' she said. 'Oh, how could I forget him? I can't leave him to Papa; he will punish him for my sin. He has been punishing him for it all his short life. My happiness will be built on his misery.' Her face crumpled at the thought.

'Yes, I see that.' Brandon was thoughtful. 'No matter. There is a way out. Do not worry. Trust me.'

Yes, she would trust him.

The walk to Gillyflower Hall was a slow one, for Nan was tired, and when they entered the last stretch of it, on the gravelled sweep, he gave a short exclamation at the sight of her white face, and the great blue smudges beneath her eyes. 'This is no way to enter your future home, my darling,' he said, and swept her into his arms, to carry her up the steps and into the Hall.

He walked past the astonished butler who opened the door, and past the astonished Lydia, who had come out of the drawing-room to greet him. He carried his burden in—to stare at Sam Stone who sat comfortably there, before the tea-tray, with a footman at the far door to make matters proper.

Brandon gave a crack of laughter and announced enigmatically as Sam rose, 'Well, this seems to have settled one matter happily enough,' for both Sam and Lydia were giving off the aura of a pair of children caught in an orchard stealing apples.

He had no need to explain himself. Sam and Lydia's expressions told all, and Nan was busy thinking, as she peered at them over the shelter of Brandon's arm, how splendid for Sam that he has found someone suitable at last. And Lydia too, of course.

'What in the world. . .?' began Lydia as Brandon

gently sat Nan down in a big armchair before telling
the footman to bring more tea, and something for Miss
Fielding to eat.

'Miss Fielding,' announced Brandon, once the footman
had gone, 'has just done me the honour of accepting
my proposal and consenting to be my wife. Her papa
being rather exercised over his discovery that she is the
author of *Sophia*, my future wife has appealed to me
for temporary asylum—something which I need not
dwell on, and the details of which will be confidential
to us all.'

This grandly ambiguous statement had Nan cough-
ing, Lydia looking startled, and Sam starting to his feet
and exclaiming, 'The ungrateful old devil! I feared this.
My dear,' he said, turning to Nan. 'He has not turned
you out, I hope?'

Nan decided to be slightly more truthful than
Brandon, but no less ambiguous. 'No, indeed. I suppose, in a sense, I have turned myself out. But not for
long, I trust.'

'And you, my dear Lydia,' Brandon addressed his
sister, still in the same grand manner which he had
employed earlier, as though he were conducting a
board meeting, 'will consent to be my future wife's
chaperon, I hope.' He decided that he rather liked
saying 'my future wife'. It gave him great pleasure and
made Nan blush in the most charming way.

'Of course, Brandon!' exclaimed Lydia warmly. 'But
we are being most remiss. We have not congratulated
you on your news. I cannot tell you how happy I am to
see you fixed at last, and with such a suitable wife.'

She walked over to Nan and kissed her. 'Welcome,
my dear,' she said.

Her good wishes were followed by Sam's, who took
the opportunity to say quietly but sternly to Brandon,
'You will look after her properly, my dear fellow. No
one has ever done so before, and she deserves the best,
the very best, from life.'

Brandon bowed to the only true friend whom Nan

had possessed before he and Lydia had arrived in Broomhall. 'And she shall have the best, my dear sir. I promise you that. As I have promised her.'

Tea arrived, and sandwiches and cake, and then Lydia insisted that Nan retire. 'For, my dear, you are looking very tired, and I know that my brother, however much he loves you, has so much energy himself that he sometimes fails to recognise that other people may not always be so blessed.'

The two lovers looked at one another. Joy reigned on Nan's face, but those with her could not but see that excitement, pain and even the knowledge that she had reached harbour at last had taken their toll of her.

She whispered to Brandon. 'I don't want to leave you.'

'We shall have all our days together soon,' was his answer to that. 'Tonight I shall send word to the Rectory that you are safe at Gillyflower Hall and that I hope to see your papa tomorrow, and then we may be married in as short a time as possible.' He stopped, and had the grace to blush. 'You see, my love, I brought a special licence back from London with me, so that once you had accepted me we need not wait.'

All three of them reacted in their own way to this piece of supreme impudence. Nan said faintly, 'Oh, Brandon, were you so sure of me?'

And Lydia said, 'For shame, Brandon, before you had so much as asked your future wife!'

And Sam said, 'By God, Tolliver, Nan's fate was sealed once you had arrived in Broomhall. You leave nothing to chance.'

'I never do.' Brandon was brief. 'Come, my love.' And he escorted Nan to the bottom of the stairs where the lovers clung together and kissed, before the maid allocated to Nan arrived with a candle to escort her to her bedroom where she found herself lapped in the kind of luxury which she had never encountered before.

Downstairs, Brandon walked back into the drawing-room to be confronted by both Sam and Lydia.

'Now, Brandon,' cried his sister imperiously, 'the truth, if you please, of your and Nan's goings-on.'

But he shook his head at her, and quoted the late Francis Bacon, '"What is truth? said jesting Pilate; and would not stay for an answer."'

No more did Brandon.

CHAPTER SEVENTEEN

NAN woke up refreshed, to greet a glorious morning. Not a glorious dawn, for it was already past ten of the clock and she had been allowed to sleep on.

The little maid came in with fresh undergarments, and a dress of Lydia's, for which, she was informed, her new chaperon had no further use. Breakfast was in the dining-room at the back of the house.

Could it be true? Was she really to marry Brandon? It seemed that she was. Lydia, who had breakfasted much ealier, was waiting for her, and Nan ate her largest meal in years.

There was no sign of Brandon. 'He has already gone to see your papa,' Lydia told her, joining her in a cup of coffee. 'To ask for you hand, and for him to marry the pair of you as soon as may be.'

'Papa *will* be surprised,' returned Nan, with the sort of giggle which she had left behind over eleven years ago, before Chaz's birth. Accepting Brandon seemed to have given her her youth back.

Lydia privately thought that the whole of Broomhall, Highborough and the surrounding district was going to be surprised, but sensibly did not say so. Instead, putting her head on one side, she remarked, 'That dress suits you better than it ever did me. We are much of a size, and I thought that you would prefer something a little fresher than the gown you arrived in.'

She might have added that Nan's dress looked as though she had been crawling through half the undergrowth between the Rectory and Gillyflower Hall, but that was another thought she did not voice.

It was strange to be idle and waited on, to be doing nothing in the middle of the morning, when by now, at the Rectory, her duties would have been in full flow.

Even stranger to have Lydia say briskly to her, as they chatted happily on the lawn below the terrace in comfortable chairs which had been carried out for them by the footmen, 'Now that I have come to know you, I am so glad that Brandon is marrying you and not one of the witless girls who have been chasing him. You will be so good for him. He needs a wife as strong-minded as he is. You will never bore him.'

A little later Nan saw the man she would be so good for striding towards them along the terrace. He looked particularly splendid. He had put on his London finery to visit Parson Fielding and had taken the chaise to go to the Rectory by the long way, taking the main road which ran towards Broomhall and which passed Gillyflower Hall's gates. He had been determined to arrive at the Rectory in full command of himself.

He was arriving back in that state, too. His coat and breeches were charcoal-grey, his shirt spotlessly white. His cravat was an extravagant dream. His hat, which he still held under his arm, and then threw on the grass beside the chair which was already set out for him, was from a hatter's heaven. His boots were like mirrors, so shiny were they. He had never, Nan decided, looked so stunningly and alarmingly handsome.

Nothing was said of his visit until Lydia, after a few moments' conversation with him, rose and said, 'I think that you are old and serious enough to be left on your own for a little. I have duties to perform, so I will leave you.'

'Good,' Brandon replied. 'We have several things to discuss, Miss Fielding.' He offered Nan his arm. 'You will allow? A quiet walk would do miracles for both of us, I think, and remove us from the gaze of the house.'

Nan took his arm and they walked away, down the slope, towards the tiny lake and the small gazebo where they had been private together once before. He handed her on to the marble bench where he had found her then, before sitting down beside her.

'Now, Miss Fielding,' he said. 'Allow me to tell you

that your papa is on his highest ropes at the prospect of having Mr Brandon Tolliver as his wealthy and well-connected son-in-law. He told me so himself, and he will marry us when we wish, although he is a little perturbed that the unthinking might consider the haste with which we are marrying a trifle odd. But no matter. If that is what we wish, then it shall be so.'

Nan was bemused. 'Oh, Brandon, whatever did you say or do to make him so amenable? Whatever did you promise him? I vow that I was fearful that he would insist that I was a fallen woman, and therefore not worthy of you.'

Brandon began to laugh whole-heartedly. 'Oh, my love. I can see that we shall never be dull if you understand so quickly the way in which I operate! Of course, I bamboozled him into doing whatever we wanted. Before I left London I arranged with an old friend that if you accepted me your father would be given the rich living of a parish near Oxford where he will be able to use the Bodleian Library whenever he wishes, and meet again the many old friends whom he has lost sight of since coming to Highborough. He would have given me the Crown Jewels after that, never mind your hand!

'I told him that I was aware of what a treasure you were to the family, and that only by offering him such a prize could I compensate him for taking you away.'

He did not say that before the bribe had been offered her father had tried to blow upon her reputation, and that he had answered him in his most arrogant manner, 'You will, of course, say nothing against Nan to me, sir. She is the woman I love and mean to marry, come what may.' That had silenced the parson.

'And then,' he went on, 'we came to Chaz. I said that seeing that he was the child of your father's middle age, and consequently looking after him must be something of a trial, we were prepared to have him visit us on a regular basis, to relieve his burden. Of course, I said, Charles would shortly go on to Eton and then to Oxford, and I would be only too happy to bear the expense of him doing so, for, I told him, what were riches for but to enable us to make our friends and relatives happy?'

He drew her into his arms. 'So, you see, you have not lost Chaz. I think that he will be ours, for your father has, I regret to say, little feeling for any of his children, and none for Chaz.'

Enthusiastic kissing, stroking and moaning followed, until, his clothing in some disarray, Brandon sat up and gasped, 'For God's sake, Nan, I wanted you to arrive at the altar in three days' time untouched—or at least not touched vitally. But at this rate we shall not last the day. We had better sit a little apart and contemplate the view.'

Nan, lacing up her bodice, was inclined to agree. 'Oh, by the by,' he added, 'your papa was gaining plenty of practice in dealing with future sons-in-law. Your sister Jane accepted George Alden the other evening, and today he was there before me! The Reverend Caleb and Mrs Fielding will be a happy pair now that they have lost all their encumbrances.'

'Oh, that is of all news the best,' Nan said, smiling. 'Jane and George are well-suited and neither of us will sit about thinking that we have cheated Jane in any way by falling in love with one another.'

'No, indeed,' replied Brandon lazily, watching her straighten her hair, which had, as usual, come down during their last bout. 'There is only one young woman to whom I wish to be "*most* particular", and that is the future Mrs Brandon Tolliver who is sitting by me. I can't wait to see you in Broomhall Church. Your papa has most particularly asked for us to be married there.'

'And Lydia has spent all morning deciding what I am to be married in,' Nan said happily. 'Oh, Brandon what a good thing it was that you lost your way and found yourself in the pantry!'

'Even more that I saw you up a tree,' Brandon announced naughtily. 'I have been longing for another look at the most splendid pair of legs I have ever seen, and now I have only a short time to wait. But I want to see you in your wedding-dress first.'

And so he did. And he and all Broomhall were agreed that no one would have thought what a handsome bride Nan Fielding would make, and small wonder, if he could cause her to look like that, that Mr Brandon Tolliver had decided to marry her.

And her legs were every bit as beautiful as Brandon had thought they were. . .

A LADY OF INDEPENDENT MEANS

by

Sarah Westleigh

Dear Reader

A Lady of Independent Means was interesting to write. I loved inventing the main characters: Louisa, who was unaware of the secrets in her aunt's life, and who had no need to consider marriage unless she wanted to; and Hugh, who thought people visiting the battlefield were ghouls, and who particularly disliked what he saw as Louisa playing with the affections of the young men around her.

He can't resist trying to guide Louisa, who much resents his efforts, but who finds her attempts to teach him a lesson backfire on her. Getting them to admit their love for each other took a deal of ingenuity! Happy reading!

Sarah Westleigh.

Sarah Westleigh has enjoyed a varied life. Working as a local government officer in London, she qualified as a Chartered Quantity Surveyor. She assisted her husband in his Chartered Accountancy practice, at the same time managing an employment agency. Moving to Devon, she finally found time to write, publishing short stories and articles, before discovering historical novels.

Other titles by the same author:

The Inherited Bride*
Set Free My Heart*
Loyal Hearts*
Heritage of Love
A Most Exceptional Quest
Escape to Destiny
Chevalier's Pawn*
Felon's Fancy
The Outrageous Dowager
Seafire
A Highly Irregular Footman
Jousting with Shadows
The Impossible Earl

* linked

CHAPTER ONE

LOUISA hung over the rail of the packet boat knowing she was about to die and wanting to. Wind, rain and salty spray lashed at her, soaking her garments and whipping her disordered hair into dripping rat's-tails. Her stylish bonnet hung from its ribbons, the feathers dripping poppy-red dye which spread into the silk and dropped on to her new pelisse, but she scarcely noticed any of these discomforts.

Her stomach heaved again but it had long been empty. A trickle of bile rose to her mouth and she wiped her lips for the hundredth time, wielding a sodden handkerchief with a shaking hand.

Why had she allowed Aunt Nazeby to cozen her into coming? She would die long before she reached France.

'Are you ill? May I help?'

The sound of the deep, rather languid voice, which carried clearly above the howl of the wind, the lashing of the waves and the creaking of the rigging, merely made her shudder. 'Go away,' she croaked. Apart from the crew, who after a shout of warning had paid her no attention at all, and the deck passengers huddled in a bunch towards the stern, she was alone, having sought solitude in which to endure her misery. She wanted no one to witness her present distress.

But instead of obeying her the man moved nearer, peering round to glimpse a fine brow, a bony nose and a wide mouth set in an oval face presently pale and tinged with green.

'You would feel better lying down,' he advised. 'Allow me——'

Louisa cut him short. 'Thank you, but no! I will not return to that cabin.'

The sentence finished on a gulp. She did not see the

273

compassionate if rather amused smile that crossed his face, being busily engaged in trying to bring up the non-existent contents of her stomach.

'Then lie on the deck,' he suggested, placing a strong hand on her shoulder. 'Come, ma'am, you will be much better off.'

She seemed unable to resist the gentle pressure he exerted. Reluctantly, she relinquished her grip upon the rail and allowed him to turn her round.

'Wrap yourself in my greatcoat,' he urged, removing the garment as he spoke. 'Be thankful that the wind is driving us towards France, for otherwise we might be doomed to a long and stormy passage, running wherever it dictated.'

Louise felt the heavy garment descend about her shoulders. She looked up to protest and met concerned grey eyes under a furrowed brow, which yet held a glimmer of wry amusement. He, curse him, was not in the slightest bit affected by the tossing motion of the little vessel. Under a wide-brimmed tall hat, which he had somehow managed to keep on despite the gale, his broad face, made distinctive by strong, anything but regular features, held no trace of the sickly tinge she knew must be evident in hers. For an instant, as she saw his gaze wander over her, she regretted the disastrous state of her clothes and toilette, but by the next had forgotten everything but another attack of nausea.

He waited patiently in the soaking rain and spray until it had passed. Then strong arms picked up her not inconsiderable weight to carry her across the heaving deck. He staggered slightly but managed to keep his balance with admirable skill.

Feebly, she struggled, knowing such intimacy with a complete stranger to be quite improper. But she knew she was fighting against the comforting feel of solid man as much as convention. 'Put me down!' she moaned.

He chuckled. She could feel the laugh reverberate

through his chest and on through her own body. 'Immediately, ma'am.'

He laid her down carefully, wedging her between the coaming surrounding the hatchway to the cabin and some deck tackle. His own clothes had suffered quite abominably, she noticed abstractedly. Since he had taken off his caped greatcoat to wrap it around her, his superfine coat and buff pantaloons had become exceedingly damp. The brocade of his waistcoat had suffered from contact with her wet pelisse and his cravat hung in limp folds which would be the despair of his valet. But at least his hair must have remained dry under the hat.

She realised suddenly that lying down did help. Her head had stopped swimming. She had been incapable of thinking as clearly as this while leaning over the rail. A small smile of gratitude touched her lips.

'Thank you, sir,' she managed.

'Remain where you are. I will secure you something to drink.'

He departed abruptly and Louisa felt bereft. She had noticed him earlier, sitting alone in the cabin, aloof and somewhat bored, scanning a newspaper. That had been before the sudden summer storm hit the packet, rendering most of its passengers incapable.

She wondered how Aunt Nazeby was feeling. That lady, used to the crossing to Ireland where her son, the present earl, possessed estates brought to him by his wife, had declared herself immune to seasickness; but she had not altogether escaped the effects of this storm. Louisa had left her in the midst of other stricken passengers, looking decidedly sickly herself while attempting to brace their wretched lady's-maids.

Not, of course, that her rescuer had been in the least stricken. She wondered who he could be, but with only vague interest. She felt too ill to concentrate on anything but her own misery.

He returned quickly. He had another greatcoat draped around his shoulders—his servant's, she sur-

mised by the cut and inferior quality, and why he hadn't
sent his man up to tend her she couldn't imagine.
Unless that individual was ill, too. But his master had
come bringing a bowl and towel as well as a goblet of
watered wine acquired, presumably, from a steward
below.

'Drink this,' he instructed, squatting as nearly at her
side as he could get. His top boots and damp pantaloons
seemed overwhelmingly near her face.

'I can't. I'll be ill again,' moaned Louisa, who did not
want to move for fear of bringing back the nausea.

'Yes, you can. Even if you bring most of it up again,
it will do you good. Come, now, ma'am, let me lift your
head.'

He put a square, capable hand under her wet curls
and urged her up. Reluctantly, but without the strength
to resist, Louisa allowed him to raise her head, eventually putting down an elbow to support herself. He held
the goblet to her lips and she drank. At least it took
the taste of bile from her mouth.

And then, of course, it all came surging up again. He
held the bowl for her.

'I told you so,' she gasped when she was able. She
had never felt so wretchedly mortified in her life.

'I know. But you will feel better now.'

He stood up and went to the lee rail, paddling
through the water surging in and out of the scuppers as
the packet heeled in a strong gust. When he came back
he placed the empty bowl near at hand, jammed among
the tackle.

'I will leave you to recover now, ma'am. The storm
is almost over and I fear I am needed below in the
cabin. We shall be in Calais within the hour if this wind
prevails. I will inform Lady Nazeby that you are safely
resting, and come back to assist you to disembark. Your
servant, ma'am.'

With a courteous bow, just as though they were in a
drawing-room instead of on a streaming, heaving deck,

he withdrew. She heard him descend the companion-way and close the hatch behind him.

She did feel better. In fact Louisa suspected after-wards that she dozed off, because the sound of barked orders and renewed activity all around made her start up. The sun had appeared again and its warmth was making the wet deck steam. The motion of the ship had lessened. Because the wind had abated and veered the crew were engaged in shaking out the reefs and reset-ting the sails.

Slowly, Louisa stirred. She sat up, leaning her back against the coaming. His coat was still about her shoulders. Her own garments were soaked beneath its comforting warmth. On land the day had been warm, but the storm and the wind at sea had caused the temperature to drop alarmingly. Now it was rising sharply again. Perhaps she should try to dry herself off. She moved cautiously, still feeling queasy, then stag-gered across to sit upon the barrel of one of several cannons carried as defence against attack by pirates. Spreading her skirts, she lifted her face to the sun, careless of her complexion. She needed to dry her hair as well as her clothes.

Who was he? The question returned to nag at her mind. She ought to know him, for he spoke as a gentleman and his garments were of top quality and cut even although he could not be described as a glass of fashion, tending rather to conservative tastes. He must move in first circles, for he apparently knew the Dowager, yet she could not remember seeing him in either drawing-room or ballroom. Not, she thought, that he seemed the sort to be comfortable in either. He hid himself in the card-rooms, perhaps. If he attended such functions at all.

She drowsed, soaking up the warmth of the sun. And awoke again to hear her aunt's anxious voice.

'There you are, Louisa, my love. I had thought you would return to the cabin once the storm abated, but here you sit as though you were nothing but a deck passenger! Have you no regard for your complexion? Where is your parasol?'

Shrugging, Louisa said, 'In the cabin, I suppose.'

'Then we must make sure to recover it! Come, my love, we must make ready to disembark!'

'Are we there already?' Louisa looked ahead and saw the coast of France looming near. 'I must have dozed off,' she explained ruefully. 'This seat is quite comfortable, you know, and I needed to dry off.'

She ran her fingers through her short curls and replaced her stained, misshapen hat, tying the ribbons securely beneath her chin.

'The feathers are in a sad state,' she observed, 'but the hat will have to do until we reach the shore. Who was that man, Aunt? The one who came to my aid.' She stroked the cape of his greatcoat, her fingers lingering on the damp, expensive material.

'Didn't you know? No, I suppose you might not. I did not recognise him at first. He's the Duke of Chadford's son. We had met before, so did not need further introduction.'

'Not Alnbridge,' said Louisa decidedly. 'I'd have recognised him.'

'No. Lord Hugh Deverill, the Earl's brother. Did a Season once, before you came out, but none of the belles could fix his interest, though plenty tried, despite Deverill's only being a younger son. Then he practically retired from Society, attached to the Foreign Office, so they say, no time for idling about in drawing-rooms, which is why I did not recognise him at once.'

'But plenty of time to conduct an *affaire*, if rumour is true. I have heard of him, though I've never met him, as far as I know. Isn't Lady Kingslea his latest flirt?'

'Possibly. Rumours did circulate when he was in London last. Mostly to the effect that he had become Maria Kingslea's latest victim. Don't sound so disapproving, Louisa. Most unmarried men have a mistress; there'd be something wrong with 'em if they didn't, in my opinion——'

'Married men have them, too,' interrupted Louisa bitterly, 'but gentlemen have no need to attach other men's wives. There must be plenty of widows or members of the muslin company available to meet their needs.'

'Really, Louisa, you shouldn't use such terms,' scolded Lady Nazeby, her eyes twinkling. 'And it takes two, you know. No one forces a woman to be unfaithful to her husband.'

'I know, or a man to his wife. When I remember the misery poor Mamma suffered. . .'

'Don't refine upon it too much, my dear Louisa. your father was a rake, no one denies that, but few men are such bad lots as he turned out to be, and I'm sure Hugh Deverill is not one of 'em. I'd have heard.'

'I wonder where he's bound?' muttered Louisa as she rose reluctantly to her feet. Her shoes were still wet, her pelisse damp and her skirts inclined to drip. She had never felt so wretchedly turned out in her life. She thrust his lordship's greatcoat into her aunt's hands. 'Are you climbing down into the cabin again? Take this back and give it to him,' she begged. 'I do not wish to speak with him again.'

'My dear, you must offer your thanks——'

'You can do that for me, Aunt Nazeby. I'll wait here until it is time to go ashore. I cannot face that cabin again. I do declare, next time I cross the Channel I shall travel as a deck passenger!'

'And be herded behind the mast with only a tarpaulin to shelter you from the elements?'

'Infinitely better than that stuffy cabin!' laughed Louisa. Please God, next time she took to the sea it would remain calm!

'I'm glad you're feeling more cheerful, my dear,' smiled Lady Nazeby fondly. 'I'll go back and deliver this coat and thank his lordship, then. Rose and Betty should be feeling up to scratch by now. I wonder how Dench is?'

'Wet, I should think,' said Louisa. Their footman had chosen to be an outside passenger.

'I hope not. And if he was sick I hope he has recovered. We need him to help carry our hand luggage.'

So saying, Lady Nazeby swayed back to descend the companionway and return Lord Hugh Deverill's coat to its owner.

Sighing, Louisa went to the rail to watch Calais draw nearer. A further trying time lay ahead. She did not mind so much going to Paris, where the *ton* was taking up residence *en masse*, but she did wish her aunt had not insisted on visiting Brussels and Waterloo first. The very thought of viewing the field of battle turned her cold. Such a ghoulish desire, she considered it, to wish to see the spot where over forty thousand men had died, many of the Englishmen among them the young, gallant officers who had graced the ballrooms of London, Brighton and Bath over the past years. Yet it was the thing to do, so her aunt insisted. One simply had to inspect the site of Wellington's famous victory or be deemed unpatriotic.

The packet began to dock. Luckily the tide was up, so they would not need to take to the faring boats to land. Louisa moved from the rail to join her aunt as the latter emerged from the cabin and handed her her parasol. Together, the two women, followed by servants laden with bandboxes and a trail of porters humping trunks, prepared to cross the gangplank to French soil.

'Are you quite recovered, Miss Finsham?'

Louisa recognised the voice immediately. She swung round, determined not to blush. At five and twenty she was far too old and seasoned to be overset, at however much of a disadvantage fate had placed her. Her parasol, at least, had not suffered, and she twirled it defiantly.

He did not wait for a reply, but turned immediately to her aunt. 'I would account it a great honour, Lady Nazeby, if you would introduce me to your companion.'

'Not my companion, my lord. Louisa is my niece, though she has chosen to reside with me and keep me company. Louisa, my love, may I introduce Lord Hugh Deverill?' Her eyes twinkled. 'I believe you have already met informally. My lord, Miss Louisa Finsham.'

'Servant, Miss Finsham.' His lordship bowed with easy grace despite his large frame. He was not stout, she conceded, but solidly built, with broad shoulders under the superfine coat. And her inspection confirmed her previous impression of strong, shapely limbs stretching the fawn pantaloons. To her mortification she noticed a spot of poppy-red marring the perfect whiteness of his crumpled cravat.

'My lord.' Louisa returned his bow with a neat curtsy, formally polite.

Other passengers, anxious to disembark, jostled behind them. Dench, loaded with several bandboxes, nevertheless proved himself quite able to help his employer down the narrow gangway. Louisa found Lord Hugh hovering at her elbow.

'Allow me, Miss Finsham.'

Without asking, he relieved her of the damp pelisse, which she had removed and was carrying, and offered his arm. Louisa could scarcely refuse to take it, though she wished she were not so aware of the muscles hidden beneath the tight-fitting sleeve. His man followed them down, carrying his master's greatcoat, like her own pelisse no longer required, and a large valise.

All was bustle on the quay, where a number of carriages awaited the packet's passengers and a contingent of surly-looking, armed *douaniers* in dark green uniforms and cocked hats stood ready to inspect passports, collect duty and intercept any contraband.

'I will see your luggage through Customs and loaded on the chaise, my lord,' said Deverill's man impassively, for his master showed little inclination to oversee the disposition of his trunks himself.

Deverill nodded. 'I'll not be long.' He smiled down at the woman on his arm, apparently not at all disturbed by her dishevelled appearance. 'Do you have your passport handy?'

'I have it here.' Louisa delved into her reticule and produced a damp document. 'I hope it will be readable!'

Deverill glanced at it briefly. 'Eminently. The paper is merely moist. The man will not question it.' He handed both documents to a waiting *douanier*. As the man returned the papers and he handed hers back, he asked, 'Are you bound for Paris too, Miss Finsham?'

'Eventually, my lord. We are to travel via Brussels.'

A frown immediately formed between his intelligent, deep-set eyes. 'Indeed, ma'am. You are making an excursion to view the battlefield?'

Distaste informed his voice and expression. Resenting his implied criticism, Louisa removed her hand from his arm.

'Indeed, sir. It is quite the thing, you know. We should be considered quite out if we did not.'

'And that would matter to you?' he enquired coldly.

'But of course. My aunt would never forgive me were I to shirk such an obvious duty. To see where our brave young men died, you know.'

'Forgive me if I cannot admire such a sentiment, Miss Finsham. To me this passion for viewing the site of tragedy on such a grand scale is nothing short of repulsive.'

'Perhaps you do not rejoice in the great victory, my lord? You would prefer that monster Napoleon to remain in power? To see Europe in constant turmoil?'

He shook his head. 'Not at all.'

'But then,' she said kindly, 'you are not a soldier, I collect. Perhaps you resent the admiration our army and its commander have so deservedly gathered to themselves.'

He executed a frigid bow. 'You must think as you wish, Miss Finsham. If your desire is to tread upon the bones of the dead I have nothing to say. No doubt we shall meet again in Paris. Until then, I will bid you adieu.'

He turned on his heel and strode to where Amelia, the Dowager Countess of Nazeby, was busy instructing the maids and Dench upon the best disposition of their mountain of luggage. The *douaniers* appeared to have lost interest in their possessions, Louisa was relieved to see.

She watched as Deverill made his devoirs to Lady Nazeby. It seemed his displeasure did not extend to that lady.

Why had she reacted so defiantly? wondered Louisa, feeling rather guilty. After all, it seemed their opinions on the subject were similar. She had allowed his inexcusable attitude to provoke her into asserting her aunt's views, not her own.

Well, it hardly mattered. If he appeared as much in Society in Paris as he did in London they would scarcely be likely to meet. He had done her a service but cancelled any debt by his censorious words. Tread upon bones, indeed! No, she would not mind if she never set eyes on Lord Hugh Deverill again.

Brussels reeked of gangrene and typhus. Wounded soldiers, most of them French, still lay about the streets begging for help. A few people were doing what they could to relieve the suffering, but it was little enough. And the majority carried on with their lives as though the poor fellows did not exist. In particular, those members of the *ton* still in residence there seemed determined to exact the last fragment of enjoyment from their social activities. On the very day of arrival they received a number of visitors at the rooms they had rented for their stay, cards were left and invitations to several soirées and drums delivered.

Louisa was appalled. 'How can they, Aunt?' she wailed, thinking how Hugh Deverill's lips would curl in disgust.

'Life must go on, my love,' Amelia pointed out. 'The

world cannot come to a halt because some poor souls have died and others are suffering.'

But she did not look as though she believed what she said. Louisa eyed her aunt anxiously. Since arriving in Brussels a kind of pall seemed to have descended to dampen her usually ebullient spirits.

'Do you wish to attend the Richmonds' soirée tonight?'

Amelia sighed. 'No, my dear, I do not believe I do. The journey has been most trying. But if you would like——'

Louisa cut her off quickly. 'No, Aunt. It is the last thing I want to do. There is too much suffering in this city for me to contemplate such a frivolous occupation.'

'Then we will remain in. Dench shall go out and bring back Ordinaries from the nearest inn.'

Next day, while her aunt continued to rest, Louisa dispensed considerable sums of money to help some of the poor derelicts find shelter and others to pay their way home. The following morning after breakfast she announced her intention of visiting the hospital in order to volunteer her services there.

'I cannot possibly countenance such a thing, Louisa,' cried her aunt, scandalised. 'Nursing men! Besides, you could so easily catch the fever and die, and what good would that do to anyone, I'd like to know? I wish I had listened to you and not come here, but no one had told me what Brussels would be like. We have a hired house—an *hôtel*, as the French call it—waiting for us in Paris. We will leave for there tomorrow.'

'Without viewing the battlefield?' asked Louisa in relief.

'By no means! That was our reason for coming here and I am quite determined to do so. But once we have seen it we may go.'

The set of Lady Nazeby's jaw indicated the impossibility of arguing with her. Louisa tried all the same.

'But——'

Lady Nazeby continued as though she had not spo-

ken. 'We will drive out there this morning. There will
be plenty of time before dinner. I will ring for Dench
and send him to acquire a hired carriage immediately.
By the time he returns we shall be ready.'

As her aunt suited actions to words, Louisa swallowed her disappointment. She owed Lady Nazeby so
much; she had been the only one to care for her since
her mother's death, and she loved the old lady dearly.
She could not argue more against this expedition, which
for some reason she seemed so determined to make.
Nor could she bring herself to refuse to accompany the
Dowager.

The hired coachman, well used to such expeditions, took them to join a string of other sightseeing
vehicles lined up on the road just below the ridge the
Allied army had defended so bravely. He pointed out
Wellington's strong points, the château of Hugemont to
the west, the farm of La Haye Sainte with its orchard
in the centre, and the farm of Papelotte to the east.
Beneath them stretched the trampled cornfields across
which Napoleon had thrown all his men into the attack.
In the distance they fancied they could see the knoll
near La Belle Alliance from which Napoleon had
directed his army.

Lady Nazeby made no attempt to descend from the
landaulet and stroll about, as the driver expected and
the other visitors were doing. Their voices, the high-
pitched shrieks of the women, floated up to them,
incongruous in that otherwise empty landscape. The
hood of their carriage was down since it was another
fine day. The Dowager Countess simply sat and stared.
As she did so the tears began to gather and then to fall.

Louisa, hardly able to bear to look upon the ruined
buildings, the devastated countryside which even yet
bore the debris of battle, traces of those who had died
there, kept her eyes steadfastly fixed on the silk gloves
covering hands gripped together in her lap.

So at first she did not notice her companion's distress.
Eventually, though, her aunt's silence made her look

up. Despite the concealing brim of a large bonnet she saw the tears streaming down the lined cheeks and immediately her own feelings were forgotten.

'Dear Aunt,' she cried, 'I should have tried harder to dissuade you from coming here! Do not fret yourself so, I beg you! Coachman,' she called in schoolroom French, which was all she knew, 'return to Brussels at once, if you please!'

The man, who had been holding his horses' heads, returned to the box and set the carriage in motion. Louisa took hold of Lady Nazeby's hand and clasped it in both of hers, not understanding her aunt's distress and afraid to speak for fear of making things worse.

'I'm sorry to be such a watering pot, m'dear,' wavered Lady Nazeby. 'I declare, I cannot imagine what has come over me!'

She did not seem able to stem her tears, however, and the return journey was accomplished in silence. With Dench sitting impassively beside the driver Louisa did not feel free to speak as she would have liked.

Once they were settled in their own private sitting-room, however, Louisa could restrain herself no longer. Her aunt's eyes were still suspiciously moist and she seemed upset beyond all comprehension.

'Dear Aunt,' she began, 'do please tell me what is amiss. I do not like to see you so overset. You appeared so determined, so anxious to follow everyone else to the battlefield. You must have known it would be a harrowing experience. What can have caused you such distress?'

Lady Nazeby dabbed at her eyes with a dainty lace handkerchief and sniffed the tears back with sudden determination. Her voice, however, still wavered.

'Did I seem so very heartless to you, my love? I knew, of course, that it would not be pleasant. But I had my own reasons for wishing to see the field of battle for myself. 'Twas not simply a desire to be in the fashion.'

'Was it not, Aunt? Then what was your reason?' asked Louisa gently.

'I have never confided this to anyone before,' sighed Amelia, who, now she had started, seemed to have gained a better command over her voice, 'apart, of course, from the dear friend who adopted him. I had a son, Louisa. He—was not Nazeby's.'

Louisa caught her breath. 'You did, Aunt?'

'Yes, my love. Your respectable aunt. I fell in love, you see. Perhaps that is why I can understand other wives... But no matter. When I discovered my state I went into retirement and had my lover's son. I travelled with a friend, a woman who desperately needed a son to keep the love of her husband. She had a property up in Yorkshire and we announced we were going there to rusticate. Our husbands did not mind. Thought it rather a joke, left 'em free to live bachelor lives for a while.'

'And you did not mind that?'

'Nothing new. Trouble with arranged marriages is if you don't suit it's hard on a man. Has to find his pleasure elsewhere. Love's worse, though. Plays the very devil with the emotions. Raises too many problems.'

'Unless you're free to marry the person you love,' murmured Louisa.

'I know very well why you've hung out for someone special but you mustn't delay too long, my dear Louisa; you're not quite past your last prayers yet, but you're not getting any younger——'

'I have no need to marry,' put in Louisa quickly. 'Thanks to the foresight of my grandmother I have enough fortune to live in reasonable style for the remainder of my life, and do not intend to allow some rake to drink and gamble it away. I know my husband will not control my fortune, thank God, but I would be hard pressed to refuse him help should he demand it. But do go on, Aunt. What happened?'

'Together, we planned everything and no one suspected the child was not my friend's. Wrote back to say

she was increasing a month after we arrived. Her
husband posted up with all haste, but since it was too
early for anything to show it didn't matter. Told him
we were set on remaining in Yorkshire and not to come
again, babies were a woman's affair. With which he
thoroughly agreed. He'd see it soon enough after it was
born.'

'And he did as he was told?'

'Of course. Men ain't much interested in a woman
when she's in a delicate condition. After that we were
left to ourselves. Had it been a girl my friend would
have been disappointed, but she would still have taken
her, for she would at least have had a child to love even
if it weren't the son her husband wanted.'

'But it was a boy,' prompted Louisa, since her aunt
had fallen into a reverie.

'Yes. Such a beautiful baby. Very like his father, you
know.'

'Who was he?'

'The father?' A wistful smile lit Amelia's face for a
moment. 'That I will never divulge. Even my friend
who brought him up did not know. But he was a peer.
The boy's pedigree could in no way be considered at
odds with his supposed father's consequence.'

'What became of him?'

'He inherited the title. Wed and produced an heir.
And died honourably on the field we have just seen.'

'Oh, Aunt!'

Compassion filled Louisa's voice as she dropped to
her knees at Amelia's side. However much she might
dislike infidelity there was something about her aunt's
story that caught at her emotions. Amelia had not been
happy with Nazeby and had not mourned his death.
How many women suffered a lifetime of unhappiness
because their husbands had been chosen for them by
parents blind to the consequences of forcing conflicting
characters into a marriage devoid of affection, let alone
love? And were the ones who took lovers simply seeking consolation, hoping to find that joy and closeness

denied them in their lawful union? How thankful she was that her father had died before he could arrange such a joyless match for her.

After a moment of silent sympathy Louisa returned to her questions.

'So your grandson has inherited. How old is he?'

'Twelve,' said Amelia baldly.

'Poor little fellow! So much consequence to bear! Is his mother sensible?'

'Only marginally. I could never understand why R——' She cut herself off quickly. 'Why my son married her. She was pretty, of course, in an insipid way. No accountin' for a man's taste. And my friend, the boy's grandmother, is no longer able to follow his progress as she would like.'

'She is ill?'

'Not precisely. But she suffers considerably with her joints and can no longer travel. We have both outlived our spouses. They were much older than us, of course.'

'You are still able to keep an eye on him.'

The words were spoken quietly. Amelia glanced at her niece, a flush of colour staining her cheekbones. 'Why we're goin' to Paris,' she muttered. 'Standin' in for her. His mother insisted on taking the boy there. Wanted diversion to take her out of her mopes, she said. Didn't want to miss the chance of catching another husband, in my opinion.'

'You don't like her,' observed Louisa wryly.

'Don't think anything about her. Just hope she don't spoil the boy.'

'Dear Aunt, if you could bring yourself to tell me who he is, I'd look out for him, too.'

Amelia's eyes filled with tears again. 'I could happily trust him to your care, my love. I am getting to be an old woman.'

'Nonsense, Aunt! That's not what I meant at all! You are going to live for years and years yet! What would I do without you? But I thought we might share the burden, in the way we share so much else.'

'It's true, though. And I would feel happier about the boy if I knew you were keeping an eye on his welfare after Muriel and I are gone. James Grade. Thurrock.'

Louisa's eyes widened. 'The new Earl of Thurrock? His must be one of the richest inheritances in the kingdom! I trust his wealth is securely tied up in trusts!'

'You may depend upon it. The Thurrock fortune always is. Families are beginning to show some sense. No good preserving the entail to prevent estates being split up if there ain't any money left to run 'em.'

'No,' agreed Louisa. 'Though it is hard on the younger sons,' she added thoughtfully. 'I often think they must resent the eldest inheriting everything.'

'I suppose they may. Most go into the army. As heir, Robert should never have been allowed to purchase his pair of colours, but there was no stopping him. Mad on it. Ensign at seventeen. Fought all through the Peninsula. Couldn't resist Wellington's call when Napoleon returned. Rallied to the flag and, like Tom Picton, got himself killed.'

'At least he left an heir.'

The glamour of the red coat had never attracted Louisa. She knew fighting was necessary to stop someone like Napoleon, but men seemed to glory in it and that she could not understand.

Yet, despite holding these sentiments herself, she had taunted Lord Hugh Deverill on not being a military man. And he had been piqued. Had climbed up on his high ropes and taken a disdainful leave.

Why should she think of Hugh Deverill now? she asked herself in irritation. She hoped never to see him again. Such an encounter could only prove too mortifying to be endured.

CHAPTER TWO

PARIS had changed. Or so said those who had known it before the Revolution. Amelia, who had visited in her youth, decided that little had physically altered. But the large mansions of the *aristos*, once so splendid, were mostly dilapidated from years of shuttered neglect or, worse, had suffered wanton destruction. A few had been used by the Revolutionary movement as centres of government or had been lived in by its leaders. But their treatment had not been kind and with but few exceptions all exuded an air of decay.

However, the city was far from dead. The *ton* of several countries had gathered there and social life in the highest circles had never been more lively. Horsemen and carriages thronged the streets. For the lower orders of Parisian inhabitants, however, life was far from rosy. With a combined force of sixty thousand encamped near by, soldiers from the victorious Prussian, Russian and Austrian armies were everywhere, terrorising the ordinary inhabitants and leaving a trail of broken lives and shattered homes behind them.

'Thank God,' remarked Louisa, shuddering as they watched a poor, weeping woman being deprived of her furniture, 'there are no redcoats among them.'

'Prussians, I believe,' grunted Amelia, noting the blue jackets, white breeches and knee-boots of the offenders. 'The guard on the gate did say that the British soldiers needed passes to enter the city and have orders to pay for whatever they take.'

'I trust the commanders will ensure that their men obey the order,' said Louisa fervently. 'I should hate for our army to be guilty of such conduct. By what I've heard, many of our senior officers have taken up residence within the city so they should be able to keep an eye on the lower ranks.' As the carriage passed on towards the centre of the town she felt constrained to remark, 'It doesn't appear too difficult to obtain a pass, judging by the number of red coats to be seen on the streets.'

'True, but note, my love, they are behaving exactly as they would in London.'

'Parading to display their uniforms,' chuckled Louisa. 'Particularly the officers!'

The Duke of Wellington had taken over Marshal Junot's house, situated on the corner of Place Louis XV near the Place Vendôme. The Dowager Countess's hired residence stood near by. The procession which drew to a halt before its ornate if dilapidated façade consisted of two carriages, each drawn by four horses, escorted by six outriders. Dench, in bob wig and the Duchess's blue and white livery, the coat lavishly decorated with gold frogging, sat up behind his mistress in the first. The second vehicle accommodated their maids and most of the luggage.

As the Dowager's train drew up before their temporary residence Louisa was so absorbed in looking up at the elaborate carvings and decorative ironwork smothering the front of the building that at first she failed to see the party gathered on the step before the double doors. Even when she did lower her fascinated gaze her eyes alighted first on Lady Nazeby's groom, Pershaw, who ran forward to hold the leaders' heads.

He was quickly relieved of this task by others and, as Dench sprang down to help his mistress alight, Pershaw bowed to her respectfully.

'Well, Pershaw! So you are arrived! My horses are safe, I trust?'

'Indeed, your ladyship. We had a pleasant crossing, and I took the journey here in easy stages, you may be sure. The bays arrived in splendid condition, Miss Finsham's black, too.'

He made another bow, in Louisa's direction this time,

and she smiled at the wiry little man, who had served the old Earl before his death and had continued in the employ of the Dowager, to whom he was devoted. She suspected he was only slightly less devoted to herself. She seemed to have known him forever; it was he who had taught her to ride and afterwards all she wanted to know about horses, for she had been a frequent visitor with the Countess ever since her mother's early death, and it was Lady Nazeby who had brought her out. When her father's demise, some three years ago, had finally left her a lady of independent means able to indulge her independent whims and live the way she chose, it had seemed natural to make her permanent home with her aunt Nazeby.

'Hello, Pershaw,' she greeted the groom. 'How nice it is to have a familiar face to welcome us! Have Prince Hal saddled and ready for me at seven tomorrow morning, will you? And be ready to accompany me. I know I can trust you to have discovered the best rides.'

Pershaw returned her smile. She knew that not only was he always happy to accompany her on her spirited excursions, he positively enjoyed them, feeling supremely superior to those poor grooms forced to idle along behind a mistress barely able to control a docile hack. They shared a moment of complete understanding.

'Certainly, miss. There are still some excellent rides in the Bois de Boulogne despite part of our army's being encamped there.'

They could not linger long with Pershaw, however, for the party on the doorstep had moved forward to greet them.

For the first time, Louisa consciously registered its presence. She immediately recognised the elegant figure of Sir Charles Stuart, the British Ambassador, for they had often met in London. He was already making his devoirs to the Countess. Over his bent head her eyes passed on to the tall man standing at his shoulder, waiting to make his bow.

It couldn't be. But it was.

She crushed down the mortification threatening to overwhelm her. Remembered gratefully the style in which they had arrived. Lifted her chin under the fashionable bonnet with its frilled brim and bunch of blue ribbons, the colour of which exactly matched the smart pelisse-robe she had chosen to wear for the journey. On this occasion she had absolutely no cause to feel at a disadvantage.

So there could be no possible reason for sight of him to put her to the blush. She was in full command of herself now, and if he chose to condemn her for visiting Waterloo it could scarcely signify.

She stepped forward with deliberate dignity and apparent aloof calm to receive the ambassador's greeting and made a curtsy which included both men. Lord Hugh Deverill had already swept a dutiful bow, removing his tall, curly-brimmed hat to reveal thick black wavy hair. His deep-set eyes held little expression, though she was close enough and fit enough to see that the grey of the iris became a mottled blue near his pupil. She had never before seen eyes quite like them and found it surprisingly difficult to tear her own away. There appeared to be something mesmerising in their neutral depths.

She had been feeling too ill to take in his appearance aboard the packet properly. Now, having at last managed to detach her gaze from his, she dazedly appreciated how attractive his smile was, lighting his ruggedly handsome face despite the fact that it did not reach his eyes.

'Miss Finsham.' His deep voice touched some nerve inside her, causing it to vibrate. 'You are fully recovered, I collect?'

'Indeed, my lord.' She met his gaze again bravely. She would *not* quake! 'Seasickness soon passes once the motion ceases, as I am certain you are aware. I must thank you again for your timely assistance on the packet boat.'

He acknowledged her thanks with a slight inclination

of his head. 'It was nothing. I trust you will enjoy your residence in Paris.'

She returned his polite gesture with the merest movement of her own head, feeling such a formal welcome required no verbal response, and was glad when Sir Charles intervened.

'Deverill has been sent by the Foreign Office to assist me here, now the numbers of English visitors have increased so dramatically. If you ladies have need of advice or help at any time, you have only to call upon either of us and we will be entirely at your service.' He swept another deep bow.

'That is most kind of you, Sir Charles,' Amelia replied for them both, 'and I greatly appreciate the courtesy of your being here to greet us. But do let us go inside! I am vastly curious to see what manner of mansion my agent has chosen.'

'One of the best available, Lady Nazeby, I do assure you.' Sir Charles gave another bow, less flourishing this time. 'I think you will find the *maître d'hôtel* highly efficient. I recommended him myself.'

He ushered the Dowager forward and Louisa found herself mounting the steps beside Lord Hugh Deverill. Unaccountably, she stumbled. Instantly, his hand, warm and sustaining, grasped her elbow. The effect took her breath as currents of sensation flowed up her arm and through her body.

'Thank you,' she gasped as she recovered her balance. His hand was immediately removed. 'Such a shallow step! You must think me inordinately weak and foolish!'

His reserved manner broke. He laughed. 'Really, Miss Finsham! *You*, weak and foolish?'

His manner teased and she could not resist smiling back. 'Well, I always seem to be thanking you for your assistance, my lord!'

'Which it gives me great pleasure to afford.'

She had reminded him of their previous encounter.

The laughter left his face and he regarded her thoughtfully as they passed through the entrance doors.

'I was surprised to be informed of your imminent arrival,' he remarked. 'I had imagined you to be planning on a longer stay in Brussels.'

'We found nothing to delay us there, my lord,' responded Louisa neutrally. The pleasant intimacy of moments earlier had deserted them. Louisa knew the reason and regretted the loss.

'Your journey was agreeable, I trust?'

'Tolerable, I thank you. We had feared molestation by vagrants or mayhap by revolutionary peasants who resented our presence, but fortunately our fears proved groundless.'

'You were right to be cautious and to travel well-protected.'

He had the air of a man forcing himself to keep up the polite conversation. His continued reservations over her movements irked. Yet she would be lacking in conduct were she to allow her irritation to show in public.

'Even in England there are dangers,' he was going on, 'but here the nation is somewhat naturally still in turmoil. Napoleon may be finally defeated but the Bourbon dynasty has never been popular and the people suffer its restoration only because they have no choice.'

Her interest caught, her pique forgotten, she asked sharply, 'The return of King Louis is not welcome?'

He shook his head. 'No. Most Frenchmen cherish the freedom they have purchased with their blood. Many acquiesced in the Terror which so shocked us——'

'How could they?' shuddered Louisa, appalled at the very idea.

'It is perhaps difficult for you to understand, but at first it was their feudal lords and oppressors who went to the guillotine. In the end, of course, the holocaust swallowed up even its own creators.'

She turned to him indignantly. 'You have the right of

it, my lord! I find it impossibly difficult to understand! The *émigrés* I have met have all been highly civilised people——'

'But haughty?' he demanded with a quizzical smile. His manner had relaxed again. This was no longer a conversation conducted for the sake of courtesy. 'A little high in the instep? Imperious in the demands made upon their inferiors?'

Louisa flushed. 'Some, my lord,' she admitted. 'But others——'

'There are good and bad in every circle, Miss Finsham. And many of the *émigrés* had of necessity to practise humility, being dependent upon the charity of others. You must know that there are plenty of Englishmen who would welcome a revolution there.'

'The Jacobins!' exclaimed Louisa scathingly.

To her relief they had caught up with Sir Charles and Amelia, who was about to greet a long line of servants gathered in the hall for her inspection. The conversation, which had threatened to become a heated argument, ended.

The tall, spare major-domo stepped forward and bowed, all stiff formality from his bewigged head to his white-stockinged legs and polished shoes. '*Bonjour, mesdames.* Welcome to the Hôtel des Fleurs, milady.'

'This,' said Sir Charles, 'is Chausson, the *maître d'hôtel.*'

The Frenchman bowed again. 'Me, myself and my staff are entirely at your service, milady.'

'Chausson gained an excellent command of English during his service in England, where he sought refuge with his master during the Revolution,' Sir Charles went on to explain. 'His master unfortunately died in exile. I believe several of the more senior servants, including the chef, are likewise able to speak our language, for similar reasons.'

Amelia beamed happily. 'Capital! For I know scarcely any French! What I learned in the schoolroom many years ago has long since been forgotten!'

'Most ladies find the knowledge returns to them when required, ma'am.'

'I do not count on it,' muttered Amelia, who considered herself too old to be re-learning old tricks.

Having booked from afar, the ladies had scarcely known what to expect of their accommodation. The agent had assured them that the house would be large enough for modest entertaining but they had not expected such lavish, if rather tarnished opulence. Nor under-servants who, without appearing obsequious, were so obviously eager to please and employed in such numbers.

'My!' exclaimed the Countess as they passed along the row acknowledging bows and curtsies. 'Where did you find all these people to staff the house, Chausson?'

'Many were employed in great households before ze Revolution, milady, and are pleased to resume zair former tasks. Eet was not ze work zey ab'orred, but zair masters. The feudal system 'as at last been abolished in France and will not return. France, she is free.'

'I see,' returned the Duchess drily. 'I trust they will not come to abhor us!'

'I sink not, milady. Ze English are more considerate.' He bowed in the direction of the two men from the embassy.

'We have a reputation to live up to, I collect,' said Louisa, unable to repress a wry grin.

'I am sure you will not find that difficult,' murmured Hugh Deverill, still seemingly glued to her side.

'And should we fail you would no doubt rejoice to see us sent to the guillotine!' returned Louisa sharply.

'Me, Miss Finsham?' He sounded startled. 'Why should you think that?'

'You speak like a Jacobin, my lord.'

She knew he was not. Some devilish imp had made her accuse him. The mischief sparked from her eyes.

He grinned. 'In my profession I must appreciate every point of view,' he defended himself lightly. 'There is always more than one side to any question. I cannot afford to be blinkered in my outlook.'

Implying that I am? wondered Louisa. If so, she had only herself to blame. But she had gone too far in this enlivening conversation to back down now. 'And one of them must be right!' she retorted smartly.

He shook his head, the smile still lingering on his lips. 'There you mistake, Miss Finsham. Both sides often have much to recommend them. That is where diplomatic compromise is required.'

'Ah, yes! Compromise!'

What scathing remark she would have made next neither of them knew, for before she could think of one, 'We must take our leave,' announced Sir Charles. 'We have already delayed your settling in for too long. But before I go I am commissioned by Lady Stuart to extend an invitation to you both to attend a reception she is giving tomorrow evening, at the embassy. There, you will meet everyone who is anyone in Paris at the present moment.'

'The pleasure will be ours,' responded Amelia, delighted. 'Where have you set up your embassy?'

'In the building Lord Wellington chose, last year. The Hôtel de Charost, in the Rue du Faubourg St Honoré. It was acquired by Napoleon. His sister used to live there and it is one of the few mansions not sadly in need of repair. I will see that cards are sent to you immediately, my lady. May I also send a carriage for you tomorrow evening?'

'Thank you, but that will not be necessary. I have instructed Pershaw to hire an adequate coach, and I have my own horses already here. We will look forward to tomorrow.'

The men made their formal farewells. Louisa watched their retreat, her eyes lingering on the form of Hugh Deverill. Most of the men she met were either podgy or willowy. She could not imagine why. Lord Hugh was neither. Broad shoulders tapered to slim hips which allowed the square tails of his frock-coat to hang with exquisite elegance. He wore narrow trousers, she noted, with a stirrup under his shoes to keep them taut. Quietly attired rather than dressed in the first stare of fashion, he nevertheless cut an admirable figure.

She had enjoyed their sparring once he had dropped his insufferably critical attitude. She could even begin to think him attractive.

For days now Hugh's mind had been filled with pictures of an urchin-like creature dealing courageously with the discomforts of seasickness. Now he found his mental vision completely engaged by a bewitching face peeping from beneath the brim of an outrageously becoming bonnet to challenge and tease him.

After the instinctive revulsion he had felt at the discovery of her intention to follow fashion and make a macabre visit to Waterloo, he should have put her firmly from his mind. Somehow he had not been able to. Now, such a course seemed even more impossible. Had it not been for that— He pulled his thoughts up short. They were leading to realms he would rather not contemplate, situated as he was.

Thankfully, he turned to Sir Charles, who was demanding his attention with an ironic enquiry as to whether Lord Hugh would stop wool-gathering and pay attention to the point under discussion.

As Chausson led the two ladies up the impressive curved staircase with its ornate balustrade Hugh Deverill continued to dominate Louisa's thoughts. Throughout their recent exchange she had sensed the reserve underlying his manner towards her. She resented it. Men did not normally take exception to her or her opinions. What right had he to condemn her, whatever she chose to do or think? She should not let his opinion concern her. Yet, perversely, it did.

On the first floor Chausson paused and she had to jerk her mind back to what he was saying.

'Ze withdrawing-room is 'ere, milady, and through

those doors the dining-room. Behind is ze morning-room and over there a smaller reception-room. And now please allow me to show you up to the bedrooms. François!' He called imperiously to a footman labouring up under the weight of several pieces of luggage, and went on to address him in French. 'Stand aside for the Countess!'

The Dowager was shown into the master bedroom, which had a dressing-room and boudoir attached. Both ladies exclaimed over its size and the elegance of its furnishings.

'You have always loved pink and cream!' cried Louisa. 'I cannot wait to see what my room is like!'

Shown into a large, airy chamber overlooking the gardens which, judging by the profusion of blooms in the neglected beds, must have given the house its name, Louisa expressed her delight.

'Green and silver are so cool and restful! Do you not think it delightful, dear Aunt?'

'I must confess to being quite in raptures over the entire establishment, Louisa, but now I must leave you. Chausson informs me dinner will be ready to be served within the hour so we must make haste to change.'

Betty soon had the huge canopied bed buried under garments extracted from travelling boxes, piling them up ready for ironing and hanging. As the older woman left what she was doing to assist her to change, Louisa realised that her maid's normally cheerful countenance wore a gloomy expression.

'Come, Betty, what is the matter?' she chided. 'Do you not find Paris to your liking? You did not object to Brussels, I collect, despite its sad state. Paris appears to be a fine city, with plenty of sights to see and no immediate aftermath of battle to render it uncongenial. Or is it this establishment which you find not to your liking?'

'It's not anything like that, Miss Louisa,' Betty confessed. 'Though I could do without seeing that Bastille place and the prison where the poor King and Queen

were locked up before they were murdered. And I
hope they've taken that dreadful guillotine away.'

'I'm sure they have,' Louisa reassured her. 'But what
is it, then? You do not normally wear such a glum
look.'

'Well, Miss Louisa, if the truth be told I'm worried.
It seems to Rose and me that there must be plenty of
smart French lady's-maids out of work over here, and
both you and the Countess might prefer to have one of
them to look after you.'

Astonished, Louisa spread her hands in a helpless
gesture. 'Do not be foolish, Betty,' she chided. 'Have I
ever shown the slightest displeasure with your work?
Are we not on the best of terms? How should I be able
to confide in a French maid, when I do not speak the
language above a word or two?'

'I am getting old, Miss Louisa,' muttered Betty. 'You
might prefer someone younger, more up-to-date in her
ways.'

'Nonsense, you ridiculous creature!' Louisa gave the
older woman a warm hug. 'You are scarcely in your
dotage yet! Have you not been with me since I was
deemed old enough to need a maid? Did you not see
me through my come-out? We know each other's ways.
I should dislike vastly to have anyone else look after
me, I can assure you! Come now, arrange my hair and
stop fretting. Do your best to see that I present a
splendid appearance at dinner, even though we are to
dine alone. Show these French servants what an English
one can do!'

Thus reassured and challenged, Betty excelled herself. So far Louisa had not taken to wearing a cap, not
having entirely resigned herself to spinsterhood. She
descended the stairs dressed in fine white muslin over
cornflower-blue silk, her curls threaded with matching
blue ribbon in a most becoming style. A pity, she
thought with a soft chuckle, that there would be no
guests to enjoy the undoubted excellence of her *toilette*.
And if one particular guest she had in mind happened

to be Hugh Deverill that was simply because of the challenge he presented. She wished to force him to admire her, to break through his coolly critical attitude. The gentleman was altogether too sure of himself. He badly needed to have his self-consequence shaken.

The lack of guests had not daunted the French chef, who, anxious to impress his new if temporary employer, had prepared a splendid dinner which Chausson saw served with great formality in a dining-room which would accommodate a minor banquet. A huge expanse of table stretched between the two ladies as they were ushered to their allotted places.

'This looks quite delicious, Chausson,' observed Lady Nazeby, 'and the covers are laid out beautifully, but in future when we dine alone we will have the meal served in the small dining-room. Meanwhile, please have Miss Finsham's place removed to this end of the table, or we shall be unable to converse.'

Chausson bowed his acquiescence and Louisa, shaking with mirth internally while maintaining a dignified outward appearance with some difficulty, took her place at her aunt's right hand. Servants often stood upon protocol and dignity far more stiffly than did their masters.

Lady Nazeby had survived the journey well, considering her age. She, too, looked the picture of elegance in a gown of rose-pink, the colour suiting her fair complexion and the white hair escaping the confines of a matching turban. She had kept her figure remarkably well and the low neckline revealed skin only slightly dried and baggy with age.

'You,' pronounced the Dowager, eyeing her niece critically as she sat, 'will take Paris by storm, my love.'

'I hardly think so, Aunt. You are prejudiced. I still lack looks, just as I did at seventeen.'

'Nonsense!' snorted Amelia. 'You never lacked looks, though I admit you are no classical beauty. You possess something far more valuable, my dear: individuality and character. And now you are older your looks have matured into striking perfection. What man of sense wants to take a beautiful simpleton to wife?'

'Your son, for one,' muttered Louisa defensively, and then could have bitten out her tongue. The last thing she wished to do was to hurt her mentor.

But Amelia brushed the remark aside. 'Amy is no simpleton, though I must admit Robert was led astray by what he considered to be a diamond of the first water. She has sad defects of character, not brain. However, you are evading the issue, my love. You have had plenty of offers, you just refuse to consider them.'

'One I did not,' Louisa reminded her aunt quietly.

Amelia snorted again. 'Do not tell me you are still refining over that worthless stripling Radburn! He has his just deserts. A shrewish wife——'

'Who brought him twenty thousand a year,' inserted Louisa grimly. 'I thought he loved me, Aunt. It seems he loved money more.'

'Most young men hang out for a rich bride; *you're* no simpleton, you know that. Besides, his uncle arranged the match, if you remember, against his will and over his head. There was not much he could do.'

'Except stand on his own two feet and refuse to be coerced! We could have managed quite well on my five thousand.'

'So you thought, my love, but he was an expensive young man, and knew it. I never liked him,' added Amelia flatly. 'Could never understand what you saw in him.'

Louisa sighed. 'He was very good-looking and amusing. But neither can I, now. At the time, though. . .'

'You were young and romantic, my love, and you have let that experience put you off marriage altogether.'

'Not off marriage, Aunt, but off the men who have since offered! I will not settle for a convenient match. I must want it with the whole of my being. Heart, mind and soul.'

'Don't forget body.' Amelia watched her niece blush

and smiled unrepentantly. 'You should bring judgement and common sense to bear, as well as inclination and emotion. You can afford to be selective,' she granted, 'but do, I beg of you, refrain from being too difficult to please. I can imagine no worse fate than to become a lonely old woman with no family to depend upon.'

'I shall have plenty of nephews and nieces to cheer my old age. I shall make a splendid great-aunt!'

'You may joke now, Louisa, but——'

Louisa cut her aunt off. 'Do let us drop this unrewarding subject! You're doing it a bit too brown, you know. How shall we spend tomorrow, before the reception?'

'You, I collect, are riding out on Prince Hal.'

'Before breakfast, yes. But afterwards?'

Louisa could tell her aunt was reluctant to drop a subject near to her heart. Aunt Nazeby's dearest wish was to see her comfortably settled. The Dowager's face mirrored her internal struggle before she gave a resigned shrug and her expression drifted into a smile.

The last of the covers had been removed, the dessert set upon the polished table and the servants dismissed before she spoke again. 'Pershaw tells me he has managed to hire a splended coach for our stay which will hold four comfortably and six at a pinch. I will have the bays put to and we shall drive about Paris in order to leave cards with all our friends and acquaintances. Perhaps we may make a call or two. Once people know we are in residence they will call and the invitations will begin to arrive.'

'Yes, we must do the pretty, despite our attendance at the embassy later, when I suppose we shall meet them all. And,' added Louisa, 'if you will agree to lend me your bays, dear Aunt, I shall ask Pershaw to see if he can find me a light carriage to drive. The weather is fine and I cannot abide being shut in a closed conveyance for long!'

'I shall trust my horses to your care with pleasure, my love. I have every confidence in your ability as a whip. If Pershaw is able to find a suitable vehicle you may most certainly borrow them.'

With this assurance Louisa felt herself relax. Next to riding on horseback, she found her greatest pleasure in driving. And she had a new city to explore.

The morning dawned fair and cool while promising a warm day. Dressed in her newest riding habit, of a dark maroon corded material decorated with gold frogging, Louisa adjusted the white stock at her neck and set the becoming top hat more firmly on her light-brown curls. The ends of a matching gauze veil, swathed around the crown, hung in soft folds about her shoulders. After a final, critical glance in the tall mirror she pulled on her gloves, picked up her crop and went down to find Pershaw, who would be waiting in the yard of the stables and coach houses serving a group of residences of which theirs was one. This was approached from the street through a high arch, and from the house through the gardens.

Pershaw had ridden one of the Dowager's lesser horses from England, leading the carriage horses and Louisa's Prince Hal, while his boy assistant used post ponies. So he would be tolerably well mounted and not reliant upon some hired hack when he accompanied her.

When she had bought him, Prince Hal had been considered by many to be too strong for her. But Pershaw had recommended the purchase and she'd known she could trust his judgement. The wiseacres had soon been proved wrong. She enjoyed an instinctive rapport with the animals; they seemed to know she loved them and gave her their affection and obedience in return. A shared enthusiasm for horses had sealed the bond between the elderly groom and his erstwhile pupil.

That morning Hal blew his greeting, nudged her shoulder affectionately, pushed his nose beneath her arm, nipping at her habit, telling her how pleased he was to see her again.

Louisa slapped his gleaming black neck, fondled his muzzle and pushed him off with a laugh, feeding him the expected sugar.

'Yes, Hal, I'm glad to see you, too, old fellow.'

Pershaw threw her up. Hal danced a little to show he felt lively and then they moved off, Pershaw setting a sedate pace through the streets.

Louisa lost no time in mentioning her intention to hire a carriage. 'My aunt has given me permission to drive her bays, Pershaw. I shall be obliged if you will find a carriage for me. One similar to the phaeton I drive at home would suit.'

'I will see to it later today, Miss Louisa. There should be little difficulty.'

They turned into a broad, wide, rather muddy avenue, the leaves of the elm trees rustling overhead in the morning breeze.

'What is this place?' Louisa asked, looking about her with undisguised pleasure.

'They call this the Champs Elysées,' Pershaw replied. 'I am reliably informed that the road was laid out in 1670 by Le Nôtre, the man who created the royal gardens. The places of entertainment on either side have been added more recently.'

As they progressed Louisa eyed what she could see of the pleasure gardens curiously. 'Are these places like Vauxhall or Battersea Gardens?'

'Very possibly, miss. They are mostly intended for the amusement of the lower orders, I believe.'

'In other words, no lady would be seen there?'

'Just so, miss.'

'A pity. But there must be one the *ton* visits!'

'I have heard mention of the Tivoli gardens, miss.'

'I must enquire,' smiled Louisa. The atmosphere in Paris was quite different from that in London. London represented home, and she loved it. But Paris released from the grip of revolution spelt romance, adventure, a liveliness in excess of even that found during the Season in London. Even the streets smelt different.

They shortly approached a massive structure, impressive despite still being incomplete. She eyed it speculatively.

'This must be Napoleon's triumphal arch.'

'Yes, miss.'

'Will it ever be finished, do you think?'

'I couldn't say, miss.'

Pershaw never overstepped the bounds of his position despite their very real friendship, based on mutual respect. Information he would provide, within his power, but he seldom ventured an opinion other than one connected with his job. Louisa had not expected other than a non-committal reply to a question she considered rhetorical. They continued on in companionable silence.

Having traversed another broad avenue, named after Napoleon's *Grand Armée*, they entered the Bois de Boulogne. It soon became clear to Louisa that this must be Paris's equivalent of Hyde Park.

A few keen horsemen were already out riding, most of them officers in uniform. In addition a number of grooms were to be seen, exercising their masters' animals. Louisa drew a happy breath.

This was the time of day she enjoyed most. She could indulge in a gallop while the rest of the town still lay abed. Later on, were the Bois anything like the Park, the bridle-paths would be crowded with the fashionable parading on horseback or in carriages, intent on seeing and being seen rather than on exercise. She would join them, with Aunt Nazeby, later on. But for the moment she had this part of the Bois virtually to herself. A long, empty stretch of perfect bridleway lay ahead.

'Come, Pershaw!' she cried, setting the eager Hal into a gallop. 'To the far end!'

Hal's hooves thundered over the dry ground. Louisa knew that Pershaw's slower animal would soon be left behind. But as she flew along, her veil streaming out behind her, she became aware of another set of hooves thudding close behind, threatening to overtake.

She did not know who it was—not Pershaw, of that she could be certain—and she had no time to look over her shoulder to find out. Pershaw had not called a warning, so no danger threatened. Whoever it was had therefore thrown down a challenge she was not about to ignore. Exhilaration gripped her as she urged Prince Hal to even greater efforts and triumphantly reached the end of the ride slightly ahead of her pursuer.

She drew rein and wheeled her sweating horse to face her challenger, who reined in his huge grey with consummate skill.

Lord Hugh Deverill doffed his beaver hat, bending from the waist in elaborate greeting.

CHAPTER THREE

LOUISA's heart, which had been pumping with exertion, missed a beat. Why the mere sight of Hugh Deverill should cause her such confusion she failed to understand. No man had had the power to do so since the year of her come-out. Grey eyes met greeny hazel and held.

'Good morning, Miss Finsham.'

On this occasion his smile did reach his eyes. The lines radiating from them, together with the softened curve of his intriguing mouth, improved the amiability of his looks considerably.

'That is a prime animal you have there,' he went on admiringly. 'May I congratulate you on your horsemanship? I have seldom enjoyed a gallop more.'

Louisa acknowledged his greeting coolly, ignoring the preposterous curl of warmth forming inside her at sight of him, while wondering whether his appearance was due to coincidence or the fact that he had overheard her order to Pershaw yesterday and had sought the meeting deliberately. 'You are too kind, my lord.'

His heavy brows rose and his smile took on a wry, engaging twist. 'I but state a fact, Miss Finsham.' He patted his horse's neck. The animal tossed its aristocratic head, setting its harness jingling and its dark mane flying, blew in appreciation of the gesture but sidled edgily away from Prince Hal, who was dancing about, his energy unabated despite his run. 'Kismet can catch most other horses,' went on his lordship somewhat ruefully. 'I expected to overtake you easily.'

At that moment Pershaw cantered up. He threw Louisa an enquiring glance while keeping a respectful distance. Louisa reassured him with a slight nod.

'You should be congratulating Lady Nazeby's head

groom, Lord Hugh. Pershaw here——' she indicated her old friend with her crop '—selected Prince Hal for me. I did but agree with his choice.'

Hugh Deverill glanced across and gave the groom a friendly acknowledgement. 'You undoubtedly have an excellent eye for a horse, Pershaw. But this fellow was surely an unlikely choice of mount for a lady?'

'But then,' inserted Louisa quickly, 'Pershaw taught me to ride. He knew my capabilities. Others warned me that I'd break my neck, but so far their prediction has not been fulfilled.'

Deverill threw back his head and laughed. 'You confound me, Miss Finsham! By what I witnessed this morning such an eventuality is most unlikely. Pershaw has my hearty congratulations on choosing a mount which matches your own spirit so exactly!'

The smile he now turned upon her appeared warm and almost caressing. Louisa wondered whether she had been forgiven her excursion to Waterloo. She decided it could do no harm to return his good humour. He certainly deserved a set-down but that could come later. Being in high spirits herself after her exercise, she positively beamed back.

For a split-second the sight of her radiant face seemed to shock him into immobility. In that moment something almost tangible seemed to flow between them. Then, 'Shall we ride on?' he murmured, and added quickly, 'Perhaps you will accept my escort back to your *hôtel*?'

'With pleasure, my lord.' She gestured Pershaw to follow as the two horses fell in skittishly side by side. Both were high-spirited animals, hers a gelding, his an entire, not a showy animal but well-found. 'If we can persuade our mounts to tolerate each other's company!' she added on a laugh.

He chuckled. 'They'll soon settle down. I'll warrant that before many days have passed they will be the best of friends.'

That could only mean he intended to ride with her

again. A flutter of excitement stirred Louisa's senses. She was finding Hugh Deverill an attractive creature when he relaxed—and when he stopped criticising, she thought, still harbouring slight resentment. But on the other hand they did appear to share a liking for horse-back riding. His presence would provide added zest to her morning excursions.

'Is the horse yours, my lord, or hired?' she ventured to enquire.

'Mine, though but recently purchased. He is ex-cavalry, a splendid animal.'

'His former owner is dead?' asked Louisa flatly.

Deverill glanced at her quickly. 'I fear so. An officer of the Greys who died of his wounds.'

'War,' observed Louisa grimly, 'is horrible. I wonder at you, in particular, considering the purchase of such an animal. He is bound to remind you of something you would rather not refine over.'

He studied her brooding face and his own expression lightened further. 'The sale will help his dependants,' he said gently. 'I paid a good price.'

Louisa stared at him for a moment and then nodded her understanding. 'Thus relieving the tragedy a little for a few people,' she acknowledged.

They rode on in silence for a while, Louisa harbour-ing melancholy thoughts of Amelia's son, who had ridden to his death in a cavalry charge. The silence had not been strained. Rather, it had seemed companion-able. Nevertheless, she felt it time to speak again.

'Do you ride early every morning, my lord?'

Hugh brought his own wandering thoughts back to answer her.

'Most mornings, when I have no duty to prevent it.'

Her eyes shone bright with unshed tears. Had he misjudged her? Or had her visit to Waterloo proved salutary? Deverill adjusted his ideas, decided that he might have been too harsh. She held an elusive attrac-tion for him that he could neither explain nor deny. Even caught in the throes of seasickness she had exuded some quality he found quite entrancing. He would have pursued the acquaintance immediately but for that unfortunate exchange at Calais. And, he admitted to himself wryly, for the fact that he knew Lady Nazeby's niece to be an heiress. He wanted no entanglement that could cast him in the role of fortune-hunter.

But he had set out to meet her this morning unable to resist the temptation offered by that overheard order to the groom. Now he was glad he had for her attitude seemed to have changed since Calais and the memory was fading. He could seek her company with a clearer conscience, if not a quieter mind. He smiled again, unable to resist the delight he found in her company.

'And you?'

Louisa's defences began to crumble before the battery of so much charm. When he tried he was able to turn it on to quite ruinous effect. He must have something about him to attract such a reputation for seduction, she supposed, and as far as she knew it was neither fortune nor rank, for younger sons, even of dukes—especially impoverished dukes, as Chadford was reputed to be—were considered of little account. Yet according to Amelia he had not lacked chances to wed a fortune. And according to rumour he did not lack for mistresses.

'Yes,' she admitted, fiddling quite unnecessarily with Hal's harness in order to avoid having to look at him and lose her countenance completely. 'Unless I have been up to all hours the previous night,' she added, a trifle breathless despite the sedate pace of their progress.

'Ah! Balls do tend to continue into the early hours, do they not? The social round here can be exhausting—several receptions, soirées and parties are held every night, not to mention the balls. Lady Stewart is to hold one on the sixteenth. I have little doubt you will receive an invitation once she knows you are here.'

'You already have yours?'

'Attached to the British Embassy as I am, I am the recipient of invitations to almost every function and am obliged to attend most, for in addition to discharging my duties to the English community I am required to cement relations with the French and other foreign leaders here.'

'Oh, lud!' exclaimed Louisa. 'That should prevent you enjoying yourself.'

He laughed. 'Not at all! It is something I seem to be good at! I don't in the least mind. But evening parties are not the only entertainments to be found in Paris.'

Louisa had recovered her poise enough to meet his eyes, her own dancing. 'There are more delights?' she breathed in mock-awe.

'Oh, many more!' His tone had become light and bantering, matching hers. 'It is a pity you arrived too late to see the Allied review of the sixty-five thousand troops stationed around the capital. I am certain you would have enjoyed the spectacle.'

'It must have been some sight! Tell me about it, pray.'

He smiled a little and prepared to oblige. 'It was indeed an impressive sight. Most of the troops looked exceptionally smart and the Duke's manoeuvres were accomplished extremely smoothly, to the admiration of all!'

'I could wish the troops' behaviour in Paris matched their parade-ground discipline!'

'Lord Wellington's command is superior in that as in every other way. He will brook no laxity on the part of his commanders. The British troops are well-disciplined at all times.'

'So I am given to understand.'

Hugh nodded. 'You would have enjoyed the cavalry,' he continued, his tone becoming enthusiastic. 'I have never before seen such handsome horses. Our own Guards—those who survived that disastrous charge,' he added on a more sombre note, 'were magnificent, as you would expect, as were the Royal Horse artillery.

All taken together it was a splendid show, a grand occasion. The Emperor of Russia and the Duke of Wellington took the salute. Everyone was there.'

'I am sure it must have been. War may be dreadful but a military parade always stirs the emotions. One cannot help but be proud of one's army.'

'Very true. And parades have the virtue of being harmless entertainment.'

'Indeed they do! How people can drive out to watch them in action——' She pulled herself up. Noting Hugh's quizzical look, she quickly changed the subject, having no wish to revive the question of her visit to the battlefield. 'How is the Duke?' she asked. 'I have not seen him this age, since he was in London last year, receiving his share of the adulation during the visit of the Allied Sovereigns.'

'He is well. The most important and influential man in Paris, of course. And enjoying the adoration and company of the fair sex. But you will be able to judge the Duke's condition for yourself this evening. He will be at our reception, you may be sure. He goes everywhere.'

Louisa suspected she could detect a degree of censure in his voice, which surprised her, given his own reputation. With her background she was bound to have her own reservations about the Duke of Wellington's friendships with women but had not expected Deverill to share them.

'You disapprove of him?' she enquired, voicing her surprise.

'Not at all, my dear Miss Finsham. Why should I? As with me, it is his duty to be present.'

'Of course,' agreed Louisa, wondering at the endearment, surprised to discover that she did not resent it. 'But—in other ways, perhaps?' she ventured. 'There have been so many rumours circulating about him in London and here. Did not Lady Shelley ride with him at the review we have been speaking of?'

'She did. Many remarked on the fact.'

His tone was non-committal. Louisa probed further.

'I had heard that Lady Frances Wedderburn-Webster was his latest flirt.'

'She was reputedly so, in Brussels.' Hugh gave a short laugh which lacked humour. 'But this is scandal-mongers' tattle, and I would prefer not to indulge in it further,' he declared.

Louisa could not resist a dig. 'Very wise, my lord. After all, he is not the only man who attracts the attention of the gossips.'

Hugh looked at her sharply, suspicious of her bland tone. To her satisfaction she saw a tinge of red appear on his broad cheekbones.

'Not all rumour is true,' he pointed out stiffly.

'Indeed, happily it is not.' Was he implying that the rumours concerning him were untrue? She did not dare pursue the subject, but how she wished she could! 'As you have reminded me, it is unwise to indulge in scandalous discussion,' she said instead. 'Especially for a diplomat.'

'A poor one, I fear, Miss Finsham,' he responded rather grimly.

'Oh, I don't know. I have heard that you travelled to America and did much to negotiate the peace with our former colony. That must have required considerable skill.'

The tone of her voice denied the admiration implicit in her words. She saw his colour deepen.

'More tittle-tattle, ma'am. No man can do more than his best, however threadbare that may be.'

'But you gained the admiration of Lord Castlereagh,' she persisted archly, some devil of mischief driving her on.

'I perceive, Miss Finsham, that I have offended you in some way. If that is so, I apologise. May we not drop this unprofitable subject and ride in amity?'

Louisa drew a sharp breath. She refused to fence with words any longer. The air must be cleared between them. 'Why should we, my lord? You seem to bear me some grudge for showing an interest in the battlefield at Waterloo. Is it wrong to be proud of our army's victory?'

He sighed. His broad shoulders drooped slightly under the dark green riding-coat, then straightened again. 'No, Miss Finsham. If I appeared to criticise I regret my lapse. I, too, rejoice in the Allied victory, and admire the Duke for what he achieved with such an infamous—to use his own term—army at his command. Had he had more of his experienced Peninsula divisions to rely upon the outcome might not have been such a near run thing. It was a dearly bought victory. The Duke himself regrets the loss of so many fine men. He spent some days in Brussels after the victory mourning them.'

'Of course he must, as do we all.' In particular Robert, the late Earl of Thurrock, she thought, her expression brooding. She had known and admired him, without knowing him to be her aunt's son. Her own cousin.

'It was Lord Wellington's defensive skills which won the day, holding on until the Prussians arrived.' Hugh steadied his horse and emitted another short laugh. 'Had old Marshal Blücher not been determined to keep his word to the Duke and insisted on marching on to Waterloo after his army's defeat at Ligny, Bonaparte's plan would have worked. He set out to divide and conquer. He expected the old man to do what Allied commanders had always done in the past—retreat towards their communications and thus save their own army at the expense of another.'

'But Blücher was made of sterner, more honourable stuff! If only that lesson had been learned earlier!'

'Indeed. Miss Finsham, I congratulate you. I did not expect you to understand the import of his actions so readily. And this morning I discover that you, too, find the business of war disagreeable.' He hesitated a moment, collecting his thoughts before going on. 'I have always failed to understand the morbid curiosity which takes so many people on a visit to the battlefield. I hear that making up a party for the purpose is currently the main source of amusement in Brussels. To walk about and pick up anything to be found—any residue of battle—even, perhaps, a soiled letter.'

The question was implicit, but there. Louisa remembered his remark at Calais and winced. So that was what he had alluded to. She stared straight ahead as she answered.

'I think it a minority who indulge in such macabre souvenir-hunting. Has it never occurred to you, Lord Hugh, that some people may be going because they lost a loved one there? That they are making a kind of pilgrimage?'

He looked suddenly stricken and turned to challenge her gaze. 'You?'

She shook her head, meeting his eyes candidly. 'No. But my aunt lost someone she was fond of. I accompanied her.'

He reined in sharply and she did likewise. He stared at her, a kind of horrified desperation on his face. 'How can I ever apologise enough? Please forgive me, dear Miss Finsham.'

She nodded, and a small smile curved the corners of her wide mouth. Greeny hazel eyes sparkled into his. He thought there were tears there.

The endearment was back in front of her name and she was glad. She had need to steady her voice before she spoke. 'You are forgiven, my lord. Your motive, I collect, was honourable.'

'And is why I have attempted to use any skill I may possess in the diplomatic field in the pursuit of peace.'

'A worthy aim which I fully endorse.'

'So, we are friends, dear Miss Finsham?'

'Friends, Lord Hugh.'

The declaration gave her spirits a decided lift. He had received his set-down—mild, as it had turned out, but she'd succeeded in discomfiting him for a few moments—and now the rift was healed. After a moment's silence she spoke again, a note of regret in her voice. 'I fear I must return to the Hôtel des Fleurs soon, or my aunt will wonder what has become of me.' She turned a mischievous smile on him. 'So, my lord, shall we race for the gates? A guinea on it!'

He accepted the challenge immediately. 'Kismet is already straining at his bit! A guinea it shall be!'

The horses raced like the fine steeds they were. Neck and neck they thundered along, the few other riders scattering to let them through. Prince Hal began to lose ground and Louisa urged him to greater effort. But, though Hal went faster than he had ever gone before, still the grey edged ahead and Louisa knew his rider would not hold him in to allow her to win. She was flattered by his lordship's obvious appreciation of her abilities and surprised by his care for her sensibilities.

Kismet won by half a length. Panting, laughing, Louisa eased Prince Hal into a walk and the two blowing, sweating animals moved through the gates and into the avenue side by side. Pershaw was gaining on them quickly, and would soon take his place a few lengths behind.

'Thank you, my lord!' Louisa's happy voice rang out despite her lack of breath. 'I have not enjoyed myself as much this age! I find it difficult to find a worthy opponent. Pershaw's mount is not fast enough, and most gentlemen think it necessary to hold their horses to allow me to win. Thank you for not doing so. I owe you a guinea. You shall receive your due this evening!'

His grey eyes, which seemed more blue than they had yesterday, actually twinkled. 'I could not impede the spirit of either horse or rider, dear Miss Finsham. A race, like a battle, should be fought to win. Any other course betrays either a lack of enthusiasm or an ulterior motive in the loser.'

'What possible ulterior motive could a gentleman have for allowing me to win?' demanded Louisa. 'I had always thought it a matter of chivalry!'

He grinned. 'They may think it the best way to fix your interest.'

Louisa's snort made Prince Hal's ears flatten. 'Then more fool they! But you did not think it to be so, my lord?'

Flirtation was a game she had practised for many years, using it to hold off her admirers. Much of the conversation that morning would have been considered too outspoken for a properly brought up young lady to indulge in with a gentleman and had held little of coquetry on her part. But Louisa was no longer a young miss and in any case had always spoken her mind. Rashly, she was asking him whether he wished to fix her interest. Despite the flirtatious manner in which her question had been posed she was now inviting a set-down. But the devil in her wanted to make this man uncomfortable again.

But he didn't look in the least uncomfortable. 'I had not made up my mind,' he returned blandly.

Made up his mind to what? Insufferable creature! Now he had *her* mortified at having exposed herself so!

But he ignored her heightened colour and, as they passed the embryo Arc de Triomphe and moved into the Champs Elysées, began to point out the various places of amusement lining its muddied, leafy path.

The carriage Pershaw had chosen proved adequate in every way. After a morning spent roaming the quarter of Paris where the *haut ton* resided leaving their cards, and afterwards having partaken of a light luncheon, Louisa and the Dowager joined the throng of fashionable carriages parading along the Champs Elysées at the end nearest to the Place de la Concorde. This, apparently, was where those in the first circle promenaded as an alternative to the Bois de Boulogne. Between the road and the river rose the Grand Palais and the Petit Palais. On the far side of the Place, where a regiment of soldiers was being drilled, could be glimpsed the Jardin des Tuileries, and beyond that the

royal Palace of the Louvre. The Palais Royal must be
visible in the distance somewhere, but she could not
make it out.

'Paris has a vast number of palaces within its bound-
aries,' Louisa remarked as she nodded and smiled to an
old acquaintance.

'I should like to see Versailles,' murmured the
Dowager. 'Oh, look, there is the Countess Lieven! She
is smiling at us! I wonder whether she will attend the
reception tonight? And, I do declare, there is Amy
Thurrock, parading the boy for all to see! I suppose she
wishes to impress her consequence as widow of one and
mother of another English earl!'

Louisa craned her neck to catch a glimpse of
Amelia's grandson. She was acquainted with his
mother, of course, but had never met the boy, since he
was too young to move in Society. At first she could
see very little, for the coachman and footman on the
approaching carriage's box obscured her view, and
Pershaw and Dench on their box were in the way too.
But as the two carriages met she obtained a clearer
view.

The Dowager Countess of Thurrock acknowledged
the Dowager Countess of Nazeby and her companion
with an artificial smile and a slight inclination of her
head. Louisa returned the greeting politely before turning her attention to the new Earl.

He resembled his father, she thought, from what she
could remember. Robert had been a little darker, but
the boy had his open countenance. His blue eyes took
in everything going on about him. Both mother and son
were, of course, wearing mourning; Amy looked pale
and ethereal in her black, the young Earl sombre and
rather subdued.

Amelia had Pershaw halt the carriage and Amy could
not do otherwise than order her coachman to draw up.
The footmen sprang down to hold the horses.

'My dear Amy!' cried Amelia with false warmth.
'How delightful to see you! We shall give ourselves the

pleasure of calling upon you shortly! And you, my lord!' she addressed the good-looking boy cheerfully. 'James, my dear boy! So you are the Earl now!'

'I wish Father had not been killed,' responded James. His voice shook. 'I would rather *never* have inherited than that Papa should have died!' he added fiercely.

'We all share in your grief,' Amelia assured him, her own voice far from steady. 'To think he came through the Peninsula campaign only to die now! War is cruel.'

'But I must shoulder my responsibilities bravely,' asserted young James, no doubt repeating a lesson relentlessly instilled. 'How do you do, ma'am?' he added rather tardily, lifting his hat and making a grave bow.

'Well enough, I thank 'ee.' Amelia indicated Louisa with a wave of her hand. 'My lord, may I present Miss Finsham, my very dear niece? I do not believe you have previously met.'

Louisa smiled at Amelia's grandson, a slight mistiness before her eyes. What an excellent creature he was! Showing such sensibility at so young an age! She loved him already. But she could see that he needed protection from his mother's less agreeable nature. Amy Thurrock was prodding him in the ribs.

'Don't stare, boy! Make your bow as you've been taught!'

Colour rushed into the lad's face. He had been gazing as though mesmerised at the lovely, fashionable woman giving him such a warm smile. 'P-pleased to make your ac-acquaintance, Miss Finsham,' he stuttered.

'My lord,' murmured Louisa. 'I am honoured to make yours.' She flashed him a reassuring smile. 'Do you ride horseback?'

'Of course!' He had recovered his composure quickly and now sounded rather indignant that she should feel the need to ask.

'Then perhaps I may see you in the Bois de Boulogne one morning. I often ride there before breakfast.'

'Really, Miss Finsham?'

His enthusiasm was plain. Louisa decided to push her luck.

'My groom and I could call for you one day, if that would suit?'

'He has his own grooms!' cried his mother indignantly. 'If he wishes to ride he will be accompanied by his tutor and a groom from his own household.'

'But, Mama, there can be no need to trouble——'

Amy cut him off firmly. 'They are paid to be troubled! If you wish to ride you will do so with them in attendance. But,' she added, shafting an insincere smile at Louisa, 'I am sure your offer was well-meant, Miss Finsham, and I thank you for taking an interest in a fatherless boy.'

'I was used to ride with Papa when he was home,' gulped James, near to tears but swallowing them down manfully. 'I shall look out for you, ma'am.'

'And I you.'

Further civilities having been exchanged, the two carriages moved on, for they were causing a blockage.

'So,' said Amelia. 'What do you, think?'

'He is a fine boy,' said Louisa sincerely, 'and stands up to his mother well, but he needs help. I trust we shall become friends.'

That evening Louisa chose her dress with especial care. In due course she would order new gowns from one of the distinguished French mantua-makers who plied their trade in Paris but meanwhile she had plenty of elegant English gowns to choose from.

'Which one, Betty?' she wondered, eyeing the selection laid out on the bed. A profusion of white crêpe and muslin, some sprigged, of yellow gauze, and silks of palest pink, forget-me-not blue, leaf-green, primrose, ivory, lilac, and a light brown rather like milky tea, met her eyes.

'The green suits you, Miss Louisa.'

'I know—but I think it must be the white crêpe for

my first appearance. The bugle beads are all securely attached, I trust?'

'Of course, Miss Louisa.' Rather indignantly, Betty picked up the garment and spread it for her mistress's inspection. The pearl-like white beads decorating the tiny bodice shone satisfactorily in the late afternoon sunlight. 'I ironed the satin petticoat only today, and the ribbon trimmings are fresh as the day the dress was made.'

'Yes.' Louisa fingered the satin and the tiny pink and blue flowers nestling among the ruched ribbon encircling the low neckline and the hem, the only touch of colour the mantua-maker had allowed. 'I have had it only a short time and worn it very little. It will do splendidly. Is the hot water ready?'

'It should be here any moment. I don't know what those lazy Frenchies are about!'

Whereas only yesterday Betty had gone in fear of losing her position, now she was treating the French servants with superior scorn. At that moment the pitcher of steaming water arrived and Betty was able to receive it with a sniff and an 'About time, too!' which the young maidservant probably did not understand, thought Louisa, amused.

An hour later, with the last of the sun casting a rosy glow over her, Louisa slipped the dress over her chemise and inspected the result in the ormolu-framed cheval mirror.

Betty had excelled herself in arranging her hair, threading her brown curls with beads and ribbons to admiration. The scandalously low-necked bodice, permissible in a woman of her more advanced years, emphasised her feminine shape, the little puffed sleeves the slenderness of her arms. The skirt hung in gentle folds from the fashionable, slightly lower waistline to an elaborately decorated hem easing into a train.

Louisa twisted this way and that, assuring herself that all was as it should be. She could do nothing about her colouring, which lacked the pale fairness fashion demanded, though her complexion remained clear enough *and* without the use of Gowland's Lotion. Against the whiteness of her gown it had taken on an ivory hue. But she had accepted this limitation on her fashionable appearance many years ago and in truth had suffered little from its consequences. Satisfied at last, she draped a fine scarf over her arm, smoothed down the long trailing ends of the satin bow flowing from beneath her bust and picked up her feathered fan and tiny silk reticule. A final glance in the mirror assured her that she was fit to make her first entrance into Parisian Society.

They were by no means the first to arrive. Judging by the attendance, Sir Charles and Lady Stuart were well-liked and offered fine hospitality. They greeted the Dowager and herself warmly.

Lord Hugh Deverill, Louisa noted, was engaged in serious conversation with a group of gentlemen at the far end of the glittering salon. Though no Corinthian unable to move for the skin-tightness of his garments, he appeared to advantage in evening dress. She could not help but notice him, for he stood out as a fine figure of a man among so many less well-endowed in stature. One in particular, whom she later discovered to be Prince Talleyrand, had a club foot, which did not improve his awkward, heavy, shapeless appearance. Even from a distance she took a dislike to his ugly features and his unpleasant laugh. She pitied Lord Hugh for having to converse with such men.

Her attention was soon distracted by the greetings of friends and by introductions to those she had not met before. The Dowager found a chair on which to sit and coze amicably with ladies of her own age, leaving Louisa to mix as she would.

Soon Louisa's voice could be heard exchanging lively conversation with a group of younger guests, among whom were a blue-coated dragoon captain, a couple of red-coated officers of the line regiments and a hussar distinguished by his golden tassels and fine boots. Uniforms representing most of the allied armies were scattered about the salon, their buttons and metal accoutrements scintillating in the light from myriad candles set in chandeliers and sconces, their brilliant colours mingling with the delicate shades of the ladies' gowns. Every glittering detail was reflected in the huge mirrors lining the walls.

Although almost surrounded by admirers, she was not surprised, shortly afterwards, to hear a deep voice she instantly recognised speak at her shoulder. She had known he would seek her out.

'Miss Finsham. My apologies for not being free to greet you on your arrival. I am happy you are able to be here.'

Louisa swung round to receive his formal bow. She curtsied in response, smiling her pleasure at seeing him again.

'Do not apologise, my lord! I have been well-entertained!'

He produced a wry smile. 'So I have observed.'

For some mysterious reason her court had melted away. That Hugh Deverill could have such an effect upon perfectly self-assured young men had not previously occurred to her. And had he been watching her? Flattering if he had. She flashed him a brilliant smile.

'Here, my lord! I do not forget my debts!'

She opened her reticule and dug in its depths, bringing out a golden guinea. He accepted the coin with a grave bow belied by the laughter in eyes which sought hers.

'I will afford you the chance to recoup your losses soon, dear Miss Finsham.'

Again that promise to ride with her! Louisa's heart began to flutter—a feat it seemed determined to perform every time she met Hugh Deverill.

Just behind him stood an older man, almost as tall as himself, possessed of a good figure and a pleasant countenance, accompanied by an elegant woman of about Amelia's age. Louisa had met neither of them before.

Hugh turned to include them in the conversation. 'May I present Monsieur Alexandre d'Arblay and his wife, Madame d'Arblay, Miss Finsham?' Everyone made their devoirs. 'Monsieur d'Arblay was chief of staff to the Maquis de Lafayette,' Deverill went on, 'and is a liberal constitutionalist helping to put France on its feet again. His wife you may know best as Miss Fanny Burney, the famous novelist. I thought you would be interested to meet her.'

'Of course!' exclaimed Louisa with pleasure. 'Dear ma'am, I have read all your books with such delight! My aunt, the Dowager Countess of Nazeby, subscribed to *Camilla*! It is indeed an honour to meet you.'

'You flatter me, Miss Finsham.'

'If you will excuse us, I fear Monsieur d'Arblay and I must return to our discussion with Prince Talleyrand and the others. But,' Hugh added, looking straight into Louisa's eyes, 'I shall look forward to speaking with you again later.'

The men departed and Louisa soon discovered how Fanny Burney had met her husband while he was living in exile at Juniper Hall, in Surrey.

'He had been dispossessed of all his lands and fortune and was very depressed,' explained Madame d'Arblay. 'I met him when I went to stay with my sister, who lived near by. Quite a colony of exiles lived at Juniper Hall. Have you met Madame de Staël yet?'

'No, *madame*. We arrived but yesterday.'

'She does not appear to be here tonight, which is strange. But you will no doubt attend her salon before long. She is a fellow authoress, a great debater, and wields great influence.'

Louisa laughed. 'I shall look forward to meeting her!'

Madame d'Arblay chuckled. 'She is quite formidable, I assure you! And men adore her, despite her unfortunate looks.'

'But not Monsieur d'Arblay, I suspect!'

'No, indeed, although he admires her greatly. Thank God my husband was able to return to France under Napoleon, for he endured his exile with great chafing of the spirit. Now he feels he can truly serve his country once again.'

'And you do not mind making your home in France, ma'am?'

Fanny d'Arblay smiled. 'I am no exile. I am able to visit England whenever I wish. Besides, home to me is where my husband is.'

Louisa wondered for a moment whether she could ever be happy living in some foreign land, whomever it was with. But she had little time to ponder the question, for a stir at the door interrupted her thoughts.

'The Duke has come at last,' murmured Madame d'Arblay. 'It is his habit to arrive late. See how the ladies cluster around him!' She laughed slightly. 'He is besieged wherever he goes.'

'His was a famous victory,' murmured Louisa non-committally. 'He is coming this way.'

'Since Waterloo he is become the most important personage of the day. I have the honour of knowing him quite well, and admire him enormously.'

'Despite his liking for the ladies?'

'Even the best of men can behave foolishly when flattered by a woman. Unfortunately he is susceptible to the fair sex.'

'It is his wife I pity.'

'And I. But she is quite unsuited to the position he now holds. He proposed as a young man, you know. The marriage has proved to be a sad mistake.'

'But he is wed, and the flirtations in which he indulges cannot, surely, be excused by a man who protests to behave with honour!'

'His conscience is his own, my dear. I only know that I find him a most agreeable friend.'

It would have been inexcusable to pursue the matter

further. Louisa silently watched the famous man's progress.

He had entered quietly with a dark woman on his arm.

'La Grassini,' murmured Madame d'Arblay helpfully under her breath. 'The Emperor's erstwhile mistress. She has found favour with the Duke, too.'

'And the lady now claiming his other arm is Frances, Lady Shelley, I see. I have not met her this age.'

'She would not be far behind! He has been paying her marked attention lately.'

'But where is Lady Frances Wedderburn-Webster?' wondered Louisa.

'In retirement. The creature is expecting to be confined at any moment,' murmured Louisa's companion somewhat tartly.

As he approached them, the Duke greeted both women as old friends, immediately effecting introductions to the ladies on his arms.

'Madame d'Arblay!' he went on effusively. 'You appear in splendid health! And Miss Finsham. Oh, yes. My dear young lady, at last to have the pleasure of your company here! Your appearance is positively enchanting tonight. It does a man good simply to look at you.'

Doing it a bit too brown, thought Louisa. He was in his mid-forties, no longer young, but not old, either. And as for his heavy-handed compliments—she supposed she should be used to them by now. She kept a smile on her face and greeted the great man charmingly. After all, as Madame d'Arblay had found, there was much to admire about Arthur Wellesley even if his hair was thinnning and his nose seemed to protrude more noticeably than ever. Most women found him attractive. She did not happen to be one of them.

She was about to make a curtsy and send him on his way when she caught a glimpse of Deverill, standing behind the Duke, his expression forbidding.

His eyes seemed to be boring into her. Did he think

her about to succumb to the allure of power? How dared he look at her like that?

Her gaze returned to Wellington's face. He still smiled at her, clearly desiring to prolong their exchange despite the two women already hanging on his arms. An idea sprang into her head. She would show Hugh Deverill exactly how much his displeasure meant to her! She laughed, albeit rather shrilly.

'My lord, I do not think I have yet paid tribute to your victorious generalship!' Quite deliberately, she stepped towards him. 'How else may I show my appreciation of your great victory but with a kiss?'

CHAPTER FOUR

LOUISA reached out, took his face between her hands and kissed him on both cheeks in the approved French style.

The Duke, not at all embarrassed, gave one of his neighing laughs and said, 'You are not the first to offer me such a charming salute, Miss Finsham.'

'Your Grace,' responded Louisa, curtsying again, wishing heartily that she had not indulged her pique with Hugh Deverill in such a manner. Not understanding her friend's action but sensing her acute embarrassment, Madame d'Arblay intervened.

'We all thank God that the Legislature demanded Napoleon's abdication and negotiated peace so that Paris itself did not have to be conquered by force of arms, your Grace. The city escaped without need of battle.'

Wellington smiled. 'I too am glad we did not have to fight in the streets of Paris, Madame d'Arblay. Blücher's men merely harried Bonaparte's troops to its gates.'

'Those of us who reside here have no fault to find with the British soldiery,' went on Fanny d'Arblay earnestly, 'but we could wish that other victorious armies of occupation would behave with more restraint. They trample the cornfields and ransack the homes of those less fortunate than ourselves.'

Wellington frowned, his face grave. 'Blücher is a famous old fellow but seems unable to stop his troops from plundering. Have you met him?'

Both ladies admitted that they had not yet had the privilege of meeting the Prussian marshal.

'He's over there.' The Duke indicated an elderly man with a large moustache who was engaged in some

331

uproarious joke with his companions. 'Allow me to effect the introductions.'

She could scarcely refuse. As Louisa joined the throng of ladies now surrounding the hero of Waterloo and followed him across the room, she noted that Lord Hugh Deverill had disappeared.

Hugh found himself more disturbed than he was prepared to admit by the scene he had just witnessed. Louisa knew the Duke—why should she not speak with him? She must greet him, or be accused of lack of conduct. What concerned him was her reaction to catching his own eye as he watched the great man. Why had she behaved in such an extraordinary manner?

He caught a glimpse of her across the salon. She had been drawn into the Duke's immediate circle and he did not like it. Gossip would be bound to follow. She had already invited it. But the consequences of that rash action of hers might die a quick natural death if she could be persuaded to drop out of the Duke's set.

He took no conscious decision, but it was not long before he had excused himself from the small crowd of guests gathered around him and made his way to her side.

Louisa could never afterwards decide quite how he had done it. She discovered Hugh Deverill at her elbow and tried to ignore him but, with a skill she assumed to be the result of long practice, he had soon detached her from the Duke's court and steered her out of the salon.

He had smiled, murmured, 'Come with me, I have something to show you,' and she had obeyed.

She was still wondering why when they reached the comparative calm of the hall. People were strolling about and servants passed to and fro but there was no crush here.

'Well, my lord,' she demanded, assuming a coolness she did not feel, for she knew she had behaved outrageously, and conscience and embarrassment were assaulting her, 'what is it you wish me to see?'

His hand touched her elbow, turning her towards open double doors. 'The ballroom,' he told her. 'It is magnificent, as are many of the other rooms. This was a palace, after all. And I think the library would interest you.'

'You intend to give me a personally conducted tour? I am honoured, my lord.'

'No need to be.' He grinned, all his charm directed towards lifting her from her present mood. ''Twas merely an excuse to avail myself of your company. But I believe you will appreciate what you see.'

Louisa was not proof against his persuasive manner. She smiled back. 'In that case, let us proceed!'

'May I offer you my arm?'

'Thank you, my lord.'

The tour began. Louisa was certainly impressed by the size of the rooms and the splendour of the decorations and furniture, but far more affected by the extensive knowledge and intimate manner of her companion. Finally, he led her into the library.

The room was empty and although the door stood open, for convention's sake, they were essentially alone. She had forgotten the Duke and all that had gone before in the pleasure of Hugh's company. She gave an exclamation, dropped his arm, and started forward.

'What a wonderful collection of books!' she cried, turning impulsively to demand of her escort. 'Are they all in French?'

'By no means! There are many here belonging to the embassy. You like reading, dear Miss Finsham?'

'Above everything!'

'I fear there are few novels in this collection.'

'That does not signify,' said Louisa. 'My aunt teases me about the learned books I read!'

He chuckled. 'Independent in all matters, including your choice of reading, I collect, my dear Miss Finsham!

I can see no reason why you should not borrow from here, if any of the books interest you.'

'Really?' Louisa's eagerness and gratitude shone from her eyes. He actually seemed to approve, whereas most men, while not critical, were condescending in their attitude. 'Thank you. Mayhap I can come one day and inspect them?'

He smiled. 'Indeed you may. I will mention it to Sir Charles.'

Louisa ran her finger along the spines of the nearest volumes and turned back to him. 'But now, my lord, grateful as I am and much as I appreciate your company, I feel I should return to the salon. My aunt will be wondering what has become of me.'

His face immediately sobered. 'Will you return to the Duke's company?' he asked.

Louisa's eyes opened wide. Memory returned. 'Why should I not?'

He appeared to hesitate, but then proceeded somewhat apologetically to say, 'I would account it the height of foolishness. You would become the object of gossip.'

She had already laid herself open to that, and knew it. But what business was that of Hugh Deverill's? How dared he lecture her? Had he shown her over the embassy in order to create an opportunity to do so? Disappointment gave her voice an added edge.

'Were I to avoid every gentleman the gossips tease I should feel free to address very few!' she returned smartly.

'True again, my dear Miss Finsham. But in his position the Duke would be wise to show more discretion. The tattle-mongers scarcely need to utter a word.'

'Nonsense! He merely enjoys the company of attractive women!'

She knew she was defending the Duke against all her true instincts. Hugh Deverill had that effect upon her. He stood looking at her, and the look in his eyes made her long to be at peace with him. Yet she could not bring herself to admit to an error of judgement. She had enjoyed independence for too long to be dictated to over such a matter now. She drew a breath.

'And because you do not approve my conduct I must in future ignore a great man? Is that the truth of it?'

He shook his head in denial. 'I have only your reputation at heart, Miss Finsham.'

'My reputation is of consequence to no one but myself, my lord! And now, if you will excuse me, I will return to my aunt!'

She flounced round and left the library before he could see the tears in her eyes.

Independence, thought Hugh, could be charming. He admired it. Yet it could also lead to uncomfortable consequences. With the best intentions in the world he had managed to alienate her.

He did not take exercise in the Bois the next morning; or if he did it was not within sight of her. James did not appear, either. Despite the advent of several young gentlemen with whom she had become acquainted the previous evening, all vying with each other to ride by her side, Louisa returned to the Hôtel des Fleurs feeling unusually depressed.

The previous evening had proved a disaster. The Duke, she realised, thoroughly enjoyed the adoration to which he was subjected. But if the *ton* hoped to discomfit her by their gossip, Louisa determined that they should not succeed. At least to all appearances.

They were, after all, in Paris, where no one but the English would dream of making a great work out of so innocent a salute. She would quote St Ambrose's dictum. Point out that he had advised that when in Rome one should live in the Roman style, and so she could surely allow herself a small excursion into the ways of the Parisians!

A perverse streak in Louisa's nature had driven her to join the sycophantic throng in the face of Hugh

Deverill's obvious displeasure. When, later in the evening, he had sought her out, she had so enjoyed his company until he had tried to warn her off involvement with the Duke. She hadn't needed warning, and his interference still rankled.

Her reaction, on returning to the salon, had been to behave in a lively manner, flirting with the Duke and his ADCs and with officers of other nationalities, too. Her laugh had rung out while all the time, inside, all she'd felt was confusion. Just because Hugh Deverill had taken her to task she'd found herself behaving in a fashion quite at odds with her normal demeanour, and she didn't exactly know why. She was usually lively, yes. She often flirted mildly, too. But last night some inner turmoil had driven her on to an extreme of behaviour she now sincerely regretted.

The result had been to ensure her a bevy of admirers wherever she went and life was too full of reviews, balls, receptions, soirées and visits to the theatre for her to refine over anything for long. She managed to push Hugh Deverill to the back of her mind and ignore his intrusion there. Well, almost.

The invitations poured in. July drifted into August. Hugh Deverill never again appeared in the Bois to ride with her, but thrusting him from her mind completely proved difficult, for he was at every function she attended, hovering in the background and, she was quite certain, watching her every move.

To her delight young James appeared in the Bois one morning, accompanied by his tutor, a gentleman named William Coynd, the youngest son of a landed family forced to put his Oxford education to good use in the earning of a living. He had no expectations and would be condemned to tutoring all his life unless he could wed a fortune. He was a personable young man and Louisa found him agreeable.

Her friendship with James grew apace. He had a passion for horses so, despite the disparity in their ages, they had plenty of interest in common.

'You ride awfully well, Miss Finsham,' he remarked after a particularly fine gallop.

His pony had struggled gamely to keep up with Prince Hal. Since it had not been called a race, Louisa had held Hal back so that they could remain side by side.

'So do you, my lord. Do you not find this time of day quite splended for riding? I so enjoy the early morning.'

'Mama did not wish me to come,' confessed James, 'but I persuaded her to allow it. I shall be glad when I am old enough to please myself without having to ask her permission for everything I do.'

'I am sure she has your best interests at heart,' murmured Louisa, mentally crossing her fingers for what she suspected to be a lie.

'Papa had resigned his commission, you know. He had to return to the colours, of course, when the call came. I wish he had not died. He was very brave.'

His voice wavered and the tears were not far away but he manfully thrust them back. 'I miss him most terribly,' he confessed. Louisa wished she could stretch out a hand to comfort him but the size of James's pony rendered that impossible.

She offered what solace she could. 'I knew him, a little. We met on several occasions when he was on leave from the Peninsula, and during last autumn. I thought him a fine gentleman.'

'Did you?' James's face lit up. 'Where did you meet? What did he say?'

He wanted to talk about his father, and Louisa obliged, as far as she was able. If she exaggerated the extent of her acquaintance with the dead Earl, she told herself she was justified by the pleasure her reminiscing brought his son.

'I shall ride every morning,' announced James as they parted that first day. And he did.

Others continued to attend her. The hussar, Major Hewitson, became a constant companion. Mr Coynd, the tutor, soon proved himself another admirer, keeping as close as he could to Louisa and joining in the lively conversations. She detected some rivalry between him and the major but could not bring herself to set him down. He was, after all, the grandson of a peer, however impoverished and forced to occupy a menial position.

They were sometimes joined by the Duke himself, often accompanied by Lady Shelley, proudly riding one of the Duke's horses, sometimes even Copenhagen.

'I am so honoured!' she exclaimed on one such occasion, patting the chestnut's neck. 'Do you attend the review tomorrow? I am to accompany dear Wellington again, riding this creature.'

'Yes, I shall be there. You are a splendid horsewoman, ma'am,' said Louisa. 'No doubt he appreciates that.'

'Well, so are others, I'm sure, including yourself, Miss Finsham. I am certain you could manage Copenhagen as well as I!'

'But I have my own Prince Hal,' returned Louisa, and the conversation languished.

Amelia watched her niece, worried by the change in her. After eight years of holding down an exemplary position at the pinnacle of Society she had thought Louisa beyond such frenetic and immodest behaviour.

'Really, Louisa,' she chided at last, 'I cannot imagine what has got into you recently! You are like to become the talk of the town if you do not stop rattling about and encouraging the Duke—who ought to be old enough to know better—and all those young men as you do!'

'The officers know it is all a tease, Aunt. And you call attending the salons of the *ton*—of Lady Castlereagh and Madame de Staël, among others— "rattling about"?'

'Not precisely, but. . .' Amelia sighed and trailed off.

Louisa immediately suffered a pang of guilt. 'Do you

not enjoy accompanying me, dear Aunt? I had not thought how tedious you might find such occasions!'

'My love, it is not the tedium I object to, for I have my gossips to keep me amused, but your lack of decorum. You have set the old tabbies gossiping behind their fans!'

'Am I really behaving so very badly, Aunt? I do not mean to. There must be something infectious in the atmosphere here, for I declare all the ladies behave just as I do!'

'Just because others make spectacles of themselves over our national hero there is no call for you to do the same! I had thought you more sensible, Louisa. And they do not all venture out in the early morning as you do, to ride with the Duke and all those young men!'

'What harm can there be in that? I am always accompanied by Pershaw or another groom. Lady Shelley is often present.' She ignored Amelia's scornful snort at that information, adding quietly, 'And I have achieved our aim of making friends with Jamie. I believe I have his confidence.'

'That at least is something to be grateful for. Forgive me for ringing a peal over you, my love, but I have only your best interests at heart.'

'Of course you do, Aunt, but I think you refine too much over a little tardy giddiness on my part. The war is finally over. Having surrendered to the navy off Rochefort, Napoleon is now on his way to exile in St Helena, so I hear, and we are in Paris celebrating a great victory!'

'I dare say you are right. In any case, you are no green girl; you have been out too long for me to govern your behaviour now. But do give heed to what I say.'

Louisa could accept such strictures from her aunt. She went over to Kiss Lady Nazeby fondly. 'I will, Aunt,' she promised.

The ladies had been waiting for their first morning callers to arrive. As Louisa finished assuring her aunt that she would indeed consider mending her ways—

indeed, she shocked herself at times with her flirtatious behaviour and was beginning to wish she had had the sense to take Hugh Deverill's warning in the spirit in which it had been intended, having become increasinly certain that he had not meant to offend her—Chausson announced the Countess of Thurrock.

Amy entered with a flounce of self-importance, her cheeks aglow and her pale blue eyes bright with suppressed excitement.

Once greetings had been exchanged—Amelia and Louisa hiding their surprise, for James's mother did not often grace their rooms with her presence—their visitor produced some newspapers to flourish before their eyes.

'Have you seen them?' she demanded.

'Seen what?' enquired Amelia carefully. She exchanged an anxious look with Louisa which their guest fortunately failed to notice in her excitement. Could Miss Finsham's excesses have reached the pages of the Press?

'What is being said in the *St James's Chronicle*, of course!'

'You have received copies from London?' put in Louisa, her curiosity piqued. Not to mention her apprehension. But of course whatever had been written could not possibly concern her! 'No, we have not seen them. What do they say?'

'Oh, they make a great play on the letter W. "Fashionable Alliteration", the author calls it, but goes on to record a report supposedly prevalent in the first circle here that the Duke—although it does not name him, of course, but refers to a "distinguished commander"—is captive to the charms of a certain lady. Lady Frances Wedderburn-Webster, of course! It surmises that the affair will end in criminal conversation! And it claims that the husband—the obnoxious Captain James W-W, you know—is suing the fortunate lover for fifty thousand pounds' damages! What do you think of that?'

'Rumours have been surrounding the Duke this age,' shrugged Amelia. 'She was here then and went on to Brussels when Bonaparte returned. But she was not the only one. Lady Shelley was there, too, riding beside him at his reviews, as she does now.'

'But the rumours surround Lady Frances Wedderburn-Webster, not Frances, Lady Shelley. Captain W-W's wife is the one likely to find herself divorced!'

'And the Duke may now be using Lady Shelley as a smokescreen,' mused Louisa.

'Not to mention yourself, Miss Finsham.' Amy Thurrock smiled in malicious triumph. 'You have been much in his company recently. What is your opinion of this scandal?'

'I have nothing to say to it, ma'am. I was not there and cannot judge.'

She was rescued from further personal questioning by the advent of several other ladies of their acquaintance. Louisa remained silent while the company enjoyed some enlivening *on dits* over the current scandal and the possibilities of damages and crim. con.

At length, 'He cannot possibly make every young woman he admires his mistress,' stated Amelia firmly. 'He enjoys the company of young people, both gentlemen and ladies. I believe his interest to be purely avuncular.'

'Would you agree with that, Miss Finsham?' asked Amy, all wide-eyed innocence.

'Certainly, my lady,' replied Louisa with all the aplomb she could muster. 'Think how fond he becomes of his ADCs! And Lady Frances was already heavily pregnant at the time of the supposed adultery. No one denies the Duke had mistresses in India and the Peninsula. But I am persuaded that this is not so unusual in an active gentleman of his disposition so often, of necessity, stationed away from home.'

'Really, Miss Finsham!' Outrage informed the voice of an elderly tabby as she clutched at her breast as though on the point of swooning. 'How shocking! A young lady of your breeding to speak so plainly of things about which you should know nothing!'

'Fustian!' exclaimed Louisa roundly. 'How could I fail to know? Were I a simpering miss at her come-out you might be excused your shock. But even you, Miss Cunningham, have spoken openly before me and at five and twenty I believe I am as entitled as you to know something of such matters!'

The tabby's gasp and Amy's titter were lost in the arrival of another visitor.

Having drawn the company's attention by means of an ostentatious cough, 'Lord Ew Deverill,' announced Chausson in sonorous tones.

Louisa's heart stopped for an endless moment. Hugh Deverill, here? He had made no duty calls on them until now, apart from one made early on when she had been visiting the modiste. She had often wondered since whether he had chosen that precise time specifically in order to avoid her. It would not surprise her in the least if he had. Apart from polite murmurs of greeting when contact was unavoidable, they had scarcely addressed a word to each other since that first, disastrous evening.

Now, having resumed its beat, her heart leapt and jumped at sight of the tall, elegant figure bending over the Dowager's hand and making his general, polished devoirs to the other ladies.

He approached Louisa last. For too long he had watched from a distance, reluctant to interfere again. Now, it seemed, he could render her a service. He bowed over her hand.

Louisa was aware that her hand trembled in his warm clasp, that the brush of his lips across her knuckles—an unnecessary contact, for he had not kissed any other hand and the gesture indicated an intimacy they did not share—sent a shiver down her spine.

He sat in a chair close beside her, which had unfortunately been vacant. His near presence made her extremely uncomfortable.

He crossed his long legs, adopting an easy, elegant

posture, prepared to listen politely to the ladies' chatter for the prescribed twenty minutes of his visit.

They, however, could not feel free to continue with their pleasurable speculations with a gentleman present. Apart, that was, from the Countess of Thurrock who, rising to take her leave, could not resist taking a parting shot at Louisa.

'My son appears to enjoy riding with you in the Bois, Miss Finsham. I am so thankful no scandal attaches to *your* name, or I would be unable to sanction his expeditions. Of course, Lady Frances, being so close to her confinement, has retired to the Wedderburn-Webster estate. Just as well,' she ended significantly, 'for I could not allow him to join a party which included *that* lady.' She turned the battery of her wide, ingenuous eyes on Hugh. 'Have you see these copies of the *St James's Chronicle*, Lord Hugh?'

He lifted negligent brows as he rose gracefully to acknowledge her parting curtsy. 'Copies are regularly delivered to the embassy, my lady.'

'Then you must have seen the ones I have here. How long it has taken for them to reach me!'

'Just so. Ours only arrived this morning. No doubt adverse winds in the Channel account for some of the delay. But as to the articles to which I am certain you refer, they do but repeat gossip which has been current for some time. I collect that it can cause no further anoyance to the parties concerned. I would advise an action for libel against the proprietors of the paper. Were it me I would consider actions for slander, too.'

Why did Louisa get the firmest impression that Hugh Deverill had presented himself that morning to show his solidarity with her, knowing that she had laid herself open to the spite of the gossips? Had his early profession of friendship meant more than mere words, after all? Had the warmth she had sensed survived the intervening coolness between them?

All her confused emotions, of resentment and guilt, excitement and apprehension, were swallowed up in her pleasure at his championship. And the look of consternation on Amy's suddenly flushed face made her ready to forgive him anything.

Once the Dowager Countess of Thurrock had departed, no doubt to spread her gossip in other establishments despite Hugh's veiled threat, the remaining ladies felt constrained to change the subject, with Hugh Deverill present. There was plenty to occupy their tongues, quite apart from the Duke's scandalous affairs.

Louisa, grateful for his presence and wishing to restore goodwill between them, took courage and addressed her somewhat silent companion.

'I have not had the pleasure of meeting you while riding in the Bois recently,' she murmured.

He scrutinised her face, his own breaking into a rueful smile.

'You are always surrounded by others, Miss Finsham. What chance could a dull dog like me expect of gaining your attention while you are entertained by illustrious dukes, youthful earls, gallant hussars and all their attendants?'

Louisa's eyes widened in a mildly flirtatious manner designed to hide the sudden thumping of her heart. Could it be that he was jealous? The idea had a most peculiar effect on her ability to breathe.

'Come, sir,' she chided gaily, glad that her state of inexplicable inner turmoil was not reflected in her voice, 'if you appear dull it is entirely your own fault! Now were you to exert yourself to show greater pleasure in the company about you——'

Her roasting could not be mistaken for anything else. His answering smile was wry.

'You have noticed my tendency to impatience with idle chatter, I collect!'

'And with idle flirtation, I believe.' Greeny hazel and grey-blue eyes met squarely. The grey-blue held a watchful, slightly questioning expression which unsettled her anew. 'But, you know,' she went on mischievously, enjoying the exchange despite her wayward emotions, 'one must give the Great Man his due in adoration. He is undoubtedly the saviour of Europe.'

'You know I do not argue with you there, dear Miss Finsham.' The smile in his eyes deepened in response to her obvious mockery. 'I would even go so far as to say of the world, since Bonaparte's ambitions knew no bounds.'

'And so, you see, we must all pay court! And some will no doubt fall victim to his consquence and power, if not his personal charm.'

'But not you, I collect, Miss Finsham,' he commented quietly.

When had the conversation turned serious? A sudden suspicion made her bite her lip. Had he overheard her answering Lady Thurrock, just before Chausson announced him? Was that why his attitude had changed? Yet that could not explain his presence here in the first place.

'He is always most courteous and kind. But even were I tempted to engage in a more intimate relationship I should not be able to forget the Duchess Kitty. And I should undoubtedly be quite ruined,' she added in mock-tragic tones.

'What is that you say, Louisa? Why should you be ruined?'

Lady Nazeby's sharply agitated tones cut across their exchange and Louisa realised she had allowed her voice to rise in her enjoyment of an entertaining if improper conversation. She beamed reassuringly.

'I shall not, dear Aunt. I was funning.'

'Well, I'm very glad to hear it! But you should not say such a thing even in jest, my love! You are tempting fate! And to say it to a gentleman! Really, Lord Hugh, you should not encourage my niece in her rackety ways!'

'My lady, my admiration for your niece is in part due to her refusal to bow entirely to Society's ideas of correct behaviour. The strait-jacket imposed upon young ladies of spirit must be irksome in the extreme.

Yet I do not believe Miss Finsham would ever stray beyond the limits of true propriety.' Rising, he bowed to his hostess. 'Regrettably I must take my leave or I shall outstay my welcome. Your servant, ladies.'

His eyes did not meet hers, for which Louisa was vastly thankful. She knew she would be unable to hide the utter confusion his words had provoked.

And then, before Amelia could ring for Chausson, the major-domo had flung open the door.

'Is Grace, ze Duke of Villainton and Madame Grassini.'

Seldom had Louisa felt so ready to sink. She was not the fluttery, fainting kind and had never pretended to be so, but at that moment she would have given much for a sniff of her aunt's hartshorn.

Wellington and Deverill exchanged greetings in passing with the utmost civility, Lord Hugh bowed to the songstress with impeccable formality, and then the Duke and the opera star were making their devoirs with practised ease. Everyone knew that Wellington had been enraptured by La Grassini's singing and by her person ever since he had first heard her perform in Paris the previous year.

At close quarters Louisa found La Grassini's features disappointing. On the stage, of course, she was too distant for fair criticism. But even here she had managed to make a theatrical entrance.

She began to chatter in her heavily accented French, which she interspersed with Italian when she could not think of the word she wanted. Louisa found the gravest difficulty in understanding what the woman said. She suspected the others of being similarly at sea.

Polite, pleasant as ever, the Duke, in his grey frock-coat and high boots, soon put a stop to her chatter and himself demanded the attention of all the ladies present, those whose residence it was and those who had already greatly overstayed their correct twenty-minute welcome.

Madame Grassini, he interpreted, had wished to call

upon the Dowager Countess to pay her respects and he had escorted her. Louisa listened apparently attentively to the conversation flowing about her, her mind occupied elsewhere.

The Duke appeared worried beneath a veneer of normality. She suspected him to be more concerned over the reports circulating than he would openly admit. It was fortunate for him that, being in such a delicate condition, Lady Frances Wedderburn-Webster had been unable to appear in Society recently, leaving him free to concentrate his attentions upon La Grassini. His friendship with Lady Shelley and her husband—and with herself as well, more recently—had been designed to obscure any former indiscretions.

But he was a ladies' man and that was that. It did not make him any the less a great general. He had defeated Napoleon. And, like everyone else, she could not help liking as well as admiring him.

Just as she liked Hugh Deverill. His mistress had not followed him to Paris. Rumour said Lady Kingslea had been kept at home by an ailing husband. Would he marry the widow if Lord Kingslea died? Louisa found that proposition even less appealing than his present relationship with the woman.

They had been invited to a supper party at Lord Castlereagh's the following day, a signal honour. The prospect did not, however, prevent Louisa from taking her usual morning exercise.

Inside the gates she found James Grade, Earl of Thurrock, Viscount Thurston, awaiting her, mounted upon a large chestnut gelding. The youngster sat his new mount well, thought Louisa as she drew Prince Hal to a halt beside the boy, who was bristling with pride.

He did not forget his manners and greeted her with an exquisite formality, which brought a small tilt to the corners of her mouth, before allowing his excitement to spill over.

'What do you think of him, Louisa? Isn't he a splendid animal?' he demanded.

Louisa inspected the horse with knowledgeable and admiring eyes before saying, 'Splendid indeed. Pershaw!' She turned to the groom with a smile. 'Am I not correct in agreeing with Lord Thurrock?'

Thus consulted, Pershaw dismounted and stepped forward to run his experienced hands from the chestnut's powerful crest along its strong neck, on down its muscled shoulder to its knee before picking up the leg to inspect the neat round hoof, making soothing noises to reassure the horse all the while. Then his hand ran over the flank and hind quarter, down the thigh to the hock, fetlock and another hoof. He eyed the horse critically as he circled it to perform the same inspection on its other side.

'Walk him round if you please, my lord.'

Full of confidence mixed with expectation, Jamie did as asked. 'Well?' he demanded as he drew up before the groom.

'Excellent piece of horseflesh, my lord,' Pershaw pronounced at last, giving a last soothing stroke to the horse's delicate head. Its ears twitched and it whickered softly in appreciation of the fondling. As though aware of receiving admiration, it lifted its head, setting the creamy mane rippling. 'Deep-chested, sound in wind and limb. Possibly,' Pershaw added diffidently, 'a little too strong for your lordship as yet?'

'Oh, no,' said Jamie confidently. 'I can handle Conker. He's obedient, and I'm very strong.'

'Where did you buy him?' asked Louisa, thinking that such an animal must have cost a small fortune and wondering at Amy's allowing the expense.

'I didn't, he's from the stables at home. Father promised him to me the moment I reached thirteen, which I did, last week.'

'Congratulations,' murmured Louisa. Yes, she'd known that—Amelia had been sad not to be able to

attend the celebrations. Supposing his mother had both-
ered to organise any.

'So I had Percy——' he grinned conspiratorially at his
groom '—send for him.'

He was fast finding the courage to exert his natural
authority. Louisa wondered whether his mother had
raised any objection. He answered her without knowing
it.

'Of course, Mama would rather I continued to ride
the pony, but I'm almost a man now, and I told her so.
So she shrugged and said she supposed I could break
my neck if I wanted to, but not to blame her.' He
grinned suddenly, a wide, boyish smile that went
straight to Louisa's heart. 'Not that I'd be able to, of
course, if I were dead.'

'Don't talk such nonsense,' she admonished with
mock-severity. 'How would you like to race Prince Hal
to the end of this ride?'

His young face lit up with enthusiasm. 'Do you mean
it, Louisa?'

Of course!' At that moment her attention was drawn
to a lone rider approaching on a massive grey. So he
had taken her hint and intended riding with her again!
'And look, here comes Lord Hugh Deverill on Kismet.
I will introduce you and we will invite him to race with
us.'

Thank God, she thought, the Duke had not put in an
appearance that morning. She and Lord Thurrock were
riding side by side, with Major Hewitson and Mr Coynd
a few paces behind, the grooms bringing up the rear.

Louisa drew rein as Deverill approached, wishing
that his appearance did not always so affect her breathing. It was quite ridiculous; she was past the age to go
into vapours over a man.

He lifted his hat and inclined his body in greeting,
punctiliously polite. 'Good morning, Miss Finsham.'

'Why, Lord Hugh!' The sun had risen and was slant-
ing across him through the trees, gilding the ends of his
black hair. The little burst of joy in her heart at sight of

him could not be denied, and she allowed herself to indulge it for a moment before she went on in what she hoped was the merely friendly tone she would use with any acquaintance. 'I do not believe you have met his lordship, James Grade, Earl of Thurrock. Jamie, may I present Lord Hugh Deverill?'

Their devoirs made, Jamie eyed the man with interest. He appeared to like what he saw, for he smiled his eager, boyish smile. 'I have heard of you, sir. My mother has spoken of you.'

'Nothing to my detriment, I trust?'

James flushed and looked uncomfortable. Louisa wondered exactly what Amy had been saying in front of the child.

'Oh, no, sir!' he assured an amused Deverill. 'Well,' he added honestly, 'not more than she usually says about everyone! I believe she admires you, sir.'

'You are acquainted with Major Hewitson of the Hussars, my lord, but you may not have met Mr Coynd, Lord Thurrock's tutor,' put in Louisa hurriedly, seeing the wry twitch of Lord Hugh's lips at this information. Amy's admiration was not necessarily something to be desired. She had observed him exercising his excellent manners to the full in an attempt to be polite on numerous occasions, and after yesterday's set-down she wondered how much longer Lady Thurrock would continue to speak well of Lord Hugh Deverill!

But Deverill's attention had already been diverted. After acknowledging the stiff greeting of Hewitson, he turned to the other man with raised eyebrows. 'William Coynd!' he exclaimed. 'Can it be you?'

'Indeed, my lord.' Coynd appeared rather less than eager to acknowledge the acquaintance. 'It is many years since we last met.'

'Coynd came up during my last year at Oxford,' explained Deverill easily.

'Lord Thurrock has a new mount, and we were just about to prove its speed in a race,' Louisa explained. 'Will you join us, my lord?'

'With pleasure, ma'am.'

'Major, will you not take part as well?' invited Louisa. Coynd's horse would not be up to the competition, but she was feeling kindly disposed towards him. 'You too, Mr Coynd. Come, sirs! Lay your bets! Pershaw shall start us!'

Both the Hussar and the tutor agreed, though with little enthusiasm, their expressions disapproving of such a display of unfeminine behaviour in a young lady. She should be content to ride sedately through the Bois, exchanging gentle and charming conversation with her escorts, not placing bets on the result of her own hoydenish intention to race in public!

On this occasion, thought Louisa with secret elation, Lord Hugh seemed rather more approving than critical, and the smile he sent her as they attempted to bring the horses into line for the start discomposed her so much that for a critical instant she lost control of Prince Hal who, excited and eager for the gallop, took the opportunity to leap forward. The other animals took off after him and Pershaw was left staring after them, his improvised starter's flag—his handkerchief—fluttering uselessly in his hand.

CHAPTER FIVE

THE whoops and shouts, the sound of thundering hooves behind, told Louisa that the race was on. Her sense of guilt at having set off before the rest of the field soon died in the excitement of the competition, for Jamie's Conker and Deverill's Kismet were soon drawing level and Hal, responding to the challenge, was galloping as though his life depended upon it.

However, Conker was younger, his chest deep, Kismet stronger, with more endurance. By the time the steaming horses reached the designated finish Conker led Kismet by a head, Hal's nose was on a level with Deverill's knee. Hewitson pounded in from two lengths behind and poor Coynd, on one of Lady Thurrock's lesser hacks, trailed in a miserable last.

'I cannot remember when I have enjoyed myself more!' cried Louisa, her face flushed with exertion and excitement, her eyes sparkling with the joy of living. 'Jamie, you have a capital creature there! Mind you, he had a lighter burden to carry! Otherwise I do believe Kismet might have won! What say you, my lord?'

'Lord Thurrock won fair and square. My only doubt, ma'am,' said Hugh Deverill, his attempt at a grave air unable to disguise the grin he could not suppress, 'is over your own lamentable attempt to gain an advantage at the start.'

Louisa knew he was roasting her and laughed, but Coynd, coming up at that moment, took the reprimand seriously.

'Look here, Deverill,' he began belligerently, 'I'll not have you casting doubts on the lady's honour! I may deprecate her desire to race like a man, but I cannot believe she would cheat. Her horse was too strong for her, she couldn't hold it.'

'Oh, I am absolutely certain you have the right of it, Coynd. I did not believe for a moment that the lady had intended to cheat, and if I gave that impression I am all contrition.'

'Don't be so addle-witted, Mr Coynd,' snapped Louisa, although Deverill's air of assumed humility made her want to laugh. 'Of course Lord Hugh did not imply anything of the kind! You may depend upon it, he was funning! And Hal is not too strong for me. I lost concentration for a moment, that was all.'

'Miss Finsham is above suspicion,' murmured Hugh.

Coynd suddenly turned away, but not before Louisa had caught sight of the high flush suffusing his cheeks. He had not taken her remark kindly. She could sympathise, and regretted her sharpness.

'Come, gentlemen,' she said lightly, trying to make amends, 'it does not signify. The race is done, and Lord Thurrock is undoubtedly the winner despite my irregular start. Let us settle our debts. Jamie, here is my guinea.'

Since that first race with Deverill Louisa had always carried a coin or two in her pocket against such a time as this. As she handed him his winnings, James beamed. 'I didn't think you cheated, Louisa, I saw what happened— you were looking at Lord Hugh when your horse decided to go. I didn't try to stop Conker from following, and none of the others held back.'

Louisa willed the flush this revealing comment provoked to recede. 'You rode him splendidly, Jamie. Your father was right, he suits you well.'

She and the young Earl had been on first-name terms almost from the beginning of their acquaintance. The deference due to his rank was offset by Louisa's additional years and they had quickly adopted each other as friends.

'Well,' said Jamie, his honesty forcing the confession, 'Conker's very obedient, otherwise he would be too strong. But we get along like anything and he tries to please me.'

'That is by far the best relationship to have with your animal, my lord,' observed Hugh, handing over his dues with a smile. 'Make a friend of your horse and it'll do anything for you.'

Hewitson paid up handsomely and with rather less good grace Coynd discharged his debt to his pupil. The party began to ride easily along another bridleway. She found Coynd and Hewitson crowding her, while Jamie and Lord Hugh rode ahead.

'I do admire your spirit, Miss Finsham,' offered the major with a stiff smile. Everything he did was stiff, Louisa thought; he seemed unable to relax. Perhaps it was the uniform. Though other Hussars managed to behave in an easy manner, so it couldn't be entirely that. 'I wonder Lord Wellington does not invite you to review the troops with him,' he went on, unconsciously adding to the irrational annoyance Louisa already felt towards him.

'I have no desire for that honour, sir,' she returned, stiff herself at an implication she would rather not pursue. 'I have no intention of becoming an object of ridicule. So far as I am concerned, His Grace must content himself with the company of his official ADCs.'

'I am glad to hear it,' put in Coynd severely. 'Such a public display would not become a lady.'

'Oh, I would not entirely agree there,' returned Louisa perversely. 'Lady Shelley is an excellent horsewoman and behaves with perfect propriety when she accompanies him at his revues. *She* cannot be considered an object of ridicule. And without such a diversion, I am persuaded that the occasions must become tedious in the extreme to someone of His Grace's character.'

Take that how you like, she thought tartly.

Far from being critical of such an opinion, however, the gentlemen vied with each other to agree with her, even Major Hewitson admitting such parades to be irksome to those taking part.

Suddenly tired of their implied criticisms of her behaviour and their less well-concealed eagerness to obtain her good opinion and engage her interest, Louisa spurred Hal forward, edging him between the two riders ahead, who readily parted to allow her to join them. Until now she had enjoyed the company of the major and the Earl's excellent tutor, who was well-educated, entertaining and polite. But today both men seemed dull, and had contrived to irritate her beyond measure.

She addressed Deverill, still riding easily and companionably, apparently oblivious of the exchanges taking place behind. 'Do you attend Lord Castlereagh's supper party later, Lord Hugh?'

'I do. Both you and Lady Nazeby are also invited, I believe.'

'Indeed, my lord, and look forward to the occasion with eagerness.'

'You will find yourself in an exclusive but mixed company. His Lordship must invite anyone of consequence who is in Paris, as well as those French ministers the Allies nominated to govern the country under King Louis XVIII.'

'Excellent! I have not yet had an opportunity to enter into converse with Talleyrand or Fouché, and although I have seen them at evening functions such occasions are always such a sad squeeze one cannot hope to speak with everyone present. I trust their characters are more agreeable than their appearances would suggest.'

Deverill chuckled. 'I will leave you to judge that for yourself. I dare not venture an opinion on such a delicate matter!'

'They're hideous,' stated young Jamie with conviction. 'Everyone says so.'

'"Everyone" being your mother, I collect,' murmured Louisa.

'And Mr Coynd,' averred Jamie stoutly.

'I should not,' advised Hugh mildly, 'voice that opinion in strange company, my lord, or you may cause an international incident!'

'I am never in strange company, so I can't,' muttered

Jamie morosely. 'I'm not old enough. It's awful to be young.'

'Not a bit of it,' differed Deverill briskly. 'Though to enjoy your youth properly you should live in the country, not in a town. I remember spending days roaming the estate at home, sometimes on horseback, sometimes on foot, speaking to the tenants, fishing in the stream, helping to bring in the harvest. . .'

The nostalgia in his voice brought Louisa's eyes to his face, to discover its hard planes softened by memory. He loved his home; of that there could be little doubt. Here was a man with a heritage rooted in the land. What a pity he had not been born the eldest son, able to indulge his love of it.

'But,' he was saying now, 'you have this park and a wonderful city to explore. Does Mr Coynd not take you to see the sights, the museums and art galleries? Have you never ridden out to Malmaison or Versailles?'

Jamie pulled a face. 'We've been to a few places in Paris. But they're most awfully dull.'

'Then he is not explaining them to you properly. Perhaps, one day, you will allow me to escort you on a tour of the city?'

'That would be absolutely splendid, my lord! Could Miss Finsham come, too?'

Hugh Deverill slanted a quizzical smile in her direction. 'I would account it a great honour were she to consent to accompany us.'

Louisa felt the blush rising and fought to contain it. 'I should be delighted to engage for such an expedition, my lord.'

She thought William Coynd might resent the interference, but forbore to comment. The prospect was too attractive to be dimmed by the casting of any doubt.

'Then I will arrange it.'

'Mama will not mind *you* taking me,' put in Jamie eagerly. 'She greatly approves of you, my lord.'

'I am flattered. Meantime, may I have the honour of escorting you to Lord Castlereagh's, Miss Finsham?'

He was offering his protection again. Louisa almost refused it, for she certainly needed no such thing!

But then the appeal of appearing in Society on the arm of such an eminently eligible escort overcame her rebellious spirit. 'Thank you, my lord,' she accepted meekly.

The smile he turned on her in reply reduced her to breathless silence.

Lord Castlereagh, the Foreign Secretary, was of course Hugh Deverill's ultimate superior. Only Sir Charles Stuart, the ambassador, stood above him, and both men had been invited to the supper.

Lord Hugh entered the salon with Louisa on one arm and Amelia on the other. Both ladies, he acknowledged, did him credit, but it was Louisa who, from the first moment of seeing her awaiting his arrival in their drawing-room, had claimed his stunned attention.

She wore an undergown of fine bud-green silk covered by a soft, hazy gauze, giving an overall effect similar to the shining grey-green of the underside of a willow leaf. Trimmed with satin ribbons in shades of bronze and brown, it suited her to admiration. As she moved the silk clung to every curve of her shapely figure, temptingly caressed the long line of her limbs. The low neckline revealed the tops of soft, creamy breasts. A string of pearls encircled her slender throat, taking their lustre from her glowing skin. Several shades of ribbon had been ingeniously threaded in her hair, asking to be pulled out so that he could run his fingers through the abundant curls. Some heady perfume wafted about her person, sending Hugh's already heightened senses into a spin. He found it difficult to keep his breathing even.

He had thought her perfect before, in that white creation she had worn to Lady Stuart's reception. That had been designed *décolleté* enough to leave little of her lovely figure to the imagination. This dress had a higher neckline and concealed rather more of her breasts but its effect was the same. And to him her looks surpassed even their previous excellence. His imagination ran riot over what that bodice concealed. He had to confess himself enchanted.

She stirred his senses so much it had become painful. In his imagination he could still feel the softness of her in his arms as he carried her across that heaving deck. And, he realised helplessly and rather angrily, he had lost all desire to bed with any other woman since that moment. The much publicised affair with Maria Kingslea had never in fact taken place anywhere but in her imagination. Her husband was his friend, her pursuit of himself an embarrassment. He heaved a small, unconscious sigh. Setting Maria down kindly was proving somewhat difficult. Soon, he would have to be brutal in his rejection.

But he must not forget that Louisa was unmarried. If he broke all the rules of acceptable behaviour and paid her marked attention it could lead to his being trapped into matrimony, a state he had long since resigned himself to eschew, regarding marriage as impractical since he did not command the means to keep an establishment worthy of the name.

To enter into a wedlock with Louisa would be asking to be branded a fortune-hunter, a breed he despised. So why had he laid himself open to attack from the scandal-mongers and matchmakers by entering Castlereagh's salon with her on his arm? The plain answer was because he had not been able to help himself.

Quite apart from her undoubted attraction for him he found her intriguing. He could not make her out. She did not approve of the Duke's infidelities and he would lay odds that she did not fancy herself in love with the fellow, as so many of the women who flocked about that powerful figure did. Why she had allowed herself to be flattered into joining the Duke's court was part of her mystery, though he could see why the Duke encouraged her. All the women he favoured were either clever, like Madame de Staël, or beautiful, like Lady Shelley, but mostly both. Louisa was both. But since her arrival in Paris her behaviour had been too flighty to accord with the decorum required in an unmarried woman of her years. Talk had been rife. And because of that he had discovered that she carried no previous reputation for indiscretion. Just a lively, independent spirit. Which was, perhaps, why she had not wed years ago. . .

He glanced down at her animated, quite lovely face and could see no guile there. He did not know what to think, except that he should tread warily and keep a tight rein on his senses, for her capable hand in its silken mitten was burning a hole through the cloth covering his arm. And, despite everything, in the teeth of all his excellent intentions, he felt protective of her, just as he had on board the packet, when she had been a complete stranger. Then, he had not known who she was. Pleasant dalliance had beckoned enticingly. Now, every fibre of his being was shouting, Beware!

She would never arrive anywhere unnoticed, for she possessed style. Her natural elegance, her vivacity and unconventional looks attracted attention the moment she entered a room. He could hear the buzz that went round at their appearance together. She had made a conquest. He had made a conquest. Whichever it was the gossips were whispering he found he no longer cared. If being the butt of speculation was the price of spending an evening in her exquisite company it was a cost he was prepared to pay.

'Where would you like to sit, Aunt?'

Louisa's low, musical voice floated into his consciousness and he realised he had become so absorbed in his thoughts that he was in danger of neglecting his duty as escort.

'Oh, I do not mind, my love. But look, there is Clarissa Marchant! I have not spoken with her this age! I believe I will go and sit with her!'

Having comfortably settled Lady Nazeby in congenial company, Hugh again offered Louisa his arm and they circulated among the other guests. Her usual train of admirers soon gathered, but never for a moment did she allow them to break the intimacy between herself and her escort, keeping them at a distance with charm and diplomacy.

Hugh marvelled. Not that he would have allowed any one of her swains to detach the beauteous creature from his arm, but her social skills were abundant, a word here, a smile there, a witty rejoinder always at her command. How was it, he wondered again, that she had not been snapped up many seasons ago? What had her father been thinking of? Or Lady Nazeby, for that matter, since she had stood as substitute mother for so many years? Between them they should have contrived to have her settled long before this. No gentleman could wish for a more accomplished wife. Should any gentleman wish to become leg-shackled. Which he most certainly did not.

Louisa had heard that earlier sigh and now noticed a slight tensing of the hard muscle under her hand. She found the particular attention he was paying her exceedingly pleasant and wanted nothing to disturb their present amity. Yet she could not ignore that signal of withdrawal. He was not entirely relaxed. Perhaps he was regretting his offer to escort her. After all, she had made herself the object of gossip over the last weeks and, although her friends knew her too well to criticise openly, others less kindly disposed did not scruple to do so. And Hugh Deverill had a position to uphold.

So, at the first opportunity she removed her hand. He cast her a quick, enquiring glance which brought the ready furrows to his brow, though only for an instant. They quickly smoothed out as he gave her an amiable smile.

'We should seek our seats in the music-room,' he suggested neutrally. 'I believe Madame Grassini is to honour us with a song.'

'That will be delightful. I had not realised how attractive a contralto voice could be until I heard her sing at the opera the other evening.'

'The Duke,' observed Hugh mildly as they strolled through to join others assembling for the concert, 'has found a seat in the front row, with Lady Shelley and Madame de Staël. Where would you like to sit, Miss Finsham?'

'Oh, anywhere. I would suggest that we join Lady Nazeby and Lady Marchant, but I see they have found seats with several of their gossips.'

'I see vacant chairs in the row in front of her.'

Louisa had acknowledged Wellington upon his arrival but indulged in no further converse with him. To regain Hugh Deverill's good opinion had, for some reason, become of some importance. She therefore accepted his polite ushering of her to a seat out of harm's way near Amelia with a certain wry amusement.

Everyone enjoyed Giuseppina Grassini's superb performance, though Louisa found the Duke's unconcealed enchantment distasteful. Poor Duchess Kitty, she thought. To have one's husband paying court so openly to another woman must be dreadful. And to be forced to suffer the scandal of the Wedderburn-Webster affair and rumours of his other indiscretions as well. She feared she would never be able to trust any man enough to marry him. A sadness settled over her features. She would like to be wed, would like a family, but could any joy children might bring compensate for the pain of a husband's infidelity?

Hugh noticed the gloom settle over her features. Was it the song she found melancholy, or the fact that Wellington was so enraptured with the songstress? A longing smote him to see rapture on *her* face. Rapture for him. He closed his eyes, attempting to control his libido, to shut out the disturbing presence at his side. The attempt proved a dismal failure.

The music was just a harmonious background for Louisa's distracted thoughts. She could not concentrate on it with Hugh Deverill's thigh bare inches from her own. What was wrong with her? She had never been so affected before! Even being held in Radburn's arms, whom she had loved, had not made her tremble and caused the blood to rush around her veins so wildly that she had to shake out her fan and flirt it rapidly to cool herself.

'Are you too hot, my love?' whispered Amelia, leaning forward and speaking rather too loudly, thus earning herself hostile glances and a hiss or two. When La Grassini was singing, no one dared to chatter, as they did while lesser mortals performed.

Louisa shook her head and grew even more heated as Lord Hugh's glance rested on her again.

The endless concert finished at last and Louisa rose to her feet with relief.

'Delightful,' enthused Amelia as Hugh escorted them through to the supper-room. 'I can forgive that woman anything! She has such a divine voice!'

'Indeed she has, my lady,' agreed Hugh politely, conscious only of the divine creature on his arm.

Tables had been scattered about the room and were already laden with delicious food. Other dishes had been placed on trestles to one side, from which Lord Castlereagh's guests could serve themselves to additional delicacies should they so desire. Despite this, a battalion of servants stood ready to keep the covers full and to serve the wine.

With a degree of necessary determination, Lord Hugh ushered them towards a table already occupied by several people.

He bowed to those already assembled and then addressed a splendid figure sitting at the head. 'Your Excellency, my lords, may we have the privilege of joining you?'

All immediately rose to their feet and Lord Hugh introduced the ladies first to the splendid figure of Prince Metternich, the Austrian chancellor. His appearance completely eclipsed that of either the ill-formed Talleyrand or the ferret-faced Fouché, who had both managed to convince the Allies that, although they had in the past served Napoleon, they should nevertheless be included in the new French government.

Metternich bowed elegantly over the ladies' hands. 'Delighted, Lady Nazeby. *Enchanté*, Miss Finsham.'

His exquisite manners quite disarmed Louisa although she mistrusted the way he looked at her. His expertise in the *boudoir* had become one of the *on dits* of Paris and Louisa had no intention of falling victim to his supposed charms. She acknowledged the introduction with becoming reserve. Even to annoy Hugh Deverill she could not risk giving this flirtatious nobleman the slightest encouragement.

Not that she wished to annoy Lord Hugh that evening. He was behaving with the utmost courtesy and had not glowered at her once, reserving a diplomatically muted glance of disapproval for the over-effusive Austrian prince.

They were then presented to Prince Talleyrand and Joseph Fouché, the regicide chief of police, recently elevated to the dukedom of Otranto. The latter man was a thin, sallow creature, and Louisa did not trust him at all.

'I believe you are already acquainted with Monsieur and Madame d'Arblay,' went on Hugh smoothly, and Louisa greeted the couple with genuine pleasure.

'Dearest Louisa, I fear you will find the conversation here very dull. When these gentlemen get together they can speak of nothing but politics,' observed Fanny as the men filled their plates with a variety of cold meats, pâté and tartlets. The two had quickly come to first-name terms after their initial meeting. Louisa greatly valued the friendship of the older woman, who had undertaken to improve Louisa's French.

'You find it boring?' asked Louisa in surprise. She herself found the political situation quite fascinating.

'Oh, no, not personally. My husband is concerned, and so, naturally, I take an interest.'

'I do not anticipate finding it dull,' smiled Louisa. 'I

rather wish women were allowed to enter into politics.
Or almost any profession,' she added wryly. 'I find the
social round intensely confining, but what else is there
for me to do? You found an outlet for your energies in
the writing of novels. I wish I had the talent to do the
same.'

'My chief happiness has come from raising a family,'
remarked Fanny, and added, 'Why have you not wed,
Louisa?'

The enquiry had been made so gently that Louisa
could not take offence. She shrugged. 'I escaped the
bonds of an arranged marriage in the first flush of my
youth, thanks to my father's happy indifference to my
fate, and since coming of age I have failed to find a
gentleman I felt I could trust with my future happiness.
I prefer independence to becoming the slave of a man
I do not love.'

'Too particular by half,' snorted Amelia, overhearing.
'Try to put some sense into her head, will you, dear
Madame d'Arblay?'

Fanny smiled. 'I do not think Louisa requires any
lessons in sense, ma'am. I myself did not marry until
late in life, and then only because I became greatly
attached to Monsieur d'Arblay.'

'An excellent creature, I'm sure, but a foreigner!
Don't you marry a foreigner, Louisa.'

'I cannot positively undertake not to, dear Aunt, but
I will do my best to please you in my choice when I
make it,' laughed Louisa, diverted by her aunt's forthright speech. 'But do remember, Aunt, you are sitting
among foreigners here.'

'They are talking in French,' shrugged Amelia,
though looking a little contrite, 'and are paying no
attention to what we may say.'

'But understand and speak English excellently,
ma'am,' pointed out Fanny with a smile.

As if at some pre-arranged signal, Monsieur d'Arblay
glanced towards his wife, who took him to task. 'It
would be polite to conduct your conversation in

English, Monsieur d'Arblay. Miss Finsham can understand a little French, but the Countess has only a slight knowledge of your language.'

'Don't trouble about me,' began Amelia, but the gentlemen's attention had been drawn and Lord Hugh immediately reverted to English.

'Our apologies, ladies! Gentlemen! We are boring the ladies with our conversation.'

'Not necessarily,' protested Louisa quickly. 'How can we know whether we are bored, when we cannot understand? Pray continue your conversation, but in English, if you please!'

Metternich laughed and immediately offered his profuse apologies. 'To me,' he explained, 'language is seldom a barrier! I am at home in German, French, English, Russian and Italian.'

'I wish,' sighed Louisa, 'that I could say the same!'

'You have an ear for languages,' offered Madame d'Arblay with a knowing inclination of her head. 'You are improving your French at great speed.'

'Are you interested in languages, Miss Finsham?' asked Lord Hugh, his face breaking into the magnetic smile that set Louisa's pulse beating, for some reason she refused to admit. 'If so, I could offer my services to teach you a little German and Italian.'

'You appear fluent in French, my lord. Do you then have the same command of the other languages?' Louisa had wondered what hidden talents he possessed to fit him for such a responsible position in the Foreign Office, and was beginning to find out.

The smile broadened. How much more attractive it was than Metternich's smooth, practised charm.

'I trust so, Miss Finsham. Together with a smattering of Russian but lately acquired, and enough Dutch to make myself understood.'

'That must be useful when speaking with the Prince of Orange,' chuckled Louisa, smiling across to where the gentleman in question sat at a table graced by the presence of Wellington and his court. 'He appears to be recovering from the injuries he sustained at Waterloo.'

'Indeed, I believe he is.' Lord Hugh's lips twitched. 'And the Prince speaks good English. I fear my Dutch is wasted on him.'

'If only we all spoke the same language!'

'Indeed, Miss Finsham,' said Metternich, 'that might contribute to the united and peaceful Europe I would like to see.'

'As would we all, Your Excellency.'

The new voice was that of their host, doing his duty by circulating among his guests. What a contrast, thought Louisa, between the brilliant, accomplished Austrian, the truth of whose words, so 'twas said, was always in doubt and who loved to gain his ends by trickery, and the courtly, handsome Englishman, whose word was his bond, whose morals were impeccable, and who was incapable of deceit. Both of them had opposed the Revolution and its subversive violence and, in their different ways, both had succeeded.

Lord Castlereagh did not remain in conversation with them for long, moving on with charming courtesy to speak with other guests. After his departure the conversation at the table continued in English, ranging over the entire field of European politics. Louisa noted that Lord Hugh spoke knowledgeably but never took sides, and could only admire his skill in guiding the talk into amicable paths. And she came to understand why the Allies had insisted on Talleyrand's and Fouchés being put into office.

They were both clever, devious men. Talleyrand had fled France on the fall of the monarchy, returning after the death of Robespierre to become Minister for Foreign Affairs under the Directory and, subsequently, under Napoleon. As chief of police Fouché, a survivor if ever there was one, had an unenviable reputation. But, by virtue of his network of spies and a ruthless police system he had a firm grip on a population which, above all, needed to be returned to law and order. Both had their own interests firmly at heart and were ready to serve any master who offered them power. So long as they toed the Allied line, their positions were assured. The Allied powers knew that both men would be assiduous in their efforts to govern France and could be relied upon to protect the restored Bourbon dynasty from further revolt. Their own futures depended upon its survival.

Thoroughly stimulated by the discussion, Louisa found herself joining in from time to time, challenging an opinion here, offering her own there. Fanny d'Arblay did, so why should not she? Amelia had long since lost interest and excused herself, moving to join more congenial company.

Eventually the party broke up and Lord Hugh made ready to escort the ladies home.

'Ma'am,' he said, addressing the Dowager, 'I failed in my duty to amuse you during the evening. I trust you did not feel too neglected. I must ask you to forgive my regrettable manners.'

'Nonsense,' rejoined Amelia robustly. 'I was not bored, I just could not listen to that dreadful murderer Fouché and the grotesque Talleyrand a moment longer!'

Lord Hugh smiled, not for one moment taken in by this protestation. 'Then I must apologise for introducing you to them. But I collect your niece was not so nice over the company she kept. I believe, Miss Finsham, you enjoyed the discussion.'

He inclined his head in her direction and offered her his arm. Louisa took it, her earlier discomfort at such close contact much reduced by the elation of her spirits.

'Indeed, my lord, I must thank you for the chance to listen and learn! I found the evening most stimulating. How I wish I were a man! I would become a politician, I declare!'

'I,' said Lord Hugh quietly, 'am exceedingly glad you are not a man.'

They had reached their carriage and a footman was

assisting Amelia to climb in. Grateful that her aunt had not heard this last provocative remark and that it was too dark, despite the flambeaux, for anyone to see her blushes, Louisa flirted her fan, although the evening was cool. Now, of course, she was alarmingly aware of the firm muscles beneath her fingers. But she replied with spirit.

'You, my lord, can have no idea of the frustrations we females endure! I have received a good education, languages apart, which is a pity since I seem to have a gift for them, only you see my governess was English and could not teach me more than she knew—but to what purpose? According to you gentlemen all I am fit for is to run a household and bear your children! I,' she added defiantly, when she had recovered her breath, 'should like above everything to do something different, but I am not allowed!'

'Many women who marry and bear children also wield great influence,' he responded quietly. 'Madame de Staël is a case in point.'

'But her husband was Dutch Ambassador!'

'And Countess Lieven, although of German extraction, reports everything she sees and hears to Tsar Alexander's foreign office.'

'And *she* is married to the Russian Ambassador in London! Those women are the fortunate exceptions, my lord, you must see that!'

'Perhaps. But if you truly desire to find some worthwhile activity inside or outside of marriage, you, Miss Finsham, will do so, of that I am convinced. But now the carriage awaits. We are delaying your aunt's departure. Allow me to help you to mount the step.'

CHAPTER SIX

'I *vow* I have never known it so hot,' grumbled Amelia, fanning herself vigorously. 'I declare, had we been in England, we would have left London for Minchingham by now!'

'Do you wish to return, Aunt?'

Louisa kept her voice neutral with an effort. Quite the last thing she wanted at that moment was to depart from Paris, however hot and uncomfortable it had become.

'And leave Jamie here at the mercy of that woman? No, my love,' said Amelia in a resigned voice, 'I shall remain here as long as Amy Thurrock does. And I collect she will not wish to miss Lady Stewart's ball on the sixteenth or the Duke's banquet two days later or all the other exciting events of this victorious summer.'

Smiling, Louisa admitted, 'Neither should I! I am glad you are decided to stay. If the open curricle would not be too uncomfortable for you, would you like me to drive you out of Paris after breakfast? I missed my ride this morning because of the storm, but it is over now and the countryside should be fresh after the rain. Mayhap,' she added on sudden inspiration, 'Lady Thurrock would allow Jamie to accompany us! There would be room to squeeze him between us.'

'I wonder——'

'It's worth a try! Shall we not send a note, asking her?'

'It would certainly be preferable to riding about the airless streets of the city in a closed carriage leaving cards and making calls!'

Soon a footman was speeding round to the nearby Thurrock establishment with the invitation. To both ladies' delight he returned with an affirmative answer.

369

But Mr Coynd and a groom were to ride escort to the smart rig Pershaw had found for Louisa to drive. Dench would travel on the step behind them.

The outing proved a great success. Louisa revelled in the feel of the two spirited horses responding effortlessly to her every command and sprang the bays the moment they had passed through the village of Montmartre. Jamie made no attempt to conceal his admiration of her skill with the ribbons. Mr Coynd rode faithfully behind, his gaze fixed on the slender figure handling the matched pair with such ease.

Since acquiring the use of the curricle Louisa had often driven herself about Paris on errands and visits, with Betty and Dench in attendance, but this was the first occasion on which she had ventured into the surrounding countryside. Doing so without a suitable escort would be unwise, for one could meet up with a group of ill-disciplined soldiers or, worse, armed malcontents. So William Coynd and Jamie's groom, Percy, both armed, were not unwelcome additions to the party.

The ladies had brought a cold collation, a light nuncheon aimed largely at Jamie's youthful appetite. After driving for an hour they came across a most pleasant spot where meadows and trees bordered a narrow stream, with not a soldier of any description in sight. Louisa slowed her cattle.

'What do you think, Aunt?'

'An excellent spot! Such a beautiful view, and with room to draw the carriage off the road, too.'

Louisa nodded and drew up. Dench jumped down to lead the horses off the carriageway. Coynd leapt from his horse, threw the reins to Percy and hurried forward to hand the ladies from the curricle.

While Percy and Dench dealt with the horses, watering them in the stream before tethering them and leaving them to crop the grass, Louisa sent Coynd for the hamper and proceeded to unpack it.

The servants took their food to a little distance and

sat apart to eat. Mr Coynd partook of his meal with
them, of course, and once more proved himself an
entertaining companion. But since the morning of his
meeting with Lord Hugh Louisa had discovered in
herself a growing aversion to his manner. He presumed
upon their acquaintance, attempting to turn it into a
warmer relationship than she for one was prepared to
accept. The Dowager, however, concentrating upon
pleasing her grandson, appeared not to notice his
tutor's encroaching ways.

'May I take the ribbons? Please, Louisa!' pleaded
Jamie eagerly as they set off for home.

'Have you driven before?' asked Louisa cautiously.

'I can drive a pony trap, and Papa was used to let me
drive his curricle and pair about the estate—he was
teaching me,' replied the boy. 'He said it was never too
young to learn. And I'm thirteen now!'

'Then you may,' said Louisa, handing over the reins
and whip with a smile. 'But do not forget we may meet
with other traffic on a public highway.'

'I'll drive carefully,' promised his lordship with a
wide grin.

He drove exceptionally well considering his years
and lack of experience, and Louisa was not slow to tell
him so. 'You will be a fine whip one day, a most
complete hand.'

Jamie flushed with pleasure. Amelia beamed with
pride.

'Papa was a non-pareil,' he announced proudly. 'But,'
he went on, his face suddenly sunk in gloom, 'Mama
will not hear of my having a carriage of my own yet.'

'Then you should apply to your grandmama,' advised
Amelia briskly. 'She is a trustee, is she not? I am certain
she will do her best to persuade her.'

'Thank you, ma'am!' cried Jamie, his face lighting up
again. 'A splendid idea! I will!'

'But for now you had better give me back the ribbons,' Louisa suggested. 'We are nearing the city.'

Reluctantly, Jamie did as bidden. 'If I had my own

carriage I could go to Waterloo,' he observed. 'Mama won't hear of that, either.'

'She has not visited the place herself?' asked Amelia curiously.

'No. She swoons at the very thought of seeing a battlefield. But I would like to see the place where my father died.'

'Understandable enough,' murmured Amelia, swallowing. 'But I can assure you there would be little to see. In this matter I believe your mother to be wise. It is best to remember him as you saw him last.'

'Riding away in his regimentals,' sighed Jamie. 'He looked so splendid and gallant.'

'I am certain he did. I can just picture him.'

Amelia was having difficulty in keeping her voice steady and her tears at bay. Louisa broke back into the conversation, attempting both to rescue her aunt from embarrassment and to lighten the atmosphere.

'Your papa would not wish you to be sad, Jamie. He died bravely, doing his duty. That is what every man of conscience would wish to do. To meet his death in such a gallant rearguard action would have pleased him. How much bettter to die so than to be killed in an accident, or to die in bed of a fever.'

'Why did he have to die at all?' muttered Jamie rebelliously.

'That, Jamie dear, is not for us to question,' murmured Amelia. Louisa was relieved to see that her aunt had regained her composure.

They were nearing Jamie's residence when, with a strange mixture of feelings, Louisa caught sight of a familiar figure striding purposefully towards them. He was both a reminder and an escape from the memory of Brussels, for meeting him must change the tenor of the conversation.

'Look!' exclaimed Jamie, showing that his attention had not been entirely sunk in thoughts of his father. 'There's Lord Hugh!'

'So it is,' murmured Louisa a trifle breathlessly, and drew her cattle to an expert halt.

Lord Hugh had already seen them and lifted his hat, bowing and smiling to the three in the curricle and nodding pleasantly to Coynd on his horse behind.

Seeing Louisa so happily ensconced in the sporting curricle, managing Lady Nazeby's pair with consummate elegance and ease, Hugh wondered at his own current lack of enterprise in that direction. At home in the country no one enjoyed the pleasure of handling the ribbons more than he. In Hampshire he was considered a fine whip, almost a non-pareil. He had not commanded the means to cut a dash when in Town and over the years had found he could travel the crowded streets of a city so much more conveniently on foot or horseback. That being so he had not troubled to acquire an outfit. He was in Paris on business, not pleasure.

All the same, a burning desire to take Miss Louisa Finsham for a drive consumed him. Preferably into the depths of the country and unaccompanied. But the Bois would do.

Amelia, returning the greeting, became suddenly aware of her niece's agitation. Glancing at Lord Hugh, she noted his bemused gaze fixed upon Louisa's face, which had taken on a decidedly pink tinge. Amelia's smile widened. Could she at last hold out some hopes that her wayward niece had met a man who could overcome her mistrust of marriage? Amelia liked Hugh Deverill, and thought he would make a suitable if not a splendid match. Although, of course, he was likely to spend much of his life in foreign parts, a circumstance of which she could not approve.

'Miss Finsham drove us out into the country,' offered Jamie eagerly. 'She is a splendid whip, and we had a top-rate run; she allowed me to handle the ribbons! Her ladyship's cattle are absolutely prime goers!'

'I am glad to hear it, and to see that you are safely returned! I must apologise for not yet keeping my promise to escort you both on an outing, my lord, but I have been greatly occupied with official business these last days. However, I had not forgot. We will make an excursion soon.'

They were causing a blockage in the road, so could not stand for long. Once the adieus had been made, Louisa gave her horses the office to start, the groom released their heads and leapt back on his seat and Lord Hugh continued on his way, musing on the possibility of suggesting that Miss Finsham allow him to drive her in the Bois. The project presented considerable difficulty. He had no liking for the idea of hiring a turn-out of indifferent quality. Miss Finsham deserved nothing but the best he could offer. At that moment he could offer nothing. He could set about purchasing a first-rate outfit and although that would no longer put him at Point Nonplus he saw little reason for thus expending his hard-earned wealth, since it would merely satisfy a whim, not a real need. The simplest solution would be for her to allow him to drive her curricle. He doubted whether the independent Miss Finsham would even consider such a proposition, even were he imprudent enough to suggest it. He could send home. . .but to bring his curricle and pair across would take altogether too long. Cursing his own lack of foresight, he strode on. But he had not anticipated paying court to a lady. . .if he *was* paying court to Miss Louisa Finsham.

His stride faltered. Was he? And if so, to what purpose?

Lord Hugh had not offered to escort them to Lady Stewart's ball. A lapse which afforded Louisa an alarming degree of disappointment. Which led to an unwelcome bout of heart-searching.

She did not choose to ride the following morning, the morning of the ball. She could not have said precisely why, but she was sunk deep in the dismals. It must be the muggy weather, she decided, since it was definitely not due to Lord Hugh's omission of the previous after-

noon. He clearly did not wish to make his interest so
clear that his intentions would be questioned. Which
was as it should be.

Unless the weather turned cooler Lady Stewart's
ballroom would be unendurable that evening. Although
looking forward to the occasion, Louisa dreaded the
crush, the stifling atmosphere compounded of smoking
candles and overheated bodies which was bound to
prevail since it always did on such occasions.

Her aunt had decided to remain in her room until
later, so Louisa breakfasted alone in the small parlour.
She had scarcely finished her coffee when Chausson
announced a visitor for her.

'Mr Coynd?' queried Louisa in surprise. 'Whatever
can he want? I hope nothing has happened to Jamie!
Where is he?'

'I have showed heem into ze morning-room,
mademoiselle.'

Louisa hurried through, anxiety clouding her brow.
It must be Jamie; the tutor could have no other reason
for calling on her.

She entered the room, carefully leaving the door
open behind her to placate the proprieties, to find Mr
Coynd pacing impatiently. She had seldom seen him
other than on a horse, and was surprised to see how
jerky was his stride. He turned upon her entrance and
executed an elaborate bow.

'Miss Finsham!' His voice sounded strangely hoarse.

Louisa curtsied. 'Good morning, Mr Coynd!' She
walked to a chair and seated herself, indicating that her
visitor should do the same. 'You wished to speak with
me? Is it about Jamie?'

'Lord Thurrock?' He looked startled as he perched
on the edge of a nearby sofa. He was not ill-looking,
considered Louisa, being smoothly handsome, but he
lacked the address of someone like Lord Hugh. Perhaps
that was due to being forced into a semi-menial
position. 'No, it is not about James, Miss Finsham.' He
paused a moment and suddenly burst out, 'Miss

Louisa!' His voice and manner became ardent. 'You must know that I hold you in the greatest regard, Louisa. You have become the dearest object of my heart!' He flung himself on one knee in front of his startled hostess and placed a dramatic hand on his brocaded waistcoat, somewhere about the region of his heart.

'Mr Coynd! Please!' exclaimed Louisa, recovering her voice and keeping it steady with some difficulty. She had had many proposals in her time, but none as embarrassing as this one threatened to become. 'Please go no further, sir, and get up, do!'

'No, my dearest Louisa! Not until I have your answer!' he declared, ignoring the first part of her injunction. 'I beg you to make me the happiest of men by bestowing your hand in marriage upon my unworthy self!'

He reached out to capture the said hand but Louisa managed to snatch it away in time.

Despite the less favourable feelings she had entertained for him these last days Louisa had still found him generally agreeable and did not want to set him down too severely. Neither did she wish to refuse him without leaving him his dignity.

'My family is ancient and its reputation without reproach,' he was going on earnestly. 'I know I have no fortune to inherit, but I am not entirely without means——'

'And I have plenty for both of us,' murmured Louisa, beginning to see the point of his surprising proposal. He could have no idea that her husband, if she took one, would gain control merely of her income, not of her fortune, which was the subject of a complicated legal settlement. 'Unfortunately, sir, I have no desire to marry, either you or anyone else. And now, if you will excuse me——' She began to rise.

But he remained at her feet, impeding her movement. 'My dearest Louisa! You cannot be so cruel! A refusal will break my heart!'

'I think not, sir, merely dent your pride a little, for I am persuaded you cannot love me and I am certain I do not love you. I am sensible of the honour you have done me in offering for my hand, but I do not believe I have ever given you cause to hope that your suit could be successful. And I was not aware of granting you permission to address me by my first name,' she added, unable to ignore his familiarity.

Coynd struggled to his feet, now every bit as stiff in his manner as Major Hewitson. 'No,' he said bitterly. 'You were all gracious friendship until Lord Hugh Deverill appeared on the scene!'

'Lord Hugh?' Louisa took the opportunity to rise to her own feet and fixed him with a repressive eye. 'His presence could make no difference to my opinion of you. You are Lord Thurrock's tutor. As such, you were and are entitled to my courtesy. But nothing more.'

'I may be a mere tutor to you, Miss Finsham, but my blood is as good as yours! I am grandson to an earl!'

'Blood, my dear sir, has nothing to say to it. I do not wish to marry you, that is all. I bid you good day.' She reached for the bell-pull. 'Chausson will see you out.'

The butler must have been hovering, probably listening, thought Louisa wryly, for he entered the room almost before she had rung.

'Show the gentleman out if you please, Chausson.'

Chausson bowed with grave dignity. 'Zees way, *monsieur*.'

'I shall not give up hope,' said Coynd, bowing.

Louisa was surprised by his dignity in defeat and felt rather sorry for him. She inclined her head. 'That is your privilege, sir, but I must warn you, your hope is misplaced,' she told him, as gently as she could.

Relief at his departure left her trembling. What an unpleasant interview with which to begin the day! At least she would not have to face him at the ball tonight. He was not in a financial position to move much in first circles, despite the right to which his blood entitled him. For which she was truly sorry, for his sake. But Hugh

Deverill was a younger son and *he* had managed to advance his fortunes in a most creditable way.

No, she could not feel too sorry for Mr Coynd. But his presence would put a damper on her future outings with Jamie. She would just have to treat the tutor with cool reserve and hope he did not again overstep the bounds of propriety.

Louisa entered the Stewarts' residence arm in arm with her aunt. Amelia was resplendent in a gown of blue figured sarcenet with matching feathered turban. This Sir Charles Stewart, their host for the evening—confusing, she thought, to have two gentlemen of that name in Paris, although their surnames were spelt differently—was Lord Castlereagh's half-brother. He and his wife, popular and gracious hosts, waited to receive them. In the ballroom myriad candles in the chandeliers and wall-sconces lit the brilliant scene, several long mirrors on the walls reflecting men garbed either in colourful uniforms or in civilian finery: exquisite waistcoats under superfine coats worn with white breeches and stockings. Most escorted ladies in pastel muslins with flowers, ribbons and feathers in their hair. The scene was worthy of a painting, she thought, absorbing its exotic beauty with appreciation.

She herself had chosen a high-waisted gown in cream silk trimmed with primrose and violet, the skirt falling gracefully to the floor at the front, with a train behind, which could be raised by strings for dancing. An over-skirt of filmy gauze floated about her like a sunlit cloud. Betty had fashioned a matching head-dress of ribbons and feathers which she knew became her. Her greeny hazel eyes roved the ballroom, searching for sight of the tall, imposing figure on whose arm she had once anticipated entering the room.

She soon picked him out. Like most other men he was bending over a beautiful woman. He moved and looked round, as though aware of her scrutiny. His face lit up and he made as though to come across to greet her.

But Louisa had recognised the woman he was with and the shock made her gasp. She had not known that Lady Kingslea had arrived in Paris. Louisa turned abruptly, unable to keep her countenance, to find Major Hewitson at her side. Just in time, she covered her mortification with a brilliant smile.

He bowed, flushing slightly at the unexpected warmth of her greeting. 'May I claim the honour of the first pair of dances, Miss Finsham? You did promise them yesterday morning——'

'Indeed, Major, so I did!' She handed him her dance card, annoyed to notice that her hand trembled slightly. Idiotish creature! To let the presence of Deverill's mistress overset her. She had known precisely what he was. But, she acknowledged, had allowed herself to be bamboozled into forgetting! She would not forget again.

Amelia departed for the card tables, where she would spend her evening with other dowagers and chaperons. A small crowd of admirers gathered round Louisa, all anxious to mark her card. When Hugh Deverill joined them and, with natural authority and address, inserted himself ahead of the lesser mortals clustered about her, she allowed him to take her card without protest. She could scarcely make a scene here, but the look she directed at him would have withered anyone else. He lifted an enquiring brow, but otherwise ignored her frosty demeanour, putting his initials against a couple of dances and returning the card to her trembling fingers without comment, except to bow and remark, 'I shall look forward to standing up with you in due course, Miss Finsham.'

'Devilish uncivil of him,' grumbled the man he had displaced, a young captain of the ninety-fifth, dashing in his green uniform. 'Deuce take it, I was about to claim the supper dance!'

Louisa hadn't noticed which dances Hugh Deverill

had marked. Now she regarded the card with dismay.
He had claimed the pair before supper. Not only would
she be forced to dance a waltz with him, but also to
endure the entire supper break in his company!

Major Hewitson, so heavily moustached it was difficult to make out more than a well-shaped lower lip and
high cheekbones, danced surprisingly well, his apparent
stiffness being all in his manner, not in the athletic
limbs of a top-of-the-trees cavalryman. As they moved
up the set Louisa began to relax, determined to enjoy
herself, to put the thought of Hugh Deverill from her
mind until the supper dance forced her to remember
him.

Hewitson was not a great conversationalist, and he
performed the movements of the dance mostly in
silence, while Louisa chattered and smiled merrily to
hide the distress in her heart. They came together and
parted again at the dictates of the steps until they
reached the top of the set, then joined hands to gallop
down the middle to take their places at the other end.
Panting, eyes brilliant, Louisa suddenly realised that
Hewitson's blue gaze was fixed on her face with an
expression of open admiration she had not seen there
before. Her liveliness, her brilliant smiles, must be
encouraging him more than she intended, she surmised,
and realised that even in her first flush of indignation
against Hugh Deverill she had not behaved with such
boisterous, wanton disregard for conduct.

The thought sobered her. For the remainder of the
two dances she moderated her behaviour. But the
major had received enough encouragement to overcome his natural shyness with the ladies.

As he returned her to her seat he asked where Lady
Nazeby might be found. 'I should like to seek an
interview with her,' he explained.

Louisa frowned. 'To what purpose, Major?'

'Is that not obvious, my dearest Miss Finsham? I wish
to seek her permission to pay my addresses to her
niece.'

Appalled, Louisa gazed up into his ardent eyes. Not two proposals in one day! ''Twill do you no good, Major,' she told him as calmly as she could. 'Lady Nazeby's permission would be worthless. She is neither my guardian nor in truth my chaperon, since I am past the age when I need either, though she is kindness itself in accompanying me on such occasions as this to offer the protection of her presence.'

Undaunted, 'Then to whom should I apply, Miss Finsham?' he persisted.

'No one, sir. The only person to whom you could usefully apply would be me, and I must inform you now that you would be well-advised to refrain from doing so. I like you, Major Hewitson, but as a friend. I would not welcome your addresses.'

He looked so embarrassed and crestfallen that Louisa took pity.

'Do not refine over me, sir,' she advised gently. 'I am not worthy of your regard. I fear I have flirted with you most unforgivably tonight and am well-chastened by the result. If I have given cause for hurt, I beg you will feel able to forgive me.'

She stood up gazing into the Hussar's eyes, seeking reassurance that he had not been too overset by her refusal to entertain his suit. To the man watching from across the room it appeared as an intimate exchange beyond that of mere friendship. She had been flirting with the young cavalry officer throughout their dances, and now she appeared to be pleading for more of the fellow's attention. How, he wondered tersely, could the man possibly deny her anything she asked? He was surprised by the pain tearing through him at the thought. He wished he had not sought to engage her for the supper dances. She would clearly rather have spent her time with Hewitson. But, deuce take it, why should he allow the gallant major free rein? She couldn't truly entertain a *tendre* for the man. He had observed no previous sign of any such emotion in her and he'd seen them together often enough. No. When his chance came he would seize it and wipe memory of the other fellow from her mind.

At her apology the major cleared his throat and appeared more embarrassed than ever. 'I must ask you to forgive me for misreading your feelings, Miss Finsham. As for mine, they remain the same. But I shall not bother you further by expressing sentiments which must cause you distress.'

'And we may remain friends?'

'If that is your wish.'

She gave him her most warm smile. 'It is, Major. I value friendships above everything. I have no wish to marry.'

Mollified by this last statement, he made his bow and left. Louisa had little time to ponder on this latest turn of events, for she was immediately claimed for the next set, which was already forming. But although she smiled and danced energetically with a succession of partners she was careful not to incite further expressions of tender regard by a continuation of her immoderate behaviour. She had just had it forcefully brought home that to react in such a way because a certain gentleman had chosen to return to his mistress produced unfortunate consequences which affected others besides herself. And what did it matter to her if Hugh Deverill's mistress was in Paris? He was nothing to her.

A protestation which grew more loweringly unrealistic as the evening wore on.

Arriving late as usual and not, to Louisa's eye, looking his usual buoyant self, the Duke of Wellington soon presented himself before her.

'Dear me,' he remarked upon being informed that her card was already full. 'Yes, yes. But I cannot forgo the pleasure of a dance with you, my dear Miss Finsham.' Saying which, he boldly struck out the initials of one of his junior officers, substituted his own and handed back the card with a smile. 'You appear to be without the company of your aunt this evening, Miss Finsham. Will you not join my party?' He indicated the group of dashing ADCs and beautiful young women, who seemed to grow in numbers every week, gathered at one end of the ballroom.

Louisa, having quietly extricated herself from his court over the last week or so without, she hoped, giving cause for offence, did not wish to fall into that trap again. Her unaccountable reaction to Hugh Deverill seemed to have precipitated her into one indiscretion after another, and it had to stop.

She acknowledged the invitation with a grateful smile while seeking tactful words to refuse it. 'You are most kind, my lord, but I am quite comfortable here, I thank you. My aunt is but in the next room, enjoying a hand of cards. And here,' she added thankfully, 'is my next partner come to claim me!'

The Duke had no call to abide by the strict rules which governed her own behaviour at a ball. For him to dance more than twice with one of his young matrons did not cause a scandal, at least not one of the kind that could ruin a young lady's reputation, get her talked about and spoil her chances of making a good match. Lady Shelley appeared to be his favourite partner and Louisa had to admit she was as good a dancer as horsewoman. But for all his attempt at high spirits Louisa thought he often looked preoccupied that evening. More disturbing articles had appeared in the *St James's Chronicle*. She felt sorry for Wellington. For the hero of Waterloo it must be particularly distasteful to have the Press snapping at his heels like angry terriers, she thought, but, to the publishers, the more revered and famous their victim, the better they were served.

Between her worried anticipation of the coming supper dance and her indignation over the Duke's plight—he might not be above reproach, but he didn't deserve such vindictive persecution—Louisa accepted her partners, danced, made polite conversation, went through the motions like an automaton, but all the time she was acutely aware of Hugh Deverill's presence.

He had not joined any particular party, moving about the ballroom between dances, exchanging greetings and conversation with different people as he went. Doing the pretty as a diplomat, she thought with scorn. Though why she should scorn him for simply doing his duty she refused to consider. So far he had not danced twice with anyone, even Lady Kingslea, who did not lack for other partners. Louisa had to admit her to be an attractive creature, tiny, vivacious and fashionably fair. She seemed to have come with Lady Sidford. Louisa wondered why Lord Hugh had not joined their party.

There came a dance, though, the one before that for which he had engaged her, when both he and Lady Kingslea appeared to be absent from the ballroom. Her eyes searched the throng anxiously, willing one of them to be present. But neither was.

Were they together? In the conservatory, perhaps, or taking the air on the terrace? The intimate scenes presented by Louisa's imagination caused her to stumble and lose her place in the dance.

She apologised to her stout, sweating partner, a minor Russian prince, who gallantly brushed it aside. 'Understandable,' he said in his almost impeccable English. 'Many of the bourgeois present have no talent for the art of the dance. No wonder they make you lose your place.'

'Really, sir,' responded Louisa, jerked from her pre-occupation by his condescending tone, 'I have never sought to blame another's performance for my own shortcomings. In my experience many of the rich cits dance extremely well, while some members of the aristocracy do so extremely badly.'

'Your kind heart does you credit, Miss Finsham,' puffed the Prince with even greater condescension, essaying a bow, the elegance of which was badly impeded by his corset.

Louisa decided that even good manners could be taken too far and was glad when the movements of the

dance saved her from having to reply. But because of
this diversion she missed their return. When she next
saw him Lord Hugh was leaning against the wall, arms
crossed, watching her. She immediately felt a flush of
heat invade her body. For an instant she glared back,
then quickly looked away, but not before she had
noticed his expression. The candles in a nearby sconce
threw flickering shadows across his face, making it
inscrutable, apart from the fact that his mouth was set
in a tight, disapproving line.

He had the effrontery to disapprove of *her*!

She tossed her head defiantly, and felt her curls
bounce, dislodging a feather already come rather loose
from the effects of her energetic dancing. The moment
the music stopped she excused herself to the Prince and
made for the ladies' retiring-room. Lady Stewart's maid
was in attendance and soon repaired the damage.
Louisa lingered as long as she felt able, reluctant to
return to the ballroom, hoping that by the time she did
both dances would be over.

But as she approached she heard the strains of a
Viennese waltz strike up. Hesitating on the threshold,
wanting to disappear again but not quite having the
determination, she became aware that Lord Hugh had
been watching out for her and was at her side.

He bowed. 'I am flattered that you did not entirely
renege on our dances, Miss Finsham. If you are
fatigued, perhaps you would rather seek the fresh air of
the terrace?'

Dear God! She'd rather endure to dance with him
than spend even a few moments alone on the darkened
terrace in his company! If he took advantage——

'Thank you, my lord, but I am not in the least
fatigued,' she retorted sharply. 'I was forced to retire to
restore my toilet.'

He glanced at her immaculate head, let his eyes
linger on a face pink with indignation and maybe
something else, and a small smile softened his lips.
'Then let us make the most of this waltz.'

He held out an imperious hand. Louisa placed hers in it and felt his other hand at her waist. Automatically, hers reached up to rest on his muscled arm. She had no time to savour the alarming effect this close contact had upon her before she was swept into the dance by a partner who was clearly expert in the art of the waltz.

CHAPTER SEVEN

THE experience was like nothing she had known before. It lasted far too long, yet not long enough.

She could spend the rest of her life in Hugh Deverill's arms, she realised dazedly as he whirled her around in the swift steps of the dance. It was where she belonged. Some part of her had recognised it the moment he had picked her up and carried her across the deck of the packet boat, but she had stubbornly refused to give the idea credence. Now, she could no longer deny it. Not that she had to like feeling the way she did, for she profoundly disapproved of his seducing other men's wives.

That evening she had watched him proving himself a polished, accomplished member of the *ton*, dancing with more grace than his appearance might suggest, conversing easily with one partner after another. Now she was experiencing his undoubted social skills at first hand. He would have taken Almack's by storm had he deigned to seek admission there. But he had kept his talents well hidden from London Society. She wondered why.

Her steps fitted his perfectly. All too soon the orchestra speeded its tempo to bring the dance to a breathless end. As it did so Hugh tightened his hold, drew her towards him until their bodies touched, and swept her into a series of dizzying twirls. When they stopped she had to cling on for a moment until the room ceased spinning. And her vertigo could only partly be attributed to the exigencies of the dance. It had almost as much to do with the potent effect of her partner's close proximity.

She regained her balance to discover both his hands at her waist, steadying her. He was too near, his presence overwhelming. She drew a deep breath, only to become aware of the scent of him, not unpleasantly sweaty like that of the Prince, but clean and fresh, tinged with the faintest hint of sandalwood.

He, of course, was neither dizzy nor out of breath nor unduly affected by her nearness. He was, however, gazing down at her with something in his eyes which disappeared the moment she looked up. His mouth curved into a twisted smile.

'It seems we suit each other in the dance at least. Our steps match well.'

'But in very little else, I vow!'

'Do not be so sure, my dear Miss Finsham.' His eyes slid from the confused expression in hers, rested a moment on the tell-tale pulse fluttering like a trapped bird at the base of her throat, paused briefly to drink in the beauty of her breasts as they rose and fell in agitation. Then they lifted to rest on her parted lips. 'It seems to me that we suit in at least one other way.'

His hands tightened on her waist. His gaze remained on her mouth, his meaning obvious, but his thick black lashes veiled the expression in his eyes.

Louisa gasped at this forthright declaration and stepped back. He dropped his hands immediately. 'We are becoming a spectacle, sir!' she informed him sharply, realising that almost everyone else had left the floor, many already making their way out of the ballroom in search of supper. Nevertheless, too many curious glances were being thrown their way. 'I am already become an object of gossip, and I will thank you not to aid the scandal-mongers in their task!' she finished tautly.

He bowed. When he spoke his voice had become remote, icy, sending a chill through her. 'Indeed, Miss Finsham. I have been at some pains to aid you in countering their tattle, and for that reason refrained from offering my escort this evening. To appear once on my arm should have been enough to silence it, to appear twice might well have given it a new direction.

But your own behaviour so far tonight can hardly be said to have assisted your cause.'

Louisa, who had been somewhat mollified by the first part of his statement, was incensed by the remainder. 'You surely flatter yourself, my lord, to suggest that your patronage should offer me protection from the gossips! And how dare you criticise my behaviour? Although in truth you have done little else since we met!'

'I had not meant to appear critical, merely to offer you advice.'

'Oh! You. . .you hypocrite! You can stand there condemning me when your mistress. . .'

She suddenly trailed off as an amused smile lightened his face, belying the suddenly intent look in his eyes.

'Never tell me you are jealous, my love?'

'Of course not!' But she was! It was not righteous indignation she had felt at the sight of Lady Kingslea, but another, much more oversetting emotion. And how dared he call her his love? 'I simply despise men who cuckold others!' she snapped.

Again he bowed, all gravity now. 'That is your privilege, Miss Finsham. Shall we proceed through to supper?'

Louisa did not feel she could eat a thing and did not want to remain in his odious company. But people were still looking at them, suspecting a quarrel by their manner, although their voices had been kept low. She did not wish to make matters worse. So she nodded.

He offered his arm. And, because she did not want to make a spectacle of their differences, she took it.

'I had thought,' he said quietly as they paced together towards supper, 'that we had become friends. Maria Kingslea is not in Paris at my invitation.'

'She's not?' muttered Louisa uncertainly.

'No.'

'Oh.'

She considered this for a moment, surprised that he should have volunteered the information.

'Then why is she here?' she demanded.

He shrugged and looked down at her, saw the uncertainty reflected in her face and smiled deprecatingly. 'To try to persuade me into becoming her lover.' She did not possess conventional beauty but striking looks which were infinitely more attractive, he thought as he continued to drown in her wide, greeny hazel gaze. The tiny green flecks around her iris enchanted him.

'Your lover? But I thought. . .'

'You were not alone. Maria saw to that. But my visits to the Kingslea establishment were made to see my old friend, her husband. She took some convincing, but I believe that she has now finally accepted the futility of her campaign.'

Louisa dragged her eyes from his to where Maria Kingslea was flirting with a portly Prussian count. Following her gaze, Hugh felt a surge of relief. Maria's immediate pursuit of another man showed how little she had really cared for him.

Why he felt it necessary to explain himself to Louisa Hugh could not fully understand. But the contempt in her eyes had been too discomfiting. He valued her good opinion.

The supper-room was crowded. He found seats in a secluded corner, from which Louisa could watch proceedings from behind the protecting screen of a huge potted fern, and, leaving her fanning herself to stir the air from a nearby open window, went off in search of food, for the dishes had been laid entirely on sidetables in the French buffet style.

He returned unexpectedly quickly given the denseness of the crush, bearing, with commendable dexterity and steady hands, two plates laden with delicacies plus two glasses of wine.

'I thought you might enjoy this claret better than lemonade,' he remarked with a smile as he balanced his booty on the narrow ledge of the pedestal holding the potted plant, 'and I also assumed that you would not wish your wine watered.'

'Thank you, my lord. You guessed well. I have long passed the age of being obliged to consume lemonade, and have a fairly strong head. I find the wine here delicious. The addition of water ruins it.'

'Precisely.'

His absence had given Louisa time to gather her wits and to realise that her censure, and her extreme reaction, had been unwarranted. She had behaved foolishly, and deserved Lord Hugh's displeasure. But although she did not enjoy being at odds with him it would be difficult to apologise. Yet if she did not she would put in jeopardy the tentative friendship which had begun to spring up between them. On the other hand, with her new knowledge of her own vulnerability, could she afford to renew and even deepen it? She would be asking to suffer hurt again.

But he had taken the trouble to put her misapprehension right and appeared ready to be on terms again. Logic and intrinsic honesty forced her to conclude that she must do the same, although no amount of honesty could force her to admit openly to jealousy. So she must word her apology carefully. And not allow him to guess how much his nearness disturbed her.

Once he was seated, therefore, and she had enjoyed a sustaining mouthful of wine and enjoyed a first taste of a delicious pigeon patty, she began, her voice pitched as low as was consistent with his being able to hear her.

'I have to confess, my lord, that I do not accept criticism easily. It is a fault in me which I know renders me most unsuitable as a wife.' His raised eyebrows gave her pause for an agonising moment. She should not have mentioned marriage, even by implication. Colouring hotly, she rushed on. 'Since we met you have found many reasons to criticise me, my lord, and my response has been, I fear, to behave in a manner to thoroughly deserve it. I loathe infidelity and hate flirts—of either sex—who use their powers to humiliate and demean. If I have appeared on occasion to be one, then I beg you to believe that I am truly sorry. I do not seek to engage

a gentleman's interest simply to inflate my own vanity.'
Her speech ended, she bit into the patty with a determination designed to disguise her discomfiture.

'Then I must apologise most sincerely, for, as I have
already said, I did not wish to offend you. If I drove
you to an extreme of behaviour by my ill-advised words
I am truly sorry.'

Louisa swallowed convulsively and felt the food go
down in an uncomfortable lump. She smiled. 'After
such a handsome apology, what can I do but pronounce
you forgiven?'

'And yet,' he mused, a slight smile curving his lips,
'consciously or unconsciously, your natural manner and
spirits do engage the interest of almost every gentleman
you meet.'

Not her looks, thought Louisa ruefully. She picked
up her glass and tried to wash down the lump of food
with a generous mouthful of wine.

'I cannot conceive of what you might mean, my lord.'

'No?' His tone was not unfriendly, merely quizzical.
'Tell me, dear Miss Finsham, how many proposals of
marriage have you turned down since your come-out?'

Colour flooded Louisa's face again as she remembered the two she'd received only that day. 'I cannot
remember,' she muttered awkwardly. 'But I have never
led any gentleman to hope for an acceptance should he
make a declaration!'

Only David, Lord Radburn, she thought in distress.
She had given him every encouragement, but she had
been the one to suffer the pain of rejection, not he.

'Have you not?'

'No, sir!'

He sounded mildly sceptical. It seemed important to
convince him. 'Would you say, my lord, that my dealings with Mr Coynd should have lead him to expect a
positive answer to a declaration?'

That had shaken him! He stared at her in confused
amazement before his gaze narrowed.

'William Coynd has proposed marriage to you?'

'Aye, sir. This very morning!'

He eyed her steadily. 'I confess to feeling surprise. Nothing in your behaviour that I have witnessed, admittedly in limited circumstances, had led me to believe that you favoured him above Major Hewitson or any other gentleman for that matter. Yet your general air of lively friendship may make many men feel——' He shrugged, allowing the gesture to complete the thought for him. 'I suppose he may have interpreted your interest in riding with young Lord Thurrock as a particular interest in him,' he mused, 'although I doubt it . . . he needs a fortune. . . and can be quite unscrupulous when it suits him.'

'I can assure you, my lord, that my desire to ride with the young Earl had nothing to do with the presence of Mr Coynd! On the contrary, he accompanied his lordship only on the Dowager Countess's insistence, although I confess I found him agreeable company at first.'

'And therefore treated him in your usual delightful manner. But you have not found him so agreeable latterly?'

'Since your meeting with him in the Bois he has tended to behave in an over-familiar manner.'

'I see.' He drained his glass. He had not eaten much. 'I fear you have become victim of an old jealousy, Miss Finsham, for which I apologise. I might have guessed my presence would cause him to move speedily to secure his fortune.'

'You believe it was my fortune he desired, sir, and not my person?'

He smiled suddenly, a sweet, placatory smile which rendered her rather breathless. 'Knowing him, I fear so, my dear, though I am certain he would not despise your person. And you must be aware that your fortune may have inspired many of the proposals you have received, since you protest you gave the gentlemen no conscious encouragement.'

Louisa coloured again. She had thought herself

beyond being put to the blush by anything a gentleman said, but this man seemed to have that kind of effect on her. 'I am, sir,' she retorted tartly. 'I have long suspected that my fortune accounted for the large number of suitors who have sought my hand despite every discouragement I have offered. I can think of no other reason for it.' A certain pride made her go on. 'Although I do not believe Major Hewitson to be in need of funds. He is reputedly vastly rich, so my person may not be entirely devoid of value in certain gentlemen's eyes.'

'I never suggested it was. On the contrary, I myself find it quite entrancing.' His leisurely gaze conducted an assessment of her charms, raising her temperature further. Finally his thick brows lifted, furrowing his forehead. He met her embarrassed, furious eyes, the expression in his own amused. 'So Major Hewitson was encouraged to ask for your hand, was he?'

He had seen her flirting with poor Major Hewitson earlier. Had she remembered that in time she would not have mentioned the Hussar's proposal! But she had, and could scarcely blame Lord Hugh for his reception of the news. But his attitude made her fume.

'Not precisely.' Louisa crumbled a morsel of bread between her fingers, rolling it into a small hard wad in lieu of grinding *him* into little pieces. 'But he requested permission to apply to my aunt on the subject.'

'And what answer did you give?'

He sounded lazily amused. But his fingers had tightened about the stem of his glass and his grey-blue eyes had become watchful.

'I told him that such an application would not serve, for my aunt has no say in the matter.'

'He should apply to you?'

'Yes.' Louisa faced him challengingly. 'I am in the fortunate position of being able to make my own decision over whom I marry. I also informed him that I had no intention of bestowing my hand on any gentleman at the present moment.'

'Do you not wish to wed?' he asked softly.

His gentle tone disarmed her. Her anger dissipated as swiftly as it had risen. She shrugged slender bare shoulders outlined by the low neckline and little puff sleeves of her gown. But her chin lifted in an unconsciously defiant gesture. 'Only if I can find an agreeable gentleman who does not covet my fortune and threaten to lose it by gaming or dissipate it by expensive living. Or both.' There was no call to inform his of the exact status of her dower. She never advertised it. Any man she would consider suitable as a husband would not care.

'And you have not met such a one?'

'No.'

She would not elaborate further or tell him of her youthful heartbreak. That would serve no purpose but to make her more vulnerable. Besides, David Radburn was in the past, and had been a mistake. She reached for her glass again. The wine was making her excessively hot. Having taken another sip, she used her fan energetically to cool her flushed face.

'I am sorry. You do not deserve to waste into an old maid.'

She looked at him, startled by both his words and his tone.

'I would rather that, my lord, than make a bad marriage. If only I were a man! I could take up a profession and feel of some use in the world.'

'So you have indicated before. But then the world would have lost the gracious presence of a beautiful woman and, mayhap, a distinguished hostess.'

'Really, sir! You are roasting me!' But that had not been his intention. She could see it in his eyes. She rushed on, heedless of the sudden thumping of her heart. 'As it is, I shall probably retire to the country and concentrate on farming and breeding horses on my aunt's estate. I already know all Pershaw can teach me. Aunt Nazeby can leave the estate as she wills, and has promised it to me.'

'So you have expectations, in addition to your present fortune.'

'Yes, but no one knows of my aunt's intention! They believe Minchingham will revert to the Nazeby estate. I beg you will not speak of it!'

She had said too much. Could she trust him with the knowledge? His gaze had become serious and held some element she could not quite fathom. Was it simply admiration? Compassion? Or appraisal?

'I will not. I am honoured that you felt you could entrust your secret to me,' he averred quietly.

But she hadn't felt that at all. The atmosphere between them had suddenly become so easy that she had spoken without thought! But all the same, looking into his steady eyes, knowing how many diplomatic secrets he must be obliged to keep, she knew she could trust him.

Hugh stood up. Louisa glanced at him enquiringly, fanning herself against the heated atmosphere. People and noise filled the supper-room and yet they had seemed to be quite alone behind their fern. Now he was preparing to abandon their isolation. Disappointment shot through her like a pain.

'You are feeling the heat,' he observed.

'It is the wine,' said Louisa, wishing to blame anything but his presence for her flushed appearance. 'I should have had it watered after all.'

He regarded her quizzically for a moment. Then his rough-hewn yet utterly compelling mouth curved into a smile, proving again how much more attractive were his rugged features than the foppish good looks of Mr Coynd or the classically sculpted face of Major Hewitson! 'Whatever the cause, allow me to escort you to the terrace for a breath of fresh air,' he suggested. 'It should be pleasant in the garden after the atmosphere in here. Will you need a shawl?'

Her disappointment turning speedily to anticipation, Louisa rose with alacrity, clutching her fan and tiny reticule. Somehow the thought of walking on the terrace with him had lost its terror. The prospect beckoned invitingly. And if people wished to gossip, let them!

'I shall do perfectly well as I am,' she assured him. 'The evening is so warm I cannot possibly catch a chill!'

'Exactly my sentiments.' He offered his arm. 'Shall we proceed?'

How wonderful it was to be in amity with him again. Louisa placed her fingers on the offered arm and as she did so a thrill of pleasure ran through her.

Passing among the other guests to reach the door, they were accosted by several friends and acquaintances, all of whom, Louisa was certain, were speculating as to the exact degree of intimacy between herself and her escort. Hugh appeared to have put aside his scrupulous desire not to arouse more gossip by being seen to show an interest in her. She had never considered that particular matter to be of any consequence. His partiality for her could be considered entirely proper. The Duke's, if any, could not.

He was to be seen, still surrounded by his bevy of youthful admirers, though looking rather less cheerful than normal. Her dance with him was still to come. Prince Metternich's, too. The ball was little more than halfway through.

The terrace ran right across the back of the house, accessible from several rooms. Hugh appeared to know his way, leading her down the curving staircase and through the library to a tall door standing open to the night.

A rocket shot skywards as they emerged, set off from one of the pleasure gardens lining the Champs Elysées.

'A poor show,' said Hugh disparagingly. 'Only wait until the display to be held in the Tivoli gardens next week. Shall you go?'

'I believe so.'

'Then,' he said softly, 'you must allow me to escort you.'

Louisa looked up into his shadowed face and smiled. 'That would indeed be a kindness, sir.'

A few flambeaus had been provided to cast light on the terrace and several candle-lanterns hung from trees further off. But essentially the gardens were lit by the soft rays of a full moon. People strolled in and out of the shadows, appearing and disappearing, the night air carrying their voices to the couple still standing on the terrace.

'There is a pond with a fountain beyond that greenery,' advised Hugh. 'Should you like to see it?'

Such an invitation would shock any chaperon, thought Louisa, amused. She had no idea where Amelia was; she had not seen her in the supper-room, so she was probably still engaged with her cards. There was no one to say her nay. Not that her aunt could have stopped her, but her disapproving presence would have cast a shadow over the escapade.

'Very much,' she acknowledged demurely.

Her hand remained on his arm as they trod the path towards the pond. Emerging from the shelter of the narrow band of shrubs, Louisa gave a small gasp of delight. Statuary gleamed in the moonlight and the trickling sound of water flowing from the fountain filled her senses with soothing magic.

'Charming, is it not?' murmured Hugh.

They had circled the pond when the moon disappeared behind a cloud, leaving them in almost total darkness. Hugh drew her aside, into the shelter of a large shrub. Without a word he took her in his arms and lowered his lips to hers.

David had kissed her, once. She had found it pleasant enough, but scarcely earth-shattering. Why had she ever imagined herself in love with him? she wondered as her heart began to pound and her limbs to liquefy so that she was obliged to hang on to the lapels of Hugh's coat for support.

As he felt her response, what had begun as a tender, exploratory tasting of her lips deepened into fierce demand. Despite her inexperience Louisa found her lips clinging to his, felt strange spears of delicious sensation invading her body.

This was what instinct had been telling her it would be like in the arms of a man she loved. Joy surged through her, renewing her strength so that she was able to loose her hold on his coat and lift her hands to his nape, where her fingers could tangle satisfyingly in the vibrant silkiness of his hair.

They shouldn't be doing this, yet she had expected no less when she'd accepted his invitation to walk in the gardens with him. She loved him. The temptation had been too great.

But then, dashingly, she remembered that he did not love her. He was no stranger to this kind of dalliance. It meant nothing to him. And the moon emerged from behind the cloud and voices could be heard, drawing nearer.

She used her hands to push at his shoulders. For a moment longer he savoured her lips before he let them go; but he kept her within the circle of his arms.

Shaken to the core, Louisa leant her forehead against his shoulder, recovering her composure. His breathing was ragged and his heart beating like a drum inside his chest. So he had been moved, too. That was something to cling to, although she had been led to believe that men quite easily were—moved.

She thought she felt the light touch of his lips upon her hair. 'Louisa,' he murmured.

It was the first time he had called her by her given name. The sound of it on his lips thrilled her through, but she could not allow him to guess.

'You forget yourself, my lord,' she accused, her voice low and far from steady as she extricated herself from his embrace. The soft voices were coming ever nearer, though the people they belonged to were out of sight behind intervening shrubs.

'Oh, no, my dear, that I do not,' Hugh kept his voice down and drew her deeper into the shadow of the bushes. She had to follow or risk detection. 'I have wanted to kiss you since we first met crossing the Channel. But if I have offended you by doing so I pray you will forgive me.'

The errant moon had appeared again. Its rays penetrated the sheltering branches enough for her to see his face, and its expression was grave. Yet the light in his eyes gave a hint of the suppressed elation he must be feeling at her ready surrender to his practised seduction.

Decorum and self-esteem told her to protest that he had. But the words of condemnation would not come.

'No,' she admitted instead, 'you did not offend me. When I agreed to walk out here with you I expected nothing less.'

The soft gleam of her smile caused him to catch his breath.

'Then you have felt it too! This attraction which pulls us together whether we will or no!' He reached out and captured her hands. His voice deepened. 'What shall we do about it, Louisa?'

'Do about it? Why, my lord, what do you suggest?'

'Hugh,' he murmured. 'You must call me Hugh, at least when we are not in company. As to what we do— I confess I have no inclination to wed. And—thus far I have never attempted to steal any woman's virginity.'

'Then it seems, my lord, that you can suggest nothing to the point.'

His grip tightened on her hands. 'Hugh,' he insisted. 'Say it, my dearest girl. I long to hear it on your lips.'

'Hugh.' His name came out cold and hard. Her saying it like that could not provide him with the same pleasure his speaking hers so tenderly had given her, but she could not help that. His words had killed all the lovely warmth his embrace had kindled. He had been playing with her. And she, fool that she was, had allowed him to. Now pride did come to her rescue. 'I am grateful to you for the experience—Hugh. I have reached an age when I feel at liberty to indulge my curiosity about such matters, to allow my desires a little

rein. . .up to a point. I found your kiss pleasant enough.'
A man of his experience would surely know that—it
would do no good to deny her reaction. 'I should not in
the least mind repeating it. But of course I could not
allow any deeper intimacy.'

'Until after you were wed.'

The words had been said in a flat voice, but Louisa
at once suspected them. She had to make her position
quite clear.

'Naturally.'

'You told me you had no intention to marry, at least
at the moment.'

'So I did! And I meant it!' But oh, how quickly she
would change her mind were *he* to propose! she thought
sadly.

'I see.'

'And now perhaps you will be so kind as to escort
me back to the ballroom. The dancing must soon begin
again.'

'Not so fast!' His voice and manner had lost their
tension. A smile seemed to have entered his eyes. 'I
will resist the temptation to make you an offer if you
will promise to reject it should I weaken. Having agreed
that neither of us desires matrimony we may surely
remain friends. And I, too, found the experiment of a
few moments ago exceedingly agreeable. Since I gather
you have no objection, I shall repeat it whenever opportunity presents itself.'

Before she had time to collect her wits she was back
in his arms, his lips claiming hers. For a moment she
resisted, wished those voices would come even nearer,
but they did not. On the contrary, they had passed by
and were fading into the distance. But then she forgot
all about resistance, all about others in the garden.

His lips were too persuasive. Not demanding, not
passionate, not possessive but caressingly, teasingly
tender. This was the Hugh she loved. The one to whom
she could so easily fall victim.

Had he asked her to become his mistress then she

would have agreed. Afterwards, she was to ask herself how she could possibly have lost all regard for reputation and propriety. But at that moment she knew she would gladly abandon the whole world if she could only remain in Hugh Deverill's arms.

CHAPTER EIGHT

HOWEVER, he did not ask. He finished the thoroughly unsettling kiss, released her and ceremoniously offered his arm.

'You wished to return to the ballroom. No doubt your next partner is anxiously awaiting your appearance.'

Louisa felt almost too fragile to walk. How dared he assault her senses in that practised, calculated manner? His voice had been coolly teasing—but she noticed his breathing had suffered and his hand trembled slightly. So although he tried to hide it under a careless manner he had not been unaffected by that embrace any more than the other. He had just exercised better control over his reactions.

Determined to hide her own mortifying weakness, Louisa took his proffered arm, willing her hand to remain steady and her legs to carry her. The first devastating effect of his kiss was passing, though, and she managed to stroll back to the library door quite steadily, assuming an insouciance of manner she was far from feeling.

In the dimness of the terrace, deserted now, he stopped again to take her hands and place lingering kisses on each palm, resurrecting all the wretchedly delicious shooting, melting sensations she had felt before. Yet she hadn't the resolution to stop him. For the moment the sheer, enervating pleasure of the caress held her in thrall.

'Can you find your own way back from here?' he asked quietly. 'It would be sensible for us to return to the ballroom separately. Otherwise the gossips will have a field-day.'

Louisa nodded abruptly. She had not spoken a word

on the way back, afraid her voice would betray her. Now all she wanted was to escape the disturbing, magnetic presence of this man, to recover her poise before being forced to dance again.

He, of course, was proving once more how adept he was at conducting this kind of intrigue. Whatever he protested about his affair with Maria Kingslea being nothing more than rumour, they had both been absent at the same time, returning separately to the ballroom. Now he was sending her back on her own. Yet she had only herself to blame for her predicament. She had invited his caresses. Which made it all the more lowering to realise how little the interlude had meant to him.

He remained behind on the terrace when she turned and almost ran in. Still in a flutter, she made her way up to the ladies' retiring-room. Since no strains of music reached her ears the after-supper dancing could not yet have begun. She had time.

'Why, Louisa, my love! There you are!' Lady Nazeby turned from one of the ornately gilded mirrors to greet her niece. 'I had wondered where you could be.'

Several other ladies looked round at this and Louisa found herself flushing guiltily. But a glance beyond her aunt into the mirror told her she had nothing to fear from her appearance. Her hair and costume were still in perfect order. Hugh's hands had not wandered. Had done no more than hold her tightly against him. His lips had wreaked only invisible devastation.

'It was so hot. I merely sought a breath of fresh air,' she informed her aunt rather breathlessly. Her lack of breath could be explained by her having climbed the stairs too quickly.

'Alone?'

Surely Aunt Nazeby must realise she did not wish to answer such a question! Ignoring the curious looks, Louisa retorted with the truth. 'No. Lord Hugh escorted me.'

'Oh,' said Amelia blandly. 'I do believe Deverill to be quite the most agreeable and considerate gentleman here. He even took the trouble to seek me out in the card-room earlier, in order to pay his respects.'

'Earlier?' repeated Louisa faintly.

'Yes, shortly before the supper dance. He said he was taking you in, and wanted to make certain I did not disapprove. As though I would!' she added airily.

Relieved to the point of jubilation, castigating herself for another excursion into the realms of unjustifiable distrust, Louisa concentrated on the unnecessary task of rearranging the neckline of her dress. Closer inspection in the mirror showed her lips to be swollen to a new ripeness. So some of the devastation he had wrought did show. As she dabbed her skin with eau-de-Cologne she prayed no one else would notice.

'I must hurry,' she said. 'The orchestra is tuning up. They will be standing up for the next set soon, and my partner will be waiting.'

'You have every dance taken, I'll be bound,' smiled Amelia happily. 'You always do, my love.'

Her aunt, thought Louisa, seemed inordinately smug about something. She wondered what.

The remainder of the evening seemed endless. Louisa had developed a headache and at one point decided to leave early, but finding her aunt happily immersed in her card game hadn't the heart to tear the older woman away. Hugh Deverill sat at a nearby table deeply engrossed in a hand of whist. He did no more than glance up and acknowledge her with a slight nod and she looked quickly away. She supposed he considered he had done his duty by dancing until supper and now he intended to enjoy himself.

She returned to the ballroom reluctantly, to be claimed by a succession of partners, including General Alva, the Duke's Spanish ADC, Sir Charles Stuart the ambassador, Prince Metternich and Wellington himself. She should be feeling flattered by so much elevated attention, she knew, but somehow her success brought little satisfaction. If she could not dance with Hugh she did not want to dance with anyone. He had quite spoilt her evening. Maria Kingslea, she noted, was concentrating her undoubted charms on the Prussian count and had already stood up with that foreign nobleman at least four times.

Of Hugh there continued to be no sign in the ballroom, but she knew where he was. Not that the knowledge did her a bit of good. Unable to follow him with her eyes, she found herself doing so in her imagination instead. It really was most inconvenient to be so affected by a man. She could only hope that her stupid infatuation would soon die.

'Did you enjoy yourself, my love?' demanded Amelia in the darkness of the carriage on the way home. 'I thought it a splendid occasion. And I won handsomely at the card table.'

'You were always lucky at cards,' smiled Louisa, evading her aunt's question.

'Skilled, I would say,' protested Amelia good-humouredly. 'I cannot understand why you do not play. I am certain that with your brain you would make a handsome profit.'

'But being a woman I am not allowed to have a brain,' teased Louisa. 'Besides, I prefer other forms of amusement, Aunt. And I would risk losing, which I could ill afford.'

'You amaze me, Louisa. So spirited and adventurous in some ways and so cautious in others! You invite scandal by your rash behaviour yet will not risk a few guineas on a hand of cards!'

'I have moderated my behaviour, Aunt Nazeby. Do not ring a peal over me, I beg. I have developed such a headache!'

'You spent too long in the garden,' observed Amelia with an ingenuousness Louisa knew to be deceptive. Lady Nazeby did not miss much concerning her niece.

The carriage passed a flambeau at that moment and Louisa hoped its light would not reveal her discomposure.

'It was so beautiful out there,' she offered defensively.

'And the company delightful, I have no doubt. I wish that young man might speak for you, my love. He has not done so yet?'

Stunned, Louisa could only stare at the pale blob which was all she could see of her aunt's face now the flambeau had been left behind. 'No, Aunt, he has not, and will not.' Her voice sounded lamentably strangled. 'He has no more wish to wed than I have!'

'So you have spoken of it,' murmured Amelia artlessly. 'It is plain to see you have developed a *tendre* for him, and he is far from indifferent to you, my love. You should try to fix his interest. You are unlikely to find a more suitable candidate for a husband.'

'Oh, do not tease me so, Aunt! I have developed no such thing! I have said many times that I do not wish to marry. And my head aches so!'

'I wonder why? Oh, very well, my love,' she agreed, at Louisa's exasperated snort, 'but do not blame me when you are old and lonely——'

'Aunt!'

'Forgive me, my love.'

Subdued at last, Amelia subsided into silence. The rattle of the iron wheels on the cobbles, the clip-clop of the horses' hooves were now the only sounds to disturb Louisa's throbbing head. And, to her relief, they too soon stopped as the carriage drew up before their *hôtel* and she was able to alight. Once inside she bade her aunt a hasty but affectionate goodnight and made for the sanctuary of her room.

She could not sleep. Long after Betty had been dismissed she sat by the open window listening to the night noises drifting in. The chirrup of a nesting bird, the neigh of a horse in the nearby stables, the distant grinding of carriage wheels and sound of hooves as some late-night reveller returned home soothed rather than offended her jangled nerves. Her head still throbbed, but not so badly, for she had taken just a little laudanum. But not enough to send her to sleep. Mayhap she should have taken more.

The moon threw its light over the scene, reminding her of those magic moments in Sir Charles and Lady Stewart's garden.

But what was the use of remembering? It only brought pain to overlay the pleasure. She had found a man she would be happy to wed, in the right circumstances. Aunt Nazeby was correct there. But Hugh Deverill was not the marrying kind. And he had believed her when she had protested her reluctance to enter into the state of matrimony.

He was charming, courteous, no idle fop but a conscientious and, some said, brilliant diplomat. And she tended to believe, now, that his reputation for seduction was highly exaggerated. He was all she had ever wished for in a husband.

But he had absolutely no reason to wed. He could take his pleasure, satisfy his needs where he willed, just as other single men did. And many married men, too, she reminded herself sternly. Yet she would be prepared to take the risk if she could wed Hugh Deverill.

She attracted him. There was little doubt on that point, she thought, becoming hot at the remembrance of his kisses, elated yet alarmed, for she could scarcely understand or trust her own astonishing response. But he had firmly closed the door on any idea of marriage between them. Only one course remained open to her. She must recover from this nonsense, avoid proximity, treat him merely as a friend and make quite certain never to give him another opportunity to kiss her.

Louisa abandoned her early morning ride for the next couple of days, preferring to avoid those who had—and the one who had not—proposed marriage to her. She missed the contact with Jamie and felt rather guilty at allowing her personal feelings to prevent her from keeping an eye on Amelia's grandson. She sent him a message of regret, saying she hoped to resume her morning exercise shortly.

Meanwhile another challenge loomed ahead. She had to face Lord Hugh at the Duke of Wellington's banquet in honour of the Emperor of Russia and the King of Prussia. With any luck at all, in such a large company, she might avoid having to speak to him at all.

She knew she was not looking her sparkling best and therefore took care with her toilet. But nothing could hide the tired lines about her eyes, the result of two almost sleepless nights.

Betty tutted over her mistress's sad looks as she fiddled with frills and ribbons and carefully arranged her curls to best effect. Amelia kept a discreet silence, simply eyeing her niece from time to time in thoughtful contemplation.

Thanks largely to Betty's efforts Louisa presented an elegant and attractive appearance when she arrived at the Duke's residence, a few yards from their own. Amelia had not ordered the carriage out to carry them so short a distance, the ladies preferring to walk, escorted by two stalwart footmen. Seeing the crush of carriages waiting their turn to disgorge their passengers at the Duke's door, Amelia remarked that although it might not be quite genteel to arrive on foot it was certainly more convenient. Holding her train clear and picking her way carefully over the dusty ground, Louisa agreed.

Lady Castlereagh was acting as Wellington's hostess. She and Amelia were old friends. The Duke had a special word for Louisa and they passed on into the reception-room to discover the seating arrangements.

Hugh was already there. He came forward, smiling easily, his hair arranged *à la Titus*, dressed more dashingly than she had seen him before in a splendid blue silk cut-away tailed coat over a cream brocaded, collared waistcoat studded with coloured stones and embroidery. Cream small-clothes descended over his powerful thighs to white silk stockings and polished black pumps. Expensive Brussels lace frothed from his shirt-front. His cravat had been tied with complex and faultless artistry. He must consider this a very special occasion.

The tumultuous reaction the sight of him provoked shocked Louisa. But she had been ready for the meeting and managed to greet him with formal courtesy and without a blush.

'We are to be dinner partners, I find,' he murmured. Seeing the consternation she could not hide, he smiled wryly. 'Do not be alarmed, my dearest Miss Finsham.'

Amelia's attention had fortunately been diverted by the arrival of the Duke of Alva, deputed her partner for the occasion. Wellington's Spanish ADC bowed before the older woman with elaborate courtesy and led her away. Louisa watched her aunt's departure with a sense of having been abandoned in her hour of need.

When Hugh resumed their conversation it was essentially private. 'I promise to serve you with perfect decorum despite the provocation of your delightful presence,' he whispered wickedly.

Louisa had to swallow before she was able to reply. The highly correct Hugh Deverill in flirtatious mood was something she had not seen before and therefore had not expected. Yet his manner did lighten the atmosphere between them. She could treat the entire situation as a joke.

'I am persuaded that there will be others at the table, my lord, which will safely inhibit any liberties you may feel inclined to take,' she returned archly.

But nothing could dampen the effect of sitting beside him for the entire banquet. The thought almost made her swoon. If she did, of course, she would be excused attendance. Many ladies would have resorted to a strategic and interesting faint in the circumstances, but Louisa was made of sterner stuff. Such cowardice would only deprive her of the opportunity to be present at a function to which all the nobility of England and all the leaders of the Allied nations had been invited. She would not allow Hugh Deverill's presence to spoil her evening. Particularly as she had begun to wonder what strings he had pulled to acquire her as his partner for the evening.

He chuckled and the sound made Louisa's toes curl. He knew exactly how she was feeling and relished her discomfort.

'May I be permitted to say how well your gown suits you, my dear Louisa?'

Louisa covered her acute discomfort at his tone and the familiarity with a rush of words. 'I had it designed by a modiste here in Paris.' She touched the bows and embroidery decorating the extremely low neckline and smoothed down the panel at the front of her skirt, which was outlined with ruched ribbon and dotted with finely worked star motifs. 'She suggested that white silk with gold ornamentation would suit this occasion to admiration.'

'Then she is a clever woman, and her judgement exceptionally sound.'

'I shall tell her of your approval, my dear Hugh. I am certain she will be quite in raptures to hear of it.'

His smile held genuine amusement. 'Well taken, my love. But depend upon it, I meant it. I have never seen you looking more desirable.'

He covered her gasp of outrage with a chuckle and presented his arm. 'Come, Miss Finsham. They are forming up to go in.'

There was no avoiding it. Louisa placed her fingers on blue silk and joined the queue awaiting the signal to move through to the banqueting hall.

The Duke always did things in lavish style and this was a particularly grand occasion so no expense had been spared. The covers were already laid as they took their places. Silver sparkled in the sunlight streaming in through several large windows, overpowering the flames of candles set in exquisitely wrought branches placed at intervals along the tables. Beautiful silver epergnes loaded with exotic fruit had been set between them.

Louisa found herself seated next to Walter Scott, Madame d'Arblay's partner for the evening. The ladies greeted each other warmly. Louisa was not much impressed by the other famous author, for his club foot made him awkward, and his gerneral appearance did not inspire admiration. She did, however, admire his writings and she soon forgot his appearance.

'I am honoured to meet you, sir,' she murmured as Fanny introduced them.

Once everyone was seated and grace said, it was the gentlemen's duty to serve their partners.

'What will you have?' asked Hugh politely, turning back to her after having made himself pleasant to a French lady on his other side. 'The trout look good, or perhaps you would prefer a portion of lamb? It looks splendidly young and tender.'

'Thank you,' responded Louisa, 'but if you could reach it I should prefer a little of the salmon cooked in pastry.'

The dish looked delicious, the pastry scales brown and glistening, and Louisa thought that if anything could tempt her suddenly lost appetite that might. Hugh drew it towards him, carefully cut the large fish in half, carved out a portion from the middle and placed it upon her plate, adding a slice of lemon.

Polite acknowledgement of his service seemed the best approach to a difficult situation. 'I admire your skill in keeping the pastry intact,' murmured Louisa. 'My thanks.'

'The skill was all the chef's, I fear. But the fish it surrounds looks capital. I believe I will have the same.' He cut himself a portion. 'I will call for glasses of white Bordeaux wine, if that will suit?'

Louisa having assented, he ordered the wine. When it arrived he bowed to her and both drank, as custom demanded. His eyes still held a devilish glint which betrayed Louisa into a blush and forced her into mindless chatter.

'I do wish,' she said as she pinched salt over her fish, 'that they had salt spoons in this country!'

'Give them time,' grinned Hugh.

But Louisa did not intend to fall victim to that smile or any of the other things about Hugh Deverill which made her heart throb so uncomfortably. Besides, she would never have a better opportunity to speak with the famous author on her other side. She therefore concentrated her attention on Walter Scott and Fanny d'Arblay, leaving Hugh Deverill rather isolated, since the French lady was well engaged with her own dinner partner.

Still far too aware of him beside her, she noted that he did not seem in the least disturbed. Whenever she looked his way he appeared to be absorbed in consuming his own food while watching and listening to all those about him. He could be quite self-contained when he chose. She almost felt piqued because he did not seem overset by her rather pointed neglect.

As each course was served she was forced to return her attention to him, of course, for he had to serve her with her choice of food and order more wine. For her second course she chose jugged pigeon and for the third tried a custard tart flavoured with cheese and found it delicious.

Hugh dipped his napkin in his finger glass to wipe his mouth before dessert. 'Madame Grassini and Madame Catalini are about to sing, I believe,' he remarked.

'Delightful,' murmured Louisa, rinsing her fingers.

Having allowed her to ignore him for most of the evening, he now seemed determined to recapture her attention. 'I see you are now on intimate terms with Madame d'Arblay. I trust your French has improved?'

'Considerably, I thank you, my lord. Madame d'Arblay has been so kind as to say I have an ear for it.'

'I promised to instruct you in the German language,'

he went on, switching without warning to French, 'but have so far lacked the opportunity. However, I could call at your establishment for an hour most mornings after breakfast if you still wish to learn.'

Torn, Louisa lowered her eyes. How could she refuse such a tempting offer? Yet she did not relish the idea of being forced to deal more intimately with Hugh Deverill. Though should she accept propriety would demand that they were not left alone together. Her aunt or Betty would always sit with them.

And she did so enjoy extending her knowledge of foreign tongues. Her mind had always devoured learning, to everyone else's dismay. 'It is not ladylike,' her aunt protested whenever she found her niece avidly reading a weighty tome borrowed from some friend's library. 'Besides, you will give yourself brain fever!'

'Nonsense!' Louisa always responded.

At least Hugh Deverill did not seem to think it strange that she should wish to learn. Languages were, of course, a generally accepted exception to the belief regarding a lady's need to absorb knowledge. But still.

Her decision made, she looked up again and gave him her first genuine smile of the evening. He had a quizzical, expectant look on his face which made Louisa wonder whether he thought her delay in answering due to incomprehension on her part. The smile turned mischievous. She would delight in surprising him.

'Thank you, my lord,' she returned in the same language. 'I accept your offer most gladly. Should we meet while riding in the Bois, perhaps you would agree to partake of breakfast with us. We can then begin the lessons immediately afterwards.'

He was grinning with open amusement. 'Capital, Miss Finsham! Your French is now quite excellent. And in so short a time! I can see that you will have little trouble in mastering German, or any other language.'

'But I had the advantage of some small knowledge of French. I have none of German.'

'Then I'll wager I can teach you enough in two

months to enable you to converse with Marshal Blücher.'

'I may not remain here for two months.'

'You are thinking of leaving?'

Did he sound dismayed? Louisa thought she must be imagining it. 'We have no firm plans as yet. Lady Nazeby will decide upon the time of our departure. And her decision rests upon—certain considerations beyond her control.'

'I see.' He looked faintly puzzled by her last statement, but to her relief chose not to pursue it. 'Well, should you still be in Paris on the nineteenth day of October, we will put my abilities as a teacher to the test. Agreed?'

'Agreed. But I will not wager on it, for to win I have only to pretend not to be able, or perhaps to neglect, to learn.'

'But you would do neither,' he offered softly. ''Twould be worse than holding your horse in a race.'

'You are right, of course,' Louisa acknowledged ruefully. 'So, ten guineas on it, sir?'

'Done.'

Solemnly, they shook hands, just as the orchestra struck up, signalling that the opera stars were about to sing.

'I shall have to present myself at your breakfast-table in all my dirt if I do as you suggest,' he murmured.

'I do not suppose, sir, that you will inconvenience us in the least. And we can in any case offer you the facility to wash.'

'Then I am happy to accept your generous offer, Louisa.'

No one else could have heard the familiarity. But it made Louisa aware that he had no thought of abandoning his intention to pursue a more intimate connection. Thankfully, she turned her attention to the recital. And for the remainder of the evening he behaved towards her with punctilious correctness. Yet the memory of those more personal exchanges could not be eradicated.

Their relationship could never truly return to what it had been before Lady Stewart's ball.

Louisa discovered that she did not want it to.

As he handed her into her carriage, 'I shall not be riding early tomorrow,' Hugh informed her. Her stab of disappointment quickly changed to indignation as he went on, 'I will call for you at three. A drive in the Bois will be pleasant, I believe, and we can then discuss my proposed tutoring in the German Language in more detail.'

'You assume too much, my lord! I may not be free tomorrow afternoon!'

'But you are, are you not?' he demanded, using his quizzing-glass for the first time that Louisa could remember in order to regard her through it. The smile on his lips incensed her further.

'You did not ask, my lord. I may not wish to drive with you!'

'I have arranged to borrow a carriage. It is available for tomorrow only.' And he added, low, 'Please, Louisa?'

'Do not be so ungracious, Louisa!' Her aunt's voice came from the depths of the carriage, where she was already seated. 'You are making unnecessary difficulties. You have no engagement tomorrow you cannot break! No doubt your man—Dutton, isn't it?—will accompany you, Lord Hugh?'

'He will, ma'am.'

Louisa wanted to go. It was his high-handed assumption that she would fall in with his plans that had made her argue. But his low-voiced plea had already softened her resolve, before ever her aunt had swept any grounds for objection aside. Aunt Nazeby, thought Louisa wryly, seemed determined to forward Hugh's suit. She would never be persuaded that his intentions were not serious.

'Very well,' she acquiesced. 'I will expect you at three.'

'Until tomorrow,' he murmured, and lightly brushed her fingers with his lips.

Watching from the drawing-room window, Louisa saw the splendid equipage draw up before the door. A sporting curricle with enormous springs, painted and gilded, the seats luxuriously padded and upholstered in red velvet. Unusually, a small seat had been inserted behind for a groom or footman. Dutton sat impassively as Hugh brought the spirited pair of matched chestnuts to a halt. He had no reason to jump down, for a footman had run out to take their heads.

Hugh lodged his whip, sprang from the vehicle and threw down the reins. Louisa bit her lip. She had not expected either him or his borrowed outfit to look so fine. They would be the centre of attention in the Bois. He was making his interest too plain.

Everyone would think he entertained thoughts of marriage. She would be left in a mortifying position when he withdrew his attentions, as he surely must. . .

But she would be returning to England soon. Perhaps he foresaw that as a natural end to a pleasant flirtation. If so, she would enjoy his friendship while she could.

A servant announced him. He strode into the room, every inch the handsome, virile gentleman, and bent over her gloved hand. No wonder her heart began to flutter!

Louisa controlled her emotions and greeted him coolly. She had dressed in her best apricot carriage dress and wore a chip-straw bonnet tied under her chin with matching ribbons. A large spray of white ostrich feathers curled about the brim.

'Enchanting,' he murmured. 'Thank you for being ready. The carriage is outside.'

'I saw it,' said Louisa, scorning subterfuge. 'It is quite splendid. Where did you discover it?'

He grinned. 'It belongs to Prince Metternich. He was so good as to offer me its use when I spoke of my wish to drive in the Bois.'

'Last evening?' enquired Louisa as they made their way downstairs.

'Just so. The port put him into an excellent mood.'

Louisa had to laugh. 'So it would appear!' They descended the steps and she halted to examine the carriage at closer quarters. 'I wonder he would allow such an expensive carriage and exceptional pair to be driven by anyone but himself!'

'But then,' grinned Hugh, handing her up, 'I have a persuasive tongue. When I particularly want something I am a difficult man to refuse.'

'Then,' said Louisa quietly as he gathered the reins and gave the horses the office to start, 'I must strengthen my defences.'

He did not answer for a moment, being occupied in negotiating his team round a corner and into a stream of other traffic. As they settled into a steady trot he turned his head to her.

'Do not do that, I beg. I engage not to ask you for more in the way of friendship than you are willing to give. But I should enjoy to ride with you, to drive with you on occasion, and sometimes to be accorded the honour of escorting you and Lady Nazeby to your engagements.'

His flirtatious manner had dropped from him as though it had never been. He had never appeared more serious. Louisa did not know whether to be glad or sorry. She had enjoyed their sparring, she realised. And did he not mean to kiss her again?

'Lud, sir,' she laughed, 'do not take my words too seriously! I should hate to have you revert to the disagreeably critical creature you were!'

His eyes twinkled. 'Was I so very disagreeable?'

'To me you seemed so.'

He negotiated the gate into the Bois with casual ease. He was an excellent whip, Louisa noted with interest.

'You would rather suffer the occasional kiss?' he suggested outrageously.

Louisa considered. She shot him a glance from the corners of dancing eyes. 'Almost,' she admitted.

'Then I shall be constrained to consider my conduct most carefully.'

She gurgled with laughter. 'I am persuaded that you always do, my lord.'

They were on terms again and she was glad. They drove in amicable silence among the throng of other carriages in the Bois, exchanging nods and smiles with acquaintances, stopping occasionally to speak with a person with whom one or both of them enjoyed greater intimacy. The stares of interest they received were embarrassingly obvious.

'We are giving the scandal-mongers much food for their tongues,' remarked Louisa at last. 'Perhaps we should not have done this, Hugh.'

'Do you mind?' His voice held sudden concern.

Louisa pursed her lips. 'Not really. It is flattering for a woman of my age to be seen to be pursued.'

He grimaced, acknowledging the accusation. 'Since you are determined on dwindling into an old tabby I am surprised lack of flattery should concern you.'

'Ah, but I would prefer it to be plain that I choose not to marry. If no gentleman paid me attention Society might begin to whisper that I could not catch a husband.'

'That must be patently untrue.'

'Perhaps. But you are laying yourself open to gossip, Hugh. Your motives will be questioned.'

'My motives are my own affair. I shall not allow gossip to influence my actions. Apart——' he suddenly grinned '——from keeping me within the bounds of perceived propriety.'

A question had been burning Louisa's tongue ever since the previous night. Now she asked it. 'Why did you borrow a curricle to drive me in the Bois, Hugh?'

He glanced at her sideways. 'Because I wanted to.'

'Why?'

His lips twitched. 'Vanity. I wanted to be seen parading with the most stunning lady in Paris.'

'Flummery, sir!'

He viewed her heightened colour with amusement. 'You do not know your own charm, Louisa.'

He had avoided answering her question. She could not pursue the subject further.

'I told you last evening,' he went on calmly. 'I wished to discuss the German lessons I have engaged to give you.'

'Oh. What is there to discuss?'

'Not much. You have paper and pen, of course. I will provide a dictionary and books to read.'

It was an excuse, of a certainty, but she did not challenge it. Instead, for the remainder of the outing she assiduously questioned him on the German language and, to his amusement, insisted on being taught a few words.

'What is a horse?'

'Just as in English there are many words to describe the precise kind animal, but 'a horse' is *ein Pferd*.'

She repeated the words. 'And a tree?'

'*Ein Baum.*'

By the time he deposited her at her door she had acquired a vocabulary of some dozen words. Whether she would remember them until the following morning they both doubted. But the exercise had been fun.

Back in her room Louisa reviewed their conversation. Whatever Hugh had promised, she knew she must keep to her determination not to drift into a situation where he could kiss her. If she did and he took advantage of the chance, she would be lost.

So began a strange interlude for Louisa. She saw Hugh Deverill almost every day, spent intimate hours with him mastering the new language, yet they were never alone. For one thing, Jamie had expressed an interest in joining the lessons, and Louisa leapt upon the idea. Lady Thurrock being amenable, since William Coynd had no knowledge of German and the lessons would be free, he returned to the Hôtel des Fleurs with Louisa and Hugh, breakfasted with them, and left when Hugh did. And Mr Coynd, appearing as reluctant to accompany the boy as Louisa was to have him do so, persuaded his employer that her son would be in excellent hands and there would therefore be no need for him to waste his time at Lady Nazeby's. A groom in attendance would suffice. Since this reasoning was extended to the early morning horseback-riding as well, Louisa was completely relieved of the embarrassing presence of Mr Coynd.

Major Hewitson, Lord Wellington and several other gentlemen continued to join her party, however. She therefore had little difficulty in avoiding any close encounter with Hugh Deverill until the moment came for them to return to the Hôtel des Fleurs. Then Jamie acted as a buffer. During the return ride they spoke in French, for his benefit.

'Mr Coynd is not much good, you see,' the boy confided. 'And I must be able to speak French if I want to travel. . .' He trailed off.

'Travel where?' asked Louisa.

'My Grand Tour,' explained Jamie rather hurriedly. Louisa thought it was not what he had meant to say, but let it pass.

'Then you had better learn Italian as well.'

Jamie glanced quickly at the speaker. 'Do you know it, Deverill?'

'Sufficiently well. But two languages are quite enough for you to begin with. Leave Italian until you have mastered the others. You have plenty of time.'

Jamie seemed content to accept this advice. 'Yes. And I could learn Italian best when I reach Italy, I suppose.'

Hugh smiled. 'If I am able, my lord, I will be glad to give you a grounding in the language before you set out.'

* * *

In September Lord Byron arrived in Paris, as did the Lambs. The arrival of Lady Caroline and her husband caused no little stir.

Neither her husband's nor Byron's presence prevented Lady Caroline from pursuing the Duke by every means at her disposal.

She began to appear in the Bois, dressed in an eye-catching purple riding habit. Louisa blushed for her. The Duke appeared indulgently amused by the young woman's excessive attentions. Louisa wondered uncomfortably if her own brief foray into flattery had amused him as much.

'Did you notice how she was dressed the other evening?' she asked Hugh on the way back to breakfast one morning. Jamie had sent his regrets, finding himself confined to bed with a cold. 'She appeared half-naked!'

'She wore a scarf,' observed Hugh mildly, his eyes dancing.

Louisa snorted. 'That flimsy thing! I have never seen anything so outrageous as the way she dresses. She invites condemnation!'

'She is an exhibitionist,' grinned Hugh, amused by Louisa's vehemence while wondering whether she could possibly be jealous over the other woman's undoubted success with the Duke and other gentlemen. But he immediately dismissed the thought as unworthy of the woman he had come to know. Deuce take it, she had a large enough court of admirers of her own. 'I feel sorry for William Lamb,' declared Louisa. 'She quite ignores him.'

'Do not many married women cut their husbands from their lives?'

'Perhaps they do,' admitted Louisa, 'but I cannot agree with it. However the marriage was brought about, one has made one's vow before God. That, I think, is why I shall never marry. I could not trust my husband to keep his.'

Hugh eyed her thoughtfully. 'You hold to a most unfashionable philosophy.'

Louisa realised she had been led to reveal more than she had intended. 'Lud, sir,' she said lightly, 'how serious we are become, when I was merely indulging in tabbyish criticism of a notorious woman! But——' she lifted questioning brows '—I have heard little said against her from one quite famous for his critical tongue! Can it be that you overlook Lady Caroline's misdemeanours while challenging others for similar offences?'

'I do not need to exercise myself over Lady Caroline, Louisa. Her behaviour does not in the least concern me.'

CHAPTER NINE

To Louisa it felt as though something had hit her in the chest. He could only mean that he *did* care what *she* did!

Why should he? Even now? And in the beginning, when it had all started, he had not even known her.

At that moment they reached the house and she was able to avoid answering because it became necessary to dismount and hand the reins to a groom to lead Prince Hal away. Hugh did the same with Kismet and the two horses clip-clopped off to the stables as the humans mounted the steps to the door.

She no longer suffered quite the same degree of agitation in Hugh's presence. Familiarity, she supposed, had worn the edge off her reactions. But unfortunately for her that did not mean she loved him the less. On the contrary, as she explored his mind, her love grew.

'Louisa knows an awful lot,' Jamie had remarked during one of their earliest breakfasts, when earnest discussion had seemed to flow naturally with the coffee. 'Fancy her knowing all about economics. I must ask my tutor if I can read Adam Smith.'

'Never tell me I am attempting to teach a bluestocking!' Hugh had exclaimed in mock-dismay. 'She knows a deal about so many subjects, not to mention the breeding of horses.'

'And the latest developments in farming,' Amelia had supplied with a sniff. 'I tell her it is most unladylike to read such earnest books as she does, but she don't take a bit of notice. I've told her, if she develops brain fever, she has only herself to blame!'

'I am sure you cannot really believe learning induces brain fever, Lady Nazeby.' Hugh had smiled. 'Such out-of-date nonsense! And to believe that women cannot learn! Elizabeth Montagu and her set of bluestockings proved otherwise quite convincingly fifty years ago!'

'But women's brains are smaller——' Amelia had begun, only to be interrupted.

'Men's are not all the same size, dear ma'am. But is a man with a small head necessarily less able to learn than one with a large one? It is quite obvious that very often the opposite applies.'

'Well, the large one might be empty,' Amelia had muttered, not to be worsted in the argument.

Louisa had laughed. 'Really, Aunt! I cannot believe you truly hold to such fustian ideas! I think you only advance them because you wish me to emulate certain feather-brained women who have gained themselves husbands. Lady Nazeby,' she had explained to Hugh, 'does not believe any man would be willing to burden himself with an educated wife.'

'It might be inconvenient if *he* was not very clever,' Jamie, who had been listening with growing interest, had put in. 'He wouldn't want to be made to look a fool, even if he *was* light in the attic himself.'

At this the company had dissolved into laughter, though Amelia, determined to have the last word, had added, 'What did I tell you, my love?'

'But,' Hugh had murmured to no one in particular, 'think of the boredom of sitting down to breakfast each morning with someone only capable of chattering about clothes and the latest *on dit*.'

'Oh, there's nothing to that,' Amelia had replied carelessly. 'The gentleman simply buries himself behind his newspaper.'

'And never the two minds shall meet!' Louisa had exclaimed with asperity. 'Well, Aunt, I categorically refuse to live my life unable to communicate with my husband! I should,' she'd added less forcefully and with a chuckle, 'rather dwindle into an old maid.'

This reference to previous conversations had brought a gleam of appreciation to Hugh's eyes. 'I cannot believe there to be a great risk of that.'

'You,' Amelia had responded darkly, 'cannot be aware of my niece's obdurate nature!'

'There, ma'am, I think you do me an injustice.'

Louisa had hastily changed the subject, suddenly recognising the intention behind her aunt's voicing of such archaic ideas. She'd appeared far too smug at having elicited such an admission from Lord Hugh. But Hugh had looked no more that amused.

Now, as she went to her room to change from her riding habit into a morning gown of becoming sprigged muslin, she reviewed Hugh's recent behaviour. Since their excursion in the Bois when the broken fences between them had been at least partially repaired he had made no attempt to be alone with her. No attempt to claim the kisses he had threatened on the evening of the ball. He had escorted both her and her aunt to the Tivoli gardens to enjoy the dancing and the lavish and spectacular firework display. But, despite her apprehension—and, she had to admit, her traitorous anticipation—he had spent the entire evening in courteous and proper attendance upon both ladies, claiming only one dance from her and making no attempt to lure her into one of the convenient paths leading to secluded glades.

Louisa knew his attention meant nothing of significance. He had offered and she had accepted his escort before the incident at the ball. He had merely been keeping an engagement already arranged. But her aunt had been quite in raptures, her opinion of the gentleman soaring to excessive heights. Which was, Louisa supposed sourly, why Lady Nazeby had provoked that discussion over breakfast a couple of days later.

Since then he had escorted them on several occasions, as he had proposed during that ride in the Bois. And he had kept his promise to behave. Louisa did not know whether he was exerting self-control, or had lost any desire to dally with her. The uncertainty wore at her nerves.

He had also organised the projected visit to places of

interest in Paris, when most of his attention seemed to be directed towards keeping Jamie entertained and informed. They had gone in her curricle, with Hugh driving. Her aunt had been quite unconcerned at the thought of his taking the reins of her precious bays.

'His reputation as a whip is second to none, my love. Of course I shall not object!'

Why she had been forced to discover his ability for herself Louisa could not fathom. Except, she supposed, that in London other, more important things had occupied her attention and any such information concerning a gentleman she did not know had passed over her head. Only his reputed excursions into adultery had made any impression upon her mind then, due no doubt to her sensitivity over such matters.

That day had, though, only served to deepen her admiration for the man. His knowledge proved prodigious and his method of imparting it commanded both interest and respect. All the places made famous during the Revolution came under their scrutiny as well as buildings of more general and cultural interest.

Jamie had returned home almost hopping with excitement. 'I wish you were my tutor, Lord Hugh!'

'Do not make too great a work of this expedition,' Hugh had warned quietly. 'You will offend Mr Coynd who, I have no doubt, is in most ways an excellent tutor. He cannot be expected to excel in every department of his duties.'

Louisa had thought this a generous speech, considering the hostility Mr Coynd had shown.

'Are you to come on Lord Wellington's expedition to Versailles next week?' Jamie had asked. 'Please do!'

'I believe so, Jamie. Unless some urgent diplomatic duty prevents my attendance.'

'Capital!'

But for Louisa that had turned out to be an equally informative but frustrating occasion. Versailles had demanded her admiration and awe. But Hugh, although as attentive as ever, had travelled in the Stuarts' coach and had not once overstepped the bounds of propriety. She was becoming excessively frustrated.

But now, what was she to make of his assertion—although not made in so many words—that he cared for her? Her hard-won composure in his presence was under grave threat as she entered the breakfast parlour. She felt like some foolish chit just out of the schoolroom, all of a flutter. What could he have meant?

She was to find out after an unusually quiet meal. Of course, Jamie's absence could account for the lack of lively conversation. But even Amelia seemed susceptible to some atmosphere pervading the air and consumed her coffee and rolls in near silence. Until Hugh suddenly spoke.

'I have news which means I shall be forced to leave Paris within the month. Possibly before the end of the lessons I engaged to give you, Louisa.' He addressed her by her given name now before Amelia or Jamie. 'Of necessity, I fear our wager must be cancelled.'

'News?' exclaimed Amelia. 'What news?'

Louisa simply looked at him, her heart turning several somersaults before sinking to her shoes. Recently, she had been living from day to day, not daring to look to a future which did not include Hugh Deverill. Now she was forced to recognise exactly how bleak such a prospect was. Her expectations, which had been so elevated by his earlier remark, descended with a thump.

'I have been honoured by a considerable promotion. I am to be appointed His Britannic Majesty's Ambassador to Austria.'

Amelia's cries of congratulation obscured Louisa's less voluble and rather unhappy reception of this news. She smiled, tried to look pleased and remarked, 'At least you know Prince Metternich well.'

He inclined his head gravely. 'That will indeed be an advantage. Had he not agreed to my appointment, I doubt it would have been made.'

'So—we are to lose your company.' Amelia sounded

less enthusiastic over the news as its implications sunk in.

'I fear so, ma'am. I shall, of course, return to England periodically and we may renew our acquaintance there.'

'Not,' said Amelia tartly, 'if you continue to ignore London Society as you have done in the past!'

Hugh smiled. 'I shall give myself the honour of calling on you in Grosvenor Square the instant I return to the capital.'

He did not look at Louisa yet she was overwhelmingly conscious that he would be calling to see her rather than her aunt. The thought did little to alleviate the sudden ache of loss which had settled in the region of her heart.

'But we must not be selfish! We do rejoice over your good fortune, do we not, Louisa?'

'Certainly, Aunt.'

Her voice sounded flat, but she could not help it. Somehow she could not summon the reserves of energy needed to put on a brave and sparkling front.

Hugh noticed her sudden loss of spirits and took comfort in the fact. Perhaps his object would not be so difficult to achieve as he had feared.

'If you are ready, Louisa, we could begin the lesson,' he suggested quietly. At Louisa's nod of assent he turned to the older woman. 'But I must beg you, Lady Nazeby, to allow me a few moments alone with your niece before you join us.'

Amelia glanced swiftly from him to Louisa who, surprised as she was at the request, gave another slight nod of assent. She did not think Hugh Deverill had dalliance in mind, although what his object could be in seeking a private interview with her she refused to guess. He could have said anything he had to say on the way back from the Bois. Unless... Normally a gentleman had only one reason for——

Her mind balked.

He held the door for her and she walked through to another small parlour, where the lessons were usually given. He shut the door firmly behind them and she did not protest.

Too agitated to sit, Louisa took up station before the empty fireplace. She moistened her lips and cleared her throat.

'You wished to speak with me, Hugh?'

'I did.' As he moved to join her he indicated a chair. 'Will you not be seated, my dear Louisa?'

Because they were alone he was not only calling her by her given name but adding an endearment. Suddenly weak in the knees, Louisa sank down on the nearest elegantly padded chair.

Hugh himself appeared unusually restive. Having seen her seated, he paced backwards and forwards a couple of times before swinging round to face her. His stance became peculiarly aggressive.

'Miss Finsham—Louisa. You must know that my feelings for you have been growing for months now and I can resist them no longer. You know how deeply I admire you. I beg you to do me the honour of accepting my hand in marriage. Louisa, my dear, dear girl, will you marry me?'

Oh, those sweetest of sweet words! Yes! cried her heart. Yes, I will marry you, my dearest Hugh.

But her lips would not form the words.

'No,' she heard herself say. 'I am sensible of the honour you do me, Lord Hugh, but I regret I cannot marry you.'

He went white. His eyes, almost slate-grey with emotion, held an incredulous, dazed expression. 'Why not?' he demanded. 'Is it because of what I said at the ball? When I asked you to refuse me should I weaken and ask? If so, I release you from your promise forthwith!'

'No!' cried Louisa. 'Of course not!'

'Then why? Is it my lack of fortune? I had not thought——'

'Do not insult me with such an accusation, sir! You know very well it is not! But you have no true desire to wed,' said Louisa, her voice gaining sad conviction with every word. 'You have told me so often enough. Mayhap you need a wife now, for you will require a hostess in your new appointment. But I will not marry you simply for your convenience, my lord.'

'My convenience!' he spluttered. 'Louisa, what are you implying? You know how much I desire you and— I know you did not find my wretchedly improper advances distasteful,' he added, his voice sinking to a rueful growl. He made a helpless gesture. 'Louisa, you must marry me!'

'Indeed, sir, that I must not. I repeat, I will not be wed for convenience, be it for domestic reasons or to gratify a gentleman's carnal needs.'

He showed no shock at her outspoken words. 'But what of your own?' he demanded roughly. 'You cannot, in all honesty, deny your response or tell me you wish to remain forever a virgin! You must know that, together, you and I could share untold delight in a marriage bed!'

'Lust, sir!' snapped Louisa, fighting back a treacherous desire to burst into tears. 'I will not be seduced by lust!'

'No!' he denied passionately. 'My regard for you is not based simply on lust and neither is my proposal. We suit so well. Our minds meet on every point. You long for an outlet for your indisputable abilities. As my wife you would surely be able to find it and I would place no barrier in your way!'

If only he had spoken one word of love. She took a sustaining breath.

'Indeed that is so, my lord, should I wish to become your wife. Unfortunately, I do not.'

He could not leap to his feet in hurt outrage, for he was not on his knees, but he stiffened his spine and raised his chin. 'In that case, there seems little more to be said.'

'No, my lord. Except——' she tried to smile, which wavered '—can we not remain friends, at least until you depart for Vienna?' She seemed always to be asking rejected suitors for their friendship, she thought rather hysterically. Luckily those she liked mostly complied. 'Although I do not wish to marry you I do hold you in great esteem and value our discussions,' she went on, unconsciously pleading. 'I would not wish our lessons to be curtailed unnecessarily. Besides, Jamie will think it strange. . .'

He bowed formally. 'If that is your wish, Miss Finsham. Forget I ever had the temerity to address you. I should have remembered all those others you have refused, your determination to ignore you own nature and to remain a spinster. I can now fully sympathise with those other fellows' feelings.'

A flush spread over Louisa's face at his reference to her nature. Of course she wanted to be wed! And to him! But not without love. How could she make him understand?

'Not all were as honest or as sincere as you, my lord, and the damage was largely to their pride, not their feelings. If I have hurt yours, please forgive me, for I had no desire to do so. But I will not wed without love.'

So that was the trouble. He had not managed to engage her affections. He had at last achieved a position from which he could afford to support a wife and wed without being accused of seeking a fortune, only to be turned down by the one woman who could meet all his needs. Hugh stifled his disappointment and raised a rueful smile. Ignoring her painful reference to love, he said, 'Nor I to offend yours, my dear Louisa. That was ill-spoken. Shall we, then, proceed with the lesson?'

Louisa nodded, unable to trust her voice. She had given him his cue and he had ignored it. So an old tabby she would become.

When Amelia cautiously entered the room five minutes later they appeared to be deeply immersed in German declensions. Only they knew that neither mind could concentrate on the lesson.

* * *

'What did he want?' demanded Lady Nazeby the moment Hugh had departed.

Louisa told her.

'To marry you! How wonderful! But why did you not say, you dreadful creature, so that I might offer my congratulations?'

'Because I refused him.'

Amelia slumped in her chair. Visibly. 'Refused him?' she gasped in a strangled voice. 'But why? He is so *right* for you!'

'Except that he does not love me, Aunt. He wants me, he needs me, but he does not love me.'

'Love!' snorted Amelia, not for the first time. 'You are obsessed by the word. What is love but affection, understanding, consideration, the desire to put the other's happiness before one's own? Hugh would give you all those things. And passion, too, I do not doubt.'

'But loyalty? Could I depend upon his not taking a mistress the moment he began to tire of me?'

'As to that, my love,' answered Amelia ruefully, 'I could not say. Many men do, of course, but as many others do not. He admires Lord Castlereagh, I perceive, who is a model husband. You must learn to trust a little, Louisa.'

In the heat of her emotions she would have accepted Hugh had he loved her. But in the aftermath of turmoil all her insecurities flooded back to haunt her, making her glad she had not succumbed to her own feelings.

Her father's lifestyle and her mother's unhappiness had thrown a shadow over her childhood, her father's neglect a cloud over her youth. And Amelia herself had suffered unhappiness in her marriage. So how could the Dowager advocate it so strongly?

Because, Louisa realised, her aunt had made the best of her circumstances, had had the courage to take a lover, had immersed herself in the bringing up of her children, found joy in the love of her family, lavished her love on them and had had enough left over to extend to her niece. Now she was concerning herself

over her grandchildren, most particularly at the
moment over Jamie, and, as ever, over her.

A wave of affection brought her to kneel at her
aunt's side.

'Dear Aunt, you refine too much over me. I know
you are right. When the time comes for me to trust a
man, I shall know.'

She should trust Hugh. He approved of Castlereagh
and disapproved of the Duke and his indiscretions.
Could I have managed without his love? she asked
herself. Did I make a mistake?

Doubts assailed her constantly from then on but she
could not bring herself to be more than politely friendly
when she next met Lord Hugh, fearing where it might
lead if she allowed herself to behave with all the
warmth she still felt towards him. She wanted to make
love with him so much. He would lead her into realms
of unimaginable delight.

He had been right. She was denying her own nature
in refusing to have him as her husband. Yet the barriers
of her doubts stood solidly between them.

Jamie rejoined the morning sessions and the lessons
continued as before for a few days, until Hugh
announced that he must return to England to make a
start on setting his affairs in order before taking up his
new appointment in November.

He had not needed to make this extra journey. Another
visit to London would still be necessary before his
departure to Vienna. Officials at the Foreign Office
would require to see him, to give him his instructions.
And there would be last-minute personal arrangements
to make, farewells to be taken from family and friends.
He could have combined all his business into the one
trip.

Pacing the deck of the packet carrying him back to
France and remembering that other passage, Hugh
recognised that his brief visit to the family estates had
been an excuse to quit Paris for a time. He had hoped

that separation from the first object of his desire might cool the flames of passion, might cure the strange ache he felt whenever he thought of his lovely Louisa. But it had not. He could not wait to see her again.

As it happened his visit had turned out to be opportune. He had discovered himself to be the beneficiary of a childless cousin's will.

'We were about to inform you, my lord,' the solicitor had told him. 'You know the property, of course, a small manor house set in a few acres close by your own father's estates. Your cousin held some investments, too, which bring in an additional income.'

Hugh mourned the passing of a congenial companion. But undoubtedly possession of an estate and private means revolutionised his financial situation. Together with his income from his new appointment he now had all the means at his disposal to wed in security and comfort. An establishment to which he could take his bride, and to which they could return on leave or when his ambassadorship ended.

But Louisa had turned him down. Because she did not love him.

He arrived back in Paris during the second week in October. Louisa had found life exceptionally dull without him. She was so glad to see him when he appeared in the Bois again that she greeted him with more far more warmth than she intended.

His own emotions under tight control, Hugh eyed her gravely, scrutinising the radiant smile on an otherwise rather wan face with suddenly intent eyes.

'You are well?'

'Indeed, my lord. And you?'

He looked tired, and thinner. The journey and intense activity, no doubt.

'I am in capital health, I thank you. Jamie is not riding this morning?'

'Not as yet. He has sent no message, so I expect him at any moment. He has seemed low in spirits recently.

His mother has taken up with Prince Boris. He does not like the Russian.'

Hugh's frown deepened while a twisted smile marred the normally pleasant set of his lips. 'A pity. But he is rich and royal. A potent combination for a woman.'

'For some women, mayhap. Do not judge all womankind by such as Amy Thurrock.'

'My apologies, Louisa. I had forgot. Your requirements in a man are rather more complicated.'

Louisa bit her lip. He sounded cynical. It did not suit him. She had not intended to open old wounds. Apart from Hugh's servant, Dutton, riding with Pershaw at a discreet distance behind, they were alone.

'Peace, Hugh,' she murmured. 'I have missed you.'

'Obliging of you to say so.'

The Hugh she had come to know had not been given to cynicism or bitterness. Could it be that he had truly been deeply hurt by her refusal, and not simply piqued? Or were bitterness and pique one and the same thing?

Louisa wallowed in a mire of self-reproach and singularly painful dismals, knowing that whatever she said would simply make matters worse. Etiquette precluded her from broaching the subject of his proposal again. She could attempt to give him every encouragement to renew his offer, but in his present mood she doubted whether that would serve. He had climbed up on his high ropes and it would be difficult to bring him down. And if he did ask her again, was she really willing to abandon her doubts, fling her cap over a windmill and entrust her future happiness to him?

She still wasn't certain, despite missing him so badly while he'd been away and the undisputed effect his close presence had upon her senses, sending her pulse racing so fast that breathing became difficult. So she remained silent, staring straight ahead, the sound of the horses' hooves, muffled by fallen leaves, a dull accompaniment to her mood.

So she did not see the anguish in Hugh's eyes as he gazed at her profile. She had admitted to missing him, and seemed subdued. Her smile on greeting had made him dare to hope that she had changed her mind. But if he did sink his pride and address her again what guarantee had he that her answer would be any different? She seemed determined to turn down every offer she received and remain unwed. He might have suspected her of being cold, of having a disgust of the physical aspects of marriage had he not known differently. Memories sent the blood rushing through his veins, to become an ache.

He shifted in his saddle to ease it as his thoughts swept on. He had suspected she hid a passionate nature under that vivacious manner, for it was betrayed by the wide, sensuous curve of her mouth. He was quite sure she did not yet fully realise her own emotional depths. And he could only imagine the joy of awakening her to the knowledge. The thought of another man teaching her the intimate joys of making love racked him with such jealousy that an inaudible groan escaped him. Kismet, sensing his tension, tossed his head and skittered dangerously on the slippery leaves.

God, he thought as he settled his mount with automatic expertise, I should never have come here this morning! The sooner I leave again for London and Vienna the better! Yet frustration had accompanied him to England and would surely do so to Austria. Despite—or because of—this he had not been able to resist the temptation to see her again, to share precious moments conversing in fractured German. Although, he admitted wryly, she was learning the language with exceptional speed. She would make the perfect ambassador's wife. That was not, however, the reason he had asked her to marry him, whatever she thought. He couldn't exactly explain why he had, except that his circumstances had changed, making it possible, and the thought of life without her left him feeling desolate, even desperate.

The horses seemed to sense their riders' mood and plodded along listlessly. They had had a run, so the edge had been taken from their initial energy. They did not seem to care, any more than their riders did, where they went or how slowly.

They were still progressing in this depressing way when a horse came tearing up behind them. William Coynd pulled on his reins so sharply that his sweating horse reared and staggered before coming to a lurching halt.

'Lord Thurrock is not with you?' he gasped.

Prince Hal had already stopped. Kismet drew along-side to allow Hugh to face Coynd.

'Jamie?' said Louisa sharply, jerked from her reverie by the anxiety on the tutor's face. 'No, he has not put in an appearance this morning. Why?'

Hugh's features had settled into a frown. 'Has something happened to him?'

'I don't know. He's missing. I thought perhaps he'd come here, though according to the stable lad he had his horse saddled up and left very early, before dawn, about five-thirty of the clock, he thinks.'

Hugh brought out his pocket watch. 'It is half of the hour before nine now. He's been gone for three hours. Why did no one miss him before?'

'His servant has gone with him——'

'Ah! So he is not alone.'

'No. And I had no reason to suppose he had not come here, until I went to the stables for my mount and spoke to the boy.'

'His mother knows nothing of his likely where-abouts?' demanded Louisa.

Coynd shifted uncomfortably. 'Lady Thurrock is not at home.'

'Not at home?' Hugh shot Coynd a fierce glance. 'Then where the deuce is she?'

'She has eloped with Prince Boris. They left late last evening.'

'And the boy knew?'

Coynd nodded. 'He discovered his mother's absence

when he sent his servant, Milsom, to fetch a drink from the kitchen. The servants were agog.'

'So I should imagine. So she left without saying farewell to her son?'

'Yes, Lord Hugh. She knew he would make a scene, I suspect, and just before her departure she gave me a draft on the bank here with instructions to take his lordship back to England. She also instructed me not to inform him of her departure until this morning.'

Louisa drew a painful breath. 'Typical of Amy Thurrock,' she muttered angrily. 'I do not think she bears any love for her son, only for his title. Hugh, we must find him!'

Hugh had relaxed, any tension in him now being of a different order. He looked like a racehorse straining to be off. 'Certainly. But where should we begin to look? Have you any suggestions, Coynd?'

Coynd hesitated. 'He may have gone after them, my lord.'

'Did he know their destination?'

'He knew they were headed for Russia.'

'The devil! The boy would surely not undertake a journey like that on horseback!'

'He had a bundle with him,' confessed Coynd miserably.

'Why on earth did the stable lad not wake you, his tutor? Surely he knew his young master should not be allowed out alone apart from Milsom at that hour? And what was Milsom thinking of?'

'If he could not dissuade him, Milsom would accompany him rather than let Jamie travel alone,' suggested Louisa quietly. 'Though I would have thought he might notify you of his young master's intention, Mr Coynd.'

Blood suffused Coynd's face. 'I was not there. My charge was safely asleep and is often left alone with servants until the early hours. I spent much of the night with friends.'

'You did not look in on the boy on your return?' asked Hugh.

'It seemed unnecessary. Besides, I needed my bed. I confess to having been a little foxed,' Coynd admitted.

'Hmm,' muttered Hugh. 'I can only regret your neglect, Coynd. It has served to exacerbate this disaster.'

'No one could regret it more than I.'

Louisa, caught up in swinging emotions, cried impatiently, 'We cannot sit here talking! We must do something! Jamie could be in danger! Think of the malcontents and footpads——'

'Quite. But where best to start?' mused Hugh. Pershaw and Dutton had drawn nearer, listening with growing concern to their employers. He turned to them. 'We will go back to Lord Thurrock's. Pershaw, you had best speak to the grooms and the lad who saddled the horses. See if his lordship left any clue as to his destination. We will examine his room. He may have left a note.'

'I did not see one,' muttered Coynd.

'Nevertheless, we will search. Something may present itself.'

'The portrait of his father has gone,' exclaimed Coynd some half an hour later.

Hugh turned from examining the contents of a mahogany military chest, which must have belonged to the late Earl of Thurrock, and Louisa looked round from the clothes press, where she had been attempting to assess what Jamie had worn, what he might have taken with him. It did not appear to be much.

'Where was it?' demanded Hugh.

'On top of his livery cupboard. Which,' added Coynd grimly, 'is empty apart from candles. He took the store of food and drink with him, I collect.'

'And no doubt Milsom obtained more from the kitchen. Did he have money?'

'One or two *louis*, perhaps.'

'Then that has, too.' Hugh indicated the chest. 'There is none here. They will not starve, and he will have enough to pay for lodgings at night.' He indicated an open pistol case. 'I believe he must have taken his father's side arm. The balls and primer have gone, too. Unless he was not allowed to have them?'

'He was given the chest intact, on his thirteenth birthday. His sword has gone, too,' supplied Coynd gloomily.

'Well, at least they'll have something to defend themselves with if they're attacked,' offered Louisa brightly. 'If he can't use the gun I am sure Milsom can.'

'Just so long as he does not have some romantic idea of calling the Prince out. . .'

Louisa gazed at Hugh in horror. 'Oh, surely not! He couldn't possibly imagine he would win a duel!'

'A young gentleman of his age does not always stop to think of the consequences of his actions,' said Hugh sadly. 'But I would have credited Lord Thurrock with more sense, young as he is.'

'So would I! So I believe he has taken it for defence only. That would be a sensible decision.'

They were saved further speculation by a discreet tap on the door followed by Pershaw's entry into the room, with Dutton at his shoulder.

'Pershaw, what news?' asked Louisa anxiously.

Frustration was eating at her soul. So much time wasted already!

'Not much, Miss Louisa. But something.'

Pershaw's lined face showed his concern. She suspected there was little he did not know about the relationship between his employer and the young Earl. Jamie, too, had inherited his devotion.

'What, then? Out with it, man!' exclaimed Hugh, revealing his own anxiety by the impatience in his voice.

'I questioned the lad carefully, my lord. At first there seemed nothing to go on, but then he remembered overhearing something Lord Thurrock said to his man. He says he said, "Thank you for understanding, Milsom." And Milsom said, "I do, my lord." And then the Earl said, "Now *she*'s not here, I can go at last."

The boy did not think the exchange important, since his lordship did not state where he intended to go, but——'

'Waterloo!' cried Louisa. 'He so wanted to go to the battlefield, to see where his father died. And we would not let him!'

'Then I must be off at once,' said Hugh decisively. 'They will have taken the main road, for certain. My horse is fresh, and I can change him at a post stable along the way. Dutton will accompany me. I should overtake them fairly quickly.'

'I will come with you,' said Louisa briskly. 'Luckily I have fallen into the habit of carrying my papers with me. One never knows, in France, when one will be asked to show them. Pershaw, are you willing to ride with me?' He was not, after all, her servant, although she felt sure he would obey her commands without demur. But in this matter she must offer him the choice.

'Naturally, Miss Louisa, I should not allow you to go without me. Like Lord Hugh's, our horses are fresh enough——'

'You will do no such thing!' interrupted Hugh. 'Louisa, my dear, this is a man's task——'

'Fustian! I can ride as well as you, and am closer to Jamie!'

This exchange, which indicated an unusual degree of intimacy between his lordship and Miss Finsham, elicited various responses from those observing it. Dutton and Pershaw exchanged knowing, satisfied smiles. William Coynd was heard to sigh.

Neither Louisa nor Hugh was concerned with what others thought at that moment, and all antagonism, all reserve had dropped from them in their mutual concern. But Hugh continued to argue.

'My dearest girl, I cannot allow you to accompany me without a chaperon. Your reputation would be in shreds——'

'Fustian!' repeated Louisa. 'It is not so fragile that it

cannot withstand my making such a necessary journey as this! Pershaw will be with me——'

'But you need a woman, my dear.'

'Well, there isn't one. I cannot return for Betty without causing Aunt Nazeby unnecessary distress, and in any case she would need to travel in a carriage. So would most women, come to that. Lady Shelley departed for Brussels these weeks past so I cannot ask her. And even were she still here, would you suggest that I invite gossip by asking her to join us? No, I thought not,' she went on triumphantly at Hugh's horrified look. 'So I must rely on Pershaw to chaperon me. I am certain he will do a splendid job!'

Pershaw bowed, trying to hide his amusement and not quite succeeding. 'Indeed, Miss Louisa, I will do my best. It is always difficult to control a filly with the bit between its teeth, my lord,' he murmured. 'Best to let it have its head.'

It was the first time Pershaw had ever ventured such an insubordinate remark and Louisa was astonished. Had it been any other servant she would have dismissed him instantly for insolence, but Pershaw was a friend, as well as a devoted servant, and was trying to help her.

So, 'That will do, Pershaw,' she said briskly.

'I could hire a post chaise,' mused Hugh. 'That might be faster and better for you——'

'No.' Louisa shook her head firmly. 'They are uncomfortable things and Pershaw and Dutton would have to ride alongside anyway—there would not be room inside for us all—so it would not be faster. Besides, we do not want to draw the curiosity of French postillions, and if we used a coach it would be more susceptible to hold up.'

Hugh grinned, and shrugged. Louisa, sensing victory, smiled back.

'I am ready to start without further delay. Are you?'

'I must return to my quarters at the embassy for money. We will need changes of horses and most probably lodgings for at least one night. It will not take long.'

'I shall accompany you,' put in Coynd at this point. He had been standing in the background, forgotten by both Hugh and Louisa as they argued and made their plans. 'The Countess has made me responsible for him in her absence. It is my duty to find his lordship.'

'No doubt,' returned Hugh pacifically, 'but we can do that as well as you, and Lady Thurrock has entrusted Jamie to our care in the past, and would no doubt do so now. You, Coynd, will be more useful here.'

'I cannot see——'

Hugh cut the protest short. 'Lady Thurrock left you in charge. You are the only person with enough authority to direct the household, which is already in a sad state of turmoil and will undoubtedly descend into chaos without you here. And besides, should Lord Thurrock return unexpectedly it would be well if he found you here waiting for him.'

Coynd lifted his shoulders in a resigned shrug, giving way to Deverill's superior authority without further question. 'Very well, my lord. I will bid you farewell and wish you both a successful journey.'

He bowed. They returned the courtesy and Hugh turned to Louisa again, giving her a slightly grim smile.

'Are you ready?'

'Indeed, my lord, I have been ready this age!' She grinned suddenly, her real anxiety for Jamie somewhat mollified by the knowledge of his destination and by a new sense of adventure.

'What are we waiting for?'

CHAPTER TEN

HUGH'S clock struck ten before they were ready to leave his apartments, for he had insisted that they eat some breakfast before starting out on the gruelling journey.

Louisa had argued that Jamie was just getting further ahead, but Hugh had remained adamant. It would do Jamie no good at all for them to fail in their mission for lack of sustenance.

Pershaw had only just joined them, having detoured to the Hôtel des Fleurs with a carefully worded message for Amelia, telling her merely that Louisa was visiting Jamie's house and might remain away for several nights.

'Lady Nazeby will be surprised and wonder at my missing Lady Castlereagh's drum tonight, but should not be unduly worried,' Louisa had told Pershaw as she finished scribbling the note. 'Leave this with Chausson; don't deliver it yourself; it is too early for her to be up, but if she was she would want to question you! But do not forget to collect your own papers, and tell no one where you are going or why, just that you are remaining with me. If she sends to the Thurrock establishment for information Mr Coynd will field her enquiries. In the end he might have to reveal the truth, but by that time, if no message has reached him to say Jamie is safe, she will have to be told. We cannot spare her anxiety for long.'

Pershaw occupied a snug room over the stables. He would not need to speak to anyone apart from Chausson and possibly a stable lad. 'I will be as quick as I can, Miss Louisa,' he had promised. And had been as good as his word.

Neither he nor Dutton had eaten breakfast, either,

Hugh had pointed out. Louisa could not bring herself to deny the servants the chance to eat, and was hungry herself, so in the end she had given in with good grace.

When the small party did at last set off, Hugh having obtained Sir Charles's assent to his absence, the autumnal sun, still rising to its low zenith, was behind them. Overnight rain had left the roads wet, but so early in the year the mud was not deep, as it would surely be by Christmas. Their progress was therefore reasonably fast.

At the end of the first stage they discovered that Jamie had rested his Conker and Milsom's horse before setting off again. The boy and his servant had eaten breakfast and departed on freshly watered horses some four hours earlier.

'We'll take fresh horses,' Hugh told the ostler, 'and leave ours here. We will return for them, of that you may be sure. I'll thank you to see that all four animals are properly cared for in our absence.'

A large sum of money changed hands. The ostler's eyes lit up. Louisa, watching with impatient interest, imagined the man had seldom, if ever, held as much gold in his hand before. But gold need not be the only inducement. She could offer a possibly more effective one. Money alone did not always secure loyalty. She stepped forward and gave the man her most winning smile.

'I am certain you will look after them to perfection.' She patted Hal's sweating neck fondly and kissed his nose. 'See they are well rubbed down, won't you? I should be greatly distressed to find any of the horses, even those ridden by the servants, had suffered harm while in your care.'

Quite overcome by the not inconsiderable battery of the lady's charm, 'You can rely on me, *madame*,' promised the man fervently.

'Lucky man, lucky Hal,' murmured Hugh as he passed her by to leave the stable.

Louisa flushed and followed him quickly, a tingle of

anticipation adding an edge to her exhilaration. The job horses were already saddled and waiting. Pershaw stood ready to help her to mount, but Hugh gave him no opportunity. He placed his strong, capable hands on her waist and lifted her easily into her saddle. His fingers lingered momentarily on her thigh as she sought the stirrup. She settled her other leg more comfortably in the hooked pommel and arranged her skirts. When she looked down his eyes were fixed on her face, their expression unmistakable.

She looked away quickly, afraid that hers might reveal her ardent response. It was wonderful to be with him again. But too many unanswered questions hung between them.

Since his abortive proposal Hugh had been holding his emotions under tight control, not allowing Louisa or anyone else to guess how much her refusal had shaken him. The moment he had set eyes on her again this morning he had known his situation to be hopeless.

Pain caught again at his raw emotions. He loved her so deeply. There and then he vowed to do his utmost to win her love in return and then to renew his offer for her hand.

For some time they rode in silence, both lost in their thoughts. At last, while the horses slowed to take a hill, Louisa spoke.

'When do you suppose we might catch him up?'

Hugh had been silently considering that matter, among others, for some time. Brussels lay some one hundred and fifty miles ahead. Jamie had a four-hour start. They stood scant chance of coming up with him that day. Darkness would fall before six. Had he been alone he would have ridden on, but with Louisa in the party to travel after dark was beyond consideration. In this way her insistence on accompanying him would slow him down, but he would not dream of pointing this out. Her company was too precious. As it was they must find a lodging for the night by five o'clock. Time for only one more change of horses, then.

'Not today, I fear,' he answered her after a moment's delay while he carefully guided his mount round a deep pothole filled with muddy water. 'He had too long a start, and has been making good speed. We cannot hope to overhaul him quickly.'

'He seems to command the means to pay his way without stint,' she remarked. 'Mr Coynd must have been mistaken in the *louis* he possessed.'

'True. Although he has not expended money on hiring horses.'

'He would be reluctant to part with Conker.'

'Also true. We cannot be certain what means he has at his disposal. Mayhap he had been hoarding his allowance. And possibly Milsom has some savings and can oblige his master with a loan.'

'He could no doubt obtain credit. With his title——'

'Titles, in France, are not much in favour, even now.'

Louisa gave her reluctant mount an encouraging cluck and a tap with her crop. She did not look at Hugh as she spoke. 'Is that why you do not use yours?'

She had noticed he forbore to prefix his name with 'Lord'. It made little difference, though, for, however surly, the innkeepers and ostlers he addressed automatically responded to his air of easy command. So the prospect of spending the night in a French inn did not daunt Louisa. With Hugh beside her to smooth their path she knew the best rooms would miraculously become available.

'It seems diplomatic,' Hugh responded wryly.

Louisa chuckled, looking at him at last, her eyes dancing. 'My dear Hugh, you have certainly found your vocation!'

She was roasting him! The leap in his spirits seemed out of all proportion to the simple fact. Yet it meant she felt easy with him, that the awkwardness between them following his proposal had disappeared. That perhaps she would be willing to reconsider——

Or mayhap a renewal of his addresses might simply

reintroduce the constraint between them. He must be patient. But he had vowed to win her, and he would!

'Then we may not catch up with him until we reach Brussels,' she added seriously, after a moment's consideration.

Hugh's horse shied at some imaginary threat in the hedgerow. Effortlessly, he brought it under control, glad of the diversion while he executed the more difficult task of doing the same for this thoughts. 'That is quite possible.'

'I'm sorry.'

'Sorry?' He sounded genuinely puzzled.

'That you should have to visit a place you dislike so much.'

He remained silent while they filed past a lumbering wagon, its sweating horses struggling to haul their load, encouraged by the carter's whip, then spoke in measured tones.

'I do not dislike Brussels. Neither do I despise the battle or the field upon which it was fought. I rejoice in the victory and admire the men who won it so brilliantly. It is the morbid curiosity I find distasteful. I thought I had already made that plain.'

'Well, yes, you did, but I had thought you would dislike to have to go there yourself. Personally, although I am concerned for him and anxious to see him safe, I shall be glad if we do not catch Jamie before he reaches Waterloo. I think we were wrong to stop him from visiting when he asked. He loved and revered his father. It is natural he should wish to pay his last respects at the place where he fell. There was, after all, no funeral.'

'I hope we do catch him,' returned Hugh sombrely. 'It is no pilgrimage a child of his age should make without support. He would be better served were we with him.'

Louisa could not hide her surprise. 'You would not attempt to prevent him from carrying out his mission?'

'No. You have made me see that for some it is a

necessary act of mourning. Without it he may never properly recover from his father's death. Afterwards, he should be able to place his father's memory in its proper perspective and continue with his life untrammelled by frustrated longings and regrets.'

The smile Louisa turned on him was so radiant that Hugh caught his breath. 'You have removed my last objection to catching him up! I am so glad we feel the same way about it,' she said fervently. 'I wished Aunt Nazeby wouldn't insist on going, you know, but at first I didn't know why she was so set upon it. When she told me I could understand. And she's been much consoled by the visit. Since then I believe she has quite come to terms with her son's death.'

'Her son?'

Hugh's startled query made Louisa realise her indiscretion. Her colour rose to accompany her confusion and she fiddled with her mount's trappings. 'Oh, dear!' she said as the horses rose to a canter on the far side of the hill. 'I should not have said that. She will be so vexed with me for revealing her secret.'

'It is safe with me,' Hugh assured her.

'Thank you, my lord diplomat! I am certain it is,' said Louisa with a slight laugh, wondering whether it would be wise to tell him the whole story later. His curiosity must be piqued. And the telling would explain her own rather personal involvement in Jamie's affairs, which had probably already given him cause to wonder.

After that silence reigned between them as they urged the tiring horses forward. They could scarcely expect job horses to be as fast as the splendid animals they had left behind. But Jamie's speed would be even more curtailed, for his horses would tire and need longer periods of rest. By the time they came to an inn where they could spend the night enquiry of the innkeeper elicited the information that the lad was only three hours ahead.

'We are catching up with him, but too slowly for my liking,' mused Hugh.

'We must make the earliest possible start tomorrow.'

'And do you not think he will do the same?' he asked wryly. 'But we can only do our best. You must be tired,' he added, concern informing his voice as he saw again the weariness Louisa was attempting to hide, first noticed as he'd lifted her from her horse. 'You are not used to being so long in the saddle, my dear. Go and rest while I order a meal and it is prepared. It will be at least half an hour, I am told. Water will be sent up and I will see that you are called when supper is ready.'

'This,' admitted Louisa honestly, 'is where I could do with Betty and a change of clothing! But you are right. I am longing to cleanse myself and rest for a while.'

As expected Hugh had obtained the best bed-chambers, together with a private parlour where they could eat.

The innkeeper's wife brought the hot water up herself, and exclaimed over Louisa's lack of a maid.

'I can manage perfectly well,' Louisa assured the woman, 'but I should be grateful if you could lend me a comb and a night shift. I had to leave suddenly, without luggage, you see.'

The woman gave her a knowing wink. 'Eloping, are you, *mademoiselle*? He is a fine gentleman; I cannot say that I blame you——'

'You are wrong!' proclaimed Louisa firmly, annoyed that her colour should rise at the suggestion. '*Monsieur* and I are not eloping, merely travelling together on an urgent mission. He was able to return to his residence for a few necessities and to collect his man, but for reasons I do not intend to explain I was unfortunately not in a position to do the same.'

'I see,' said her hostess, smiling in a friendly fashion but speaking in a tone of voice that said she didn't believe a word of what Louisa said. 'Would you like my daughter Marie to come and attend you, *mademoiselle*? She can bring the things you'll need and you'll find her a capable lady's maid.'

'Thank you, *madame*. I should be most grateful for the service.'

Rested, bathed and refreshed, her hair dressed with dexterity by the innkeeper's daughter, who had lent her a chemise and a cotton blouse so that she could wash Louisa's garments ready for the next day, Louisa went down to the parlour feeling more hungry than she had for many a long day. They had barely stopped for dinner, snatching some cold meat with bread and a glass of wine while fresh horses were saddled.

Once the covers were served and he was assured that they lacked nothing, the innkeeper left them. Dutton hovered about his master, offering further service, but Hugh soon dismissed him, telling him to join Pershaw in the common dining-room, where he could partake of his own supper.

The autumn evening being chilly a huge fire burnt in the grate, its glow filling the little parlour with cheerful warmth. At first Louisa found the intimate atmosphere daunting but told herself not to be so missish. No one here was likely to report back to Paris and if she could not enjoy a meal alone with a gentleman without feeling herself compromised it would be a very poor thing indeed.

'Is this their ordinary?' she asked brightly, sniffing at the delicious bowl of soup steaming on the table near a branch of candles. 'I must confess to being extremely sharp set!'

'With a few extras,' smiled Hugh, watching the soft, flickering light illuminate her face, emphasising the straightness of her narrow nose, revealing the delicate hollows beneath her high cheekbones, the fullness of her lips, the length of the lashes surrounding her lovely eyes, which appeared quite green in that light. The candles brought out the copper tints in her brown curls, simply dressed and without ornament. Heat surged through his body as he studied her delectable person. God, how he loved her!

He worked hard to keep his voice cool. 'The notice

was too short for our hostess to prepare much in the way of specialities, but she has baked some fruit tartlets and made a custard. The mutton chops, the cold ham and the savoury pancakes the French make were already on the menu.'

'It all smells delicious, and I see she has not stinted the sauces!'

'They keep a good cellar here, too. The wine is excellent. Shall I pour you a glass?'

'If you please.'

Before she had finished the soup the food and the heat of the room had made Louisa uncomfortably hot. Her thick maroon habit was suited to riding but not to eating in a warm parlour.

'I think I must remove my jacket,' she apologised, undoing the buttons concealed among the gold frogging.

He was on his feet in a moment. 'Allow me.'

He eased the jacket from her shoulders, his movements a caress. A shiver ran down Louisa's spine, disturbingly pleasurable. This was the first time they had been alone together since his proposal and, apart from the disturbing touch on her thigh that morning, the first time he had touched her in other than a purely impersonal manner since the ball.

Marie's peasant blouse with its little puff sleeves lay low on her shoulders, kept up by a drawstring around the neckline above a band of dainty smocking. Louisa longed for the courage to re-tie the bow, to draw the material up to cover her exposed flesh, for she saw Hugh's eyes drawn to the graceful column of her neck and descend to linger on the gentle swell of her breasts. Yet the blouse was less revealing than the ball gowns and evening dresses she wore every day, and she did not feel embarrassed when men looked at her then!

Had she known the temptation the bow tying the drawstring presented to Hugh's itching fingers she would have lost the last remnants of her composure. She was struggling as it was. She was so acutely aware of him. He had discarded his riding coat, retaining his waistcoat over changed linen. His shirt and immaculate cravat gleamed softly white in the candle-glow, the simple brown waistcoat with brocaded reveres affording a dignified contrast to the buff breeches tucked into his newly polished calf-length boots.

She tucked her own badly cleansed boots further under the protection of her travel-stained skirt. How she envied him his change of apparel! Dutton had probably packed a razor, too, for Hugh appeared to be freshly shaven. She raised a small and silent vote of thanks to Marie, without whose help her own appearance would have been regrettable indeed.

Hugh, having put temptation firmly aside, laid her jacket on a chair and resumed his seat. 'Have some mutton,' he suggested prosaically, although Louisa detected a slight tremor in his hand—one to match that afflicting her entire body. 'The caper sauce is delicious.'

Louisa attempted to divert both their thoughts with bright chatter. 'A small portion, then, for I must sample the pancakes! Do you know what our good landlady has used to fill them?'

Hugh had already consumed his mutton. He transferred a *galette* to his plate and investigated the contents.

'Ham, I believe, and mushrooms.' He took a mouthful and sampled the flavour. 'Cheese, too! The woman is a capital cook.'

'I agree,' said Louisa, savouring the mutton. 'She is wasted here!'

'Not so! Instead of catering to the whims of one family, she gives cheer to countless weary travellers!'

'We were fortunate to find this inn.' She finished the last of her mutton. 'Delicious! And now I shall try one of those pancakes, if you please!' He served her with smooth efficiency and as she cut into the food she thanked him before finishing her opening remark. 'We could have been forced to put up at some flea-infested hovel!'

'The main roads are well served. If Napoleon did nothing else, he kept his communications open.'

'I suppose he did have some good points.'

'Undoubtedly. He did much for France until power went to his head and he tried to subjugate the world and in the process sacrificed the flower of French manhood. In the end, you know, he was calling up sixteen-year-old boys. Those who tried to evade the conscription were sent to the front in chains.'

'Well, he's on his way to St Helena now. He will not escape again, I think.'

'God forbid!'

They completed their meal in an amicable silence only interrupted by polite enquiries as to each other's needs and fancies. The tension between them eased. Louisa sipped her final glass of wine and sighed.

'I must retire and leave you to your brandy.'

'Must you leave? I should not enjoy my brandy sitting here by myself. I have never seen the need for a gentleman to be left to drink at the table alone—unless, of course, he intends to imbibe to excess.' Louisa was already on her feet. He rose at the same time and held out his hand. 'Since we cannot retire to another room, will you not join me by the fire? We may, perhaps, drink tea together, if our hostess is capable of making it!'

'I hope she is! How I long for a dish of tea! But the French do not seem to have embraced the habit, as we have, and make it so poorly!'

He shifted her chair to facilitate her movements and, taking her hand, led her to a chair by the fire, which burnt less brightly now but still gave out a pleasant warmth.

'Are you comfortable? Would you like the tea at once?'

'Quite comfortable, thank you. And I should love to have my tea now if that would be possible. If we are to make an early start I must seek my bed soon.'

Tempted to say he would be pleased to see that she

found it and to join her there, Hugh resisted the wicked impulse in the interests of future progress. In some moods he was certain she would respond in kind to such an improper suggestion, for she was no simpering miss, but he was not sure enough of her at that moment. Instead, 'I will ring and order it,' he murmured prosaically.

He picked up the handbell and strode to the door. A serving girl answered the summons but *madame* herself brought the tray.

'Here you are, then, *monsieur, mademoiselle.*' She put the tray down on its legs and curtsied, giving them a distinctly knowing smile. 'Shall I pour it, or would you prefer to be left alone?'

Louisa did not think she could abide the woman in the room a moment longer, with her looks and innuendoes. All made in good part, of course, but highly embarrassing just the same.

'Thank you, *madame*, I will pour. Will you ask Marie to go to my room and make my things ready for the night? I shall not keep her waiting long.'

'Certainly, *mademoiselle*, though she will not mind how long she has to wait.'

The woman left them with another suggestive smile.

Hugh chuckled. 'I do believe she thinks we are up to no good!'

'She believes we are eloping,' muttered Louisa.

'Well, that's better than——' He broke off abruptly at sight of the mortification mirrored on Louisa's half-averted face. He realised that, far from welcoming the idea, Louisa was upset by it. He crushed down his own disappointment in an attempt to comfort her. 'My dear, I am sorry if you find the idea of eloping with me distasteful, but what does one common woman's mistaken opinion matter? Perhaps we should call in Dutton or Pershaw to chaperon us.'

'No,' protested Louisa fiercely. 'I will not be overset by a peasant's impertinence! I knew there could be misunderstanding when we set out. I was prepared to outface my own kind, so I am certainly able to withstand her insinuations! I will pour the tea if you will bring the tray nearer.'

Hugh did as requested, his mind in new disarray. Was it indeed the idea of marrying him that had caused her distress, or the thought of losing her reputation? He wished he knew. If it were the latter, why had she been so determined to accompany him?

'You should not have come,' he suggested softly.

'No doubt you are right.' She busied herself pouring the tea so that she need not look at him. She was a nuisance; he had not wished for her company. But he did not have the same incentive to catch up with Jamie and see him safe as she did.

'I had to.' Now was the time to explain fully. Then he could not misunderstand and think her motive had been simply to be with him... That had only been part of it. She handed him a cup of tea.

'Had to?' he probed.

'Yes. For Aunt Nazeby's sake. He is her grandson. My cousin. Although, of course, he does not know it and must never be told!'

Hugh drew a breath. 'I see! Then Muriel, Countess of Thurrock, is not his grandparent? Robert was not her son?'

'No. She was and is Aunt Nazeby's dearest friend. They arranged it between them. But of course no one must ever know, because of the succession.'

'But who was his father? And why the deception?'

'I do not know who her lover was, except that he was a man of rank. And as to why, Aunt says the deception kept two marriages together. Perhaps three. Muriel needed a son, Amelia a good home for her bastard. And her lover's marriage was saved from the effects of scandal.'

Hugh put his cup back on the tray and moved to kneel beside her chair. He looked up into her shadowed eyes, his own serious.

'And is this why you have such an aversion to a man taking a married woman as his lover?'

Louisa started. Such a thought had been far from her mind. She gave a slight, negative shake of her head. 'Not particularly. I did not know of it until we reached Waterloo. But it illustrates my reasons for disliking such irresponsible and licentious behaviour. Tell me, Lord Hugh, how many of your bastards are in line to inherit a title?'

Hugh sprang to his feet, his leap reminding Louisa of the effect of an electric shock, an amusing novelty when demonstrated among one's friends. But Hugh was not amused. A smothered curse escaped his lips as he swung round to turn his back on her.

'Do you still believe the scurrilous gossip that has been put about?' he demanded harshly. No wonder she could not love him! But he had thought her more generous-minded.

'I don't know what to think.' How Louisa controlled her voice she did not know. As it was it sounded desperately uncertain. Her deep-seated distrust of all men had led her unruly tongue to run away with her and she had offended him bitterly. She continued almost inaudibly, quite unable to meet his blazing eyes. 'But you must concede that many lofty houses may nurture a cuckoo in their nursery. With all the immorality, the infidelity, rife among the nobility I often wonder whether any ancient line is as pure as its incumbents are pleased to believe.'

'And that concerns you?'

His tone had lost its bitter edge. It had softened, become thoughtful. Emboldened, Louisa looked up and met the full force of his penetrating gaze. It held an arrested expression, yet something like tenderness lurked there too. She shivered slightly, and shrugged.

'I think it a pity. But what concerns me more is the lightness with which people, both gentlemen and ladies, take their marriage vows. They are made before God and should be sacred.'

'Yes. You must believe that, for me,' he averred soberly, 'they would be. That they are not for some men and women concerns me but in the end their conscience is their own.'

'How can they do it?' wondered Louisa.

'For many reasons. Unhappiness. Their spouse's indifference or infidelity. Boredom. Sometimes, especially for men, it is sheer promiscuity, for women, often the promise of luxuries a mean or impecunious husband cannot or will not supply. It does not take much to persuade a woman that an amorous adventure will answer all her problems, will add excitement and glamour to her life. And the acquisition of a lover proves to an older female that she is still attractive.'

Louisa stood up, her scarcely touched tea forgotten. 'I think I must retire to my room.'

Hugh made a last attempt to penetrate the barrier she had erected between them. 'How can I persuade you that I am not the libertine you think me?' he demanded softly.

'Perhaps you already have, my lord, for what it is worth.' She managed a tremulous smile. 'You must understand, though, that I find it difficult to trust any man. My father's behaviour caused my mother such pain.'

'My dear!'

'Goodnight, Hugh.'

He laid a hand on her arm as she went to sweep past him, not trusting herself to remain in his company any longer. She would burst into tears or say something else she would regret if she did.

He looked down into her face, his eyes heavy with a longing he could not disguise. In her face he saw only hostility, in her eyes anguish. He sighed and let her go.

'God grant you a good night's rest.'

Louisa left the room swiftly, before she gave in and cried against his chest. She had been so sure he meant to kiss her. Her lips had parted in anticipation while her mind, whirling with conflicting thoughts and divers emotions, had taken control of her taut nerves. She had not wanted him to see how much she longed for his kiss. Yet the desire had been there.

And now, as she made her way up the dark stairway by the light of a candle picked up and kindled at its foot, all she felt was dismay at what she had done. And acute disappointment over what he had not. Why had he not taken her into his arms and resolved all her doubts with a kiss? For if he loved her——

But she had no reason at all to believe that he did.

CHAPTER ELEVEN

LOUISA descended to breakfast in subdued mood. She should not have quarrelled with Hugh. The disagreement had arisen, she recognised, from a desperate need to resist his lure. To pick a fight had been the simplest way to prevent herself from falling into his arms. But she should not have done it. They had a purpose in common and must work together to achieve its aim, whatever their personal feelings. Of course, Jamie was probably perfectly all right and well able to look after himself with Milsom's help, but they could not rely on that or allow him to continue his impetuous journey without adequate protection.

Hugh was already in the parlour when she entered. He immediately stood and made his devoirs.

'Good morning, Louisa. You are rested, I trust?'

Louisa dipped a curtsy in response. 'Thank you, yes.' Dutton was in attendance. No doubt Pershaw was seeing to the acquisition of fresh horses. But Hugh's wary politeness was not caused by Dutton's presence. No, his manner was a direct result of last night.

She held out an appealing hand. Surprised, he hesitated fractionally before taking it into his firm clasp. Her heart, already drumming, beat faster.

'Forgive me, Hugh. I was tired last evening,' she apologised, with an unconsciously pleading smile. 'Forget the unfair accusations I made. I have no wish to be at odds with you.'

His expression softened. All hostility had disappeared from her eyes, which shone up at him like stars. 'Readily.' He turned the hand he held palm up. His lips, dry and warm, lingered on her quivering flesh. He looked up to capture her eyes again with his. 'If you will allow me to offer my sincere regrets for any pain I may have caused in return?'

He retained her hand, smiling crookedly into her tear-sheened eyes. Dutton was busily occupied at the sideboard. She could almost see the man's ears flapping. But she did not mind. She knew that he approved of her. As Pershaw approved of Hugh. Servants really did hold an extraordinary influence over one's life, she thought, when their approval or disapproval could colour one's own judgement! She accepted Pershaw's opinion over so many things. Why not over Hugh?

Because Hugh Deverill was not a horse, she thought wryly. But a good judge of a horse was often a good judge of a man.

Her whole being relaxed. She blinked back her foolish tears and gave him a sunny smile. 'You, my dear diplomat, could charm anyone into anything!'

Now he laughed, captured her other hand and kissed both palms in turn, causing delicious tremors to course through her body. Then he closed her fingers over his kisses and gave her back her hands. 'We should eat. Dawn will be breaking soon.'

Thrown completely off balance by his caresses, Louisa nodded and took her seat. Reluctantly, she uncurled her fingers to break her roll and spread butter. But the feel of those kisses remained upon her palms long after she mounted her horse and took hold of the reins. Beneath her leather gloves the tingle left by his lips continued to remind her of that precious moment when the rift between them had been healed.

There was little sun. A chill wind had sprung up overnight but the rain held off and they scarcely noticed the weather. The regular halts for changes of horses and a quick bite to eat became longed-for breaks in a relentless drive forward. Louisa had never been called upon to ride hard for so long in her life before and exhaustion threatened to overtake her. She pressed on doggedly, determined to die rather than show it and prove Hugh right when he'd tried to dissuade her from coming.

So she ignored her sore seat and aching back and concentrated on keeping up with him. He, ever solicitous, had probably cut down his own pace, she realised. Having her along was slowing down his progress. He made no comment, being too much the gentleman to do so. And Pershaw was really too old for this kind of jaunt. She had done him no favour by asking him to accompany her.

But, steadily, they were overtaking Jamie. By the time they reached Cambray, where contingents of the Allied army had been billeted, he was little more than half an hour ahead, and still riding Conker.

'We should catch him up before nightfall,' said Hugh, relieved. 'He will cross into Belgium and stop at Mons, I should guess. We can hope to find him there.'

Louisa nodded, saving her breath. They were approaching a wooded, winding stretch of road and she was thankful that, although the sun had still not quite broken through, the low, dark clouds had lifted somewhat during the day, making the tunnel through the trees less gloomy.

Determinedly keeping her eyes fixed on potholes and hazards a few yards ahead, she heard Hugh swallow an oath. He put out a warning hand to touch her horse's bridle.

'Slower!' he ordered, just loud enough for the two servants behind to hear him. 'Dutton, Pershaw, cock your pieces!'

Jerked from her concentration on the road immediately in front of her hack's hooves, Louisa focused her eyes ahead.

The scene that met he eyes brought a gasp to her lips. A coach blocked the highway, the four snorting, restive horses harnessed to it restrained by a man at the leaders' heads. Several mounted men surrounded the carriage. At least two figures lay on the ground. Another stood backed up against a wheel with his hands above his head. There seemed to be a couple of loose animals adding to the confusion.

Hugh slowed his party down to a walk as he led a cautious approach. Having assessed the situation, 'Scatter,' he ordered crisply. 'Dutton, Pershaw, follow me. Dutton, fire a warning shot into the air.'

'There are too many——' began Louisa in dismay.

'Keep out of the way!' barked Hugh, spurring his horse forward as Dutton's shot rang out.

The men holding up the coach, realising they had been interrupted, answered fire. A ball whistled past uncomfortably close to Louisa's head. She ducked, heart in mouth, but did not slow down, keeping close behind Pershaw and Dutton, who, riding well apart, followed a length behind Hugh.

He had drawn his sword. Bellowing a challenge, he spurred his horse into a charge. Unfortunately, not being Kismet, the animal responded reluctantly, pounding forward with ears laid back, its eyes rolling in fright. Pershaw and Dutton, flourishing their pistols—Louisa suspected that Dutton's needed reloading—thundered along behind.

Someone shouted from within the carriage and the muzzle of a twin-barrelled fowling piece appeared in the window. The flash of fire as it first spluttered and then went off alarmed everyone, although the single ball went harmlessly up into the trees.

The approach of three armed men and the threat posed by the second barrel of the sporting gun proved too much for the highwaymen. A cry went up to retreat. The one at the carriage cattle's heads released them and sprang into his own saddle. The leader of the band, masked like the rest, grasped the reins of a riderless chestnut horse that, to Louisa, looked alarmingly familiar.

'Conker!' she gasped.

She spurred forward and as she approached the tableau resolved itself further. Three bodies lay on the ground, two on one side of the coach, one on the other.

The man who had been standing with his hands above his head moved quickly to bend over the nearest prone figure, which groaned and moved. Louisa was more interested in the small person struggling to his feet on the far side of the coach.

'Jamie!' she cried, flung herself from her mount and rushed to his side, running round the back of the coach out of reach of its plunging horses.

'Louisa!' Utter relief washed over his face. 'We tried to stop them but they knocked me off, and hit Milsom——' He broke off, looked helplessly to where Milsom lay, one side of his face covered in blood, and then his face crumpled. 'And they've taken Conker!' he ended miserably.

'You stay here with the boy,' Hugh called to her across the backs of the coach horses. 'Dutton, come with me. We'll try to recover the stolen horse.'

'Yes, my lord.'

As though he were used to undertaking this kind of task every day, Dutton accepted the still cocked pistol that Pershaw thrust into his hand and prepared to follow his master. The two rode off without a backward glance as Pershaw sprang to control the horses attached to the coach.

Jamie appeared to be frightened but not seriously hurt, although he had a bruise on his forehead. Milsom she didn't know about. Hugh was riding full tilt into danger. She scarcely hesitated.

'Is your pistol loaded, Jamie?'

'Yes, and primed. I didn't get a chance to fire it or to draw my sword——'

'Good. Give it to me. I know how to use it. Stay here with Pershaw.'

She grasped the gun, ran back to her horse, which, now the excitement was over, was busy munching grass from the verge. 'Help me up,' she threw at the man with the fowling piece, who was just descending from the rocking vehicle.

'My dear young lady——'

'You,' said Louisa, addressing the footman and ignoring the master, since he was arguing. 'Help me to mount and then look to your horses so that Pershaw may attend the wounded.'

Her voice carried such command that the man obeyed instinctively, albeit with a glance of apology in his master's direction. Louisa rejoiced to see that the coachman, who had caught a ball in his shoulder, was very much alive, sitting propped against a wheel and groaning with pain.

Pershaw would see to everything there, she knew. And, overwhelmingly, it was Hugh who mattered. She had to be with him. To help if possible. Die with him if necessary.

The weariness had dropped from her like a cloak. She felt full of energy, alert, frightened to death and yet driven by some power above and beyond herself to ride to her love's side.

Hugh had a good start, but was not out of sight, for once through the narrow wood the track led straight across the fields. The highwaymen had not so far fired again on their pursuers, no doubt concentrating on speed and conserving their balls. Like Hugh's and Dutton's, her mount was relatively fresh. She made a light burden.

She began to overtake them, just as they were overtaking the fugitives, who found themselves hampered by a fractious Conker. Unused to such rough treatment and disliking being parted from his master, the chestnut was showing his mettle.

Before long Hugh was close enough to be within firing range. 'Stop! *Arrêtez*!' he roared.

They didn't heed his cry. Hugh fired.

Realising the captured horse was slowing them down, the leader let go of Conker's reins; Dutton returned the fire of one of the others but Louisa, clinging on with her knees, cocked Jamie's pistol and aimed for the leader; for, once free of the need to manage Conker, the man had looked over his shoulder and was pointing his pistol at Hugh.

She was too far away really. Her ball smacked harmlessly into the ground at the horse's heels, but the frightened animal leapt forward, almost throwing the man, whose shot went high and wide because of it.

Louisa's mount, frightened out of its wits by the explosion above its head, wheeled sharply, threatening to unseat her. While she struggled to remain in her saddle, handicapped by a pistol she did not wish to abandon since it was precious to Jamie, it took the bit between its teeth and bolted. Hazily, as she concentrated on clinging on and trying to regain control, she saw that Hugh, who had easily captured the loose Conker, had stopped the chase and allowed the miscreants to escape.

Relieved beyond measure to know that he was safe, Louisa was content to let her horse run. It would soon tire and since it had chosen to make straight back towards the road she had no real desire to stop it.

As the animal approached the belt of trees it decided it did not like the darkness ahead and swerved to the left.

Now Louisa did attempt to regain control, resting the hand holding the pistol and a tight rein on its withers and tugging regularly with her other. But the creature still kept the bit firmly between its teeth despite the discomfort caused by her treatment. Years of being ridden by indifferent horsemen had given it a hard mouth.

Hoofbeats from behind were drawing near. Taking a moment to glance behind, she realised Hugh had been chasing after her and that now she had changed course he was cutting across to intercept.

Before he could reach her a troop of scarlet-coated Life Guardsmen appeared from the trees ahead. Her tiring animal spotted them at once. It pricked its ears at the sight of so many other horses progressing steadily towards it, slowed its place, shook its head and responded to the bit. Louisa rode it forward before turning it to face Hugh.

By the time he drew his sweating mount alongside hers the soldiers were only a hundred yards off. They both reined in.

'You foolish creature!' he accused, breathing heavily, his voice unsteady. 'I told you to remain on the road!'

'Would you have preferred me to fall into strong hysterics?' demanded Louisa indignantly. She was panting, too. 'I am sorry, Hugh, that I am not of a fashionable disposition, but I am not in the habit of succumbing to the vapours at the veriest hint of danger.'

'I know, my dear——' he managed a smile '—and I admire you the more for it! But you cannot imagine my feelings when I thought to see you thrown, perhaps killed. . .'

His voice trailed off. Louisa looked into his eyes, saw the anguish he could not hide and a small smile touched her lips.

'But I can,' she assured him huskily. 'Why do you imagine I followed you when you rode off into danger?'

'Louisa——'

There was no time for more. The captain drew his troop to a halt and saluted.

'May I enquire your business here, sir?'

Hugh explained. 'Had you travelled another mile along the road you would have discovered the coach,' he finished.

'The highwaymen made off in that direction, did they?' mused the captain, nodding over the fields. 'I think we might give chase. Sergeant, take six men and see what you can find.'

'One of the horses,' said Hugh, 'is a piebald, and one of the men has a ginger beard.'

'Capital. You heard that? On your way, then, Sergeant. I'll accompany you back to your friends, my lord. We may be able to offer assistance to the wounded. Do you know the identity of the gentleman

in the coach?' he went on to ask as he rode between
Louisa and Hugh, the remainder of his troop trotting
behind.

'No. But he was armed and so was his coachman, I
imagine, since he got shot.'

'There was a crest on the door,' put in Louisa, 'but I
did not recognise either him or it. He was English,
though,' she added as an afterthought. 'I should have
thought I might.'

'We shall no doubt soon discover his identity,' murmured Hugh with a grin. 'It is not only members of the
ton who are entitled to crests, you know.'

'And most unwise of him to flaunt it on these roads,'
observed the captain drily.

Chatting and speculating amiably, they at last
returned to the road. As Louisa had expected, Pershaw
had everything under control—including, it seemed, the
rather choleric occupant of the coach.

'Intolerable delay!' he was spluttering as they
appeared. 'My man needs attention and I wish to reach
Paris with all speed!'

'Here comes his lordship now,' said Pershaw stiffly,
obviously relieved. 'You will be able to thank him
personally, my lord.'

So he was ennobled. But she had never seen him in
London or elsewhere and now she heard him speak
properly she could perhaps imagine why. He had the
broadest of country accents. Difficult to place.

Jamie jumped forward eagerly. 'Allow me to present
you, my lord. Lord Hugh, Louisa, this is Lord Cumnor,
of Cumnor Place in Lancashire, who has been visiting
Waterloo on his way to Paris, where he hopes to be
presented to Lord Wellington. He owns a mill and
supplies material for our army's uniforms and believes
Lord Wellington will be grateful.' Hugh and Louisa
dutifully inclined their heads. 'Miss Louisa Finsham,
the niece of Amelia, Dowager Countess of Nazeby, and
Lord Hugh Deverill, of the British Embassy in Paris,
my lord.'

Well done, Jamie, thought Louisa, giving the lad a smile as Cumnor made a stiff bow. Now everyone knew exactly who everyone else was!

Hugh indicated the captain. 'Captain Brownhill of the Life Guards, my lord. His corporal is skilled in attending the wounded. He will look at your coachman. Jamie, how is Milsom?'

'He's all right apart from a sore head, I think. He was knocked out and the wound bled a bit. And the coachman has been seen to. But, sir, you got Conker back! Dutton brought him in and said Louisa's horse had bolted!'

'You took a bump, too, by the look of it,' said Hugh, ignoring the latter part of Jamie's outburst as he dismounted and assisted Louisa from her saddle. 'Let the corporal take a look at both of you. My lord, your attackers are being pursued by some of Captain Brownhill's men. But they had a good start. I doubt whether they will be caught. You are lucky we all came along when we did.'

'I am grateful to you of course, Deverill, and was asking your man to convey my thanks, but he insisted I wait for your return.'

'Not Lord Hugh's man but Lady Nazeby's groom, my lord.' Louisa thought she had seldom met a less gracious person in her life. 'I imagine he was concerned for our safety and wished you to witness our return before taking your own departure. In certain circumstances your coach could have been essential to our survival.'

Pershaw nodded. 'Precisely, Miss Finsham.'

'Luckily we escaped unharmed,' said Hugh, his polite manner, Louisa realised, concealing considerable anger. 'Now the corporal has inspected your coachman and pronounced him fit to travel I can see no reason to delay you longer. However, I would advise you to hire some armed outriders at the next town. They should accompany you for the remainder of the journey, particularly as your crest is so prominently displayed on your carriage doors. There is safety in numbers. As no doubt Lord Thurrock has discovered.'

Jamie flushed and Louisa wished Hugh hadn't publicly criticised the boy. But Cumnor did not notice.

'I have my fowling piece. I shall not hesitate to use both barrels another time!'

'But you will have only one fit man to protect you, my lord. Take my advice and do as his lordship has suggested.'

Captain Brownhill had dismounted, too. His clipped voice brought a scowl to Cumnor's heavy face. 'I'll do as I think best. Good day to you, my lords, Captain, Miss Finsham. You will be returning to Paris? Perhaps we shall meet again there.'

Hugh bowed. 'We shall be returning when our business in Brussels is finished. Certainly within the week.'

Jamie's flush of embarrassment turned to one of eagerness. He had not missed the implication of Hugh's words. Louisa gave him an encouraging smile.

'Then I'll be on my way. Thanks again, Deverill, and to you, Thurrock.'

With the prospect of speedy departure, Cumnor was behaving with condescending grace. They watched the coach roll away with some relief.

Captain Brownhill remounted and gathered his troop behind him. He saluted. 'Pleasure to be of service, my lords, ma'am.'

'I hope you catch those rascals,' said Hugh. 'If you need us to identify them we'll be in Brussels for the next couple of days. The Duchess of Richmond will know our whereabouts. After that, we shall return to Paris.'

'I should be glad to welcome you to the barracks at Cambray, my lord, if you have time to stop in passing. We should have news by then.'

'Thank you, Captain. We may well take you at your word.'

With a brisk nod the captain called his men to order and rode off at their head.

'And now, young man,' said Hugh with paternal severity, 'I should ring a peal over your head for being such a sapskull. Not only did you endanger your own life, but that of Milsom, too.'

'I was awfully glad to see you,' confessed Jamie, subdued. 'How did you guess where I'd gone?'

'It was not difficult. And the reason I shall not make a tiresome piece of work of this matter is because Louisa has persuaded me that you should be allowed to see the field upon which your father died if you so wish. We shall therefore escort you there. If that is still your desire?'

There could be no question of that. Milsom, having been complimented for his care of his young master, was helped back on his horse.

'Are you certain you are fit to ride?' asked Louisa dubiously.

'Perfectly, thank you, Miss Finsham. I shall manage,' he said, which was a mixed sort of response, but Louisa admired the man's determination. Conker skittered about when Jamie mounted, glad to be reunited with his master. The hired horses accepted their burdens with resignation and the party proceeded into Belgium.

In view of their exchange just as the Life Guards had ridden up Louisa expected Hugh to seek to be alone with her that evening. She anticipated the moment with intense pleasure. If Hugh proposed again she would accept. He must care for her. Else why had he been so distraught at the mere thought of her being hurt? She knew perfectly well what had caused her concern over his safety. Surely he must love her just a little? Enough for her to work on in the future? And single independence had long ceased to appear as attractive to her as it had when she'd left England.

She was to be disappointed. Jamie, professing himself far from tired and quite able to manage for himself for one night, sent Milsom to bed to nurse his aching head and settled down to monopolise Hugh for the remainder of the evening. Louisa, who was desperately tired, the excitements of the day adding to her exhaustion, retired early herself. Hugh bade her a ceremonious good night, his eyes warm, his lips ardent on her hand.

It was not enough.

Arrived in Brussels, Hugh immediately called on the Duchess of Richmond. Since the Duke and Duchess had taken up residence in Brussels she had naturally become the leader of the *ton* in that city and her ball, thrown on the eve of Waterloo, had become famous. So many of the gay young officers who had danced there and left in the early hours to report for duty had not survived the battle.

Hugh returned to the inn, where the others were taking refreshment, to inform them that Her Grace had offered her hospitality. He had accepted with gratitude. Although conditions in Brussels had improved considerably over the last couple of months the inns were still crowded and the danger of infection lurked within their walls.

'My dear,' cried the Duchess after greeting Louisa, 'so brave of you to undertake such a hazardous journey! And to defy convention to do so! You must know that Lord Hugh—such an excellent young man—has explained the situation and you have my full support! My maid will attend you. She will search out a gown for you to wear—there must be something suitable in my wardrobe and if not then in Jane's or Georgy's. My daughters are in Paris but have left much of their wardrobes behind.'

'You are most kind, ma'am. I have met your daughters, of course. They are in excellent health and spirits. Lady Georgiana is a great favourite with Lord Wellington.'

'They both are! I truly believe he looks upon them as his own daughters! But come, my dear, Brigide shall show you to your room and then see to your needs.'

A bath had never been more welcome. Cleansed, her hair and skin faintly perfumed with some mixture added to the water by Brigide, Louisa gratefully accepted a complete change of linen and donned a low-necked, cream silk gown trimmed with lace, which belonged to Lady Jane. It had been selected from those available as being a good fit and of reasonably suitable design for dining at the Duchess's table. A blue sprigged muslin dress had been set aside for wear the following day.

'I will see to the cleaning of your habit, *mademoiselle*,' promised the lady's maid. 'How would you prefer your hair to be dressed?'

'You decide,' suggested Louisa.

'Well, *mademoiselle*, I think it would suit you a little shorter, with curls drawn down over your forehead and arranged around your ears to frame your face. The style would be soft yet emphasise the fine lines of your jaw.'

Louisa regarded herself in the mirror. Her hair had grown a little long and certainly at that moment, having just been dried, looked untidy. Yet— An image of Hugh, as though reflected behind her in the mirror, suddenly swam into her vision. His eyes were fixed on her unruly curls and his fingers were stretched out as if to bury themselves in their luxuriant thickness. A *frisson* of awareness ran down her spine, as though in truth his fingers were caressing her. He would prefer her hair longer; she knew it instinctively. Its brown colour was nothing exceptional. Its attraction, if it had any at all, lay in its abundance and vitality.

'No,' she decided. 'I will not have it cut any shorter just yet. But otherwise your suggestion sounds excellent. I usually have it dressed off my forehead. This will make a change.'

Brigide set about her task without further demur. She was more skilled than Betty, of that there could be no doubt. Under her expert ministrations the curls were tamed and a slight decoration to match the satin bow beneath her breasts was fixed.

'Capital!' exclaimed Louisa, rather taken aback by

the vision confronting her in the mirror. The woman was a magician! 'Thank you, Brigide!'

The Duchess's maid acknowledged the praise with a curtsy and departed to minister to her mistress.

Brigide had of necessity dressed her early, so Louisa had an hour to spare before dinner. The afternoon sun made the small parterre beneath her window appear especially inviting. She did not imagine the Duchess would object to her taking a stroll along its paths. She felt restless. As though she was on the edge of some great adventure. Mayhap she was, for Hugh must surely renew his proposal before long. And she would accept him this time. With or without any declaration of love. Of one thing she was now fairly certain. Once wed, she would have no reason to doubt his fidelity. She had worried herself needlessly on that score. Unless, of course, she failed him as a wife.

That did seem rather unlikely, unless childbirth rendered her delicate, which was not an unknown eventuality. She had to hope she would survive the dangers of that condition and emerge in good health. For who could blame a man whose wife was unable to receive him in her bed for seeking release elsewhere? She would never be so foolish as to choose to banish him. Given her health she would love him so much that he would never wish to look at another woman while she lived!

Having carefully placed a bonnet over her new *coiffure* and wrapped a thin shawl about her bare shoulders, Louisa went downstairs to seek a door leading to the garden. Directed to one by a passing servant, she strolled towards the far end of the parterre, drawn by the sight of colourful blooms and the aroma of herbs. Those which had scented her bath must have been gathered here. She drew in an appreciative breath, revelling in the mixed perfumes of the garden, at their most pungent as evening approached.

Finding a seat, she sat down to enjoy a few moments

of quiet reflection, so welcome after three days of energetic action.

Jamie was safe and well. Hugh had sent an express message back to William Coynd the previous evening, from Mons. Aunt Nazeby should hear the whole story soon and be reassured, knowing them all to be together. What she would think of her own part in the business Louisa dared not imagine. That her aunt would try to stop wagging tongues she did not doubt.

Of course, Hugh might think he now had to ask her to wed him. She was, in the eyes of many, hopelessly compromised. But—oh, dear God, if he asked her for that reason she would feel obliged to refuse him again!

The complications of the situation had not occurred to her before. Her mind had been set on rescuing Jamie and she had dismissed all the consequences of her impulsive action in accompanying Hugh without the presence of a proper chaperon as of little account. Now she stopped to think clearly on the matter it had been a foolish thing to do. But surely, as she had protested at the time, her reputation would be strong enough to withstand the malicious gossip which would undoubtedly ensue?

For years Hugh had chosen to ignore the society which so ruled her life. Until, in fact, that society had temporarily moved to Paris and his position there had forced him into taking his place in it. He would depart for Austria shortly, leaving all the gossip behind. As usual, it would be the woman who suffered censure, although Hugh might be criticised for not coming up to scratch.

Footsteps on the path brought her head up. Hugh was striding purposefully towards her. Her recent thoughts seemed suddenly most pertinent. Had he come to propose, to regularise their relationship because their presence presented an embarrassment to the Richmonds? Not that the Duchess had appeared in the least overset. . .

Her thoughts made her uneasy in his presence. He

did not appear to notice. He made his bow and indicated the space on the seat beside her.

'May I sit?'

Louisa moved a little to make more room. 'Of course. This garden is most pleasant, is it not?'

'A veritable haven of peace. I saw you sitting here and hoped you would not mind my joining you. We are within clear sight of the house.'

So he had the proprieties in mind. Louisa did not know whether to be glad or sorry. The tension inside her grew as he settled himself on the seat, his thigh mere inches from her own.

'Jamie would like to visit the battlefield tomorrow. Do you wish to accompany us?'

His abrupt words restored much of Louisa's calm. He had not sought her out to propose!

'Yes,' she said immediately. 'I see it as my duty. But you have no need——'

'Like you, I consider it a duty. Very well, we will all go. I will hire a coach which Pershaw may drive. It will make a change from horseback riding and give Conker and Milsom's horse a much needed rest.'

Louisa noded. 'When shall we begin our journey back to Paris?'

'The following day, I suggest. I must return with all speed, for I have many neglected duties awaiting my attention. If you would prefer to travel by chaise——'

Louisa cut him off. 'No. We have no luggage and may as well take advantage of the fact. We shall be a sizeable party and hardly likely to attract the attentions of highwaymen. Besides, if we hired a chaise, what would Jamie do about Conker?'

'Both horses would have to be brought back by a groom.'

'That would not please Jamie!'

Hugh grinned. 'No. I have the greatest admiration for that boy. I wonder whether his mother will return to see to his welfare?'

This question had been exercising Louisa's brain. 'If

the Prince marries her I should think not. If he does not, she is ruined and will scarcely dare. I think she has abandoned Jamie.'

'She must be a most unnatural mother!'

'She could not gain sole control of his fortune, you see. The other trustees—his grandmother and a firm of lawyers—must also be consulted whenever anything over and above his allowance is to be spent. They must approve expenditure on the estates, too. She has her jointure, of course, but that was not enough. She did not like the trust arrangements, but the Thurrock fortune has always been well hedged against dissipation by anyone other than the Earl himself—once he comes fully into his inheritance, of course.'

'So what will he do?'

'I have been thinking. I imagine the old Dowager will take up residence at Thurston, his favourite estate, and do her best to see he is happy. Lady Nazeby will always be welcome and between them the old ladies will thoroughly spoil him!'

'I can imagine,' chuckled Hugh. 'It sounds an ideal solution.'

'And should anything happen to either of them I shall step in to ensure that Jamie's welfare does not suffer.'

'If you are able.'

'I can see nothing to stop me.'

That was his cue. Louisa waited, scarcely breathing, for him to protest that there could be everything to prevent her. Instead, in a leisurely manner, he rose to his feet.

'It is growing a little chilly. I believe you should return indoors. It must be almost time for dinner.'

CHAPTER TWELVE

A FRUSTRATING evening loomed, probably to be followed by another early night. What were Hugh's intentions? wondered Louisa impatiently, toying with her food while listening with half an ear to the wide-ranging conversation he was conducting with their intelligent hosts. He had been betrayed into displaying more concern than was strictly necessary after the incident on the road the previous day. This had raised her hopes enormously. She had thought an impassioned declaration imminent. Yet it had not materialised and now his behaviour towards her, though undoubtedly attentive, remained strictly correct in every way.

Of course, while staying in the Richmond's residence their conduct must be above reproach. Louisa recognised and regretted the fact. Hugh had shown in the garden that he respected their hosts too much to attempt to snatch a few stolen moments of forbidden privacy and thus give cause for offence. So, in fact, did she—respect their hosts. But appreciating the limitations on their freedom did nothing to lessen her present puzzlement over Hugh's true feelings.

Leaving the men to sit on at the dining-table over their port and brandy, the Duchess led her guest into the drawing-room. Having settled her comfortably in an armchair, she proceeded to ply her with questions. Louisa was happy to talk about her friendship with James Grade, the new Earl of Thurrock, explaining how they enjoyed riding in the Bois de Boulogne together, where Lord Hugh Deverill, like many others, including Lord Wellington, often joined them. And how the intimacy between all three had deepened during Lord Hugh's instruction of both herself and Jamie in the German language, so that when the Countess eloped with the Russian prince, enabling Jamie to set off on his longed-for mission to Waterloo, it had seemed natural for them to ride together to his assistance.

'Hasn't Deverill offered for you yet?' asked the Duchess when Louisa stopped.

Louisa simply could not prevent the blush that rose to stain her cheeks. 'Why do you ask, ma'am?'

'You are manifestly attached to each other. It is obvious he cherishes a *tendre* for you, as, I suspect, you do for him.'

Louisa's fingers began to tremble as the import of the Duchess's words sunk in. Were her feelings really plain for all to see? And since the Duchess was correct about her, could she be right about Hugh?

She smoothed a crease in the skirt of her gown and prevaricated. 'Neither of us has any wish to marry. Especially Lord Hugh.'

'Devil take me if I ever heard such nonsense! True, as Chadford's younger son Deverill has no duty to produce heirs, but most men, sooner or later, become persuaded that they need a wife and a nursery of their own.'

'Lord Hugh will need a wife, as Ambassador to Austria.' Louisa met her hostess's eyes bravely. 'Yes, my lady, he has asked me to marry him. I refused.'

'May I be permitted to enquire why?'

Louisa suddenly felt that she could confide in this kindly, experienced woman, the mother of two young girls, one still unmarried. 'I did not wish to be wed as a matter of convenience, ma'am. I have fortune enough to render me independent for life. I have no cause to tie myself in wedlock with a man who does not love me.'

The Duchess snorted. 'You sound like my Georgie! She is hanging out after some romantic ideal, won't consider any of the matches we propose for her!'

'But you do not force her into matrimony, dear ma'am.'

'No. Unfashionable, I know, but can't bring ourselves to do it. I suppose she will marry one day,' sighed the Duchess, 'probably just before it is time for her to say her last prayers! You should do the same, Louisa. What makes you think Hugh Deverill does not love you, my dear?'

The sudden question forced Louisa to lower her eyes, unable at that moment to meet the Duchess's sharp gaze. 'He has never said so.'

'Is that all?' Her Grace sounded somewhat derisive. 'Actions speak louder than words, child, you should remember that! Some men find it difficult to put their emotions into words. Yet they are displayed for all to see in their behavior. Mayhap Deverill is such a one.'

'Perhaps, ma'am.' Louisa doubted the truth of this supposition. He was excellent at expressing himself on other intimate matters. 'But I am not inexperienced in the way of gentlemen. Others who have asked me to marry them have protested their devotion.'

'Did you believe 'em?'

'Not all of them, no.'

And the one she had had not been speaking the truth.

'So there you are!' For the Duchess that admission seemed to vindicate her argument. 'To some men a declaration of love comes as easily as a snatched kiss in the dark! To others, the emotion is too deep, perhaps even too precious a feeling to be put into words. It may not even be recognised as love.'

Louisa digested this piece of wisdom in silence. 'I hope he will not feel *obliged* to ask me again,' she said at last.

The Duchess immediately recognised the oblique reference to the present unorthodox situation in which the pair found themselves. She shrugged her elegant shoulders. 'If he possesses the fine sensibilities I believe him to, he will realise that the best way to lose you would be to allow you to imagine any such thing. Be patient, my dear Louisa, and if he dallies too long then take steps to bring him to the point again!'

'Steps, ma'am?' Louisa's eyes opened wide in seemingly innocent surprise.

'Don't play the green girl with me, my dear,' chuckled the Duchess, 'it won't wash! I've known you since you first appeared at St James's, too long to suppose you do not know what I mean! But take my advice. Wait until you are back in Paris and the scandal of your headlong rush after young Thurrock with only a groom to chaperon you has had time to be forgotten. I would wager Deverill will have spoken of his own accord by then. But if by chance he has not, you must make sure he does.'

'He leaves Paris in a few weeks,' observed Louisa despondently.

'My dear Louisa, I have never known you to be defeatist before! Depend upon it, the man loves you! But he will not address you again if he thinks another refusal likely.'

Louisa sat up straighter, a new determination written on her face. 'You are right, ma'am! I am indulging in unnecessary dismals! And,' she added ruefully, 'I have given him little enough cause to renew his offer!'

The gentlemen joined them soon after this and Louisa tried hard to enliven her thoughts. Lady Richmond was correct. She was not usually so ready to sink into gloom. But nothing, ever, had seemed so important to her as discovering whether Hugh truly loved her or not. Whether he intended to renew his offer or not. Time was so short. All her future happiness was at stake. How could she not be apprehensive?

The party set off for the battlefield after breakfast the following morning. Dutton sat on the box with Pershaw while Louisa, Jamie and Hugh rode inside the coach. Milsom had been left behind to nurse his sore head.

'We need not meet many of those who are merely sightseers,' remarked Hugh as they set off, the coach rumbling through the busy streets of Brussels, now happily almost cleared of wounded derelicts. 'The hired coachmen take their customers to Mont St John and the scene of Wellington's final victory. I propose that we travel on to La Belle Alliance, where the major met his death at the hands of Napoleon's reserves. I have instructed Pershaw accordingly.'

'Such a waste!' mourned Louisa. 'If only they had retreated in good order after routing the French *cuirassiers* and not charged on through the infantry and into Napoleon's reserve lines!'

'It was the Union Brigde that did it.' Jamie had clearly studied the reports with precocious interest. 'Lord Uxbridge—he was the commander of the cavalry, and he led the Household Brigade himself, you know—couldn't stop them. My papa died trying to cover the retreat.'

'The troopers had been served with rum to stiffen their nerve. It made them reckless,' observed Hugh grimly.

Silence reigned as the coach gathered speed along the less crowded road south out of the city. The coach lurched and bumped into potholes despite Pershaw's excellent driving. Hanging on to the strap, Louisa considered that the long journey on horseback had been preferable to one confined within a bouncing carriage. However, if the weather changed and became wet she supposed Hugh would insist upon their travelling back to Paris by coach or chaise. Either way the long journey promised to be tedious.

'I'd quite like to look across from Mont St John first,' said Jamie suddenly, jerking her thoughts back to the present. 'If there are not too many other people already there,' he added apologetically. 'It's where the charge began.'

Hugh smiled a trifle wryly. 'I collect that you will not be satisfied until you have seen everything.'

'Well, sir, he was my father.'

'I know, Jamie. You shall see whatever you wish. I'll tell Pershaw.'

Hugh thrust his head out of the window to draw the coachman's attention and gave the order to divert. He was sitting opposite Louisa and Jamie, who were facing the horses. As he drew his head back inside his eyes met Louisa's. Understanding flowed between them. Neither relished the next few hours, but Jamie deserved their support.

They passed the village of Mont St John and then the deserted farmhouse, which brought them to the ridge behind which Wellington had hidden most of his army. They descended from the coach and climbed the hill. Louisa had seen the battlefield before, but not quite from here. She had been slightly below the top of the ridge on her previous visit, on the road on its far side, unable to see what lay behind. In any case, she had not wanted to look.

Having reached the crest, Jamie stood and slowly turned full circle. 'Yes,' he said, 'I can see it now. Only the nine-pounders and a few advance troops were deployed to the south, hidden among the corn. Papa and the remainder of the army waited back there.' He waved a hand towards the ruined farmhouse.

Louisa looked about her, too, less reluctant than she had been on her first visit. She had heard enough discussion of the battle in the drawing-rooms of Paris to arouse her interest. The fields in every direction had been flattened, their crops lost, trampled into the mud by thousands of feet and hooves. Visible evidence of the carnage had been removed. The ground had begun to recover. Only the shells of the buildings remained as a reminder of the men who had died there.

Hugh had also become absorbed in the scene as he followed Jamie's explanation. It was surprising how compelling the place could become when one's interest was personal, mused Louisa. He must have read and listened to the accounts of the battle too, for he nodded his head. 'And here, behind the ridge, was where the men endured Bonaparte's eighty-gun bombardment and held the line until Blücher's Prussian reinforcements could arrive.'

Louisa tried to imagine lying in the corn on wet, muddy ground with shot and shell continually falling around her, watching comrades being killed and injured and simply having to endure. And after that to face the terrorising panoply of a Napoleonic offensive, hear the threatening beat of drums advancing at the head of a formidable army, the bearded grenadiers marching four hundred abreast and shouting at the top of their voices, the elusive *tirailleurs* running and firing ahead. It did not bear thinking about.

'And I suppose,' said Jamie after some moments of silent contemplation, 'that must be La Belle Alliance.'

He pointed across the flattened fields to the south to another ridge.

'That is what I understood from the guide when I was here before.' Louisa was glad to remove her eyes from the devastated fields near by to a point so distant that detail was obscured. 'And that knoll there is the one from which Bonaparte conducted the battle.'

'May we please go and see it?' asked Jamie.

Just below where they stood the carriages of sightseers had begun to arrive. Both Louisa and Hugh turned thankfully back to rejoin their coach.

There was little more to be seen than further devastated buildings and flattened fields on arrival at the spot from which Napoleon had directed the battle. The two great commanders had never joined directly in battle before. On that day, as so often before in his career, the Duke had proved that sound defence could break the resolve of the attacking army and win the day. It had been the Peninsula story all over again. Napoleon had rejected the advice of his veteran marshals and used his normal tactics. And been beaten.

Jamie did not have much to say as he contemplated the field on which his father had died. Eventually, hand on sword hilt, he turned to Hugh and smiled, a rather strained smile but a smile nevertheless.

'Thank you for coming with me, Lord Hugh.' He swivelled to where Louisa stood. 'You too, dear Louisa. I can imagine it all now, the noise and the smoke and the fury of battle. I should like to follow my father and purchase a commission in the cavalry when I am older.'

Louisa opened her mouth to protest that he should consider no such thing but Hugh silenced her with a look.

'That will be your privilege, my lord. Are you ready to leave now?' As he assisted Louisa over the rough ground he murmured, 'At that age I wanted to be a mail-coach driver!'

Louisa understood. There would be plenty of time for Jamie to change his mind without her lecturing him now.

'Well,' said the Duchess over dinner, 'what did you think? Such a sad, brave sight! When I think of all those gallant young men who left my ball to die on that field I sometimes wonder how I can bear it! I had asked Wellington if I should cancel the affair, for we all knew a battle must be imminent, but he said no. We were all so gay that night! Not least Wellington himself!'

'Or so he wanted it to appear. He had made his dispositions, my dear. There was nothing more he could do except to receive messages and write new orders. Although with the messages pourin' in, he did confess to me that Napoleon had humbugged him, had gained four and twenty hours' march on him. He had not expected the enemy to advance to rapidly.' The Duke of Richmond laughed slightly, wryly reminiscent. 'He asked to borrow my local map.'

'Very soon the officers took their leave, the trumpets sounded and the drums beat to arms. Brussels was alive with troops.' The Duchess shuddered. 'Then, when the wounded began pouring in. . .! My dears, it was quite frightful!'

'We need not dwell on it any longer, my love. Thankfully it is all over and that monster is safely on his way to St Helena, if he has not already arrived. He will be able to do no more harm.'

The Duke having deftly diverted the conversation, Hugh followed his lead. 'With the American war ended we may hope for a period of peace at last.'

'Indeed, my boy, and you are just the person to see to it that we do! Off to Vienna, eh? Ever been there?'

'No, Your Grace. During much of the Congress of Vienna I was engaged in assisting those sent to negotiate peace with America. The Treaty of Ghent was signed only last December. After that I spent a few months in England.'

'Well-earned rest, eh? And then they sent you over to Paris. Done an excellent job there, by all accounts. Castlereagh can't speak highly enough of you. Deserve an embassy of your own. We are not entirely cut off from news here, you know! And you, young lady, are you goin' to marry the fellow and go with him?'

Louisa could have sunk with mortification but instead she tilted her chin. How could he? As blood flooded her face she dared not even glance in Hugh's direction. What possible answer could she give?

She was saved by the Duchess. 'Really, Richmond!' exclaimed that lady. 'Don't be such a bumble! Leave the young people alone to settle their own affairs!'

Jamie, however, blurted out, 'Are you to be married? How famous! I may visit you in Vienna!'

Goaded, Louisa spoke before she thought. 'No,' she declared fiercely, 'we are not! And now, everyone, may we please change the subject?'

'Sorry,' mumbled the Duke, looking rather shamefaced but allowing a twinkle to remain in his eyes. 'Delicate subject, eh? Should've realised. Well, my dear, you'd better leave us soon, or we'll never be ready to leave for the Countess's drum. Glad you're coming, Deverill. Still a few of us left in residence here for you to meet.'

Thus prompted, the Duchess rose to lead Louisa from the room. Louisa avoided looking at Hugh. She could not imagine what his reaction to the Duke's words had been.

'I have ordered an early tea tray, my dear, and then we may be off. You will know most of the English people there, but you will meet some of the local first circle as well.'

After the Duke's unfortunate remarks Louisa did not feel she could face Hugh again that day. Let alone suffer all the curious looks and questions both strangers and acquaintances were certain to throw in her direction. She simply could not go!

'If you will excuse me, dear ma'am, I would beg your leave to remain in my room this evening. We begin our journey back to Paris tomorrow and I shall need to rest.'

'Nonsense!' declared the Duchess roundly. 'It is essential for you to come! You must realise that appearing under my patronage will scotch the gossip surrounding your arrival in Brussels. If I indicate my approval of your presence here no one else will dare to criticise. At least not openly! And the news will soon travel to Paris. Your presence tonight will secure your future acceptance in Society.'

Wise in the ways of the *ton*, Louisa had recognised the fact earlier and then forgotten it in her desperation to avoid an embarrassing confrontation with Hugh. She smiled wryly.

'Of course you are right, ma'am. It was foolish of me to forget.'

'But you feel so mortified by what my dear husband the Duke said that you wonder how you may keep your countenance in the presence of Deverill.' At Louisa's half-hearted attempt at denial, the Duchess merely smiled. 'Depend upon it, he will be feeling exactly the same. So you must both put on a brave front and behave with impeccable propriety. In that manner you may retrieve the situation, especially as I intend that you should travel back in my coach, accompanied by one of my maids.'

'Your Grace, you must not put yourself to so much trouble——'

'I can do as I like with my own coach and staff, you'll allow? We have another carriage we may use meanwhile.'

Louisa could do nothing but accept with gratitude. She wondered what Hugh would have to say to the gesture.

The evening passed off without serious incident. Louisa, still wearing Lady Jane's dress and consequently not feeling up to scratch in her appearance, did her best to appear her usual lively self. Under the auspices of the Duke and Duchess both she and Hugh were welcomed to the informal evening's entertainment given by one of the Duchess's firmest friends.

Hugh behaved with impeccable courtesy, hovering behind the ladies while they were seated, plying them with drinks as requested and asking Louisa to stand up with him for the prescribed two sets. Otherwise he did not dance, remaining with the Duchess, seating himself when Louisa's chair became available beside her, at other times standing elegantly propped against the wall, always chatting amiably to those who came to pay their respects to his hostess. The Duke had disappeared in search of the card tables.

The gathering was relatively small and the dancing informal. Louisa did not lack for partners, for some army detachments were still stationed in Brussels. All the time she danced she was acutely aware of Hugh. On the occasions when she found the courage to look, his eyes seemed to be following her. Yet he had said nothing of importance during their dances. Had shown no embarrassment, either. Gradually, under his calming influence, her own discomfort had lessened. Plainly he intended to ignore the Duke's unfortunate remarks. She would therefore do the same.

Hugh found it impossible to take his eyes from Louisa's graceful figure as she danced with lively abandon. Not the frenetic abandon of those early days in Paris, he noted thankfully, and, although she laughed with and smiled at her partners, coquetry was quite absent from her manner.

She had been truly moritfied by the wretched Duke's question. But for Hugh, busy biding his time before laying his heart at her feet, the Duke's indiscretion had proved equally distressing. For Louisa had rejected the prospect of marriage to him as though it was the last thing in the world she wished to contemplate. He had been so confident, after her words after the hold-up, that her feelings for him had deepened. He could no longer deny the true nature of his own attachment. Physical desire had exploded upon him like one of Congreve's rockets almost from the first, but love had crept up like a thief in the night, stealing his heart and soul. Without Louisa, his life would be worth nothing. Persuading her of this, after his former irregular conduct, he had expected to prove difficult. Now he wondered whether he could ever succeed and, even if he did, whether it would make any difference if her heart had not been touched. She had declared that she would not wed without love. And had sounded so entirely opposed to the idea of marrying him and accompanying him to Vienna!

The Duchess, watching his grim profile and detecting the direction of his gaze, decided not to interfere further. She had done her best to reassure Louisa. If Hugh Deverill was half the man she thought him to be he would not appreciate the advice of anyone, let alone an interfering woman's. He knew exactly what he wanted and would go his own way about getting it.

The party departed next morning after an early breakfast. One of the Duchess's personal maids, an older woman named Rhoda, travelled inside the carriage with them. The Duke's second coachman held the reins, with

Pershaw beside him to take his turn if required. Dutton and Milsom rode on the seat behind. Jamie's two horses had been tethered to the rear of the carriage. Without the weight of riders on their backs they would be able to stay fresh much longer and should prove little drag on the speed of a coach drawn by four post horses. All six men, including Jamie, carried pistols.

Louisa bade their hosts an affectionate farewell. She had always had an admiration for the Duchess of Richmond and although the Duke had caused her so much mortification she could not long hold him in disgust. She liked him and he had meant no harm.

A slight drizzle soon cleared away and those riding outside had a more pleasant journey than anticipated, despite a decidedly autumnal chill. Luckily the weather had, on the whole, been kind. Jamie and Milsom had brought a change of clothing and a caped riding coat each, as had Hugh and Dutton. Pershaw, however, had been forced to borrow a suitable garment and Louisa was glad of the travelling rugs draped over her shoulders and tucked in about her knees.

Rhoda sat beside her, with Jamie and Hugh opposite. As the coach rocked and swayed onwards Louisa listened idly to Jamie's chatter, her real attention centred on the man sitting opposite, whose knees bumped hers every time the carriage lurched and threw him forward. Whenever this happened a shock ran through her body and it was not pleasant. It should have been, of course, but it was not, for it meant nothing. Hugh was not affected by the contact. His eyes rested upon her from time to time, serious and remote. Both her own instinct and Lady Richmond must be mistaken. He could not love her.

How she longed for the brisk but unhurried journey to end, her torture to be over! Only one thing relieved the monotony—a brief visit to the barracks at Cambray.

The Life Guard captain greeted them warmly, but had no news of the miscreants they had encountered on the road.

'My men chased them for several miles, following their hoofprints until they came to a crossroads,' Captain Brownhill told them. 'Since there was no sign of the horses or of the men and they could have gone in any direction, the Sergeant abandoned the search. But my patrols are keeping a sharp eye open for them, you may be sure.'

Louisa and Jamie were fascinated by all the comings and goings, the incredible mixture of uniforms, the sight of companies of different armies all drilling in the barrack square at the same time.

'What a splendid sight they make!' Louisa commented.

Jamie's eyes were fixed on a troop of Life Guards drilling on their horses.

'There is talk of moving the Allied headquarters here,' smiled the captain, fully aware of their interest. 'Discipline must be maintained, for the Commander in Chief may visit at any time.'

'I wish the same could be said of the troops in and around Paris,' sighed Louisa. 'The Prussians and even the Russians and Austrians still leave a trail of shattered homes and ruined fields behind them. No wonder Madame de Staël and others plead so earnestly with the Duke of Wellington to reduce the numbers of the army of occupation!'

'He will not, of course,' put in Hugh, 'for we must remember, even if they find it convenient to forget, how ready some parts of the French army and many of its citizens were to welcome Bonaparte back last March. Wellington will keep a sizeable presence here until the new French leaders have proved themselves capable of ruling a peaceful country. He himself intends to remain in Paris for some time yet.'

'Such requests are regarded by those at headquarters as causing trouble. Such people will find themselves unpopular if they persist in their demands,' stated Captain Brownhill.

'Do not fear, Captain, their Lordships Wellington

and Castlereagh, ably assisted, may I say, by Lord Hugh Deverill——' Louisa risked a small smile in his direction '—are constantly putting their views on the matter to those that matter in Paris. If only discipline could be introduced into the conduct of the occupying forces I believe everyone would accept its presence as a regrettable necessity.'

'Lord Wellington does his best, of that you may be sure,' said the captain. 'But he lacks disciplinary authority over any but his own army.'

Hugh made a helpless gesture. 'No, and Blücher and the other commanders, being victorious, consider themselves justified in allowing their troops licence. There, too, persuasion is the only answer. But, Captain, we must not take up more of your time. We still have some distance to travel before nightfall.'

'I am glad to see you are well protected,' said the captain as he bade them farewell, 'and that the crest on your coach is unobtrusive. I pray you will not meet with trouble on the way.'

'Much as she enjoys ostentation, the Duchess of Richmond has an even greater regard for survival,' grinned Hugh. 'She is keenly aware of the likely consequences of blazoning her arms too obviously on continental roads.'

'I suppose,' said Louisa ruefully as the coach gathered speed, 'we shall be forced to recognise that dreadful creature, Lord Cumnor.'

'We owe him civility, no more,' responded Hugh.

'He owes you much more,' said Jamie indignantly, 'and so do I! I could not have borne to lose Conker! He was Papa's last present to me and he carried me so well on the journey.'

'You should have used post horses,' commented Louisa with a smile. 'Did it not occur to you, Jamie?'

'Yes, but I didn't think my funds would stretch to the cost, you see. As it was I had to borrow from Milsom. I do hope I can repay him when I get back.'

'Your mother left some funds with Mr Coynd, but if

you find you cannot lay your hands on ready money I will stake you until your affairs are settled,' promised Hugh. 'Did your mama say nothing, Jamie? Will she marry this Prince?'

Until then they had kept a discreet silence over the circumstances surrounding Jamie's abrupt departure. Hugh obviously thought it time to clear up a few matters before they arrived back.

'No, she didn't, and I hope she doesn't!' muttered Jamie rebelliously. 'If she sends for me I shan't go. She can't make me if my other trustees say I need not.'

'You must consult your grandmother at the earliest possible moment,' advised Louisa.

'Yes.' Jamie seemed to hesitate. 'I suppose I shall have to continue to obey Mr Coynd. But I shall insist he takes me back to England shortly.'

'Those were your mother's instructions and it would certainly seem to be the best plan,' agreed Hugh. 'I must return there myself in a few weeks. Perhaps we may travel together.'

'Capital!' exclaimed Jamie. 'Mr Coynd could have no objection to that!'

Hugh's smile was rather wry. 'I trust not.'

And that was how matters stood when at last they entered Paris, with Pershaw, leading Prince Hal, Kismet and Dutton's horse, following behind. The animals had seemed in fine fettle when they'd recovered them at the last stage. Conker had appeared quite content to continue trotting along behind the carriage so he and Milsom's horse remained tethered to it. The sight of all the riderless animals following the coach brought a smile to Louisa's face. 'What a splendid sight we make!' Then she sobered. 'But conspicuous. No one will be able to miss our return.

'No one should be allowed to do so,' mumured Hugh. 'We have done nothing of which we need feel ashamed.'

'I shall tell everybody how you came to my rescue!' cried Jamie. 'You'll be the greatest of heroes!'

'No need to make a great piece of work of it, my boy,' cautioned Hugh. 'You will be facing scandal enough as it is, with your mother eloping and you disappearing as you did. Best to play the entire episode down.'

'Oh.' Jamie looked quite disappointed. 'I was looking forward to telling everyone about the hold-up.'

'Of course you may tell anyone who asks. But keep your account brief and do not exaggerate.'

'I'll try,' muttered Jamie.

Louisa privately thought it would be a miracle if he succeeded.

CHAPTER THIRTEEN

THE sensation occasioned by Miss Louisa Finsham's scandalous behaviour quickly died. The Duchess of Richmond had entertained the couple in her home and presented them to Brussels Society; and admiration for their prompt action in riding to the rescue of the young Earl of Thurrock, so unscrupulously abandoned by his mother, won the day. Besides, since the pair concerned seemed entirely composed over the whole affair, other, more rewarding subjects for gossip soon occupied the gabble-grinders' attention.

For one thing the Duchess of Wellington was expected in Paris, informed at last by her husband that he was ready to receive her, perhaps hoping her presence would quell the rumours still rife concerning his relationship with Lady Frances Wedderburn-Webster.

For a week or so the previous year, before returning home, Kitty had tried very hard to be a duchess and fulfil the functions of an ambassador's wife in Paris. But she was not suited to the station to which her husband's success had elevated her, being altogether too homely, uninterested in his affairs, too much in awe of her famous husband to succeed. She annoyed him in almost every way, particularly by her inability to manage money, thus ending up in debt. Her arrival was therefore awaited expectantly. Would the Duke continue his addresses to La Grassini? He had not scrupled to parade his conquest before his wife the previous year. How terribly lowering for her to have to watch him escorting beautiful, talented women while she herself sat ignored until sent back to obscurity at home! But she must surely be inured to his partiality for other women by now. She could not possibly be ignorant of the string of beautiful and gifted women he had courted, trailing back through the Peninsula to India. Though of course she hadn't been married to him while he was in India.

Making her curtsy to the Duchess, Louisa could only feel sorry for the dowdy, middle-aged woman. She was making a brave effort. She adored her distinguished husband but was overawed by him. The hem of her unusually splendid gown had become torn. Doing her best to hide the damage, she cried, 'Do not tell the Duke! I pray you, do not draw his attention to it! He will be so vexed!'

Why she should think he would concern himself over such a trifle defeated Louisa. But she could see that poor Kitty could offer him no sparkling conversation, no radiant beauty, no outstanding horsemanship, no particular talent of any kind. Not even passion, by the looks of her; she was too timid. He must feel his marriage a disaster, apart from the two healthy sons Kitty had borne him.

Louisa made an effort to keep the Duchess company, to direct her myopic gaze away from the sight of the Duke paying open court to Madame Grassini and talking animatedly with the other admiring women gathered about him. She was scarcely surprised when, on several such occasions, Hugh strolled over, made his bow and proceeded to engage Kitty in conversation on mundane matters, asking after her sons and how things did in London. He had no need to consult Kitty, he had been there so recently, and the embassy was kept well abreast of the latest news from the capital. Louisa loved him the more for his kindness. He drew her into the conversation and, together, they managed to divert Kitty's attention from the Duke's neglect.

In the midst of all the speculation following Duchess Kitty's arrival, news came of Jamie's mother. The Countess of Thurrock was now a princess. Her elopement had caused enough stir. Her marriage became the subject of the latest on-dits.

James determinedly resisted her undoubtedly cool suggestion that he join her in Russia for the summer.

'I don't like him,' he confided to Louisa and Amelia, who had been in transports of relief over the safe return of both her loved ones. 'I shall never acknowledge him as my father! I am going to return to England with Lord Hugh. Grandmama Thurrock will see to it that I do not have to obey Mama's summons!'

'We all will,' declared Amelia. 'We shall return with you. We have no reason to remain in residence here for the winter. I shall prefer to be in London for the last of the Little Season and to retire to Minchingham for Christmas. Do you not agree, Louisa?'

'Of course, Aunt.'

Louisa's insides churned at the prospect of the journey. Not only would she be travelling with Hugh, but she must endure the sea crossing again, perhaps making another exhibition of herself in front of him.

Contrary to the Duchess of Richmond's prediction he made no move to declare himself again. In fact he seemed so occupied with neglected embassy business that she saw little of him. When they did meet in drawing-room or salon he held himself aloof, impeccably polite but never, by so much as a look, hinting at any intimacy between them, past or present. Only his eyes, when they rested upon her, held a look she could not fathom.

Neither Paris nor London could hold any attraction for her without Hugh's presence. The only person she would be sad to leave was Fanny d'Arblay. Otherwise she did not care whether she went or stayed, although going would prolong the bittersweet agony of seeing him for a little longer. And as for taking the Duchess's advice and precipitating matters between them—well, so far the opportunity simply had not arisen. And if it did she doubted she would have the courage to act. Hugh's apparent indifference had seriously diminished her self-confidence.

So it was with anxious foreboding that Louisa

embarked upon the journey home. Hugh's taking up of his appointment in Vienna had been delayed until the New Year. He would spend what was left of November and part of December at the Foreign Office being briefed and remain in England for Christmas. She supposed he would leave his rooms in St James's and retire to the family estate, Kidderslake Hall in Hampshire, for the festival, there to take final leave of his parents and family. She would be at Minchingham in Berkshire, some twenty miles distant as the crow flew, but it might just as well be two hundred.

He travelled with Jamie. William Coynd occupied the third pull-out seat of that hired chaise. She shared a similar conveyance with Lady Nazeby. Pershaw, his lad and Jamie's groom, Percy, were bringing all the horses separately, while the other servants followed their masters and mistresses in two post chaises, required to change vehicles as well as horses at every stage. Yet another vehicle had been hired to carry the overflow of their considerable luggage. Four chaises and sixteen sweating horses driven by postilions plus a coach and coachman with another four horses pulling that had rendered their progress quite impressive. It did not, however, bring any meaningful communication between Louisa and Hugh, who maintained his pleasantly reserved manner during all their stops and overnight halts.

At Calais Louisa eyed the packet boat with grave misgiving. Shelter on the deck was non-existent, yet she dreaded having to descend into the dark, smelly cabin. She wore her thickest pelisse and carried a large, warm travelling rug, prepared to endure the cold rather than the discomfort of the cabin, since although the day was dull it was not raining. Their luggage was being carried aboard, the process overseen by Hugh and Dutton on the quay and Jamie, with Mr Coynd and Milsom in attendance, on board. She watched it disappear into the hold with abstract interest. The surly *douaniers*, their faces still scowling under their large cocked hats, had let it through without much trouble. Everyone's papers had been in order and they were free to board. Amelia and the maids, escorted by Dench, had already begun to cross the gangplank. Louisa hung back, savouring her last moments on solid ground.

A quiet voice spoke in her ear.

'The sea is tolerably calm today and the captain does not expect the weather to worsen. We have a fair breeze and the crossing should be a fast and pleasant one.'

Louisa turned impulsively. This was the first sign of other than polite concern Hugh had shown since Brussels. His words had not been extraordinary but his tone had changed.

'You remember my weakness,' she accused wryly. 'How I wish I were a good sailor!'

'How could I forget?' His smile lit a small flame in her heart. 'You were unfortunate to experience a storm on your first voyage. This one may enable you to face future crossings with greater fortitude.'

Louisa grimaced. 'Possibly, if I am ever persuaded to make such a journey again! But I cannot sit in that stuffy cabin!'

'Then you need not. The true joy of the sea can only be experienced on deck, in the wind and the spray. Come, my dear Louisa. Take my arm. We must board soon or be left behind!'

Oh, the dear feel of him! Louisa trembled and the slight feeling of sick fear disappeared in excitement. If Hugh did not. . .then she would. . . Or would she?

The deck rocked gently beneath her feet but she scarcely noticed it. Hugh had left her to speak again with the ship's captain. Amelia, with the maids, had already climbed down below, to obtain the best seats, Louisa surmised. Jamie, watched over by a diligent William Coynd, was exploring the deck. Dench, Milsom and Dutton leant on the rail some distance away, chatting with a number of other deck passengers.

'Come,' said Hugh, returning. 'The ship is about to

sail. We must join the deck passengers behind the mast while the sailors attend to their work. Afterwards, we may go where we will.'

'You are to remain on deck, too?'

'Did you think I would leave you alone?'

He smiled at her in a way that set her heart beating faster. This was the old Hugh, attentive and charming, his smile and the expression in his eyes holding something more than friendship.

They made themselves as unobtrusive as possible while the ship was warped out of the harbour and the sails hoisted and set. The shouts of the men, the noise of creaking timbers, the sound of flapping canvas all combined to bring a sense of adventure Louisa had missed on the outward voyage, confined as she had been in the cabin below deck. Afterwards she had felt too ill to give the sweating sailors' activities more than passing attention. But now she had to admire their energy and skill as they hauled on ropes and secured the ends. The wind filled the sails and the ship heeled, sending her reeling into Hugh's ready arms.

He laughed. 'Enthralling, isn't it? They've finished now, see? They're settling down to wait for their next order and the ship is on a steady keel. Come to the weather side, here, where there is no tackle to worry us. It'll be breezy but dry.'

Louisa clutched the rug round her shoulders with one hand as she leant on his arm with the other. It was chilly, but so exhilarating! The feathers and ribbons on her bonnet blew wildly and she answered his laugh with one of her own.

The up-and-down motion now seemed no more than a gentle rocking as the ship's bow cut through the waves, sending white spray to drench the foredeck. A little drifted back to where they stood, but not enough to concern either of them.

Hugh's arm went about her shoulders and she did not object. Propriety might demand that she should, but the feel of it there was too precious. For several minutes they stood in silence, braced against the bulwarks. Despite his easy manner Louisa could feel tension in the arm across her shoulders. Hugh was not as relaxed as he appeared. She wondered what he was thinking. Her nerves responded to his rigidity by producing butterfly sensations in her stomach. She hoped she wouldn't feel sick again. But this fluttery sensation was due to pleasurable anticipation, not motion or fear.

He stirred at last, though he did not speak. Instead, he lifted her chin with his free hand and bent his head. She closed her eyes as he insinuated his head beneath her brim, knowing what was coming before ever his mouth touched hers.

They seemed to fuse together, those two pairs of lips. His tenderly demanding, hers sweetly yielding. And despite all the layers of thick clothing separating them Louisa's body, with a will of its own, melted into his. Place, time, everything was forgotten as she enjoyed the delight of his kiss. She had waited so long for him to carry out his threat that she had almost forgotten what his mouth felt like, yet instantly it was familiar, as though he had never stopped kissing her at all. His heart thudded under her hand. A small groan of pleasure escaped her and the beat quickened.

And then a loud laugh from one of the deck passengers penetrated her consciousness. She stiffened, tore her lips from his and made a feeble attempt to push him away.

'Hugh! Remember where we are! Everyone will see!'

'Capital,' said Hugh calmly, although his eyes and the give-away clenching of his jaw told her he was far from calm. His hold did not relax at all. 'If I have managed to compromise you before all these people then you will have to marry me.'

'Hugh!'

Her shocked tone brought a twinkle to his grey-blue eyes, a mischievous smile to those fascinating lips. 'My love, you were going to marry me anyway, so what does it matter?'

Stunned by his words and slightly incensed by the manner of his declaration, Louisa bridled, despite the sudden singing of the blood in her veins. 'I was not!' she denied. 'And of course it matters! A lady's reputation——'

'Yours, I confide, is not so fragile as to be damaged by so small a matter in such a public place. You said yourself, in Paris——'

'I know what I said in Paris!' Louisa's colour had heightened to a hectic red. Wretched man! To throw her own words back in her face! Then, suddenly, she had to ask. 'Why have you waited all this time to carry out your threat?'

'Threat?'

His innocent expression denied the laughter in his eyes. He would force her to say the words.

'To kiss me whenever opportunity presented itself,' she muttered.

He smiled down at her, certain now that his doubts had been groundless. That her vehement denial of any question of marriage between them had been defensive, designed to hide her true feelings. He shifted the arm about her downwards and tightened his hold.

'Because,' he said softly, serious now, 'I discovered that I could not treat you with such disrespect.'

'So you asked me to marry you instead.'

'Yes,' he admitted soberly. 'Of course, having been promoted and so being in a position to do so helped, but I did not realise, then, how much I loved you. I only knew I desired you and wanted to protect you, from yourself if necessary.'

'But I,' sighed Louisa regretfully, 'had no wish to be protected!'

'Unfortunately, no.' He grinned, but then his expression became passionate and his emotions spilled over into speech. 'My dearest girl! You must know that I adore you! You are become the first object of my heart and I find I cannot live without you!'

Louisa gazed up at him, stunned by the ardent nature

of his declaration. 'But——' she took refuge in the past '—you said you did not wish to wed. You were so set against it!'

'Because I had always sworn to myself not to wed before I had the means to support a wife in style. My pride would not allow it, and I had no wish to be branded a fortune-hunter,' he admitted. 'I was absolutely determined not to wed an heiress until I had a fortune of my own! And you, my love, not only possessed such a fortune but appeared to be rather flirtatious. How could I know what your feelings were? Even after I lost my heart I denied it to myself, afraid to admit it because it made me vulnerable. I was jealous.' He gave a slight, self-deprecating laugh. 'I could not begin to contemplate the prospect of losing you to another.'

Louisa eyed him steadily. 'My excessive flirtatiousness was occasioned by your attitude! I should not have cared, but I did.'

'I wonder why?' he murmured, his lips finding one corner of her mouth.

'I considered you horribly stuffy, quite overbearing and distinctly arrogant.'

'Charming,' he murmured, kissing the other corner.

'But I couldn't help falling in love with you,' she whispered.

He sucked in his breath sharply. 'Yet you said you did not.'

At a loss, Louisa frowned. 'When?'

'When I asked you to marry me. You said you would not wed without love.'

'Your love,' she told him softly, smiling contentedly. 'Now I know I have that, there is no problem.'

'And your mistrust of all men?' he probed. 'Do you now feel able to trust me?'

'I trust you,' she assured him earnestly. 'Love has quite overcome my fears. I realise that Papa never loved Mama.'

'As I most assuredly love you!' he declared again, and kissed her to prove it.

'And I love you,' Louisa asserted once she was able. 'Although,' she added provocatively, 'I do find your arrogant assumption that I would wed you, while still believing I did not love you, quite incomprehensible.'

'But I knew you did, after your horse bolted. Or at least I thought I knew it until you denied so roundly any intention of marrying me, at the Richmonds'. Your attitude sunk me in despondency but I could not quite forget that moment when you confessed your concern for my safety. And then, just now on the quay. You smiled at me,' he said simply.

'After weeks of polite coldness your voice held warmth,' she whispered. 'I had hoped your concern for my safety meant you loved me, Hugh, but then your attitude changed. I quite despaired.'

'I felt I must keep my distance, for your reputation's sake. Had you shown some enthusiasm for our union I would have explained my attitude to you. But I did not think you cared.'

'Oh, Hugh! Not care? My love, you cannot imagine how much I care!'

They searched each other's eyes and neither could see anything but sincerity and love reflected there. Hugh broke the spell by drawing a deep breath.

'Oh, my love! I find in you all I could ever wish for in a wife. Beauty, poise, passion, brains, an unrivalled ability to take your place in Society and a definite gift for languages. Besides all that you can ride like a dream and Pershaw tells me you know almost as much about breeding as he does. What more could I possibly desire, except your love? If I have that then I am rich beyond measure.'

'You forgot my modest fortune,' teased Louisa, snuggling closer into his arms.

The wind had whipped colour into her cheeks. Her bonnet, which she had thought so securely fixed, had become dislodged and her curls blew carelessly about her face. Hugh saw the happiness, the laughter filling her gorgeous eyes and could not resist another kiss.

'But that is yours. Lady Nazeby informed me so,' he remarked after a while. 'It will not become mine. Unlike the rest of you. And it is you I want, my love.'

'The traitor!' gasped Louisa, part annoyed, part relieved that he already knew the truth and still wanted to marry her. Then she smiled up at him. 'I wish you could have my fortune too, my love.' She discovered that she would have trusted him implicitly to look after it. He would never squander money, though his spending could be lavish at times and like all men he gambled, but in moderation. And because she loved him she wanted to keep no part of herself back. Never before had she regretted the terms of her inheritance. 'We shall need a home of our own in England,' she added as an afterthought.

'I have one!' He grinned triumphantly into her surprised face. 'It is not widely known yet, for I only discovered it for myself while I was in London, but I inherited a small estate quite near to the family acres from a bachelor cousin. There is a modest income to accompany it. I believe the house will please you and we can extend it if it grows too small. But——' his arms tightened yet again as he crushed her to him '—the trust you show in wishing you could offer me your fortune overwhelms me.'

Without her realising it Louisa's arms had risen to encircle his neck. 'I could never have married a man I could not trust with it. That is why I kept its nature secret. The revelation was to be my final test of any suitor's integrity! Aunt quite spoilt it for me!' she teased.

'Wretch!'

'I know. And I cannot tell you how glad I am that she did, for she saved me from severe embarrassment. How could I have sprung such knowledge on you without feeling ashamed of my deception? But you can possibly appreciate why I preferred to remain independent. I had no need to marry for security. Only for love, and the hope of a family.'

'The first you have, the second I shall do my best to give you,' vowed Hugh.

The kiss which followed was interrupted by a bellow from the captain followed by intense deck activity as the sailors rushed for the ropes. Hugh still had his arm about her waist as though to steady her as they made for safety behind the main mast, but Louisa knew it was because he did not want to let her go. Poker-faced servants greeted their arrival. Jamie and Mr Coynd joined them from another part of the deck. Jamie's grin almost split his face. Only then did Louisa realise that their every move must have been avidly watched. She blushed.

'Should we congratulate you, my lord?' enquired Dutton solemnly, attempting to hide his grin. 'If I might be allowed to say so, miss, Mr Pershaw will be that pleased to hear the news.'

'What news?' demanded Louisa blandly.

'Why, of your engagement, miss!'

'His lordship has not yet asked me to marry him,' responded Louisa demurely.

Hugh's brows almost disappeard into his tumbled hairline. His hat, like hers, had suffered dislodgement. It was perched at a precarious angle on the back of his head. 'Have I not?'

'No, my lord. You told me that I should marry you.'

'Ah!' exclaimed Hugh. 'I collect that I should make my offer in form. I shall do my best, though I absolutely decline to go down on one knee on the wet deck.' He glanced around the circle of the servants' studiously blank faces and beyond them to the deck passengers, whose expressions held avid interest. Without the slightest sign of either annoyance or embarrassment he turned to Louisa and made an elaborate bow. 'My dear Miss Finsham, will you do me the inestimable honour of accepting my hand in marriage?'

'Why, Lord Hugh! I do declare, you quite take me

by surprise!' Louisa entered into the spirit of the thing. If the proposal was destined to be made a public spectacle, why not make it a good one? 'But since our servants are so happily disposed to anticipate our union, how can I possibly refuse you?'

'How indeed, you little tease!'

He held out his hand and Louisa placed hers in it. He drew her nearer.

'And I'm glad, too!' Jamie's excited voice broke the threatened spell. 'It's capital news, Louisa! I must go and tell Lady Nazeby! She'll be quite in raptures!'

'Not so fast, my lord! If you will allow, I should like to be the first to inform her ladyship of my intentions.'

'Oh! Yes, of course. Are you going now?'

'Not quite yet.' Hugh looked down into Louisa's radiant face. 'My love, can you wed me before Christmas? I shall not wish to leave for Austria without you.'

'Whenever you like, my lord,' murmured the future Lady Hugh Deverill meekly.

'Capital,' murmured Hugh. And, bracing his legs against the movement of the ship, he took her in his arms and bent his head to kiss her again, ignoring the amused expressions of almost everyone present. The servants managed to maintain some semblance of gravity.

The sniggers and chuckles, the shouted words of encouragement and Jamie's cheer were quite lost on the couple swaying together on the heaving deck, each aware only of the other.

'Now,' murmured Hugh, reluctantly releasing her soft lips, 'you are, I think, sufficiently compromised. Jilt me at your peril!'

'Why, sir,' she murmured in return, 'you leave me no choice. I fear I must bow to your wicked demands.'

The rush of wind and water and the creaking of the timbers drowned their lowered voices.

'Wicked?' He gazed down into her face. The flare of his nostrils, the flame in his eyes made her shiver in happy anticipation. 'Whatever we do together, my dearest love, will never be wicked.'

'I know,' she acknowledged. 'You have given me a glimpse already. You will lead me to paradise.'

This time when they kissed no one laughed or cheered. William Coynd, a rueful smile on his face, tugged Jamie away. Everyone else, as of one accord, turned their backs to allow them privacy. A moment of such obvious tender commitment demanded nothing less.

THE *Regency* COLLECTION

Where rogues find romance

**Look out for the last volume in this limited
collection of Regency Romances from
Mills & Boon® in April 2000.**

Featuring:

His Lordship's Dilemma
by Meg Alexander

and

The Last Gamble
by Mary Nichols

Still only £4.99